BY SILVIA MORENO-GARCIA

*The Beautiful Ones*
*Certain Dark Things*
*Signal to Noise*
*Gods of Jade and Shadow*
*Untamed Shore*
*Mexican Gothic*

# MEXICAN GOTHIC

# MEXICAN GOTHIC

### Silvia Moreno-Garcia

DEL REY

NEW YORK

Published in the United States by Del Rey, an imprint of Random House, a division of Penguin Random House LLC, New York.

DEL REY is a registered trademark and the Circle colophon is a trademark of Penguin Random House LLC.

LIBRARY OF CONGRESS CATALOGING-IN-PUBLICATION DATA
Names: Moreno-Garcia, Silvia, author.
Title: Mexican Gothic / Silvia Moreno-Garcia.
Description: New York: Del Rey, [2020]
Identifiers: LCCN 2019048648 (print) | LCCN 2019048649 (ebook) |
ISBN 9780525620785 (hardback; alk. paper) |
ISBN 9780525620792 (ebook)
Subjects: GSAFD: Gothic fiction.
Classification: LCC PR9199.4.M656174 M49 2020 (print) |
LCC PR9199.4.M656174 (ebook) | DDC 813/.6—dc23
LC record available at https://lccn.loc.gov/2019048648
LC ebook record available at https://lccn.loc.gov/2019048649

Printed in the United States of America on acid-free paper

randomhousebooks.com

6 8 9 7

Book design by Jen Valero

*Para mi madre*

# MEXICAN GOTHIC

1

The parties at the Tuñóns' house always ended unquestionably late, and since the hosts enjoyed costume parties in particular, it was not unusual to see Chinas Poblanas with their folkloric skirts and ribbons in their hair arrive in the company of a harlequin or a cowboy. Their chauffeurs, rather than waiting outside the Tuñóns' house in vain, had systematized the nights. They would head off to eat tacos at a street stand or even visit a maid who worked in one of the nearby homes, a courtship as delicate as a Victorian melodrama. Some of the chauffeurs would cluster together, sharing cigarettes and stories. A couple took naps. After all, they knew full well that no one was going to abandon that party until after one A.M.

So the couple stepping out of the party at ten P.M. therefore broke convention. What's worse, the man's driver had left to fetch himself dinner and could not be found. The young man looked distressed, trying to determine how to proceed. He had worn a papier-mâché horse's head, a choice that now came back to haunt him as they'd have to make the journey through the city with this cumbersome prop. Noemí had warned him she wanted to win the costume contest, placing ahead of Laura Quezada and her beau, and thus he'd made an effort that now seemed misplaced, since his companion did not dress as she had said she would.

Noemí Taboada had promised she'd rent a jockey outfit, complete with a riding crop. It was supposed to be a clever and slightly scandalous choice, since she'd heard Laura was going to attend as Eve, with a snake wrapped around her neck. In the end, Noemí changed her mind. The jockey costume was ugly and scratched her skin. So instead she wore a green gown with white appliqué flowers and didn't bother to tell her date about the switch.

"What now?"

"Three blocks from here there's a big avenue. We can find a taxi there," she told Hugo. "Say, do you have a cigarette?"

"Cigarette? I don't even know where I put my wallet," Hugo replied, palming his jacket with one hand. "Besides, don't you always carry cigarettes in your purse? I would think you're cheap and can't buy your own if I didn't know any better."

"It's so much more fun when a gentleman offers a lady a cigarette."

"I can't even offer you a mint tonight. Do you think I might have left my wallet back at the house?"

She did not reply. Hugo was having a difficult time carrying the horse's head under his arm. He almost dropped it when they reached the avenue. Noemí raised a slender arm and hailed a taxi. Once they were inside the car, Hugo was able to put the horse's head down on the seat.

"You could have told me I didn't have to bring this thing after all," he muttered, noticing the smile on the driver's face and assuming he was having fun at his expense.

"You look adorable when you're irritated," she replied, opening her handbag and finding her cigarettes.

Hugo also looked like a younger Pedro Infante, which was a great deal of his appeal. As for the rest—personality, social status, and intelligence—Noemí had not paused to think too much about all of that. When she wanted something she simply wanted it, and lately she had wanted Hugo, though now that his attention had been procured she was likely to dismiss him.

When they arrived at her house, Hugo reached out to her, grasping her hand.

"Give me a kiss good night."

"I've got to run, but you can still have a bit of my lipstick," she replied, taking her cigarette and putting it in his mouth.

Hugo leaned out the window and frowned while Noemí hurried into her home, crossing the inner courtyard and going directly to her father's office. Like the rest of the house, his office was decorated in a modern style, which seemed to echo the newness of the occupants' money. Noemí's father had never been poor, but he had turned a small chemical dye business into a fortune. He knew what he liked and he wasn't afraid to show it: bold colors and clean lines. His chairs were upholstered in a vibrant red, and luxuriant plants added splashes of green to every room.

The door to the office was open, and Noemí did not bother knocking, breezily walking in, her high heels clacking on the hardwood floor. She brushed one of the orchids in her hair with her fingertips and sat down in the chair in front of her father's desk with a loud sigh, tossing her little handbag on the floor. She also knew what *she* liked, and she did not like being summoned home early.

Her father had waved her in—those high heels of hers were loud, signaling her arrival as surely as any greeting—but had not looked at her, as he was too busy examining a document.

"I cannot believe you telephoned me at the Tuñóns'," she said, tugging at her white gloves. "I know you weren't exactly happy that Hugo—"

"This is not about Hugo," her father replied, cutting her short.

Noemí frowned. She held one of the gloves in her right hand. "It's not?"

She had asked for permission to attend the party, but she had not specified she'd go with Hugo Duarte, and she knew how her father felt about him. Father was concerned that Hugo might propose marriage and she'd accept. Noemí did not intend to marry Hugo and had told her parents so, but Father did not believe her.

Noemí, like any good socialite, shopped at the Palacio de Hierro, painted her lips with Elizabeth Arden lipstick, owned a couple of very fine furs, spoke English with remarkable ease, courtesy of the nuns at the Monserrat—a private school, of course— and was expected to devote her time to the twin pursuits of leisure and husband hunting. Therefore, to her father, any pleasant activity must also involve the acquisition of a spouse. That is, she should never have fun for the sake of having fun, but only as a way to obtain a husband. Which would have been fine and well if Father had actually liked Hugo, but Hugo was a mere junior architect, and Noemí was expected to aspire higher.

"No, although we'll have a talk about that later," he said, leaving Noemí confused.

She had been slow dancing when a servant had tapped her on the shoulder and asked if she'd take a call from Mr. Taboada in the studio, disrupting her entire evening. She had assumed Father had found out she was out with Hugo and meant to rip him from her arms and deliver an admonishment. If that was not his intent, then what was all the fuss about?

"It's nothing bad, is it?" she asked, her tone changing. When she was cross, her voice was higher-pitched, more girlish, rather than the modulated tone she had in recent years perfected.

"I don't know. You can't repeat what I'm about to tell you. Not to your mother, not to your brother, not to any friends, understood?" her father said, staring at her until Noemí nodded.

He leaned back in his chair, pressing his hands together in front of his face, and nodded back.

"A few weeks ago I received a letter from your cousin Catalina. In it she made wild statements about her husband. I wrote to Virgil in an attempt to get to the root of the matter.

"Virgil wrote to say that Catalina had been behaving in odd and distressing ways, but he believed she was improving. We wrote back and forth, me insisting that if Catalina was indeed as *distressed* as she seemed to be, it might be best to bring her to

Mexico City to speak to a professional. He countered that it was not necessary."

Noemí took off her other glove and set it on her lap.

"We were at an impasse. I did not think he would budge, but tonight I received a telegram. Here, you can read it."

Her father grabbed the slip of paper on his desk and handed it to Noemí. It was an invitation for her to visit Catalina. The train didn't run every day through their town, but it did run on Mondays, and a driver would be sent to the station at a certain time to pick her up.

"I want you to go, Noemí. Virgil says she's been asking for you. Besides, I think this is a matter that may be best handled by a woman. It might turn out that this is nothing but exaggerations and marital trouble. It's not as if your cousin hasn't had a tendency toward the melodramatic. It might be a ploy for attention."

"In that case, why would Catalina's marital troubles or her melodrama concern us?" she asked, though she didn't think it was fair that her father label Catalina as melodramatic. She'd lost both of her parents at a young age. One could expect a certain amount of turmoil after that.

"Catalina's letter was very odd. She claimed her husband was poisoning her, she wrote that she'd had visions. I am not saying I am a medical expert, but it was enough to get me asking about good psychiatrists around town."

"Do you have the letter?"

"Yes, here it is."

Noemí had a hard time reading the words, much less making sense of the sentences. The handwriting seemed unsteady, sloppy.

*. . . he is trying to poison me. This house is sick with rot, stinks of decay, brims with every single evil and cruel sentiment. I have tried to hold on to my wits, to keep this foulness away but I cannot and I find myself losing track of time and thoughts. Please. Please. They are cruel and unkind and they will not let me go. I bar my door but still they come, they whisper at nights and I am so afraid of*

*these restless dead, these ghosts, fleshless things. The snake eating its tail, the foul ground beneath our feet, the false faces and false tongues, the web upon which the spider walks making the strings vibrate. I am Catalina Catalina Taboada. CATALINA. Cata, Cata come out to play. I miss Noemí. I pray I'll see you again. You must come for me, Noemí. You have to save me. I cannot save myself as much as I wish to, I am bound, threads like iron through my mind and my skin and it's there. In the walls. It does not release its hold on me so I must ask you to spring me free, cut it from me, stop them now. For God's sake . . .*

*Hurry,*
*Catalina*

In the margins of the letter her cousin had scribbled more words, numbers, she'd drawn circles. It was disconcerting.

When was the last time Noemí had spoken to Catalina? It must have been months ago, maybe close to a year. The couple had honeymooned in Pachuca, and Catalina had phoned and sent her a couple of postcards, but after that there had been little else, although telegrams had still arrived wishing happy birthdays to the members of the family at the appropriate times of the year. There must have also been a Christmas letter, because there had been Christmas presents. Or was it Virgil who had written the Christmas letter? It had, in any case, been a bland missive.

They'd all assumed Catalina was enjoying her time as a newly-wed and didn't have the inclination to write much. There had also been something about her new home lacking a phone, not exactly unusual in the countryside, and Catalina didn't like to write anyway. Noemí, busy with her social obligations and with school, simply assumed Catalina and her husband would eventually travel to Mexico City for a visit.

The letter she was holding was therefore uncharacteristic in every way she could think of. It was handwritten, though Catalina preferred the typewriter; it was rambling, when Catalina was succinct on paper.

"It is very odd," Noemí admitted. She had been primed to declare her father was exaggerating or using this incident as a handy excuse to distract her from Duarte, but that didn't seem to be the case.

"To say the least. Looking at it, you can probably see why I wrote back to Virgil and asked him to explain himself. And why I was so taken aback when he immediately accused me of being a nuisance."

"What exactly did you write to him?" she asked, fearing her father had seemed uncivil. He was a serious man and could rub people the wrong way with his unintended brusqueness.

"You must understand I would take no pleasure in putting a niece of mine in a place like La Castañeda—"

"Is that what you said? That you'd take her to the asylum?"

"I mentioned it as a possibility," her father replied, holding out his hand. Noemí returned the letter to him. "It's not the only place, but I know people there. She might need professional care, care that she will not find in the countryside. And I fear we are the ones capable of ensuring her best interests are served."

"You don't trust Virgil."

Her father let out a dry chuckle. "Your cousin married quickly, Noemí, and, one might say, thoughtlessly. Now, I'll be the first to admit Virgil Doyle seemed charming, but who knows if he is reliable."

He had a point. Catalina's engagement had been almost scandalously short, and they'd had scant chance to speak to the groom. Noemí wasn't even sure how the couple met, only that within a few weeks Catalina was issuing wedding invitations. Up until that point Noemí hadn't even known her cousin had a sweetheart. If she hadn't been invited to serve as one of the witnesses before the civil judge, Noemí doubted she'd have known Catalina had married at all.

Such secrecy and haste did not go down well with Noemí's

father. He had thrown a wedding breakfast for the couple, but Noemí knew he was offended by Catalina's behavior. That was another reason why Noemí hadn't been concerned about Catalina's scant communication with the family. Their relationship was, for the moment, chilly. She'd assumed it would thaw in a few months, that come November Catalina might arrive in Mexico City with plans for Christmas shopping and everyone would be merry. Time, it was merely a question of time.

"You must believe she is saying the truth and he is mistreating her," she concluded, trying to remember her impression of the groom. *Handsome* and *polite* were the two words that came to mind, but then they'd hardly exchanged more than a few sentences.

"She claims, in that letter, that he is not only poisoning her but ghosts walk through walls. Tell me, does that sound like a reliable account?"

Her father stood up and went to the window, looking outside and crossing his arms. The office had a view of her mother's precious bougainvillea trees, a burst of color now shrouded in darkness.

"She is not well, that is what I know. I also know that if Virgil and Catalina were divorced, he'd have no money. It was pretty clear when they married that his family's funds have run dry. But as long as they are married, he has access to her bank account. It would be beneficial for him to keep Catalina home, even if she'd be best off in the city or with us."

"You think he is that mercenary? That he'd put his finances before the welfare of his wife?"

"I don't know him, Noemí. None of us do. That is the problem. He is a stranger. He says she has good care and is improving, but for all I know Catalina is tied to her bed right now and fed gruel."

"And she is the melodramatic one?" Noemí asked, examining her orchid corsage and sighing.

"I know what an ill relative can be like. My own mother had a stroke and was confined to her bed for years. I also know a family does not handle such matters well at times."

"What would you have me do, then?" she asked, daintily placing her hands on her lap.

"Assess the situation. Determine if she should indeed be moved to the city, and attempt to convince him this is the best option if that is the case."

"How would I manage such a thing?"

Her father smirked. In the smirk and the clever, dark eyes, child and parent greatly resembled each other. "You are flighty. Always changing your mind about everything and anything. First you wanted to study history, then theater, now it's anthropology. You've cycled through every sport imaginable and stuck to none. You date a boy twice then at the third date do not phone him back."

"That has nothing to do with my question."

"I'm getting to it. You are flighty, but you are stubborn about all the *wrong* things. Well, it's time to use that stubbornness and energy to accomplish a useful task. There's nothing you've ever committed to except for the piano lessons."

"And the English ones," Noemí countered, but she didn't bother denying the rest of the accusations because she did indeed cycle through admirers on a regular basis and was quite capable of wearing four outfits in a single day.

*But it isn't like you should have to make up your mind about everything at twenty-two*, she thought. There was no point in telling her father that. He'd taken over the family business at nineteen. By his standards, she was on a slow course to nowhere. Noemí's father gave her a pointed look, and she sighed. "Well, I would be happy to make a visit in a few weeks—"

"Monday, Noemí. That is why I cut your party short. We need to make the arrangements so you're on the first train to El Triunfo Monday morning."

"But there's that recital coming up," she replied.

It was a weak excuse and they both knew it. She'd been taking piano lessons since she was seven, and twice a year she performed in a small recital. It was no longer absolutely necessary for socialites to play an instrument, as it had been in the days of Noemí's mother, but it was one of those nice little hobbies that were appreciated among her social circle. Besides, she liked the piano.

"The recital. More likely you made plans with Hugo Duarte to attend it together, and you don't want him taking another woman as his date or having to give up the chance of wearing a new dress. Too bad; this is more important."

"I'll have you know I hadn't even bought a new dress. I was going to wear the skirt I wore to Greta's cocktail party," Noemí said, which was half the truth because she had indeed made plans to go there with Hugo. "Look, the truth is the recital is not my main concern. I have to start classes in a few days. I can't take off like that. They'll fail me," she added.

"Then let them fail you. You'll take the classes again."

She was about to protest such a blithe statement when her father turned around and stared at her.

"Noemí, you've been going on and on about the National University. If you do this, I'll give you permission to enroll."

Noemí's parents allowed her to attend the Feminine University of Mexico, but they had balked when she declared she'd like to continue her studies upon graduation. She wanted to pursue a master's degree in anthropology. This would require her to enroll at the National. Her father thought this was both a waste of time and unsuitable with all those young men roaming the hallways and filling ladies' heads with silly and lewd thoughts.

Noemí's mother was equally unimpressed by these modern notions of hers. Girls were supposed to follow a simple life cycle, from debutante to wife. To study further would mean to delay this cycle, to remain a chrysalis inside a cocoon. They'd clashed over the matter a half dozen times, and her mother had cunningly stated it was up to Noemí's father to hand down a decree, while her father never seemed poised to do so.

Her father's statement therefore shocked her and presented an unexpected opportunity. "You mean it?" Noemí asked cautiously.

"Yes. It's a serious matter. I don't want a divorce splashed in the newspaper, but I also can't allow someone to take advantage of the family. And this is Catalina we are talking about," her father said, softening his tone. "She's had her share of misfortunes and might dearly need a friendly face. That might be, in the end, all she needs."

Catalina had been struck by calamity on several occasions. First the death of her father, followed by her mother's remarriage to a stepfather who often had her in tears. Catalina's mother had passed away a couple of years later and the girl had moved into Noemí's household: the stepfather had already left by then. Despite the warm embrace of the Taboadas, these deaths had deeply affected her. Later, as a young woman, there had been her broken engagement, which caused much strife and hurt feelings.

There had also been a rather goofy young man who courted Catalina for many months and whom she seemed to like very much. But Noemí's father had chased him away, unimpressed by the fellow. After that aborted romance, Catalina must have learned her lesson, for her relationship with Virgil Doyle had been a paragon of discretion. Or maybe it had been Virgil who had been more wily and urged Catalina to keep mum about them until it was too late to disrupt any wedding.

"I suppose I could give notice that I'll be away for a few days," she said.

"Good. We'll telegraph Virgil back and let them know you are on your way. Discretion and smarts, that's what I need. He is her husband and has a right to make decisions on her behalf, but we cannot be idle if he is reckless."

"I should make you put it in writing, the bit about the university."

Her father sat down behind his desk again. "As if I'd break my word. Now go get those flowers out of your hair and start packing your clothes. I know it'll take you forever to decide what to wear. Who are you supposed to be, incidentally?" her father asked, clearly dissatisfied with the cut of her dress and her bare shoulders.

"I'm dressed as Spring," she replied.

"It's cold there. If you intend to parade around in anything similar to that, you better take a sweater," he said dryly.

Though normally she would have come up with a clever rejoinder, she remained unusually quiet. It occurred to Noemí, after having agreed to the venture, that she knew very little of the place where she was going and the people she would meet. This was no cruise or pleasure trip. But she quickly assured herself that Father had picked her for this mission, and accomplish it she would. Flighty? Bah. She'd show Father the dedication he wanted from her. Perhaps he'd come to see her, after her success—for she could never picture herself failing—as more deserving and mature.

# 2

When Noemí was a little girl and Catalina read fairy tales to her, she used to mention "the forest," that place where Hansel and Gretel tossed their bread-crumbs or Little Red Riding Hood met a wolf. Growing up in a large city, it did not occur to Noemí until much later that forests were real places, which could be found in an atlas. Her family vacationed in Veracruz, in her grandmother's house by the sea, with no tall trees in sight. Even after she grew up, the forest remained in her mind a picture glimpsed in a story-book by a child, with charcoal outlines and bright splashes of color in the middle.

It took her a while, therefore, to realize that she was headed *into* a forest, for El Triunfo was perched on the side of a steep mountain carpeted with colorful wildflowers and covered thickly with pines and oaks. Noemí sighted sheep milling around and goats braving sheer rock walls. Silver had given the region its riches, but tallow from these animals had helped illuminate the mines, and they were plentiful. It was all very pretty.

The higher the train moved and the closer it got to El Triunfo, though, the more the bucolic landscape changed and Noemí reassessed her idea of it. Deep ravines cut the land, and rugged ridges loomed outside the window. What had been charming rivulets turned into strong, gushing rivers, which spelled doom should anyone be dragged by their currents. At the bottom of the mountains farmers tended groves and fields of alfalfa, but there were no such crops here, just the goats climbing up and down rocks. The land kept its riches in the dark, sprouting no trees with fruit.

The air grew thin as the train struggled up the mountain until it stuttered and stopped.

Noemí grabbed her suitcases. She'd brought two of them and had been tempted to also pack her favorite trunk, though in the end she had judged it too cumbersome. Despite this concession, the suitcases were large and heavy.

The train station was not busy and was barely a station at all, just a lonesome square-shaped building with a half-asleep woman behind the ticket counter. Three little boys were chasing one another around the station, playing tag, and she offered them some coins if they helped her lug her suitcases outside. They did, gladly. They looked underfed, and she wondered how the town's inhabitants got by now the mine was closed and only the goats provided the opportunity for a bit of commerce.

Noemí was prepared for the chill of the mountain. The unexpected element was therefore the thin fog that greeted her that afternoon. She looked at it curiously as she adjusted her teal calotte hat with the long yellow feather and peered onto the street looking at her ride, for there could hardly be any mistaking it. It was the single automobile parked in front of the station, a preposterously large vehicle that made her think of swanky silent film stars of two or three decades earlier—the kind of automobile her father might have driven in his youth to flaunt his wealth.

But the vehicle in front of her was dated, dirty, and it needed a paint job. Therefore it was not truly the kind of automobile a movie star would drive these days, but seemed to be a relic that had been haphazardly dusted off and dragged onto the street.

She thought the driver might match the car and expected to find an elderly man behind the wheel, but a young fellow of about her age in a corduroy jacket stepped out. He was fair-haired and pale—she didn't realize anyone could be *that* pale; goodness, did he ever wander into the sun?—his eyes uncertain, his mouth straining to form a smile or a greeting.

Noemí paid the boys who had helped bring her luggage out, then marched forward and extended her hand.

"I am Noemí Taboada. Has Mr. Doyle sent you?" she asked.

"Yes, Uncle Howard said to pick you up," he replied, shaking her hand weakly. "I'm Francis. I hope the ride was pleasant? Those are all your things, Miss Taboada? Can I help you with them?" he asked in quick succession, as if he preferred to end all sentences with question marks rather than commit to definite statements.

"You can call me Noemí. Miss Taboada sounds so fussy. That's the sum of my luggage, and yes, I'd love some assistance."

He grabbed her two suitcases and placed them in the trunk, then went around the car and opened the door for her. The town, as she saw it from her window, was peppered with winding streets, colorful houses with flower pots at their windows, sturdy wooden doors, long stairways, a church, and all the usual details that any guidebook would call "quaint."

Despite this, it was clear El Triunfo was not in any guide-books. It had the musty air of a place that had withered away. The houses were colorful, yes, but the color was peeling from most of the walls, some of the doors had been defaced, half of the flowers in the pots were wilting, and the town showed few signs of activity.

It was not that unusual. Many formerly thriving mining sites that had extracted silver and gold during the Colonia interrupted their operations once the War of Independence broke out. Later on, the English and the French were welcomed during the tranquil Porfiriato, their pockets growing fat with mineral riches. But the Revolution had ended this second boom. There were many hamlets like El Triunfo where one could peek at fine chapels built when money and people were plentiful; places where the earth would never again spill wealth from its womb.

Yet the Doyles lingered in this land, when many others had long gone. Perhaps, she thought, they'd learned to love it, though she was not much impressed by it, for it was a steep and abrupt landscape. It didn't look at all like the mountains from her childhood storybooks, where the trees appeared lovely and flowers grew by the road; it didn't resemble the enchanting place Catalina had said she would live in. Like the old car that had picked Noemí up, the town clung to the dregs of splendor.

Francis drove up a narrow road that climbed deeper into the mountains, the air growing rawer, the mist intensifying. She rubbed her hands together.

"Is it very far?" she asked.

Again he looked uncertain. "Not that far," Francis said slowly, as if they were discussing a matter that had to be considered with much care. "The road is bad or I'd go faster. It used to be, a long time ago, when the mine was open, that the roads around here were all in good shape, even near High Place."

"High Place?"

"That's what we call it, our home. And behind it, the English cemetery."

"Is it really very English?" she said, smiling.

"Yes," he said, gripping the wheel with both hands with a strength she would not have imagined from his limp handshake.

"Oh?" she said, waiting for more.

"You'll see it. It's all very English. Um, that's what Uncle Howard wanted, a little piece of England. He even brought European earth here."

"Do you think he had an extreme case of nostalgia?"

"Indeed. I might as well tell you, we don't speak Spanish at High Place. My great uncle doesn't know a word of it, Virgil fares poorly, and my mother wouldn't ever attempt to stitch a sentence together. Is . . . is your English any good?"

"Lessons every day since I was six," she said, switching from Spanish to English. "I'm sure I'll have no trouble."

The trees grew closer together, and it was dark under their branches. She was not one for nature, not the real thing. The last time she had been anywhere near a forest had been on that excursion to El Desierto de los Leones when they went riding and then her brother and her friends decided to do some practice shooting with tin cans. That had been two, maybe even three years before. This place didn't compare to that. It was wilder here.

She found herself warily assessing the height of the trees and the depths of the ravines. Both were considerable. The mist thickened, making her wince, fearing they'd wind up halfway down the mountain if they took a wrong turn. How many eager miners hunting for silver had fallen off a cliff? The mountains offered mineral riches and a quick death. But Francis seemed secure in his driving even if his words faltered. She didn't generally like shy men—they got on her nerves—but who cared. It was not as if she'd come to see him or any other members of his family.

"Who are you, anyway?" she asked, to distract herself from the thought of ravines and cars crashing against unseen trees.

"Francis."

"Well, yes, but are you Virgil's little cousin? Long-lost uncle? Another black sheep I must be informed about?"

She spoke in that droll way she liked, the one she used at cocktail parties, and that always seemed to get her very far with people, and he replied as she expected, smiling a little.

"First cousin, once removed. He's a bit older than me."

"I've never understood that. Once, twice, thrice removed. Who keeps track of such a thing? I always figure if they come to my birthday party we are related and that's it, no need to pull out the genealogy chart."

"It certainly simplifies things," he said. The smile was real now.

"Are you a good cousin? I hated my boy cousins when I was little. They'd always push my head against the cake at my party even though I didn't want to do the whole mordida thing."

"Mordida?"

"Yes. You're supposed to take a bite of the cake before it is cut, but someone always shoves your head into it. I guess you didn't have to endure that at High Place."

"There aren't many parties at High Place."

"The name must be a literal description," she mused, because they kept going up. Did the road have no end? The wheels of the car crunched over a fallen tree branch, then another.

"Yes."

"I've never been in a house with a name. Who does that these days?"

"We're old-fashioned," he mumbled.

Noemí eyed the young man skeptically. Her mother would have said he needed iron in his diet and a good cut of meat. By the looks of those thin fingers he sustained himself on dewdrops and honey, and his tone tended toward whispers. Virgil had seemed to her much more physical than this lad, much more present. Older, too, as Francis had indicated. Virgil was thirty-something; she forgot his exact age.

They hit a rock or some bump in the road. Noemí let out an irritated "ouch."

"Sorry about that," Francis said.

"I don't think it's your fault. Does it always look like this?" she asked. "It's like driving in a bowl of milk."

"This is nothing," he said with a chuckle. Well. At least he was relaxing.

Then, all of a sudden, they were there, emerging into a clearing, and the house seemed to leap out of the mist to greet them with eager arms. It was so odd! It looked absolutely Victorian in construction, with its broken shingles, elaborate ornamentation, and dirty bay windows. She'd never seen anything like it in real life; it was terribly different from her family's modern house, the apartments of her friends, or the colonial houses with façades of red tezontle.

The house loomed over them like a great, quiet gargoyle. It might have been foreboding, evoking images of ghosts and haunted places, if it had not seemed so tired, slats missing from a couple of shutters, the ebony porch groaning as they made their way up the steps to the door, which came complete with a silver knocker shaped like a fist dangling from a circle.

*It's the abandoned shell of a snail*, she told herself, and the thought of snails brought her back to her childhood, playing in the courtyard of their house, moving aside the potted plants and seeing the roly-polies scuttle about as they tried to hide again. Or feeding sugar cubes to the ants, despite her mother's admonishments. Also the kind tabby, which slept under the bougainvillea and let itself be petted endlessly by the children. She did not imagine they had a cat in this house, nor canaries chirping merrily in their cages that she might feed in the mornings.

Francis took out a key and opened the heavy door. Noemí walked into the entrance hall, which gave them an immediate view of a grand staircase of mahogany and oak with a round, stained-glass window on the second landing. The window threw shades of reds and blues and yellows upon a faded green carpet, and two carvings of nymphs—one at the bottom of the stairs by the newel post, another by the window—stood as silent guardians of the house. By the entrance there had been a painting or a mirror on a wall, and its oval outline was visible against the wallpaper, like a lonesome fingerprint at the scene of a crime. Above their heads there hung a nine-arm chandelier, its crystal cloudy with age.

A woman was coming down the stairs, her left hand sliding down the banister. She was not an old woman although she had streaks of silver in her hair, her body too straight and nimble to belong to a senior citizen. But her severe gray dress and the hardness in her eyes added years that were not embedded in the flesh of her frame.

"Mother, this is Noemí Taboada," Francis said as he began the climb up with Noemí's suitcases.

Noemí followed him, smiling, and offered her hand to the woman, who looked at it as if she was holding up a piece of week-old fish. Instead of shaking her hand, the woman turned around and began walking up the stairs.

"A pleasure to meet you," the woman said with her back to Noemí. "I am Florence, Mr. Doyle's niece."

Noemí felt like scoffing but bit her tongue and simply slid next to Florence, walking at her pace.

"Thank you."

"I run High Place, and therefore, if you need anything, you should come to me. We do things a certain way around here, and we expect you to follow the rules."

"What are the rules?" she asked.

They passed next to the stained-glass window, which Noemí noted featured a bright, stylized flower. Cobalt oxide had been used to create the blue of the petals. She knew such things. The paint business, as her father put it, had provided her with an endless array of chemical facts, which she mostly ignored and which, nevertheless, stuck in her head like an annoying song.

"The most important rule is that we are a quiet and private lot," Florence was saying. "My uncle, Mr. Howard Doyle, is very old and spends most of his time in his room. You are not to bother him. Second of all, I am in charge of nursing your cousin. She is to get plenty of rest, so you must not bother her unnecessarily either. Do not wander away from the house on your own; it is easy to get lost and the region is puckered with ravines."

"Anything else?"

"We do not go to town often. If you have business there, you must ask me, and I'll have Charles drive you."

"Who is he?"

"One of our staff members. It's a rather small staff these days: three people. They've served the family for many years."

They went down a carpeted hallway, oval and oblong oil portraits on the walls serving as decoration. The faces of long-dead Doyles stared at Noemí from across time, women in bonnets and heavy dresses, men in top hats wearing gloves and dour expressions. The kind of people who might lay claim to a family crest. Pale, fair-haired, like Francis and his mother. One face blended into another. She would not have been able to tell them apart even if she'd looked closely.

"This will be your room," said Florence once they reached a door with a decorative crystal knob. "I should warn you there is no smoking in this house, in case you partake in that particular vice," she added, eyeing Noemí's chic handbag, as if she could see through it and into her pack of cigarettes.

*Vice*, Noemí thought and was reminded of the nuns who had overseen her education. She'd learned rebellion while muttering the rosary.

Noemí stepped inside the bedroom and regarded the ancient four-poster bed, which looked like something out of a Gothic tale; it even had curtains you could close around it, cocooning yourself from the world. Francis set the suitcases by a narrow window—this window was colorless; the extravagant stained-glass panes did not extend to the private quarters—while Florence pointed out the armoire with its stash of extra blankets.

"We are high up the mountain. It gets very cold here," she said. "I hope you brought a sweater."

"I have a rebozo."

The woman opened a chest at the foot of the bed and took out a few candles and one of the ugliest candelabra Noemí had ever seen, all silver, a cherub holding up the base. Then she closed the chest, leaving these findings on top of it.

"Electrical lighting was installed in 1909. Right before the revolution. But there have been few improvements in the four decades since then. We have a generator, and it can produce enough power for the refrigerator or to light a few bulbs. But it's far from suitable lighting for this whole house. Accordingly, we rely on candles and oil lamps."

"I wouldn't even know how you use an oil lamp," Noemí said with a chuckle. "I've never even been camping properly."

"Even a simpleton can understand the basic principles," Florence said, and then continued talking, giving Noemí no chance to reply. "The boiler is finicky at times and at any rate young people shouldn't have very hot showers; a mild bath will do for you. There is no fireplace in this room, but a great large one downstairs. Have I forgotten anything, Francis? No, very well."

The woman looked at her son, but did not give him any time to reply either. Noemí doubted many people got a chance to utter a word with her around.

"I'd like to speak to Catalina," Noemí said.

Florence, who must have thought this was the end of their conversation, already had a hand on the doorknob.

"Today?" the woman asked.

"Yes."

"It's almost time for her medication. She won't stay awake after she takes it."

"I want a few minutes with her."

"Mother, she's come so far," Francis said.

His interjection seemed to have caught the woman off guard. Florence raised an eyebrow at the young man and clasped her hands together.

"Well, I suppose in the city you have a different sense of time, running to and fro," she said. "If you must meet her forthwith, then you better come with me. Francis, why don't you go see if Uncle Howard will be joining us for dinner tonight? I don't want surprises."

Florence guided Noemí down another long hallway and into a room with another four-poster bed, an ornate dressing table with a three-winged mirror, and an armoire large enough to hold a small army. The wallpaper in here was a diluted blue with a floral pattern. Little landscape paintings decorated the walls, coastal images of great cliffs and lonely beaches, but these were not local views. This was England, most likely, preserved in oils and silver frames.

A chair had been set by a window. Catalina sat in it. She was looking outside and did not stir when the women walked into the room. Her auburn hair was gathered at her nape. Noemí had steeled herself to greet a stranger ravaged by disease, but Catalina did not seem much different from when she'd lived in Mexico City. Her dreamy quality was perhaps amplified by the décor, but this was the sum of the change.

"She is supposed to have her medication in five minutes," Florence said, consulting her wristwatch.

"Then I'll take those five minutes."

The older woman did not seem happy, but she left. Noemí approached her cousin. The younger woman had not glanced at her; she was oddly still.

"Catalina? It's me, Noemí."

She placed a hand gently on her cousin's shoulder, and only then did Catalina look at Noemí. She smiled slowly.

"Noemí, you've come."

She stood in front of Catalina nodding. "Yes. Father has sent me to check up on you. How are you feeling? What's wrong?"

"I feel awful. I had a fever, Noemí. I'm sick with tuberculosis, but I'm feeling better."

"You wrote a letter to us, do you remember? You said odd things in it."

"I don't quite remember everything I wrote," Catalina said. "I had such a high temperature."

Catalina was five years older than Noemí. Not a great age gap, but enough that when they were children, Catalina had taken on a motherly role. Noemí remembered many an afternoon spent with Catalina making crafts, cutting dresses for paper dolls, going to the movies, listening to her spin fairy tales. It felt strange to see her like this, listless, dependent on others when they had all once depended on her. She did not like it at all.

"It made my father awfully nervous," Noemí said.

"I'm so sorry, darling. I shouldn't have written. You probably had many things to do in the city. Your friends, your classes, and now you are here because I scribbled nonsense on a piece of paper."

"Don't worry about it. I wanted to come and see you. We haven't seen each other in ages. I had thought you would have come visit us by now, to be frank."

"Yes," Catalina said. "Yes, I thought so too. But it's impossible to get out of this house."

Catalina was pensive. Her eyes, hazel pools of stagnant water, grew duller, and her mouth opened, as if she were getting ready to speak, except she did not. She drew her breath in instead, held it there, then turned her head and coughed.

"Catalina?"

"Time for your medicine," Florence said, marching into the room, a glass bottle and a spoon in hand. "Come now."

Catalina obediently had a spoon of the medication, then Florence helped her into bed, pulling the covers up to her chin.

"Let's go," Florence said. "She needs her rest. You can talk tomorrow."

Catalina nodded. Florence walked Noemí back to her room, giving her a brief sketch of the house—the kitchen was in that direction, the library in this other one—and told her they'd fetch her for dinner at seven. Noemí unpacked, placed her clothes in the armoire, and went to the bathroom to freshen up. There was an ancient bathtub there, a bathroom cabinet, and traces of mold on the ceiling. Many tiles around the tub were cracked, but fresh towels had been set atop a three-legged stool, and the robe hanging from a hook looked clean.

She tested the light switch on the wall, but the light fixture in the bathroom did not work. In her room, Noemí could not locate a single lamp with a light bulb, though there was one electrical outlet. She supposed Florence had not been joking about relying on candles and oil lamps.

She opened her purse and riffled through it until she found her cigarettes. A tiny cup decorated with half-naked cupids on the night table served as an impromptu ashtray. After taking a couple of puffs, she wandered to the window, lest Florence complain about the stench. But the window would not budge.

She stood, looking outside at the mist.

# 3

Florence came back for her promptly at seven with an oil lamp in her hand to light the way. They went down the stairs to a dining room weighed down by a monstrous chandelier, much like the one in the hallway entrance, which remained unlit. There was a table big enough for a dozen people, with the appropriate tablecloth of white damask. Candelabra had been set on it. The long, white, tapered candles reminded Noemí of church.

The walls were lined with china cabinets crammed with lace, porcelain, and most of all with silver. Cups and plates bearing the proud initial of their owners—the triumphant, stylized D of the Doyles—serving trays and empty vases, which might have once gleamed under the glow of the candles and now looked tarnished and dull.

Florence pointed to a chair, and Noemí sat down. Francis was already seated across from her and Florence took her place at his side. A gray-haired maid walked in and placed bowls filled with a watery soup in front of them. Florence and Francis began to eat.

"Will no one else be joining us?" she asked.

"Your cousin is asleep. Uncle Howard and Cousin Virgil may come down, perhaps later," Florence said.

Noemí arranged a napkin on her lap. She had soup, but only a little. She was not used to eating at this hour. Nights were no time for heavy meals; at home they had pastries and coffee with milk. She wondered how she'd fare with a different schedule. *À l'anglaise*, like their French teacher used to say. *La panure à l'anglaise*, repeat after me. Would they have four o'clock tea, or was it five o'clock?

The plates were taken away in silence, and in silence there came the main dish, chicken in an unappealing creamy white sauce with mushrooms. The wine they'd poured her was very dark and sweet. She didn't like it.

Noemí pushed the mushrooms around her plate with her fork while trying to see what lay in the gloomy cabinets across from her.

"It's mostly silver objects in here, isn't it?" she said. "Did all of these come from your mine?"

Francis nodded. "Yes, back in the day."

"Why did it close?"

"There were strikes and then—" Francis began to say, but his mother immediately raised her head and stared at Noemí.

"We do not talk during dinner."

"Not even to say 'pass the salt'?" Noemí asked lightly, twirling her fork.

"I can see you think yourself terribly amusing. We do not talk during dinner. That is the way it is. We appreciate the silence in this house."

"Come, Florence, surely we can make a bit of conversation. For the sake of our guest," said a man in a dark suit as he walked into the room, leaning on Virgil.

*Old* would have been an inaccurate word to describe him. He was ancient, his face gouged with wrinkles, a few sparse hairs stubbornly attached to his skull. He was very pale too, like an underground creature. A slug, perhaps. His veins contrasted with his pallor, thin, spidery lines of purple and blue.

Noemí watched him shuffle toward the head of the table and sit down. Virgil sat too, by his father's right, his chair at such an angle that he remained half enveloped in shadows.

The maid didn't bring a plate for the old man, only a glass of dark wine. Maybe he'd already eaten and had ventured downstairs for her sake.

"Sir, I'm Noemí Taboada. It's nice to meet you," she said.

"And I am Howard Doyle, Virgil's father. Although you've guessed that already."

The old man wore an old-fashioned cravat, his neck hidden under a mound of fabric, a circular silver pin upon it as a decoration, a large amber ring on his index finger. He fixed his eyes on her. The rest of him was bleached of color, but the eyes were of a startling blue, unimpeded by cataracts and undimmed by age. The eyes burned coldly in that ancient face and commanded her attention, vivisecting the young woman with his gaze.

"You are much darker than your cousin, Miss Taboada," Howard said after he had completed his examination of her.

"Pardon me?" she asked, thinking she'd heard him wrong.

He pointed at her. "Both your coloration and your hair. They are much darker than Catalina's. I imagine they reflect your Indian heritage rather than the French. You do have some Indian in you, no? Like most of the mestizos here do."

"Catalina's mother was from France. My father is from Veracruz and my mother from Oaxaca. We are Mazatec on her side. What is your point?" she asked flatly.

The old man smiled. A closed smile, no teeth. She could picture his teeth, yellowed and broken.

Virgil had motioned to the maid, and a glass of wine was placed before him. The others had resumed their silent eating. This was to be, then, a conversation between two parties.

"Merely an observation. Now tell me, Miss Taboada, do you believe as Mr. Vasconcelos does that it is the obligation, no, the destiny, of the people of Mexico to forge a new race that encompasses all races? A 'cosmic' race? A bronze race? This despite the research of Davenport and Steggerda?"

"You mean their work in Jamaica?"

"Splendid, Catalina was correct. You do have an interest in anthropology."

"Yes," she said. She did not wish to share more than that single word.

"What are your thoughts on the intermingling of superior and inferior types?" he asked, ignoring her discomfort.

Noemí felt the eyes of all the family members on her. Her presence was a novelty and an alteration to their patterns. An organism introduced into a sterile environment. They waited to hear what she revealed and to analyze her words. Well, let them see that she could keep her cool.

She had experience dealing with irritating men. They did not fluster her. She had learned, by navigating cocktail parties and meals at restaurants, that showing any kind of reaction to their crude remarks emboldened them.

"I once read a paper by Gamio in which he said that harsh natural selection has allowed the indigenous people of this continent to survive, and Europeans would benefit from intermingling with them," she said, touching her fork and feeling the cold metal under her fingertips. "It turns the whole superior and inferior idea around, doesn't it?" she asked, the question sounding innocent and yet a little bit mordant.

The elder Doyle seemed pleased with this answer, his face growing animated. "Do not be upset with me, Miss Taboada. I do not mean to insult you. Your countryman, Vasconcelos, he speaks of the mysteries of 'aesthetic taste' which will help shape this bronze race, and I think you are a good example of that sort."

"Of what sort?"

He smiled again, this time his teeth visible, the lips drawn. The teeth were not yellow as she'd imagined, but porcelain-white and whole. But the gums, which she could see clearly, were a noxious shade of purple.

"Of a new beauty, Miss Taboada. Mr. Vasoncelos makes it very clear that the unattractive will not procreate. Beauty attracts beauty and begets beauty. It is a means of selection. You see, I am offering you a compliment."

"That is a very strange compliment," she managed to say, swallowing her disgust.

"You should take it, Miss Taboada. I don't hand them out lightly. Now, I am tired. I will retire, but do not doubt this has been an invigorating conversation. Francis, help me up."

The younger man assisted the waxwork and they left the room. Florence drank from her wine, the slim stem carefully lifted and pressed against her lips. The oppressive silence had settled upon them again. Noemí thought that if she paid attention, she would be able to hear everyone's hearts beating.

She wondered how Catalina could bear living in this place. Catalina had always been so sweet, always the nurturer watching over the younger ones, a smile on her lips. Did they really make her sit at this table in utter silence, the curtains drawn, the candles offering their meager light? Did that old man try to engage her in obnoxious conversations? Had Catalina ever been reduced to tears? At their dining room table in Mexico City her father liked to tell riddles and offer prizes to the child who piped up with the correct answer.

The maid came by to take away the dishes. Virgil, who had not properly acknowledged Noemí, finally looked at her, their eyes meeting. "I imagine you have questions for me."

"Yes," she said.

"Let's go to the sitting room."

He grabbed one of the silver candelabra on the table and walked her down a hallway and into a large chamber with an equally enormous fireplace and a black walnut mantel carved with the shapes of flowers. Above the fireplace hung a still life of fruits, roses, and delicate vines. A couple of kerosene lamps atop twin ebony tables provided further illumination.

Two matching faded green velour settees were arranged at one end of the room, and next to them there were three chairs covered with antimacassars. White vases collected dust, indicating that this space had once been used to receive visitors and supply merriment.

Virgil opened the doors of a sideboard with silver hinges and a marble serving surface. He took out a decanter with a curious stopper shaped like a flower and filled two glasses, handing her one. Then he sat on one of the stately, stiff, gold brocade armchairs set by the fireplace. She followed suit.

Since this room was well illuminated, she was presented with a better picture of the man. They had met during Catalina's wedding, but it had all been very quick and a year had passed. She had not been able to recall what he looked like. He was fair-haired, blue-eyed like his father, and his coolly sculpted face was burnished with imperiousness. His double-breasted lounge suit was sleek, charcoal gray with a herringbone pattern, very proper, though he'd eschewed a tie, and the top button of his shirt was undone as if he were trying to imitate a casualness it was impossible for him to possess.

She was not sure how she should address him. Boys her age were easy to flatter. But he was older than she was. She must be more serious, temper her natural flirtatiousness lest he think her silly. He had the stamp of authority here, but she also had authority. She was an envoy.

The Kublai Khan sent messengers across his realm who carried a stone with his seal, and whoever mistreated a messenger would be put to death. Catalina had told her this story, narrating fables and history for Noemí.

Let Virgil understand, then, that Noemí had an invisible stone in her pocket.

"It was good of you to come on such short notice," Virgil said, though his tone was flat. Courtesy, but no warmth.

"I had to."

"Did you really?"

"My father was concerned," she said. There was her stone, even as his own badge was all around him, in this house and its

things. Noemí was a Taboada, sent by Leocadio Taboada himself.

"As I tried to tell him, there is no need for alarm."

"Catalina said she had tuberculosis. But I don't think that
quite explains her letter."

"Did you see the letter? What did it say exactly?" he asked,
leaning forward. His tone was still flat, but he looked alert.

"I did not consign it to memory. Enough that he asked me to
visit you."

"I see."

He turned his glass between his hands, the fire making it glint
and sparkle. He leaned back against the chair. He was handsome.
Like a sculpture. His face, rather than skin and bone, might have
been a death mask.

"Catalina was not well. She ran a very high fever. She sent that
letter in the midst of her sickness."

"Who is treating her?"

"Pardon me?" he replied.

"Someone must be treating her. Florence, is she your cousin?"

"Yes."

"Well, your cousin Florence gives her medicine. There must be
a doctor."

He stood up and grabbed a fireplace poker, stirring the burning logs. A spark flew through the air and landed on a tile dirty
with age, a crack running down its middle.

"There is a doctor. His name is Arthur Cummins. He has
been our physician for many years. We completely trust Dr. Cummins."

"Doesn't he think her behavior has been unusual, even with
tuberculosis?"

Virgil smirked. "Unusual. You have medical knowledge?"

"No. But my father did not send me here because he thought
everything was as *usual.*"

"No, your father wrote about psychiatrists at the first possible
opportunity. It's the thing he writes about, over and over again,"

Virgil said scornfully. It irritated her to hear him speaking in such a way about her father, as though he were terrible and unfair.

"I will speak to Catalina's doctor," Noemí replied, perhaps more forcefully than she should have, for at once he returned the poker to its stand with a quick and harsh movement of his arm.

"Demanding, are we?"

"I wouldn't say demanding, exactly. Concerned, more like it," she replied, taking care to smile, to show him this was really a small matter that might be easily resolved, and it must have worked, for he nodded.

"Arthur comes by every week. He'll stop by Thursday to see Catalina and my father."

"Your father is also ill?"

"My father is old. He has the aches that time bestows on all men. If you can wait until then, you may speak to Arthur."

"I have no intention of leaving yet."

"Tell me, how long do you expect to remain with us?"

"Not too long, I hope. Enough to figure out if Catalina needs me. I'm sure I could find lodging in town if I'm too much of a nuisance."

"It's a very small town. There's no hotel, not even a guest-house. No, you can remain here. I'm not trying to run you out. I wish you'd come for another reason, I suppose."

She had not thought there would be a hotel, although she would have been glad to discover one. The house was dreary, and so was everyone in it. She could believe a woman could sicken quickly in a place like this.

She sipped her wine. It was the same dark vintage she'd had in the dining room, sweet and strong.

"Is your room satisfactory?" Virgil asked, his tone warming, turning a bit more cordial. She was, perhaps, not his enemy.

"It's fine. Having no electricity is odd, but I don't think anyone has died from a lack of light bulbs yet."

"Catalina thinks the candlelight is romantic."

Noemí supposed she would. It was the kind of thing she could imagine impressing her cousin: an old house atop a hill, with mist and moonlight, like an etching out of a Gothic novel. *Wuthering Heights* and *Jane Eyre*, those were Catalina's sort of books. Moors and spiderwebs. Castles too, and wicked stepmothers who force princesses to eat poisoned apples, dark fairies cursing maidens and wizards who turn handsome lords into beasts. Noemí preferred to jump from party to party on a weekend and drive a convertible.

So maybe, in the end, this house suited Catalina fine. Could it be it had been a bit of a fever? Noemí held her glass between her hands, running her thumb down its side.

"Let me pour you another glass," Virgil said, playing the role of the attentive host.

It could grow on you, this drink. Already it had lulled her into a half sleep, and she blinked when he spoke. His hand brushed hers as he made a gesture to refill her glass, but she shook her head. She knew her limits, traced them firmly.

"No, thanks," she said, setting the glass aside and rising from the chair, which had proven more comfortable than she might have guessed.

"I shall insist."

She shook her head prettily, defusing the denial with that tried and proven trick. "Heavens, no. I will decline and wrap myself in a blanket and go to bed."

His face was still remote, yet now seemed infused with more vitality as he surveyed her very carefully. There was a spark in his eye. He'd found an item of interest; one of her gestures or words struck him as novel. She thought it was her refusal that amused him. He was, likely, not used to being refused. But then, many men were the same.

"I can walk you to your room," he offered, smooth and gallant.

They went up the stairs, him holding an oil lamp hand-painted with patterns of vines, which made the light emanating from it turn emerald and infused the walls with a strange hue: it painted the velvet curtains green. In one or other of her stories Catalina had told her the Kublai Khan executed his enemies by smothering them with velvet pillows so there would be no blood. She thought this house, with all its fabrics and rugs and tassels, could smother a whole army.

# 4

reakfast was brought to her on a tray. Thank goodness she did not have to sit down to eat with the whole family that morning, although who knew what dinner might bring. The chance for solitude made the porridge, toast, and jam she had been served a bit more appetizing. The drink available was tea, which she disliked. She was a coffee drinker, preferred it black, and this tea had a definite, faint, fruity scent to it.

After a shower, Noemí applied lipstick and lined her eyes with a little black pencil. She knew her large, dark eyes and her generous lips were her greatest assets, and she used them to excellent effect. She took her time going through her clothes and picked a purple acetate taffeta dress with a full, pleated skirt. It was too fine to be worn as a day dress—she had rung in 1950 in a similar outfit eight months before—but then she tended toward opulence. Besides, she wanted to defy the gloom around her. She decided that this way her exploration of the house would be more entertaining.

There certainly was a lot of gloom. Daylight did not improve High Place. When she walked the ground floor and opened a couple of creaky doors she was inevitably greeted by the ghostly sight of furniture covered with white sheets and draperies shut tight. Wherever the odd ray of sun slipped into a room, one could see dust motes dancing in the air. In the hallways, for every electrified sconce with a bulb there were three that were bare. It was obvious most of the house was not in use.

She had assumed the Doyles would have a piano, even if it was out of tune, but there was none, and neither could she find a radio or even an old gramophone. And how she loved music. Anything from Lara to Ravel. Dancing too. What a pity that she'd be left without music.

She wandered into a library. A narrow wooden frieze with a repeating pattern of acanthus leaves, divided by pilasters, encircled the room, which was lined with tall, built-in bookcases stuffed with leather-bound volumes. She reached out for a book at random and opened it to see it had been ravaged by mold and was perfumed with the sweet scent of rot. She clapped the book shut and returned it to its place.

The shelves also contained issues of old magazines, including *Eugenics: A Journal of Race Betterment* and the *American Journal of Eugenics*.

*How appropriate*, she thought, remembering Howard Doyle's inane questions. She wondered if he kept a pair of calipers to measure his guests' skulls.

There was a terrestrial globe with countries' names out of date in a lonesome corner and a marble bust of Shakespeare by a window. A large, circular rug had been placed in the middle of the room, and when she looked down at it she realized it showed the image of a black serpent biting its tail against a crimson background, with tiny flowers and vines all around it.

This was probably one of the best maintained rooms in the house—certainly one of the most used, judging by the lack of dust—and still it seemed a tad frayed, its curtains faded into an ugly green, more than a few books blighted by mildew.

A door at the other end of the library connected with a large office. Inside it, the heads of three stags had been mounted on a wall. An empty rifle cabinet with cut-glass doors was set in a corner. Somebody had hunted and given it up. Atop a desk of black walnut she found more journals of eugenics research. A page was marked in one of them. She read it.

The idea that the half-breed mestizo of Mexico inherits the worst traits of their progenitors is incorrect. If the stamp of an inferior race afflicts them, it is due to a lack of proper social models. Their impulsive temperament requires early restraint. Nevertheless, the mestizo possess many inherent splendid attributes, including a robustness of body . . .

She no longer wondered if Howard Doyle had a pair of calipers; now she wondered how many he kept. Maybe they were in one of the tall cabinets behind her, along with the family's pedigree chart. There was a trash can next to the desk, and Noemí slid the journal she had been reading into the can.

Noemí went in search of the kitchen, having been informed of its location by Florence the previous day. The kitchen was ill lit, its windows narrow, the paint on its walls peeling. Two people sat on a long bench, a wrinkled woman and a man who, though noticeably younger, still sported gray in his hair. He was fifty-something, surely, and she probably closer to seventy. They were using a round brush to clean the dirt off mushrooms. When Noemí walked in, they raised their heads but did not greet her.

"Good morning," she said. "We weren't introduced properly yesterday. I'm Noemí."

Both of them stared at her mutely. A door opened and a woman, also gray-haired, walked into the kitchen carrying a bucket. She recognized her as the maid who had served them during dinner, and she was of an age with the man. The maid did not speak to Noemí either, nodding instead, and then the couple who were seated on the bench nodded too before placing their attention back on their work. Did everyone follow this policy of silence in High Place?

"I'm—"

"We're working," the man said.

The three servants then looked down, their wan faces indifferent to the presence of the colorful socialite. Perhaps Virgil or Florence had informed them Noemí was someone of no importance and that they should not trouble themselves with her.

Noemí bit her lip and stepped outside the house using the back door the maid had opened. There was mist, like the previous day, and a chill to the air. Now she regretted not wearing a more comfortable outfit, a dress with pockets where she could carry her cigarettes and her lighter. Noemí adjusted the red rebozo around her shoulders.

"Did you have a good breakfast?" Francis asked, and she turned around to look at him. He'd also come out through the kitchen door, wrapped in a snug sweater.

"Yes, it was fine. How's your day going?"

"It's all right."

"What is that?" she asked, pointing at a nearby wooden structure, made hazy by the mist.

"That's the shed where we keep the generator and the fuel. Behind it is the coach house. Do you want to take a look at it? Maybe also go to the cemetery?"

"Sure."

The coach house seemed like a place that might have a hearse and two black horses inside, but instead there were two cars. One was the luxurious older vehicle that Francis had driven; the other was a newer but much more modest-looking car. A path snaked around the coach house, and they followed it through the trees and the mist until they reached a pair of iron gates decorated with the motif of a serpent eating its tail like the one she'd seen in the library.

They walked down a shady path, the trees so close together only a smattering of light made it through the branches. She could picture this same graveyard once upon a time in a tidier state, with carefully tended shrubs and flower beds, but now it was a realm of weeds and tall grasses, the vegetation threatening to swallow the place whole. The tombstones were blanketed with moss, and mushrooms sprouted by the graves. It was a picture of melancholy. Even the trees seemed lugubrious, though Noemí could not say why. Trees were trees.

It was the sum of it, she thought, and not the individual parts that made the English cemetery so sad. Neglect was one thing, but neglect and the shadows cast by the trees and the weeds clustered by the tombstones, the chill in the air, served to turn what would have been an ordinary collection of vegetation and tombstones into a fiercely displeasing picture.

She felt sorry for every single person buried there, just as she felt sorry for everyone living at High Place. Noemí bent down to look at a headstone, then another, and frowned.

"Why are all these from 1888?" she asked.

"The nearby mine was managed by Spaniards until Mexico's independence and left alone for many decades because nobody believed much silver could be extracted. But my great uncle Howard thought differently," Francis explained. "He brought modern English machines and a large English crew to do the work. He was successful, but a couple of years after reopening the mine there was an epidemic. It killed most of the English workers, and they were buried here."

"And then? What did he do after? Did he send for more workers from England?"

"Ah . . . no, no need . . . he always had Mexican workers too, a large contingent of them . . . but they're not all buried here. I believe they're in El Triunfo. Uncle Howard would know better."

A rather exclusive spot, then, though Noemí supposed it was for the best. The families of local crew members probably wanted to visit their loved ones, to leave flowers on their graves, which would have been impossible in this place, isolated from the town.

They walked onward until Noemí paused before a marble statue of a woman standing on a pedestal, flower wreaths in her hair. She flanked the doorway to a mausoleum with a pedimented doorway, her right hand pointing at its entrance. The name *Doyle* was carved in capital letters above this doorway along with a phrase in Latin: *Et Verbum caro factum est.*

"Who's this?"

"The statue is supposed to be the likeness of my great aunt Agnes, who died during the epidemic. And here, the Doyles are all buried here: my great aunt, my grandfather and grandmother, my cousins," he said, trailing off, dipping into an uncomfortable silence.

The silence, not only of the cemetery but of the whole house, unnerved Noemí. She was used to the rumble of the tram and the automobiles, the sound of canaries chirping in the inner courtyard by the gleeful fountain, the barking of the dogs and the melodies pouring from the radio as the cook hummed by the stove.

"It's so quiet here," she said and shook her head. "I don't like it."

"What do you like?" he asked, curious.

"Mesoamerican artifacts, zapote ice cream, Pedro Infante's movies, music, dancing, and driving," she said, counting a finger as she listed each item. She also liked to banter, but she was certain he could figure that out on his own.

"I'm afraid I can't be much help with that. What kind of car do you drive?"

"The prettiest Buick you've ever seen. A convertible, of course."

"Of course?"

"It's more fun driving without the hood on. It makes your hair look movie-star perfect. Also, it gives you ideas, you think better," she said, running a hand through her wavy hair jokingly. Noemí's father said she cared too much about her looks and parties to take school seriously, as if a woman could not do two things at once.

"What kind of ideas?"

"Ideas for my thesis, when I get to it," she said. "Ideas about what to do on the weekend, anything really. I do my best thinking when I'm in motion."

Francis had been looking at her, but now he lowered his eyes. "You're very different from your cousin," he told her.

"Are you also going to tell me I lean toward a 'darker' type, both my hair and coloration?"

"No," he said. "I didn't mean physically."

"Then?"

"I think you're charming." A panicked look contorted his face. "Not that your cousin lacks charm. You are charming in a special way," he said quickly.

*If you'd seen Catalina before*, she thought. If he'd seen her in the city with a pretty velvet dress, going from one side of the room to the other, that gentle smile on her lips and her eyes full of stars. But here, in that musty room, with those eyes dimmed and whatever sickness had taken hold of her body . . . but then, perhaps it wasn't that bad. Perhaps before the illness Catalina still smiled her sweet smile and took her husband by the hand, guiding him outside to count the stars.

"You say that because you haven't met my mother," Noemí replied lightly, not wishing to voice her thoughts on Catalina. "She is the most charming woman on Earth. In her presence I feel rather tacky and unremarkable."

He nodded. "I know what that is like. Virgil is the family's heir, the shining promise of the Doyles."

"You envy him?" she asked.

Francis was very thin; his face was that of a plaster saint haunted by his impending martyrdom. The dark circles under his eyes, almost like bruises against that pale skin, made her suspect a hidden ailment. Virgil Doyle on the other hand had been carved from marble: he exuded strength where Francis irradiated weakness, and Virgil's features—the eyebrows, the cheekbones, the full mouth—were bolder, entirely more attractive.

She could not judge Francis ill if he wished for that same vitality.

"I don't envy him his ease with words or his looks or his position, I envy his ability to go places. The farthest I've ever been is El Triunfo. That's it. He's traveled a bit. Not for long, he's always quick to return, but it's a respite."

There was no bitterness in Francis's words, only a tired sort of resignation as he continued speaking. "When my father was still alive he'd take me to town and I'd stare at the train station. I'd try to sneak in to look at the sign with the departure times."

Noemí adjusted her rebozo, trying to find warmth in its folds, but the cemetery was terribly damp and chilly; she could almost swear the temperature had dropped a couple of degrees the more they'd pressed into it. She shivered, and he noticed.

"I'm so stupid," Francis said, removing his sweater. "Here, have this."

"It's fine. Really, I couldn't let you freeze for my sake. Maybe if we start walking back I'll be better."

"Well, fine, but please, wear it. I swear I won't be cold."

She put on the sweater and wrapped the rebozo around her head. She thought he might pick up the pace since she was now walking in his sweater, but he didn't rush back home. He was probably used to the mist, the shady chill of the trees.

"Yesterday you asked about the silver items in the house. You were right, they came from our mine," he told her.

"It's been closed for a long time, hasn't it?"

Catalina had said something about that; it was why Noemí's father had not been keen on the match. Virgil seemed to him a stranger, maybe a fortune hunter. Noemí suspected he'd let Catalina marry him because he felt guilty about driving away her previous suitor: Catalina had loved him truly.

"It happened during the Revolution. That's when a host of things happened, one thing led to another and operations ceased. The year Virgil was born, 1915, that was the absolute end of it. The mines were flooded."

"Then he is thirty-five," she said. "And you are much younger."

"Ten years younger," Francis said with a nod. "A bit of an age gap, but he was the one friend I had growing up."

"But you must have gone to school eventually."

"We were schooled at High Place."

Noemí tried to think of the house filled with the noise of children's laughter, children playing hide and seek, children with a spinning top or a ball between their hands. But she couldn't. The house would have not allowed such a thing. The house would have demanded they spring from it fully grown.

"Can I ask you a question?" she said, when they were rounding the coach house and High Place was visible, the curtain of mist having parted. "Why the insistence on silence at the dining table?"

"My great uncle Howard, he's very old, very delicate, and very sensitive to noises. And the sound travels easily in the house."

"Is his room upstairs? He can't possibly hear people talking in the dining room."

"Noises carry," Francis said, his face serious, his eyes fixed on the old house. "Anyway, it's his house and he sets the rules."

"And you never bend them."

He glanced down at her, looking a little perplexed, as if it had not occurred to him until now that this was a possibility. She was certain he'd never drunk too much, stayed out far too late, nor blurted the wrong opinion in his family's company.

"No," he said, once again with that resigned note in his voice.

When they walked into the kitchen, she took off the sweater and handed it back to him. There was one maid now, the slightly younger maid, sitting by the stove. She did not look at them, too occupied with her chores to spare them a single glance.

"No, you should keep it," Francis said, ever polite. "It's rather warm."

"I can't be stealing your clothes."

"I have other sweaters," he said.

"Thanks."

He smiled at her. Florence walked into the room, again decked in a dark navy dress, her face severe, glancing at Francis and then at Noemí, as if they were small children and she was trying to determine whether they had scarfed down a forbidden box of sweets. "If you'll come with me for your lunch," she said.

This time it was the three of them at the table; the old man did not materialize and neither did Virgil. The lunch was conducted quickly, and after the dishes were cleared Noemí went back to her room. They brought up a tray with her dinner, so she supposed the dining room had been just for the first night and the lunch was also an anomaly. With her tray they also brought her an oil lamp, which she set by the bedside. She tried to read the copy of *Witchcraft, Oracles, and Magic Among the Azande,* which she'd brought with her, but kept getting distracted. Noises did carry, she thought, as she focused on the creaking of floorboards.

In a corner of her room there was a bit of mold upon the wallpaper that caught her eye. She thought of those green wallpapers so beloved by the Victorians that contained arsenic. The so-called Paris and Scheele greens. And wasn't there something in a book she'd read once about how microscopic fungi could act upon the dyes in the paper and form arsine gas, sickening the people in the room?

She was certain she'd heard about how these most civilized Victorians had been killing themselves in this way, the fungi chomping on the paste in the wall, causing unseen chemical reactions. She couldn't remember the name of the fungus that had been the culprit—Latin names danced at the tip of her tongue, *brevicaule*—but she thought she had the facts right. Her grandfather had been a chemist and her father's business was the production of pigments and dyes, so she knew to mix zinc sulfide and barium sulfate if you wanted to make lithopone and a myriad of other bits of information.

Well, the wallpaper was not green. Not even close to green; it was a muted pink, the color of faded roses, with ugly yellow medallions running across it. Medallions or circles; when you looked at it closely you might think they were wreaths. She might have preferred the green wallpaper. This was hideous, and when she closed her eyes, the yellow circles danced behind her eyelids, flickers of color against black.

# 5

atalina sat by the window again that morning. She seemed remote, like the last time Noemí had seen her. Noemí thought of a drawing of Ophelia that used to hang in their house. Ophelia dragged by the current, glimpsed through a wall of reeds. This was Catalina that morning. Yet it was good to see her, to sit together and update her cousin on the people and things in Mexico City. She detailed an exhibit she had been to three weeks prior, knowing Catalina would be interested in such things, and then imitated a couple of friends of theirs with such accuracy a smile formed on her cousin's lips, and Catalina laughed.

"You are so good when you do impressions. Tell me, are you still bent on those theater classes?" Catalina asked.

"No. I have been thinking about anthropology. A master's degree. Doesn't that sound interesting?"

"Always with a new idea, Noemí. Always a new pursuit."

She'd heard such a refrain often. She supposed that her family was right to view her university studies skeptically, seeing as she'd changed her mind already thrice about where her interests lay, but she knew rather fiercely that she wanted to do something special with her life. She hadn't found what exactly that would be, although anthropology appeared to her more promising than previous explorations.

Anyway, when Catalina spoke, Noemí didn't mind, because her words never sounded like her parents' reproaches. Catalina was a creature of sighs and phrases as delicate as lace. Catalina was a dreamer and therefore believed in Noemí's dreams.

"And you, what have you been up to? Don't think I haven't noticed you hardly write. Have you been pretending you live on a windswept moor, like in *Wuthering Heights*?" Noemí asked. Catalina had worn out the pages of that book.

"No. It's the house. The house takes most of my time," Catalina said, extending a hand and touching the velvet draperies.

"Were you planning on renovating it? I wouldn't blame you if you razed it and built it anew. It's rather ghastly, isn't it? And chilly too."

"Damp. There's a dampness to it."

"I was too busy freezing to death last night to mind the dampness."

"The darkness and the damp. It's always damp and dark and so very cold."

As Catalina spoke, the smile on her lips died. Her eyes, which had been distant, suddenly fell on Noemí with the sharpness of a blade. She clutched Noemí's hands and leaned forward, speaking low.

"I need you to do a favor for me, but you can't tell anyone about it. You must promise you won't tell. Promise?"

"I promise."

"There's a woman in town. Her name is Marta Duval. She made a batch of medicine for me, but I've run out of it. You must go to her and get more. Do you understand?"

"Yes, of course. What kind of medicine is it?"

"It doesn't matter. What matters is that you do it. Will you? Please say you will and tell no one about it."

"Yes, if you want me to."

Catalina nodded. She was clutching Noemí's hands so tightly that her nails were digging into the soft flesh of her wrists.

"Catalina, I'll speak to—"

"Shush. They can hear you," Catalina said and went quiet, her eyes bright as polished stones.

"Who can hear me?" Noemí asked slowly, as her cousin's eyes fixed on her, unblinking.

Catalina slowly leaned closer to her, whispering in her ear. "It's in the walls," she said.

"What is?" Noemí asked, and the question was a reflex, for she found it hard to think what to ask with her cousin's blank eyes upon her, eyes that did not seem to see; it was like staring into a sleepwalker's face.

"The walls speak to me. They tell me secrets. Don't listen to them, press your hands against your ears, Noemí. There are ghosts. They're real. You'll see them eventually."

Abruptly Catalina released her cousin and stood up, gripping the curtain with her right hand and staring out the window. Noemí wanted to ask her to explain herself, but Florence walked in then.

"Dr. Cummins has arrived. He needs to examine Catalina and will meet you in the sitting room later," the woman said.

"I don't mind staying," Noemí replied.

"But he'll mind," Florence told her with a definite finality. Noemí could have pressed the point, but she elected to leave rather than get into an argument. She knew when to back down, and she could sense that insisting now would result in a hostile refusal. They might even send her packing if she made a fuss. She was a guest, but she knew herself to be an inconvenient one.

The sitting room, in the daytime, once she peeled the curtains aside, seemed much less welcoming than at night. For one it was chilly, the fire that had warmed the room turned to ashes, and with daylight streaming through the windows every imperfection was laid bare more strikingly. The faded velour settees appeared a sickly green, almost bilious, and there were many cracks running down the enamel tiles decorating the fireplace. A little oil painting, showing a mushroom from different angles, had been attacked, ironically, by mold: tiny black spots marred its colors and defaced the image. Her cousin was right about the dampness.

Noemí rubbed her wrists, looking at the place where Catalina had dug her nails against her skin, and waited for the doctor to come downstairs. He took his time, and when he walked into the sitting room, he was not alone. Virgil accompanied him. She sat on one of the green settees, and the doctor took the other one, setting his black leather bag at his side. Virgil remained standing.

"I am Arthur Cummins," the doctor said. "You must be Miss Noemí Taboada."

The doctor dressed in clothes of a good cut, but which were a decade or two out of fashion. It felt like everyone who visited High Place had been stuck in time, but then she imagined in such a small town there would be little need to update one's wardrobe. Virgil's clothing, however, seemed fashionable. Either he had bought himself a new wardrobe the last time he'd been in Mexico City or he considered himself exceptional and his clothes worthy of more expense. Perhaps it was his wife's money that allowed a certain lavishness.

"Yes. Thank you for taking the time to speak to me," Noemí said.

"It's my pleasure. Now, Virgil says you have a few questions for me."

"I do. They tell me my cousin has tuberculosis."

Before she could continue, the doctor was nodding and speaking. "She does. It's nothing to be concerned about. She's been receiving streptomycin to help her get over it, but the 'rest' cure still holds true. Plenty of sleep, plenty of relaxation, and a good diet are the true solution to this malady."

The doctor took off his glasses and took out a handkerchief, proceeding to clean the lenses as he spoke. "An ice bag on the head or an alcohol rub, that's really what all this is about. It will pass. Soon she'll be right as rain. Now, if you'll excuse me—"

The doctor stuffed the glasses in the breast pocket of his

jacket, no doubt intending to leave the conversation at that, but it was Noemí's turn to interrupt him.

"No, I won't excuse you yet. Catalina is very odd. When I was a little girl, I remember my aunt Brigida had tuberculosis and she did not act like Catalina at all."

"Every patient is different."

"She wrote a very uncharacteristic letter to my father, and she seems unlike herself," Noemí said, trying to put her impressions into words. "She has changed."

"Tuberculosis doesn't change a person, it merely intensifies the traits the patient already possesses."

"Well, then, there's definitely something wrong with Catalina, because she's never possessed this listlessness. She has such an odd look about her."

The doctor took out his glasses and put them on again. He must not have liked what he saw and frowned.

"You did not let me finish," the doctor muttered, sounding snappish. His eyes were hard. She pressed her lips together. "Your cousin is a very anxious girl, quite melancholic, and the illness has intensified this."

"Catalina is not anxious."

"You deny her depressive tendencies?"

Noemí recalled what her father had said in Mexico City. He'd called Catalina melodramatic. But melodramatic and anxious were not the same thing at all, and Catalina had definitely never heard voices in Mexico City, and she hadn't had that bizarre expression on her face.

"What depressive tendencies?" Noemí asked.

"When her mother died, she became withdrawn," Virgil said. "She had periods of great melancholy, crying in her room and talking nonsense. It's worse now."

He had not spoken until then, and now he chose to bring that up, and not only to bring it up but to speak with a careful detachment, as if he were describing a stranger instead of his wife.

"Yes, and as you said her mother had died," Noemí replied. "And that was years and years ago, when she was a girl."

"Perhaps you'll find certain things come back," he said.

"Although tuberculosis is hardly a death sentence, it can still be upsetting for the patient," the doctor explained. "The isolation, the physical symptoms. Your cousin has suffered from chills and night sweats; they're not a pretty sight, I assure you, and codeine provides temporary relief. You cannot expect her to be cheery and baking pies."

"I'm concerned. She's my cousin, after all."

"Yes, but if *you* begin to get agitated too, then we won't be better off, will we?" the doctor said, shaking his head. "Now, I really must be going. I'll see you next week, Virgil."

"Doctor," she said.

"No, no, I will be going," the doctor repeated, like a man who has become aware of an impending mutiny aboard a ship.

The doctor shook Noemí's hand, grabbed his bag, and off he went, leaving her upon the grotesque settee, biting her lips and not knowing quite what to say. Virgil took the spot the doctor had vacated and leaned back, aloof. If there ever was a man who had ice in his veins, it was this one. His face was bloodless. Had he really courted Catalina? Courted anyone? She could not picture him expressing affection toward any living thing.

"Dr. Cummins is a very capable physician," he said with a voice that was indifferent, a voice that indicated he would not have cared if Cummins was the best or worst physician on Earth. "His father was the family's doctor, and now he watches over our health. I assure you, he has never been found lacking in any way."

"I'm sure he is a good doctor."

"You do not sound sure."

She shrugged, trying to make light of it, thinking that if she kept a smile on her face and her words were airy, he might be more receptive. After all, he seemed to be taking this whole matter lightly. "If Catalina is ill, then she might be better off in a sanatorium close to Mexico City, somewhere where she can be tended to properly."

"You don't believe I can tend to my wife?"

"I didn't say that. But this house is cold and the fog outside is not the most uplifting sight."

"Is this the mission that your father gave you?" Virgil asked. "That you would come here and snatch Catalina away?"

She shook her head. "No."

"It feels like it," he said briskly, though he did not sound upset. The words remained cold. "I realize that my home is not the most modern and most fashionable there is. High Place was once a beacon, a shining jewel of a house, and the mine produced so much silver that we could afford to cram armoires with silks and velvet and fill our cups with the finest wines. It is not so anymore.

"But we know how to take care of ill people. My father is old, he's not in perfect health, yet we tend to him adequately. I wouldn't do any less for the woman I've married."

"Still. I would like to ask, perhaps, what Catalina needs is a specialist in other matters. A psychiatrist—"

He laughed so loudly she jumped a little in her seat, for until now his face had been very serious, and the laughter was unpleasant. The laughter challenged her, and his eyes settled on her.

"A psychiatrist. And where might you find one around these parts? You think he might be summoned out of thin air? There is a public clinic in town with a single doctor and nothing more. You'll hardly find a psychiatrist there. You'd have to head to Pachuca, maybe even to Mexico City, and fetch one. I doubt they'd come."

"At least the doctor at the clinic might offer a second opinion, or he might have other ideas about Catalina."

"There's a reason why my father brought his own doctor from England, and it's not because the health care in this place was magnificent. The town is poor and the people there are coarse, primitive. It's not a place crawling with doctors."

"I must insist—"

"Yes, yes, I do believe you will insist," he said, standing up, the striking blue eyes still unkindly fixed on her. "You get your way in most things, don't you, Miss Taboada? Your father does as you wish. Men do as you wish."

He reminded her of a fellow she'd danced with at a party the previous summer. They had been having fun, briskly stepping to a danzón, and then came time for the ballads. During "Some Enchanted Evening" the man held her far too tightly and tried to kiss her. She turned her head, and when she looked at him again there was pure, dark mockery across his features.

Noemí stared back at Virgil, and he stared at her with that same sort of mockery: a bitter, ugly stare.

"What do you mean?" she asked, challenge peppering the question.

"I recall Catalina mentioning how insistent you can be when you want a beau to do your bidding. I won't fight you. Get your second opinion if you can find it," he said with a chilling finality as he walked out of the room.

She felt a little pleased to have needled him. She sensed that he had expected—as had the doctor—that she would accept his words mutely.

That night she dreamed that a golden flower sprouted from the walls in her room, only it wasn't . . . she didn't think it a flower. It had tendrils, yet it wasn't a vine, and next to the not-flower rose a hundred other tiny golden forms.

*Mushrooms*, she thought, finally recognizing the bulbous shapes, and as she walked toward the wall, intrigued and attracted by the glow, she brushed her hands against these forms. The golden bulbs seemed to turn into smoke, bursting, rising, falling like dust upon the floor. Her hands were coated in this dust.

She attempted to clean it off, wiping her hands on her nightgown, but the gold dust clung to her palms, it went under her nails. Golden dust swirled around her, and it lit up the room, bathing it in a soft yellow light. When she looked above, she saw the dust glittering like miniature stars against the ceiling, and below, on the rug, was another golden swirl of stars.

She brushed her foot forward, disturbing the dust on the rug, and it bounced up into the air again, then fell.

Suddenly, Noemí was aware of a presence in the room. She raised her head, her hand pressed against her nightgown, and saw someone standing by the door. It was a woman in a dress of yellowed antique lace. Where her face ought to have been there was a glow, golden like that of the mushrooms on the wall. The woman's glow grew stronger, then dimmed. It was like watching a firefly in the summer night sky.

Next to Noemí the wall had started to quiver, beating to the same rhythm as the golden woman. Beneath her the floorboards pulsed too; a heart, alive and knowing. The golden filaments that had emerged together with the mushrooms covered the wall like a netting and continued to grow. She noticed, then, that the woman's dress was not made of lace, but was instead woven with the same filaments.

The woman raised a gloved hand and pointed at Noemí, and she opened her mouth, but having no mouth since her face was a golden blur, no words came out.

Noemí had not felt scared. Not until now. But this, the woman attempting to speak, it made her indescribably afraid. A fear that traveled down her spine, to the soles of her feet, forcing Noemí to step back and press her hands against her lips.

She had no lips, and when she tried to take another step back she realized that her feet had fused to the ground. The golden woman reached forward, reached toward her, and held Noemí's face between her hands. The woman made a noise, like the crunching of leaves, like the dripping of water onto a pond, like the buzzing of insects in the pitch-black darkness, and Noemí wished to press her hands against her ears, but she had no hands anymore.

Noemí opened her eyes, drenched in sweat. For a minute she didn't remember where she was, and then she recalled she had been invited to High Place. She reached for the glass of water she'd left by the bedside and almost knocked it down. She gulped down the whole glass and then turned her head.

The room was in shadows. No light, golden or otherwise, dotted the wall's surface. Nevertheless, she had an impulse to rise and run her hands against the wall, as if to make sure there was nothing strange lurking behind the wallpaper.

# 6

Noemí's best bet for obtaining a car was Francis. She didn't think Florence would give her the time of day, and Virgil had been absolutely irritated with her when they had spoken the previous day. Noemí remembered what Virgil had said about men doing as she wanted. It bothered her to be thought of poorly. She wanted to be liked. Perhaps this explained the parties, the crystalline laughter, the well-coiffed hair, the rehearsed smile. She thought that men such as her father could be stern and men could be cold like Virgil, but women needed to be liked or they'd be in trouble. A woman who is not liked is a bitch, and a bitch can hardly do anything: all avenues are closed to her.

Well, she definitely did not feel liked in this house, but Francis was friendly enough. She found him near the kitchen, looking more washed out than the previous days, a slim figure of ivory, but his eyes were energetic. He smiled at her. When he did, he wasn't bad looking. Not quite like his cousin—Virgil was terribly attractive—but then she thought most men would have had a hard time competing with Virgil. No doubt that's what had hooked Catalina. That pretty face. Maybe the air of mystery he'd had about him too had made Catalina forget about sensible matters.

*Genteel poverty*, Noemí's father had said. *That's what that man has to offer.*

Apparently also a rambling, old house where you were liable to have bad dreams. God, the city seemed so far away.

"I'd like to ask you for a favor," she said after they'd exchanged morning pleasantries. As she spoke she linked her arm to his with a fluid, well-practiced motion, and they began walking together. "I want to borrow one of your cars and go into town. I have letters I'd like to post. My father doesn't really know how I'm doing."

"You need me to drive you there?"

"I can drive myself there."

Francis made a face, hesitating. "I don't know what Virgil would say about that."

She shrugged. "You don't have to tell him. What, you don't think I can drive? I'll show you my license if you want."

Francis ran a hand through his fair hair. "It's not that. The family is very particular about the cars."

"And I'm very particular about driving on my own. Surely I don't need a chaperone, and you'd make a terrible chaperone, anyway."

"How so?"

"Who ever heard of a man playing chaperone? You need an insufferable aunt. I can lend you one of mine for a weekend if you'd like. It'll cost you a car. Will you help me, please? I'm desperate."

He chuckled as she steered him outside. He picked up the car keys hanging from a hook in the kitchen. Lizzie, one of the maids, was rolling bread upon a floured table. She did not acknowledge either Noemí or Francis even one bit. The staff at High Place was almost invisible, like in one of Catalina's fairy tales. *Beauty and the Beast*, that had been it, had it not? Invisible servants who cooked the meals and laid down the silverware. Ridiculous.

Noemí knew all the people who worked in her house by name, and they certainly were not begrudged their chatter. That she even knew the names of the staff at High Place seemed a small miracle, but she'd asked Francis, and Francis had obligingly introduced them: Lizzie, Mary, and Charles, who, like the porcelain locked in the cabinets, had been imported from England many decades ago.

They walked toward the shed, and he handed her the car keys. "You won't get lost?" Francis asked, leaning against the car's window and looking down at her.

"I can manage."

True enough. It wasn't as if one could even attempt to get lost. The road led up or down the mountain, and down she went, to the little town. She felt quite content during the drive and rolled her window open to enjoy the fresh mountain air. It wasn't such a bad place, she thought, once you got out of the house. It was the house that disfigured the land.

Noemí parked the car by the town square, guessing both the post office and the medical clinic must be nearby. She was right and was quickly rewarded with the sight of a little green-and-white building that proclaimed itself the medical unit. Inside there were three green chairs and several posters explaining all matter of diseases. There was a receiving desk, but it was empty, and a closed door with a plaque on it and the doctor's name in large letters. *Julio Eusebio Camarillo*, it said.

She sat down, and after a few minutes the door opened and out came a woman holding a toddler by the hand. Then the doctor poked his head through the doorway and nodded at her.

"Good day," he said. "How can I help you?"

"I'm Noemí Taboada," she said. "You are Dr. Camarillo?"

She had to ask because the man looked rather young. He was very dark and had short hair that he parted down the middle and a little mustache that did not really age him, managing to make him look a bit ridiculous, like a child mimicking a physician. He also wasn't wearing a doctor's white coat, just a beige-and-brown sweater.

"That's me. Come in," he said.

Inside his office, on the wall behind his desk, she indeed saw the certificate from the UNAM with his name in an elegant script. He also had an armoire, the doors thrown open, filled with pills, cotton swabs, and bottles. A large maguey lay in a corner in a yellow pot.

The doctor sat behind his desk and Noemí sat on a plastic chair, which matched the ones in the vestibule.

"I don't think we've met before," Dr. Camarillo said.

"I'm not from around here," she said, placing her purse on her lap and leaning forward. "I've come to see my cousin. She's sick, and I thought you might take a look at her. She has tuberculosis."

"Tuberculosis? In El Triunfo?" the doctor asked, sounding quite astonished. "I hadn't heard anything about that."

"Not in El Triunfo proper. At High Place."

"The Doyle house," he said haltingly. "You are related to them?"

"No. Well, yes. By marriage. Virgil Doyle is married to my cousin Catalina. I was hoping you'd go check on her."

The young doctor looked confused. "But wouldn't Dr. Cummins be taking care of her? He's their doctor."

"I'd like a second opinion, I suppose," she said and explained how strange Catalina seemed and her suspicions that she might require psychiatric attention.

Dr. Camarillo listened patiently to her. When she was done, he twirled a pencil between his fingers.

"The thing is, I'm not sure I'd be welcome at High Place if I showed up there. The Doyles have always had their own physician. They don't mingle with the townsfolk," he said. "When the mine was operational and they hired Mexican workers, they had them living at a camp up the mountain. Arthur Cummins senior also tended to them. There were several epidemics back when the mine was open, you know. Lots of miners died, and Cummins had his hands full, but he never requested local help. I don't believe they think much of local physicians."

"What sort of epidemic was it?"

He tapped his pencil's eraser against his desk three times. "It wasn't clear. A high fever, very tricky. People would say the oddest things, they'd rant and rave, they'd have convulsions, they'd attack each other. People would get sick, they'd die, then all would be well, and a few years later again the mystery illness would strike."

"I've seen the English Cemetery," Noemí said. "There are many graves."

"That's only the English people. You should see the local cemetery. They said that in the last epidemic, around the time the Revolution started, the Doyles didn't even bother sending down the corpses for a proper burial. They tossed them in a pit."

"That can't be, can it?"

"Who knows."

The phrase carried with it an implicit distaste. The doctor didn't say, "Well, I believe it," but it seemed there might be no reason why he shouldn't.

"You must be from El Triunfo, then, to know all of this."

"From near enough," he said. "My family sold supplies to people at the Doyle mine, and when they shuttered it, they moved to Pachuca. I went to study in Mexico City, but now I'm back. I wanted to help the people here."

"You should start by helping my cousin, then," she said. "Will you come up to the house?"

Dr. Camarillo smiled but he shook his head, apologetic. "I told you, you'll get me in trouble with Cummins and the Doyles."

"What can they do to you? Aren't you the town's physician?"

"The health clinic is public, and the government pays for bandages, rubbing alcohol, and gauze. But El Triunfo is small, it's needy. Most people are goat farmers. Back when the Spaniards controlled the mine, they could support themselves making tallow for the miners. Not now. There's a church and a very nice priest here, and he collects alms for the poor."

"And I bet the Doyles place money in his contribution box and the priest is your friend," Noemí said.

"Cummins places the contributions in the box. The Doyles

don't bother with that. But it's their money, all the same, everyone knows it."

She didn't think the Doyles had much money left; the mine had been closed for more than three decades. But their bank account must have a modest balance, and a little bit of cash might go a long way in an isolated town like El Triunfo.

What to do now? She thought it over, quickly, and decided to take advantage of those theater lessons her father had considered a waste of money.

"Then you won't help me. You're afraid of them! Oh, and here I am without a friend in the world," she said, clutching her purse and standing up slowly, her lip quivering dramatically. Men always panicked when she did that, afraid she'd cry. Men were always so afraid of tears, of having a hysterical woman on their hands.

At once the doctor made a placating motion and spoke quickly. "I didn't say that."

"Then?" she pressed on, sounding hopeful, giving him the most fetching of smiles, the one she used when she wanted to get a policeman to let her go without a speeding ticket. "Doctor, it would mean the world to me if you helped."

"Even if I go, I'm no psychologist."

Noemí took out her handkerchief and clutched it, a little visual reminder that she could, at any moment, break into tears and start dabbing at her eyes. She sighed.

"I could head to Mexico City, but I don't want to leave Catalina alone, especially if there's no need for it. I may be wrong. You'd save me a long trip back and forth; the train doesn't even run every day. Will you do me this little favor? Will you come?"

Noemí looked at him, and he looked back at her with a dose of skepticism, but he nodded his head. "I'll stop by Monday around noon."

"Thanks," she said, standing up quickly and shaking his hand, and then, remembering the fullness of her errand, she paused. "By the way, do you know a Marta Duval?"

"Are you going around talking to every specialist in town?"

"Why do you say that?"

"She's the local healer."

"Do you know where she lives? My cousin wanted a remedy from her."

"Does she? Well, I suppose it makes sense. Marta does a lot of business with the women in town. Gordolobo tea is still a popular remedy for tuberculosis."

"Does it help?"

"It's fine enough for coughs."

Dr. Camarillo bent down over his desk and drew a map on his notepad and handed it to her. Noemí decided to walk to Duval's house, since he said it was nearby, and it turned out to be a good idea, because the path that led to the woman's house would have been no good for a car and the way there was a little convoluted, the streets following no plan, growing chaotic. Noemí had to ask for directions, despite the map.

She spoke to a woman who was doing her laundry by the front door of her house, scrubbing a shirt against a battered washboard. The woman put down her bar of Zote soap and informed Noemí she had to go uphill a little farther. The town's neglect was more obvious the farther you moved from the central square and the church. The houses became shacks made of bare brick, and everything seemed gray and dusty, with scrawny-looking goats or chickens stuck behind rickety fences. Some dwellings were abandoned, with no doors or windows left. She supposed the neighbors had scavenged whatever wood, glass, and other materials they could take. When they'd driven through town, Francis must have taken the most scenic of roads, and even then her impression had been of decay.

The healer's house was very small and stood out because it was painted white and was better taken care of. An old woman with her hair in a long braid, wearing a blue apron, sat outside by the door on a three-legged stool. She had two bowls next to her and was peeling peanuts. In one bowl she threw the discarded shells, in another she threw the peanuts. The woman did not look up as Noemí approached her. She was humming a tune.

"Excuse me," Noemí said. "I'm looking for Marta Duval."

The humming ceased. "You've got the prettiest shoes I've even seen," the old woman said.

Noemí glanced down at the pair of black high-heeled shoes she was wearing. "Thank you."

"I don't get many people with pretty shoes like that."

The woman cracked another peanut open and tossed it into the bowl. Then she stood up. "I'm Marta," she said, looking up at Noemí, her eyes cloudy with cataracts.

Marta went into the house carrying a bowl in each hand. Noemí followed her inside, into a small kitchen that also served as the dining room. On a wall there was a picture of the Sacred Heart and a bookshelf held plaster figurines of saints, candles, and bottles filled with herbs. From the ceiling there also hung herbs and dried flowers, lavender and epazote and branches of rue.

Noemí knew there were healers who made all sorts of remedies, gathering herbs for hangovers and herbs for fevers, and even tricks to cure the evil eye, but Catalina had never been the type to seek such cures. The first book that had gotten Noemí really interested in anthropology had been *Witchcraft, Oracles, and Magic Among the Azande,* and when she tried to discuss it with Catalina, Catalina would not hear of it. The mere word "witchcraft" gave her a fright, and a healer of Duval's sort was two steps removed from witchcraft, not only handing out tonics but also curing the susto by placing a cross of holy palm on someone's head.

No, Catalina wouldn't have been the type to wear a bracelet of ojo de venado on her wrist. How had she ended up at this house, talking to Marta Duval, then?

The old woman placed the bowls on the table and pulled out a chair. When she sat down there was a sudden fluttering of wings, which startled Noemí, and a parrot swooped onto the woman's shoulder.

"Sit," Marta said, taking a peeled peanut and handing it to the parrot. "What do you want?"

Noemí sat down across from her. "You made a remedy for my cousin, and she needs more of it."

"What was it?"

"I'm not sure. Her name is Catalina. Do you remember her?"

"The girl from High Place."

The woman took another peanut and gave it to the parrot, which cocked its head and stared at Noemí.

"Yes, Catalina. How do you know her?"

"I don't. Not really. Your cousin used to come to church once in a while, and she must've gotten to talking with someone there because she came to see me, told me that she needed something to help her sleep. She visited me a couple of times. Last time I saw her she was agitated, but wouldn't tell me about her problems. She asked me to mail a letter for her, addressed to someone in Mexico City."

"Why didn't she mail it herself?"

"I don't know. She said, 'Come Friday, if we don't see each other, mail this,' so I did. Like I said, she wouldn't discuss her problems. She said she had bad dreams, and I tried to help with that."

*Bad dreams*, Noemí thought, recalling her nightmare. It wasn't hard to have bad dreams in a house like that. She placed her hands on top of her purse. "Well, whatever you gave her must have worked, because she wants more of it."

"More." The woman sighed. "I told the girl, no tea is going to make her feel better, not for long."

"What do you mean?"

"That family is cursed." The woman touched the parrot's head, scratching it, and the bird closed its eyes. "You haven't heard the stories?"

"There was an epidemic," Noemí said cautiously, wondering if she meant that.

"Yes, there was sickness, much sickness. But that wasn't the only thing. Miss Ruth, she shot them."

"Who's Miss Ruth?"

"It's a famous story around these parts. I can tell it, but it'll cost you a little."

"You're rather mercenary. I'm already going to pay for the medicine."

"We've got to eat. Besides, it's a good story, and no one knows it as well as I do."

"So you're a healer and a storyteller."

"Told you, young miss, we got to eat," the woman said with a shrug.

"All right. I'll pay for a story. You have an ashtray?" she asked, taking out her cigarettes and her lighter.

Marta grabbed a pewter cup from the kitchen and placed it before her, and Noemí leaned forward, both elbows resting on the table, and lit her cigarette. She offered the old woman a cigarette and Marta took two, smiling, but she did not light either one, instead tucking them in her apron's pocket. Perhaps she'd smoke the cigarettes later. Or even sell them.

"Where to begin? Ruth, yes. Ruth was Mr. Doyle's daughter. Mr. Doyle's darling child, she wanted for nothing. Back then they had many servants. Always lots of servants to polish the silver and make teas. The bulk of those servants were people from the village, and they lived at the house, but sometimes they came down to town. For the market, for other things. And they'd talk, about all the pretty things at High Place and pretty Miss Ruth.

"She was going to marry her cousin—Michael, it was—and they'd ordered a dress from Paris and ivory head combs for her hair. But a week before the wedding, she grabbed a rifle and shot her groom, shot her mother, her aunt, and her uncle. She shot her father, but he survived. And she might have shot Virgil, her baby brother, but Miss Florence hid away with him. Or maybe Ruth had mercy."

Noemí hadn't seen a single weapon in the house, but then they must have tossed the rifle. There was only silver on display, and she wondered, incongruously, if the bullets the murderess had used might not have been made of silver.

"When she was done shooting them, she took the rifle and killed herself." The woman cracked a peanut.

What a morbid tale! And yet, this was not a conclusion. Merely a pause. "There's more, isn't there?"

"Yes."

"You're not going to tell me the rest?"

"One has to eat, young miss."

"I'll pay."

"You won't be stingy?"

"Never."

Noemí had placed the box of cigarettes on the table. Marta extended a wrinkled hand and took another one, again tucking it in her apron. She smiled.

"The servants left after that. The people who remained in High Place were the family and trusted folks they'd employed for a long time. They stayed there, stayed out of sight. Then one day Miss Florence was suddenly at the train station, off on vacation when she had never set a foot outside the house. She came back married to a young man. Richard, he was called.

"He wasn't like the Doyles. He was talkative; he liked to come down to town in his car and have a drink and chat. He'd lived in London and New York and Mexico City, and you got the feeling that the house of the Doyles wasn't his favorite place of them all. He was talkative, all right, and then he started talking strange things."

"What sort of things?"

"Talk of ghosts and spirits and the evil eye. He was a strong man, Mr. Richard, until he wasn't, and he looked rather shabby and thin, stopped coming into town and disappeared from view. They found him at the bottom of a ravine. There're lots of ravines here, you might have noticed that, well, there he was, dead at twenty-nine, left behind a son."

*Francis*, she thought. Pale-faced Francis with his soft hair and his softer smile. She'd heard nothing of this long saga, but then she supposed it was not the kind of thing anyone would like to discuss.

"It all sounds tragic, but I'm not sure I'd call it a curse."

"You'd call it coincidence, wouldn't you? Yes, I suppose you would. But the fact is everything they touch rots."

*Rots.* The word sounded so ugly, it seemed to stick to the tongue, it made Noemí want to bite her nails even though she'd never done such a thing. She was particular about her hands; ugly nails wouldn't have done for her. It was odd, that house. The Doyles and their servants were all an odd lot, but a curse? No.

"It couldn't be anything but coincidence," she said, shaking her head.

"Could be."

"Can you make the same remedy you made for Catalina the last time?"

"It's no easy thing. I'd have to gather the ingredients, and it would take me a little while. It wouldn't solve the issue. It's like I said: the problem is that house, that cursed house. Jump on that train and leave it behind, that's what I told your cousin. I thought she'd listened, but what do I know?"

"Yes, I'm sure you did. What's the price of this remedy, anyway?" Noemí asked.

"The remedy and the stories."

"Yes, that too."

The woman named a sum. Noemí opened her purse and took out a few bills. Marta Duval might have cataracts, but she saw the bills clearly enough.

"It would take me a week. Come back in a week, but I make no promises," the woman said, extending her hand, and Noemí placed the bills in her palm. The woman folded them and tucked them in her apron's pocket. "Can you spare another cigarette?" she added.

"Very well. I hope you like them," Noemí said, handing her one more. "They're Gauloises."

"They're not for me."

"Then for whom?"

"Saint Luke the Evangelist," she said, pointing to one of the plaster figurines on her shelves.

"Cigarettes for saints?"

"He likes them."

"He has expensive tastes," Noemí said, wondering if she could find a store that sold anything even close to Gauloises in town. She'd have to replenish her stock soon.

The woman smiled, and Noemí handed her another bill. What the hell. As she'd said, everyone had to eat and God knew how many customers the old lady had. Marta seemed very pleased and smiled even more.

"Well, I'm off, then. Don't let Saint Luke smoke all the cigarettes at once."

The woman chuckled, and they walked outside. They shook hands. And the woman squinted.

"How do you sleep?" the woman asked.

"Fine."

"You have dark circles under your eyes."

"It's the cold up here. It keeps me awake at night."

"I hope it's that."

Noemí thought of her odd dream, the golden glow. It had been a rather hideous nightmare, but she had not had time to analyze it. She had a friend who swore by Jung, but Noemí had never understood the whole "the dream is the dreamer" bit, nor had she cared to interpret her dreams. Now she recalled one particular thing Jung wrote: everyone carries a shadow. And like a shadow the woman's words hung over Noemí as she drove back to High Place.

# 7

That evening, Noemí was summoned once again to the dreary dinner table with its tablecloth of white damask and the candles, and around this ancient table the Doyles gathered together, Florence, Francis, and Virgil. The patriarch would have supper in his room, it seemed.

Noemí ate little, stirring the spoon around her bowl and itching for conversation, not nourishment. After a little while she could not contain herself any longer and chuckled. Three pairs of eyes settled on her.

"Really, must we tie our tongues all dinner long?" she asked. "Could we speak perhaps three or four sentences?"

Her voice was like fine glass, contrasting with the heavy furniture and heavy drapes and the equally weighty faces turned toward her. She didn't mean to be a nuisance, but her carefree nature had little understanding of solemnity. She smiled, hoping for a smile in return, for a moment of levity inside this opulent cage.

"As a general rule we do not speak during dinner, as I explained last time. But it seems you are very keen on breaking every rule in this house," Florence said, carefully dabbing a napkin against her mouth.

"What do you mean?"

"You took a car to town."

"I needed to drop a couple of letters at the post office." This was no lie, for she had indeed scribbled a short letter to her family. She had thought to dutifully send a missive to Hugo too, but then reconsidered. Hugo and Noemí were not a couple in the proper sense of the word, and she worried if she did send a letter he might interpret it as a sign of an impending and serious commitment.

"Charles can take any letters."

"I'd rather do it myself, thank you."

"The roads are bad. What would you do if your car was stuck in the muck?" Florence asked.

"I imagine I'd walk back," Noemí replied, setting down her spoon. "Really, it's not a problem."

"I imagine it isn't for *you*. The mountain has its dangers."

The words did not seem outright hostile, but Florence's disapproval was thick as treacle, coating each and every syllable. Noemí felt suddenly like a girl who'd had her knuckles rapped, and this made her raise her chin and stare back at the woman in the same way she had stared at the nuns at her school, armored with poised insurrection. Florence even resembled the mother superior a little: it was her expression of utter despondency. Noemí almost expected her to demand she take out her rosary.

"I thought I explained myself when you arrived. You must consult with me on matters concerning this house, its people, and the things in it. I was specific. I told you Charles was to drive you into town and, if not him, then perhaps Francis," Florence said.

"I didn't think—"

"And you have smoked in your room. Don't bother denying it. I said it was forbidden."

Florence stared at Noemí, and Noemí imagined the woman sniffing at the linens, examining a cup for traces of ashes. Like a bloodhound, out for prey. Noemí intended to protest, to say that she had smoked but twice in her room and both times she had intended to open the window, but it was not her fault it wouldn't open. It was closed so tight you'd think they'd nailed it shut.

"It's a filthy habit. As are certain girls," Florence added.

Now it was Noemí's turn to stare at Florence. How dare she. Before she could say anything, Virgil spoke.

"My wife tells me your father can be a rather strict man," he said, all cool detachment. "He's set in his ways."

"Yes," Noemí replied, glancing at Virgil. "At times he is."

"Florence has managed High Place for decades," Virgil said. "As we do not have many visitors, you can imagine she's quite set in her ways too. And it's quite unacceptable, don't you think, for a visitor to ignore the rules of a house?"

She felt ambushed; she thought they had planned to scold her together. She wondered if they did this with Catalina. She would go into the dining room and offer a suggestion—about the food, the décor, the routine—and they would politely, delicately silence her. Poor Catalina, who was gentle and obedient, as gently squashed down.

She had lost her appetite, which had been scant to begin with, and sipped her glass of sickly-sweet wine rather than attempt to converse. Eventually Charles walked in to inform them that Howard would like to see them after dinner, and they made their way up the stairs, like a traveling court off to greet the king.

Howard's bedroom was very large and decorated with more of the weighty, dark furniture that abounded around the rest of the house, and thick velvet curtains that could conceal the thinnest ray of light.

The most striking feature of the room was the fireplace, with a carved wooden mantelpiece adorned with what at first glance seemed to be circles, but revealed themselves to be more of those snakes eating their tails that she'd spotted before at the cemetery and in the library. A sofa had been set in front of the fireplace, and upon it sat the patriarch, swaddled in a green robe.

Howard looked even older that evening. He reminded her of one of the mummies she'd seen in the catacombs in Guanajuato, arranged in two rows for tourists to peek at. Upright they stood, preserved by a quirk of nature, and dragged from their graves when the burial tax was not paid so that they might be exhibited. He had that same withered, sunken aspect, as though he had already been embalmed, the elements reducing him to bone and marrow.

The others walked ahead of her, each of them clasping the old man's hand in greeting, then stepping aside.

"There you are. Come, sit with me," the old man said, motioning to her.

Noemí sat next to Howard, giving him a vague, polite smile. Florence, Virgil, and Francis did not join them, instead choosing another couch and chairs on the other end of the room to sit down. She wondered if he always received people in this manner, picking one lucky person who would be allowed at his side, who would be granted an audience, while the rest of the family was brushed aside for the time being. A long time ago this room might have been filled with relatives, friends, all of them waiting and hoping Howard Doyle would curl a finger in their direction and ask them to sit with him for a little while. She had seen photographs and paintings of a large number of people around the house, after all. The paintings were ancient; maybe they were not all of relatives who had lived at High Place, but the mausoleum hinted at a vast family or, perhaps, the assurance of descendants who would find their way there.

Two large oil paintings hanging above the fireplace caught Noemí's eye. They each depicted a young woman. Both were fair-haired, both very similar in looks, so much so that at first glance one might take them for the same woman. However, there were differences: straight strawberry blond hair versus honeyed locks, a tad more plumpness in the face in the woman on the left. One wore an amber ring on her finger, which matched the one on Howard's hand.

"Are these your relatives?" she asked, intrigued by the likeness, what she supposed was the Doyle look.

"These are my wives," Howard said. "Agnes passed away

shortly after our arrival to this region. She was pregnant when disease took her away."

"I'm sorry."

"It was a long time ago. But she has not been forgotten. Her spirit lives on in High Place. And there, the one on the right, that is my second wife. Alice. She was fruitful. A woman's function is to preserve the family line. The children, well, Virgil is the only one left, but she did her duty and she did it well."

Noemí looked up at the pale face of Alice Doyle, the blond hair cascading down her back, her right hand holding a rose between two fingers, her face serious. Agnes, to her left, was also robbed of mirth, clasping a bouquet between her hands, the amber ring catching a stray ray of light. They stared forward in their silk and lace with what? Resolution? Confidence?

"They were beautiful, were they not?" the old man asked. He sounded proud, like a man who has received a nice ribbon at the county fair for his prize hog or mare.

"Yes. Although . . ."

"Although what, my dear?"

"Nothing. They seem so alike."

"I imagine they should. Alice was Agnes's little sister. They were both orphaned and left penniless, but we were kin, cousins, and so I took them in. And when I traveled here Agnes and I were wed, and Alice came with us."

"Then you twice married your cousin," Noemí said. "And your wife's sister."

"Is it scandalous? Catherine of Aragon was first married to Henry VIII's brother, and Queen Victoria and Albert were cousins."

"You think you're a king, then?"

Howard reached forward and patted her hand; his skin seemed paper-thin and dry, smiling. "Nothing as grandiose as that."

"I'm not scandalized," Noemí said politely and gave her head a little shake.

"I hardly knew Agnes," Howard said with a shrug. "We were married and before a year had passed I was forced to organize a funeral. The house wasn't even finished back then and the mine had been operating for a scant handful of months. Then the years passed, and Alice grew up. There were no suitable grooms for her in this part of the world. It was a natural choice. One could say preordained. This is her wedding portrait. See there? The date is clearly visible on that tree in the foreground: 1895. A wonderful year. So much silver that year. A river of it."

The artist had indeed carved the tree with the year and the initials of the bride: AD. Agnes's portrait sported the same detail, the year carved on a stone column: 1885, AD. Noemí wondered if they had simply dusted off the old bride's trousseau and handed it to the younger sister. She imagined Alice pulling out linens and chemises monogrammed with her initials, pressing an old dress against her chest and staring into the mirror. A Doyle, eternally a Doyle. No, it wasn't scandalous, but it was damn odd.

"Beautiful, my beautiful darlings," the old man said, his hand still resting atop Noemí's as he turned his eyes back toward the paintings, his fingers rubbing her knuckles. "Did you ever hear about Dr. Galton's beauty map? He went around the British Isles compiling a record of the women he saw. He catalogued them as attractive, indifferent, or repellent. London ranked as the highest for beauty, Aberdeen the lowest. It might seem like a funny exercise, but of course it had its logic."

"Aesthetics again," Noemí said, as she delicately pulled her hand free from his and stood up, as if to take a closer look at the paintings. Truth be told she didn't like his touch, nor did she much enjoy the faint unpleasant odor that emanated from his robe. It might have been an ointment or medicine that he'd applied.

"Yes, aesthetics. One must not dismiss them as frivolous. After all, didn't Lombroso study men's faces in order to recognize a criminal type? Our bodies hide so many mysteries and they tell so many stories without a single word, do they not?"

She looked at those portraits above their heads, the serious mouths, the pointed chins and luscious hair. What *did* they say, in their wedding dresses as the brush stroked the canvas? I am happy, unhappy, indifferent, miserable. Who knew. One could construct a hundred different narratives, it didn't make them true.

"You mentioned Gamio when we last spoke," Howard said, grabbing his cane and standing up to move next to her. Noemí's attempt at distance had been in vain; he crowded her, touched her arm. "You're correct. Gamio believes natural selection has pressed the indigenous people of this continent forward, allowing them to adapt to biological and geographical factors that foreigners cannot withstand. When you transplant a flower, you must consider the soil, mustn't you? Gamio was on the right track."

The old man folded his hands atop his cane and nodded, looking at the paintings. Noemí wished that someone would open a window. The room was stuffy, the conversations of the others were whispers. If they were conversing. Had they gone quiet? Their voices were like the buzzing of insects.

"I wonder why you are not married, Miss Taboada. You are the right age for it."

"My father asks himself that same question," Noemí said.

"And what lies do you tell him? That you are too busy? That you esteem many young men but cannot find one that truly captivates you?"

This was very close to what she'd said, and perhaps if he'd intoned the words with a certain levity it might have been constructed as a joke and Noemí would have clutched his arm for a moment and laughed. "Mr. Doyle," she would have said, and they would have talked about her father and her mother, and how she was always quarreling with her brother, and her cousins who were numerous and lively.

But Howard Doyle's words were harsh and his eyes had a sickening sort of animation to them. He almost leered at her, one of his thin hands brushing a strand of her hair, as if doing her a kindness—he'd found a bit of lint and tossed it away—but no. No kindness at all as he moved that lock behind her shoulder. He was a tall man even in his old age, and she didn't like looking up at him, she didn't like seeing him bend toward her like that. He looked like a stick insect, an insect hiding under a velvet robe. His lips curved into a smile as he leaned down closer, peering carefully at her.

He smelled foul. She turned her head, and she rested a hand against the mantelpiece. Her eyes met those of Francis, who was looking at them. She thought he was a scared bird, a pigeon, the eyes round and startled. It was very hard to imagine he was related to the insect-man before her.

"Has my son shown you the greenhouse?" Howard asked, stepping back, and his eyes lost their unpleasantness as he turned toward the fire.

"I didn't know you had a greenhouse," she replied, a little surprised. Then again, she hadn't opened every door in the house, nor had she looked at the place from every angle. She hadn't wanted to, beyond her first cursory exploration of High Place. It wasn't a welcoming home.

"A very small one and in a state of disrepair, like most things around here, but the roof is of stained glass. You might like it. Virgil, I've told Noemí you will show her the greenhouse," Howard said, the loudness of his voice so shocking in the quiet room that Noemí thought it might cause a small tremor.

Virgil merely nodded and, taking this as a cue, approached them. "I'll be glad to, Father," he said.

"Good," Howard said, clasping Virgil's shoulder before he set off across the room, joining Florence and Francis, and taking up the seat Virgil had been occupying.

"Has my father been bothering you, telling you what he considers to be the finest type of manhood and womanhood possible?" Virgil asked, smiling at her. "The answer is tricky: the Doyles are the finest specimens around, but I try not to let it go to my head."

Noemí was a little surprised by the smile, but she welcomed the warmth after stomaching Howard's odd leer and his sharp grin. "He was talking about beauty," she said, her voice charmingly composed.

"Beauty. Of course. Well, he was a great connoisseur of beauty, once, although now he can barely eat mush and stay up until nine."

She raised a hand and hid her grin behind it. Virgil traced one of the snake carvings with his index finger, looking a bit more serious as he did, his smile subdued.

"I'm sorry about the other night. I was rude. And earlier today Florence made a fuss about the car. But you must not feel badly about it. You can't be expected to know all our habits and little rules," he said.

"It's fine."

"It's stressful, you know. My father is very frail and now Catalina is ill too. I'm not in the best of moods these days. I don't want you to feel we don't want you here. We do. We very much do."

"Thank you."

"I don't think you quite forgive me."

No, not quite, but she was relieved to see not all the Doyles were so damn gloomy all the time. Maybe he was telling the truth, and before Catalina had fallen sick Virgil had been more disposed to merriment.

"Not yet, but if you keep it up I may erase a mark or two on your scorecard."

"You keep score then? As if you're playing cards?"

"A girl has to keep track of a number of things. Dances are not the only ones," she said with that easy, genial tone of hers.

"I've been given to understand you are quite the dancer and the gambler. At least, according to Catalina," he said, still smiling at her.

"And here I thought you might be scandalized."

"You'd be surprised."

"I love surprises, but only when they come with a nice, big bow," she declared, and because he was playing nice, she played nice too and tossed him a smile.

Virgil in turn gave her an appreciative look that seemed to say, *See, we may yet become friends.* He offered her his arm, and they

walked toward the rest of the family members, to chat for a few
more minutes before Howard declared he was much too tired to
entertain any more company, and they all disbanded.


She had a curious nightmare, unlike any dream she'd had before
in this house, even if her nights had been rather restless.

She dreamed that the door opened and in walked Howard
Doyle, slowly, each of his steps like the weight of iron, making
the boards creak and the walls rumble. It was as if an elephant
had trampled into her room. She could not move. An invisible
thread anchored her to the bed. Her eyes were closed but she
could see him. She gazed at him from above, from the ceiling, and
then from the floor, her perspective shifting.

She saw herself too, asleep. She saw him approaching her bed
and tugging at the covers. She saw this, and yet her eyes remained
shut even when he reached out to touch her face, the edge of a nail
running down her neck, a thin hand undoing the buttons of her
nightdress. It was chilly and he was undressing her.

Behind her she felt a presence, felt it like one feels a cold spot
in a house, and the presence had a voice; it leaned close to her ear
and it whispered.

"Open your eyes," the voice said, a woman's voice. There had
been a golden woman in her room, in another dream, but this
was not the same presence. This was different; she thought this
voice was young.

Her eyes were nailed shut, her hands lay flat against the bed,
and Howard Doyle loomed over her, stared down at Noemí as
she slept. He smiled in the dark, white teeth in a diseased, rotting
mouth.

"Open your eyes," the voice urged her.

Moonlight or another source of light hit Howard Doyle's thin,
insect-like body, and she saw it wasn't the old man standing by
her bed, studying her limbs, her breasts, staring at her pubic hair.
It was Virgil Doyle who had acquired his father's leering grin,

who smiled his white smile, and who looked at Noemí like a man observing a butterfly pinned against a velvet cloth.

He pressed a hand against her mouth, pushing her back against the bed, and the bed was very soft, it dipped and swayed and it was like wax, like being pressed into a bed of wax. Or perhaps mud, earth. A bed of earth.

And she felt such sweet, sickening desire flowing through her body, making her roll her hips, sinuous, a serpent. But it was he who coiled himself around her, swallowed her shuddering sigh with his lips, and she didn't quite want this, not like that, not those fingers digging too firmly into her flesh, and yet it was hard to remember why she hadn't wanted it. She must want this. To be taken, in the dirt, in the dark, without preamble or apology.

The voice at her ear spoke again. It was very insistent, jabbing her.

"Open your eyes."

She did and woke up to discover she was very cold; she had kicked the covers away and they tangled at her feet. Her pillow had tumbled to the floor. The door lay firmly closed. Noemí pressed both hands against her chest, feeling the rapid beating of her heart. She ran a hand down the front of her nightdress. All the buttons were firmly in place.

Of course they would be.

The house was quiet. No one walked through the halls, no one crept into rooms at night to stare at sleeping women. Still, it took her a long time to go back to sleep, and once or twice, when she heard a board creak, she sat up quickly and listened for footsteps.

8

oemí planted herself outside the house, waiting for the doctor to arrive. Virgil had told her she could get a second opinion, so she had informed Florence the doctor would be stopping by and that she had obtained Virgil's permission for this visit, but she didn't quite trust any of the Doyles to greet Dr. Camarillo and had decided to serve as a sentinel.

As she crossed her arms and tapped her foot she felt, for once, like one of Catalina's characters in their childhood tales. The maiden gazing out the tower, waiting for the knight to ride to the rescue and vanquish the dragon. Surely the doctor would conjure a diagnosis and a solution.

She felt it necessary to be positive, to hope, for High Place was a place of hopelessness. Its shabby grimness made her want to push forward.

The doctor was punctual and parked his car near a tree, stepping out, doffing his hat and staring up at the house. There wasn't much mist that day, as if the Earth and sky had cleared up in advance of this visitor, though it served to make the house look more forlorn, unshrouded and bare. Noemí imagined Julio's house was nothing like this, that it was one of the shabby yet colorful little houses down the main street, with a tiny balcony and wooden shutters and a kitchen with old azulejos.

"Well, this is the famous High Place," Dr. Camarillo said. "About time I saw it, I suppose."

"You haven't been here before?" she asked.

"No reason for me to come. I've been past where the mining camp used to be. Or what's left of it, at any rate, when I've gone hunting. There's plenty of deer around, up here. Mountain lions too. You have to be careful on this mountain."

"I didn't know that," she said. She recalled how Florence had admonished her. Could she have been worried about mountain lions? Or was she more worried about her precious car?

The doctor grabbed his bag and they went inside. Noemí had been afraid Florence might come running down the stairs, ready to glare at both Dr. Camarillo and Noemí, but the staircase was empty, and when they reached Catalina's room they found the woman alone.

Catalina seemed in good enough spirits, sitting in the sunlight, dressed in a simple but becoming blue dress. She greeted the doctor with a smile.

"Good day, I'm Catalina."

"And I'm Dr. Camarillo. I'm pleased to meet you."

Catalina extended her hand. "Why, he looks so young, Noemí! He must be hardly older than you!"

"You are hardly older than me," Noemí said.

"What are you talking about? You're a little girl."

This sounded so like the happy Catalina of days past, bantering with them, that Noemí began to feel foolish for bringing the doctor to the house. But then, as the minutes ticked by, Catalina's ebullience began to fade and turn into a simmering agitation. And Noemí couldn't help but think that even though nothing was exactly *wrong*, something was definitely not right.

"Tell me, how are you sleeping? Any chills at night?"

"No. I feel much better already. Really, there's no need for you to be here, it's such a fuss over nothing. Over nothing, truly," Catalina said. Her vehemence when she spoke had a forced cheerfulness to it. She repeatedly rubbed a finger across her wedding band.

Julio merely nodded. He talked in a steady, measured tone while he took notes. "Have you been given streptomycin and para-aminosalicylic acid?"

"I think so," Catalina said, but she responded in such haste Noemí didn't think she'd even listened to the question.

"Marta Duval, did she also send a remedy for you? A tea or herb?"

Catalina's eyes darted across the room. "What? Why would you ask that?"

"I'm trying to figure out what all your medications are. I'm assuming you saw her for a remedy of some sort?"

"There's no remedy," she muttered.

She said something else, but it wasn't a real word. She babbled, like a small child, and then Catalina suddenly clutched her neck, as if she'd choke herself, but her grip was lax. No, it was not choking, but a defensive gesture, a woman guarding herself, holding her hands up in defense. The movement startled them both. Julio almost dropped his pencil. Catalina resembled one of the deer in the mountains, ready to dart to safety, and neither knew what to say.

"What is it?" Julio asked, after a minute had gone by.

"It's the noise," Catalina said, and she slowly slid her hands up her neck and pressed them against her mouth.

Julio looked up at Noemí, who was sitting next to him.

"What noise?" Noemí asked.

"I don't want you here. I'm very tired," Catalina said, and she gripped her hands together and placed them on her lap, closing her eyes, as if to shut her visitors away. "I really don't know why you must be here bothering me when I should be sleeping!"

"If you will—" the doctor began.

"I can't talk anymore, I'm exhausted," Catalina said, her hands trembling as she attempted to clutch them together. "It's really quite exhausting being ill and it's even worse when people say you shouldn't do anything. Isn't that odd? Really . . . it's . . . I'm tired. Tired!"

She paused, as if catching her breath. All of a sudden Catalina opened her eyes very wide and her face had a terrifying intensity to it. It was the visage of a woman possessed.

"There're people in the walls," Catalina said. "There're people and there're voices. I see them sometimes, the people in the walls. They're dead."

She extended her hands, and Noemí gripped them, helplessly, trying to comfort her, as Catalina shook her head and let out a half sob. "It lives in the cemetery, in the cemetery, Noemí. You must look in the cemetery."

Then just as suddenly Catalina stood up and went to the window, clutching a drape with her right hand and looking outside. Her face softened. It was as if a tornado had struck and spun away. Noemí didn't know what to do, and the doctor appeared equally baffled.

"I'm sorry," Catalina said evenly. "I don't know what I say, I'm sorry."

Catalina pressed her hands against her mouth again and began coughing. Florence and Mary, the oldest maid, walked in, carrying a tray with a teapot and a cup. Both of the women eyed Noemí and Dr. Camarillo with disapproval.

"Will you be long?" Florence asked. "She's supposed to be resting."

"I was just leaving," Dr. Camarillo said, collecting his hat and his notepad, clearly knowing himself an unwelcome intruder with these few words and Florence's lofty tilt of the head. Florence always knew how to cut you down with the succinct efficiency of a telegram. "It was nice meeting you, Catalina."

They stepped out of the room. For a couple of minutes neither one spoke, both weary and a little rattled.

"So, what's your opinion?" she finally asked as they began walking down the stairs.

"On the matter of tuberculosis I would have to take an X-ray of her lungs to get a better idea of her condition, and I really am no expert in tuberculosis in the first place," he said. "And on the other matter, I warned you, I'm not a psychiatrist. I shouldn't be speculating—"

"Come on, out with it," Noemí said in exasperation, "you must tell me *something*."

They stopped at the foot of the stairs. Julio sighed. "I believe you are correct and she needs psychiatric attention. This behavior is not usual with any tuberculosis patient I've met. Perhaps you might find a specialist in Pachuca who could treat her? If you can't make the trek to Mexico City."

Noemí didn't think they'd be making the trek anywhere. Maybe if she spoke to Howard and tried to explain her concerns? He was the head of the household, after all. But she didn't like the old man, he rubbed her the wrong way, and Virgil might think she was trying to overreach. Florence certainly would be of no help to her, but what about Francis?

"I'm afraid I've left you with a worse conundrum than before, haven't I?" Julio said.

"No," Noemí lied. "No, I'm very thankful."

She was dispirited and felt silly for having expected more of him. He was no knight in shining armor nor a wizard who might revive her cousin with a magic potion. She ought to have known better.

He hesitated, seeking perhaps to provide her with more reassurance. "Well, you know where to find me if you need anything else," he concluded. "Do seek me out if it's necessary."

Noemí nodded, watched him as he got into his car and drove away. She recalled, rather grimly, that certain fairy tales end in blood. In Cinderella, the sisters cut off their feet, and Sleeping Beauty's stepmother was pushed into a barrel full of snakes. That particular illustration on the last page of one of the books Catalina used to read to them suddenly came back to her, in all its vivid colors. Green and yellow serpents, the tails poking out of a barrel as the stepmother was stuffed into it.

Noemí leaned against a tree, standing there with her arms

crossed for a while. She walked back inside the house to find Virgil standing on the staircase, his hand on the banister.

"There was a man to see you."

"It was the doctor from the public health clinic. You did say he could visit."

"I'm not admonishing you," he told her as he finished climbing down the stairs and stood in front of her. He appeared a little curious, and she guessed he wanted to know what the doctor had said, but she also guessed he would not ask yet, and Noemí didn't want to blurt it all out either.

"Do you think you'd have time to show me the greenhouse now?" she asked diplomatically.

"Gladly."

It was very small, the greenhouse—almost like the postscript at the end of an awkward letter. Neglect had flourished, and there were dirty glass panels and broken glass aplenty. In the rainy season the water seeped in with ease. Mold caked the planters. But a few flowers were still in bloom, and when Noemí looked up she was greeted by the striking vision of colored glass: a glass roof decorated with a twining serpent. The snake's body was green, the eyes were yellow. The sight of it quite surprised her. It was perfectly designed, almost leaping off the glass, its fangs open.

"Oh," she said, pressing the tips of her fingers against her lips.

"Something the matter?" Virgil asked, moving to stand next to her.

"Nothing, really. I've seen that snake around the house," she said.

"The ouroboros."

"Is it a heraldic symbol?"

"It's our symbol, but we don't have a shield. My father had a seal made with it, though."

"What does it mean?"

"The snake eats its tail. The infinite, above us, and below."

"Well, yes, but why did your family pick that as your seal? It's everywhere too."

"Really?" he said nonchalantly and shrugged.

Noemí tilted her head, trying to get a better look at the snake's head. "I haven't seen glass like that in a greenhouse," she admitted. "You'd expect transparent glass."

"My mother designed it."

"Chromic oxide. I'd bet that's what gives it that green coloration. But there must also be some uranium oxide used here, because, see? Right there, it almost seems to glow," she said, pointing at the snake's head, the cruel eyes. "Was it manufactured here or shipped piece by piece from England?"

"I know little of how it was built."

"Would Florence know?"

"You're an inquisitive creature."

She wasn't sure whether he meant it as a compliment or a defect. "The greenhouse, hmm?" he went on. "I know it's old. I know my mother loved it more than any other part of the house."

Virgil moved toward a long table that ran along the center length of the greenhouse, crammed with yellowed potted plants, and to the back, to a bed box that held a few pristine pink roses. He carefully brushed his knuckles against the petals.

"She took care to cut out the weak and useless shoots, to look after each flower. But when she died, nobody much cared for the plants, and this is what's left of it all."

"I'm sorry."

His eyes were steadfast on the roses, pulling a blighted petal. "It doesn't matter. I do not remember her. I was a baby when she died."

Alice Doyle, who shared her initials with that other sister. Alice Doyle, blond and pale, who had been flesh once, who had been more than a portrait on a wall, who must have sketched on a piece of paper the serpent that curled above their heads. The rhythms of its scaly body, the shape of its narrowed eyes, and the terrible mouth.

"It was a violent death. We have a certain history of violence, the Doyles. But we are resistant," he said. "And it was a long time ago. It doesn't matter."

*Your sister shot her*, she thought, and she could not picture it. It was such a monstrous, terrible act that she could not imagine that it truly had happened, in this house. And afterward someone had scrubbed the blood away, someone had burned the dirty linens or replaced the rugs with the ugly scarlet splotches on them, and life had gone on. But how could it have gone on? Such misery, such ugliness, surely it could not be erased.

Yet Virgil seemed unperturbed.

"My father, when he spoke to you yesterday about beauty, he must have spoken about superior and inferior types too," Virgil said, raising his head and looking at her intently. "He must have mentioned his theories."

"I'm not sure what theories you refer to," she replied.

"That we have a predetermined nature."

"That sounds rather awful, doesn't it?" she said.

"Yet as a good Catholic you must believe in original sin."

"Perhaps I'm a bad Catholic. How would you know?"

"Catalina prays her rosary," he said. "She went to church each week, before she got sick. I imagine you do the same, back home."

As a matter of fact Noemí's eldest uncle was a priest and she was indeed expected to attend mass in a good, modest black dress, with her lace mantilla carefully pinned in place. She also had a tiny rosary—because everyone did—and a golden cross on a matching chain, but she didn't wear the chain regularly, and she had not given much thought to original sin since the days when she was busy learning her catechism in preparation for her first communion. Now she thought vaguely about the cross and almost felt like pressing a hand against her neck, to feel the absence of it.

"Do you believe, then, that we have a predetermined nature?" she asked.

"I have seen the world, and in seeing it I've noticed people seem bound to their vices. Take a walk around any tenement and you'll recognize the same sort of faces, the same sort of expressions on those faces, and the same sort of people. You can't remove whatever taint they carry with hygiene campaigns. There are fit and unfit people."

"It seems like nonsense to me," she said. "That eugenicist discourse always makes my stomach turn. Fit and unfit. We are not talking about cats and dogs."

"Why shouldn't humans be the equivalent of cats and dogs? We are all organisms striving for survival, moved forward by the single instinct that matters: reproduction and the propagation of our kind. Don't you like to study the nature of man? Isn't that what an anthropologist does?"

"I hardly want to discuss this topic."

"What do you want to discuss?" he asked with dry amusement. "I know you're itching to say it, so say it."

Noemí had meant to be more subtle than this, more charming, but there was no point in evasion now. He'd entwined her in conversation and pushed her to speak.

"Catalina."

"What about her?"

Noemí leaned her back against the long table, her hands resting on its scratched surface, and looked up at him. "The doctor who came today thinks she needs a psychiatrist."

"Yes, she very well may need one, eventually," he agreed.

"Eventually?"

"Tuberculosis is no joke. I cannot be dragging her off somewhere else. Besides, she'd hardly be accepted in a psychiatric facility considering her illness. So, yes, eventually we might evaluate specialized psychological care for her. For now she seems to be doing well enough with Arthur."

"Well enough?" Noemí scoffed. "She hears voices. She says there are people in the walls."

"Yes. I'm aware."

"You don't seem worried."

"You presume a great deal, little girl."

Virgil crossed his arms and walked away from her. Noemí protested—a curse, delivered in Spanish, escaping her lips—and quickly moved behind him, her arms brushing against brittle leaves and dead ferns. He turned abruptly and stared down at her.

"She was worse before. You did not see her three or four weeks ago. Fragile, like a porcelain doll. But she's getting better."

"You don't know that."

"Arthur knows that. You can ask him," he said calmly.

"That doctor of yours wouldn't even let me ask two questions."

"And that doctor of yours, Miss Taboada, as far as my wife tells me, looks like he can't even grow a beard."

"You talked to her?"

"I went to see her. That's how I knew you had a guest."

He was correct on the point of the doctor's youth, but she shook her head. "What does his age have to do with anything?" she replied.

"I'm not about to listen to a boy who graduated from medical school a few months ago."

"Then why did you tell me to bring him here?"

He looked her up and down. "I did not. You insisted. Just as you are insisting on having this extremely dull conversation."

He made to leave, but this time she caught his arm, forcing him to turn and face her again. His eyes were very cold, very blue, but a stray beam of light hit them. Gold, they looked for a flickering second, before he inclined his head and the effect passed.

"Well, then *I* insist, no, I *demand*, that you take her back to Mexico City," she said. Her attempt at diplomacy was a failure and they both knew it, so she might as well speak openly. "This silly, creaky old house is no good for her. Must I—"

"You are not going to change my mind," he said, interrupting her, "and in the end she's my wife."

"She's my cousin."

Her hand was still on his arm. Carefully, he took hold of her fingers and pried them loose of his jacket's sleeve, pausing for a second to look down at her hands, as if examining the length of her fingers or the shape of her nails.

"I know. I also know you don't like it here, and if you are itching to get back to your home and away from this 'creaky' house, you're welcome to it."

"Are you throwing me out now?"

"No. But you don't give the orders around here. We'll be fine as long as you remember this," he said.

"You're rude."

"I doubt it."

"I should go right away."

Throughout this whole conversation his voice had remained level, which she found very infuriating, just as she despised the smirk that marked his face. He was civil and yet disdainful.

"Maybe. But I don't think you will. I think it's in your nature to stay. It's the dutiful pull of blood, of family. I can respect that."

"Maybe it's in my nature not to back down."

"I believe you are correct. Don't bear me a grudge, Noemí. You'll see this is the best course."

"I thought we had a truce," she told him.

"That would imply we've been at war. Would you say that?"

"No."

"Then everything is fine," he concluded and walked out of the greenhouse.

He had a way of parrying her words that was maddening. She could finally understand why her father had been so irritated by Virgil's correspondence. She could imagine the letters he wrote, filled with sentences that feinted and amounted to an irritating nothing.

She shoved a pot from atop the table. It broke with a resounding crash, spilling earth upon the floor. At once she regretted the gesture. She could smash all the crockery, it would do her no good. Noemí knelt down, trying to see if the damage might be fixed, grabbing pieces of ceramic and seeing how they fit together, but it was impossible.

Damn it and damn it again. She pushed the pieces away with her foot, under the table.

Of course he had a point. Catalina was his wife, and he was the one who could make choices for her. Why, Mexican women couldn't even vote. What could Noemí say? What could she do in such a situation? Perhaps it would be best if her father intervened. If he came down here. A man would command more respect. But no, it was as she'd said: she wasn't going to back down.

Very well. Then she must remain for a while longer. If Virgil couldn't be persuaded to assist her, maybe the loathsome patriarch of the Doyle family might rule in her favor. She might be able to drag Francis onto her side of the court, she suspected that. Most of all she felt like leaving now would be betraying Catalina.

Noemí stood up, and as she did she noticed that there was a mosaic on the floor. Stepping back and looking around the room she realized it circled the table. It was another of the snake symbols. The ouroboros slowly devouring itself. The infinite, above us, and below, as Virgil had said.

$9$

n Tuesday, Noemí ventured into the cemetery. Catalina had inspired this second trip—"You must look in the cemetery," she'd said—but Noemí did not expect to find anything interesting there. She thought, however, that she might have a smoke in peace, among the tombstones, since Florence wouldn't abide a cigarette even in the privacy of her bedroom.

The mist gave the cemetery a romantic aura. She recalled that Mary Shelley had rendezvoused with her future husband in a cemetery: illicit liaisons by a tomb. Catalina had told her this story, just as she had gushed over *Wuthering Heights*. Sir Walter Scott, that had been another favorite of hers. And the movies. How she'd delighted in the torturous romance of *María Candelaria*.

Once upon a time Catalina had been engaged to the youngest of the Inclános but had broken it off. When Noemí had asked her why, since he seemed for all intents and purposes a very agreeable man, Catalina had told her she expected more. True romance, she said. True feelings. Her cousin had never quite lost that young-girl wonder of the world, her imagination crowded with visions of women greeting passionate lovers by moonlight. Well, except now. There wasn't much wonder in Catalina's eyes, though she did seem lost.

Noemí wondered if High Place had robbed her of her illusions, or if they were meant to be shattered all along. Marriage could hardly be like the passionate romances one read about in books. It seemed to her, in fact, a rotten deal. Men would be solicitous and well behaved when they courted a woman, asking her out to parties and sending her flowers, but once they married, the flowers wilted. You didn't have married men posting love letters to their wives. That's why Noemí tended to cycle through admirers. She worried a man would be briefly impressed with her luster, only to lose interest later on. There was also the excitement of the chase, the delight that flew through her veins when she knew a suitor was bewitched with her. Besides, boys her age were dull, always talking about the parties they had been to the previous week or the one they were planning to go to the week after. Easy, shallow men. Yet the thought of anyone more substantial made her nervous, for she was trapped between competing desires, a desire for a more meaningful connection and the desire to never change. She wished for eternal youth and endless merriment.

Noemí rounded a small cluster of tombs with moss covering the names and dates on them. Leaning back on a broken headstone, she reached into her pocket for her pack of cigarettes. She saw movement nearby, on a mound, a shape half hidden by the mist and a tree.

"Who's there?" she said, hoping it wasn't a mountain lion. That would be her luck.

The mist did not allow her to glimpse anything properly. She squinted and stood on her tiptoes, frowning. The shape. She almost thought it had a halo. A yellow or golden coloring, like light refracted for a quick second . . .

*It lives in the cemetery*, Catalina said. The words had not frightened her. But now, standing outside, with only a packet of cigarettes and a lighter, she felt exposed and vulnerable, and she couldn't help but wonder exactly *what* lived in the cemetery.

*Slugs, worms, and beetles, and nothing more,* she told herself, sliding her hand into her pocket, clasping her lighter like a talisman. The shape, gray and lacking definition, a blur of darkness against the mist, did not move toward Noemí. It remained still. It might be nothing but a statue. A trick of the light might have made it appear as if it were moving.

Yes, no doubt it had been a trick of the light, just like with the quickly glimpsed halo. She moved away, eager to retrace her steps and head back to the house.

She heard a rustling in the grass and, turning her head sharply, she noticed the shape had vanished. It couldn't have been a statue.

She was suddenly, unpleasantly, aware of a buzzing, almost like a beehive but not quite. It was loud. Or no, loud was not the right word. She could hear it very clearly. Like the echo in an empty room it seemed to bounce back to her.

*It lives in the cemetery.*

She ought to get back to the house. It was that way, to her right.

The mist, which had seemed insubstantial and thin as she swung the gate open, had thickened. Noemí tried to think hard whether it was to her right or her left that she should head. She did not want to end up following a wrong trail and bumping into a mountain lion or sliding off a ravine.

*It lives in the cemetery.*

Right, it was definitely right. The buzzing was also toward the right. Bees or wasps. Well, what if there were bees? It wasn't as if they'd sting her. She wasn't going to paw at their hive to get honey.

The sound, though. It was unpleasant. It made her want to go in the opposite direction. Buzzing. Maybe it was flies. Flies as green as emeralds, their fat bodies atop a piece of carrion. Meat, red and raw, and really, why must she think these things? Why must she stand like this, with a hand in her pocket and her eyes wide, anxiously listening . . .

*You must look in the cemetery.*

Left, go left. Toward that mist, which seemed even thicker there, thick as gruel.

There came the crunching of a twig under a shoe and a voice, pleasant and warm in the coldness of the cemetery.

"Out for a stroll?" Francis asked.

He wore a gray turtleneck and a navy coat and a matching navy cap. A basket dangled from his right arm. He always seemed rather insubstantial to Noemí, but now, in the mist, he appeared perfectly solid and real. It was exactly what she needed.

"Oh, I could kiss you, I'm so happy to see you," she said merrily.

He blushed as red as a pomegranate, which was not becoming and was also, frankly, a little funny because he was a bit older than her, a man made. If anyone should play the bashful maid, it should be her. Then again she supposed there weren't many young women fawning over Francis in this place.

She figured if she ever got him to a party in Mexico City he would be utterly thrilled or petrified, only one of two extremes.

"I'm not sure I've done anything to deserve that," he said, half mumbling the words.

"You deserve it. I can't seem to figure out where is what in this mist. I was thinking I'd have to spin around and hope there wasn't a gully nearby and I'd go tumbling right into it. Can you see anything? And do you know the location of the cemetery gates?"

"Of course I know it," he said. "It's not that hard if you look down. There're all kinds of visual markers to guide you."

"It feels like having a veil thrust over your eyes," she declared. "I also fear there are bees nearby and they might sting me. I heard a buzzing."

He glanced down, nodding, looking at his basket. Now that he was with her, she had regained her levity, and she peered curiously at him.

"What do you have there?" she asked, pointing at the basket.

"I've been collecting mushrooms."

"Mushrooms? At a cemetery?"

"Sure. They're all around."

"As long as you don't plan to make them into a salad," she said.

"What would be wrong about that?"

"Only the thought of them growing over dead things!"

"But then mushrooms always grow over dead things in a way."

"I can't believe you are strolling around in this fog hunting for mushrooms growing on graves. It sounds grim, like you're a body snatcher from a nineteenth-century dime novel."

Catalina would have liked that. Perhaps she'd gone mushroom hunting in the cemetery too. Or else she simply stood in this same spot, smiling wistfully as the wind toyed with her hair. Books, moonlight, melodrama.

"Me?" he asked.

"Yes. I bet you have a skull in there. You're a character out of Horacio Quiroga's stories. Let me see."

He had draped a red handkerchief over the basket, which he removed to allow her to inspect the mushrooms. They were a bright, fleshy orange with intricate folds, soft as velvet. She held a small one between her index finger and her thumb.

"*Cantharellus cibarius*. They're quite delicious, and they were not growing in the cemetery, but farther away. I merely cut through here to get back home. Locals call them duraznillos. Smell them."

Noemí leaned down closer to the basket. "They smell sweet."

"They're quite lovely too. There's an important connection between certain cultures and mushrooms, you know? The Zapotec Indians of your country practiced dentistry by giving people a mushroom which would intoxicate them and serve as an anesthetic. And the Aztecs, they too found mushrooms interesting. They consumed them in order to experience visions."

"Teonanácatl," she said. "The flesh of the gods."

He spoke eagerly. "You know about fungi, then?"

"No, not really: history. I was thinking of becoming a historian before I detoured and settled on anthropology. At least that is the plan now."

"I see. Well, I'd love to find those little, dark mushrooms that the Aztecs ate."

"Why, you don't strike me as that type of boy," Noemí said, handing him back the orange mushroom.

"What do you mean?"

"They're supposed to make you feel drunk and induce a great lust. At least that's what the Spaniard chroniclers said. Do you plan on snacking on them and going on a date?"

"No, well, I would not want them, not for that," Francis quickly babbled.

Noemí liked to flirt and she was good at it, but she could tell by the renewed redness in Francis's cheeks that he was a novice at this. Had he ever gone dancing? She couldn't picture him heading to town for a festivity, nor could she see him sneaking kisses in a darkened cinema in Pachuca, though Pachuca was unlikely in the first place since he'd never traveled far. Who knew. Maybe she'd kiss him before the trip was over, and he would be utterly shocked by the gesture.

But then, she was discovering she actually enjoyed his company and didn't wish to torture the young man.

"I'm joking. My grandmother was Mazatec, and the Mazatec ingest similar mushrooms during certain ceremonies. It's not about lust, it's communion. They say the mushroom speaks to you. I understand your interest in them."

"Why, yes," he said. "The world is filled with so many extraordinary wonders, isn't it? You could spend a lifetime peering in forests and jungles and never see one tenth of nature's secrets."

He sounded so excited, it was a bit funny. She didn't have a naturalist bone in her body, but rather than judging his passion ridiculous she was moved by his fervor. He had such life when he spoke like that.

"Do you like all plants, or are your botanical interests limited to mushrooms?"

"I like all plants and have pressed a large share of flowers, leaves, ferns, and such. But mushrooms are more interesting. I make spore prints and draw a little," he said, looking pleased.

"What's a spore print?"

"You place the gills on a paper surface and they leave an impression of it. It's used to help identify mushrooms. And the botanical illustrations, they are beautiful. Such colors. I might . . . perhaps . . ."

"Perhaps what?" she asked when he didn't continue.

He clutched the red piece of cloth in his left hand tightly. "Perhaps you'd like to see the prints sometime? I'm sure it doesn't sound exciting, but if you find yourself terribly bored it might be a distraction."

"I would like to, thanks," she said, helping him out since he seemed to have lost all knowledge of words and was looking mutely at the ground, as if the right sentence might sprout there.

He smiled at her, carefully setting the red handkerchief back on top of the mushrooms. The mist had thinned as they spoke, and now she could see the tombstones, the trees, and the shrubs.

"At last, I am no longer blind," Noemí said. "There is sunlight! And air."

"Yes. You could make your way back on your own," he replied, a note of disenchantment in his voice as he looked around. "Although you could keep me company for a while longer. If you are not too busy," he added cautiously.

She had been eager to leave the cemetery a few minutes before, but now it was all peaceful and quiet. Even the mist seemed pleasant. She couldn't believe she'd been scared. Why, the figure she had seen must have been Francis walking around and poking at the ground for mushrooms.

"I might have a cigarette," she said and lit one with nimble fingers. She offered him the pack, but Francis shook his head.

"My mother wants to have a chat with you about that," he said, looking serious.

"Is she going to tell me smoking is a filthy habit again?" Noemí asked as she took a puff and tilted her head up. She liked doing that. It enhanced her long, elegant neck, which was among her finest features and made her feel a bit like a movie star. Hugo Duarte and all the other boys fawning around her certainly thought it was a charming detail.

She was vain, yes. Though she didn't think it was a sin. Noemí looked a bit like Katy Jurado when she struck the right pose, and of course she knew what exact pose and angle to strike. But she'd abandoned the theater classes. Nowadays she wished to be a Ruth Benedict or a Margaret Mead.

"Maybe. The family insists on certain healthy habits. No smoking, no coffee, no loud music or noises, cold showers, closed curtains, mild words and—"

"Why?"

"It's the way it's always been done at High Place," Francis said blandly.

"The cemetery sounds more lively," she said. "Maybe we should fill a flask with whiskey and have a party here, under that pine tree. I'll blow smoke rings your way, and we can try and find those hallucinogenic mushrooms. And if it turns out they do indeed induce a sort of lust or frenzy and you get fresh with me, I won't mind one bit."

She was joking. Anybody would have known it was a joke. Her tone of voice possessed the dramatic intonation that takes place when a woman is giving a grand performance. But he took it all wrong, no longer blushing but paling.

He shook his head. "My mother, she would say that's wrong, to suggest . . . it's wrong . . ."

He trailed off, though it was not necessary that he elaborate. He seemed plainly disgusted.

She pictured him talking to his mother, whispering, the word *filth* on his lips and both of them nodding, agreeing. Superior and inferior types, and Noemí did not belong in the first category, did not belong in High Place, did not deserve anything but scorn.

"I don't care what your mother thinks, Francis," Noemí said as she dropped the cigarette and crushed it under the heel of her shoe with two vicious stomps. She began walking briskly. "I'm headed back. You're a complete bore."

A few steps later she stopped and crossed her arms, turning around.

He had followed her and was close behind.

Noemí took a deep breath. "Let me be. I don't need you to show me the way."

Francis bent down and carefully picked up a mushroom that she had accidentally trampled over in her mad dash toward the cemetery gates. It was satiny-white, the stem had broken off from the cap, and he held both in the palm of his hand.

"A destroying angel," he muttered.

"Sorry?" she asked, confused.

"A poisonous mushroom. Its spore print is white, which is how you can distinguish it from an edible one."

He placed the mushroom back on the ground and stood up, brushing away the dirt from his trousers. "I must seem ridiculous to you," he said quietly. "A ridiculous fool clutching his mother's skirts. You'd be right too. I dare not do anything to upset her, or to upset Great Uncle Howard. Especially Uncle Howard."

He looked at her, and she realized that the contempt in his eyes hadn't been meant for her, but for himself. She felt awful, and she remembered how Catalina had told her she was capable of leaving deep scars in people if she didn't watch her scalding tongue.

*For all your intelligence, you don't think sometimes*, Catalina had said. How true. There she was, making stories up in her head when he had said nothing cruel to her.

"No. I'm so sorry, Francis. I'm the fool, a court jester," Noemí said, attempting a sort of lightness in the delivery, hoping he understood she hadn't meant it, that they might laugh this silly quarrel away.

He nodded slowly, but did not seem convinced. She stretched out a hand, touching his fingers, which were dirty from handling the mushrooms.

"I really am sorry," she said, this time eradicating any flippancy.

He looked at her with great solemnity and his fingers tightened around hers, and he gave her a little tug, as if to pull her closer to him. But just as quickly he released her and stepped back, grabbing the red cloth he carried atop his basket and handing it to her.

"I'm afraid I've dirtied you," he said.

"Yes,"—Noemí looked at her hand, smudged with soil—"I guess you have."

She wiped her hands clean on the cloth and handed it back to him. Francis tucked it in a pocket and set the basket down.

"You should go back," he said, glancing aside. "I still need to collect more mushrooms."

Noemí didn't know if he was telling the truth or was still upset and merely wanted her gone. She couldn't blame him if he was sore with her. "Very well. Don't let the mist swallow you," she said.

She reached the cemetery's gate soon enough and swung it open. Noemí looked over her shoulder and saw a figure at a distance, Francis with his basket, the curling wisps of mist making his features vague. Yes, he must have been the silhouette she had spied in the cemetery earlier, and yet she felt it couldn't have been him.

*Maybe it was a destroying angel of a different kind,* Noemí mused, and immediately regretted such an odd, morbid thought. Really, what was wrong with her today?

She retraced her steps, followed the trail back to High Place. When she walked into the kitchen she found Charles sweeping the floor with an old broom. Noemí smiled in greeting. Just then, Florence walked in. She wore a gray dress, a double strand of pearls and her hair up. When she caught sight of Noemí she clasped her hands together.

"Finally, there you are. Where have you been? I've been looking for you." Florence frowned, glancing down. "You're trailing mud inside. Take off those shoes."

"I'm sorry," Noemí said, looking down at her high heels, which were crusted with dirt and blades of grass. She took them off, holding them in her hands.

"Charles, take those and clean them," Florence ordered the man.

"I can do it. It's no problem."

"Let him."

Charles put the broom aside and walked toward her, extending his hands. "Miss," he said, the one word.

"Oh," Noemí replied and handed him the shoes. He took them, grabbed a brush that lay upon a shelf, and sat on a stool in the corner of the room and began brushing the dirt off her high heels.

"Your cousin was asking for you," Florence said.

"Is she all right?" Noemí asked, immediately worried.

"She's fine. She was bored and wanted to converse with you."

"I can go upstairs right away," Noemí said, her stockinged feet moving quickly against the cold floor.

"There's no need for that," Florence said. "She's taking her nap now."

Noemí had already stepped into the hallway. She looked back at Florence, who was walking toward her, and shrugged. "Perhaps you could go up later?"

"Yes, I will," Noemí said, but she felt deflated and a little bad for not having been around when Catalina wanted her.

# 10

In the mornings Florence or one of the maids came by to deliver Noemí's breakfast tray. She had tried to converse with the maids, but they did not offer anything but curt yeses and nos to Noemí. In fact, when she encountered any of the staff of High Place—Lizzie or Charles or the eldest of the three servants, Mary—they inclined their head and kept walking, as if they were pretending Noemí did not exist.

The house, so quiet, with its curtains drawn, was like a dress lined with lead. Everything was heavy, even the air, and a musty scent lingered along the hallways. It felt almost as if it were a temple, a church, where one must speak in low voices and genuflect, and she supposed the servants had acclimatized to this environment and therefore tiptoed along the staircase, unwilling nuns who had made vows of silence.

That morning, however, the quiet routine of Mary or Florence knocking a single time, walking in, and setting her tray on a table was interrupted. There were three knocks, three soft rapping noises. No one walked in, and when the knocks were repeated Noemí opened the door to find Francis there, bearing her tray.

"Good morning," he said.

He quite surprised her. She smiled. "Hello. Are you short staffed today?"

"I offered to help my mother deliver this, since she's busy seeing about Great Uncle Howard. He's had pain in his leg last night, and when he does he's in a foul mood. Where should I set it down?"

"Over there," Noemí said, stepping aside and pointing at the table.

Francis carefully set the tray down. Afterward he slid his hands into his pockets and cleared his throat.

"I was wondering if you'd be interested in looking at those spore prints today. If you have nothing better to do, that is."

This was a great chance for Noemí to ask him for a ride, she thought. A bit of socializing and he was sure to do as she said. She needed to go into town.

"Let me talk to my secretary. I have a very full social agenda," Noemí replied cheekily.

He smiled. "Should we meet in the library? In, say, an hour?"

"Very well."


It was close to a social outing, this trek to the library, and it invigorated her, for she was an eager social creature. Noemí changed into a polka-dot day dress with a square neck. She had misplaced the matching bolero jacket and really she ought to have been wearing white gloves with it, but their location being what it was, it was not as if a little faux pas like that would be noticed and make it into the society pages.

As she brushed her hair she wondered what everyone was up to back in the city. No doubt her brother was still behaving like a baby with that broken foot of his, Roberta was probably trying to psychoanalyze their whole circle of friends as she always did, and she was sure by now Hugo Duarte had found a new girl to take to recitals and parties. The thought needled her for a second.

Hugo was, truth be told, a good dancer and decent company during social functions.

As she descended the stairs she was amused by the thought of a party at High Place. No music, of course. The dancing would have to take place in silence, and everyone would be dressed in gray and black, as if attending a funeral.

The hallway that led to the library was profusely decorated with photographs of the Doyles rather than paintings, as was the case on the second floor. It was hard, however, to look at them because the hallway was kept in semi-darkness. She'd need to hold a flashlight or candle to them to see anything properly. Noemí had an idea. She walked into the library and the office and pulled the curtains aside. The light filtering out through the open doors of these rooms lit up a stretch of wall, providing her a chance to examine the images.

She looked at all those strange faces that seemed nevertheless familiar, echoes of Florence and Virgil and Francis. She recognized Alice, in a pose very similar to the one she sported in the portrait above Howard Doyle's fireplace, and Howard himself, rendered young, his face devoid of wrinkles.

There was a woman, her hands tightly held in her lap, her light hair pinned up, who regarded Noemí with large eyes from her picture frame. She looked about Noemí's age, and perhaps it was that, or the way her mouth was set so hard, somewhat between aggrieved and doleful, that made Noemí lean closer to the photograph, her fingers hovering above it.

"I hope I haven't kept you waiting," Francis said as he approached her, a wooden box under one arm and a book under the other.

"No, not at all," Noemí said. "Do you know who this is here?"

Francis looked at the picture she was examining. He cleared his throat. "That is . . . that was my cousin Ruth."

"I've heard about her."

Noemí had never seen the face of a killer; she wasn't in the habit of perusing the newspapers for stories about criminals. She recalled what Virgil had said, about people being bound to their vices and how their faces reflected their nature. But the woman in the photograph seemed merely discontent, not murderous.

"What have you heard?" Francis asked.

"She killed several people, and herself."

Noemí straightened herself up and turned to him. He placed the box on the floor, and his expression was distant.

"Her cousin, Michael."

Francis pointed at a picture of a young man standing ramrod straight, the chain of a pocket watch glinting against his chest, his hair neatly parted, a pair of gloves in his left hand, his eyes rendered almost colorless in the sepia photograph.

Francis pointed at the photograph showing Alice, who looked like Agnes. "Her mother."

His hand darted between two pictures, a woman with her light hair swept up and a man in a dark jacket. "Dorothy and Leland. Her aunt and uncle, my grandparents."

He went quiet. There was nothing more to say; the litany of the dead had been recited. Michael and Alice, Dorothy, Leland, and Ruth, all of them resting in that elegant mausoleum, the coffins gathering cobwebs and dust. The thought of the party without music, the funerary clothes, now seemed extremely morbid and apt.

"Why did she do it?"

"I wasn't born when it happened," Francis said quickly, turning his head away.

"Yes, they must have told you something, there must have been—"

"I told you, I wasn't even born then. Who knows? This place could drive anyone crazy," he said angrily.

His voice sounded loud in this quiet space of faded wallpaper and gilded frames; it seemed to bounce off the walls and return to them, scraping their skin with its harshness, almost booming. It startled her, this acoustic effect, and it also seemed to affect him. He hunched his shoulders, shrank down, trying to make himself smaller.

"I'm sorry," he said. "I shouldn't raise my voice like that. The sound carries here, and I'm being very rude."

"No, I'm being rude. I can understand you wouldn't want to talk about such a thing."

"Another time, perhaps I might tell you about it," he said.

His voice was now velvet soft and so was the silence that settled around them. She wondered if the gunshots had boomed through the house just as Francis's voice had boomed, leaving a trail of echoes, and then the same plush silence.

*You have a devious mind, Noemí*, she chided herself. *No wonder you dream awful things.*

"Yes. Well, what about those prints you have with you?" she told him, because she did not want any more grimness.

They went into the library, and he spread on a table before her the treasures he carted in the box. Sheets of paper with brown, black, and purplish blotches upon the surface. They reminded her of the Rorschach images Roberta—the same friend who swore on Jung—had shown her. These were more accurate; there was no subjective meaning to be assigned. These prints told a story, as clear as her name written on a chalkboard.

He also showed her pressed plants, lovingly collected between the pages of a book. Ferns, roses, daisies, dried and catalogued with an immaculate handwriting that put Noemí's shabby penmanship to shame. She thought their mother superior would have adored Francis, with his neatness and his organized spirit.

She informed him of this, told him how the nuns at her school would have fussed about him.

"I always got stuck at 'I believe in the Holy Spirit,'" she said. "I couldn't name its symbols. There was the dove and maybe a cloud and holy water, and oh, then I'd forget."

"Fire, which transforms whatever it touches," Francis said helpfully.

"I told you, the nuns would have loved you."

"I'm sure they liked you."

"No. Everyone *says* they like me well enough, but that's because they have to. No one is going to declare they hate Noemí

Taboada. It would be crass to state such a thing while you're nibbling at a canapé. You have to whisper it in the foyer."

"Then, in Mexico City, at your parties, you spend the whole time feeling people don't like you?"

"I spend the time drinking good champagne, dear boy," she said.

"Of course." He chuckled, leaning against the table and looking down at his spore prints. "Your life must be exciting."

"I don't know about that. I have a good time, I suppose."

"Aside from the parties, what do you do?"

"Well, I'm attending university, so that eats up much of my day. But you're asking what I do in my spare time? I like music. I often get tickets to the Philharmonic. Chavez, Revueltas, Lara, there's so much good music to listen to. I even play a little piano myself."

"Do you, truly?" he asked, looking dazzled. "That is amazing."

"I don't play *with* the Philharmonic."

"Yes, well, it still sounds exciting."

"It's not. It's so dull. All those years of scales and trying to hit the right keys. I'm so dull!" she declared, as one must. To seem too eager about anything was a little vulgar.

"You aren't. Not at all," he assured her quickly.

"You're not supposed to say that. Not like that. You sound much too honest. Don't you know anything?" she asked.

He shrugged, as if apologizing, unable to match her high spirits. He was bashful and a little odd. And she liked him in a different way than she liked the bold boys she knew, different than Hugo Duarte, whom she liked mostly because he danced well and resembled Pedro Infante. This was a warmer feeling, more genuine.

"You think me spoiled now," she said and allowed herself to sound rueful, because she actually did want him to like *her,* and it wasn't for show.

"Not at all," he replied, again with that disarming honesty, as he leaned down on the table and fiddled with a couple of spore prints.

She rested her elbows on the table and leaned forward, smiling, until her eyes were level with his. They looked at each other.

"You'll think it in a minute because I have to ask you for a favor," she said, unable to forget the question she had on her mind.

"What?"

"I want to go into town tomorrow, and your mother said I can't take the car. I was thinking you might give me a ride there and pick me up, say, a couple of hours later."

"You want me to drop you off in town."

"Yes."

He looked away, evading her gaze. "My mother will not have it. She'll say you need a chaperone."

"Are *you* going to chaperone *me*?" Noemí asked. "I'm not a child."

"I know."

Francis slowly walked around the table, stopping close to her and leaning down, inspecting one of the plant specimens on display. His fingers brushed lightly over a fern.

"They've asked me to keep an eye on you," he said, his voice low. "They say you're reckless."

"I suppose you agree and you think I need a babysitter," she replied, scoffing.

"I think you can be reckless. But maybe I can ignore them this one time," he said, almost whispering, his head lowered as if to reveal a secret. "We should leave early tomorrow, around eight o'clock, before they're up and about. And don't tell anyone we're going out."

"I won't. Thank you."

"It is nothing," he replied and turned his head to look at Noemí.

This time his gaze lingered on her for one long minute before, skittish, he stepped back and rounded the table again, returning to his original position. A bundle of nerves is what he was.

A heart, raw and bleeding, she thought, and the image lingered in her mind. The anatomical heart, like in the Lotería cards, red, with all veins and arteries, rendered bright crimson. What was the saying? Do not miss me, sweetheart, I'll be back by bus. Yes, she had spent many lazy afternoons playing Lotería with her cousins, declaiming the popular rhyme that went with each card as they played and made their bets.

Don't miss me, sweetheart.

Could she get Lotería cards in town? It might give her and Catalina an activity to pass the time. It would be something they'd done before, which would conjure memories of more pleasant days.

The door to the library opened and Florence walked in, Lizzie following her behind with a pail and a rag. Florence's gaze swept across the room, coldly assessing Noemí and settling on her son.

"Mother. I didn't realize you'd be cleaning the library today," Francis said, quickly standing up straight and shoving his hands in his pockets.

"You know how it is, Francis. If we do not keep on top of things they fall apart. While a few may consign themselves to idleness, others must observe their duties."

"Yes, of course," Francis said and began gathering his things.

"I'd be happy to watch over Catalina while you do your cleaning," Noemí offered.

"She's resting. Mary is with her, anyway. There's no need for you."

"Still, I'd like to make myself useful, as you say," she declared, uttering a challenge. She wasn't going to let Florence complain that she did nothing.

"Follow me."

Before Noemí exited the library, she glanced over her shoulder and shot Francis a smile. Florence marched Noemí into the dining room and gestured to the display cases crammed with silver.

"You were interested in these items. Perhaps you might polish them," she said.

The Doyles' silver collection was quite staggering, each shelf

lined with salvers, tea sets, bowls, and candlesticks that sat dusty
and dull behind glass. A lone person could not hope to tackle this
whole task alone, but Noemí was determined to prove herself in
front of this woman.

"If you give me a rag and some polish, I'll do it."

Since the dining room was very dark, Noemí had to light several lamps and candles in order to see exactly what she was doing.
Then she set about meticulously working the polish into every
crevice and curve, sliding the rag over enameled vines and flowers. A sugar bowl proved to be exceedingly difficult, but for the
most part she managed well.

When Florence returned, many pieces lay gleaming on the
table. Noemí was carefully polishing one of two curious cups
that were shaped in the form of stylized mushrooms. The base of
the cups was decorated with tiny leaves and even a beetle. Maybe
Francis could tell her if this was based on a real mushroom spe-
cies and which one.

Florence stood there, watching Noemí. "You're industrious."

"Like a little bee, when I feel like it," Noemí replied.

Florence approached the table, running her hands over the
items Noemí had polished. She picked one of the cups up and
spun it between her fingers, inspecting it. "You expect to win my
praise this way, I think. It would take more."

"Your respect, perhaps. Not your praise."

"Why would you need my respect?"

"I don't."

Florence set the cup down and clasped her hands together, her
eyes admiring the metal objects, almost reverently. Noemí had to
admit it was a bit overwhelming to look at so many glittering
riches on display, though it seemed a pity they had all been locked
away, dusty and forgotten. What good were mountains of silver
if you didn't use them? And the people in the town, they had so
little. They didn't keep silver locked in cabinets.

"Most of this is made from silver from our mines," Florence
said. "Do you have any idea how much silver our mine produced?
God, it was dizzying! My uncle brought all the machinery, all the

knowledge to dredge it from the dark. Doyle is an important name. I don't think you realize how lucky your cousin is to be part of our family now. To be a Doyle is to be *someone*."

Noemí thought of the rows of old pictures in the hallway, the dilapidated household with its dusty alcoves. And what did she mean that to be a Doyle meant to be someone? Did that make Catalina no one before she came to High Place? And was Noemí therefore confined to a faceless, luckless band of nobodies?

Florence must have noticed the skepticism in Noemí's face, and she fixed her eyes on the young woman. "What do you talk about with my son?" the woman asked abruptly, clasping her hands again. "Back there, in the library. What were you talking about?"

"Spore prints."

"That's all?"

"Well, I can't recall it all. But now, yes, spore prints."

"You talk about the city, perhaps."

"Sometimes."

If Howard reminded her of an insect, then Florence brought to mind an insectivorous plant about to swallow a fly. Noemí's brother had once owned a Venus flytrap. It had scared her a little, as a child.

"Don't give my son any ideas. They will bring him pain. Francis is content here. He doesn't need to hear about parties, music, and booze, and whatever other frivolities you choose to share with him about Mexico City."

"I'll be sure to discuss with him the preapproved subjects you dictate. Perhaps we can erase all the cities on the terrestrial globe and pretend they don't exist," Noemí said, because although Florence was intimidating, she was not willing to hide in a corner, like a baby.

"You're very cheeky," Florence said. "And you think you have a special power simply because my uncle thinks you possess a pretty face. But that's not power. It's a liability."

Florence leaned over the table, looking at a large, rectangular serving tray with a border of stylized floral wreaths. Florence's face, reflected on the silver surface, was elongated and deformed. She ran a finger around the tray's border, touching the flowers.

"When I was younger, I thought the world outside held such promise and wonders. I even went away for a bit and met a dashing young man. I thought he'd take me away, that he would change everything, change me," Florence said, and her face softened for the briefest moment. "But there's no denying our natures. I was meant to live and die in High Place. Let Francis be. He's accepted his lot in this life. It's easier that way."

Florence fixed her blue eyes on Noemí. "I'll put away the silver, no further assistance is required," she declared, ending their conversation abruptly.

Noemí went back to her room. She thought about all the times Catalina had narrated fairy tales. Once upon a time there was a princess in a tower, once upon a time a prince saved the girl from the tower. Noemí sat on the bed and contemplated the notion of enchantments that are never broken.

# 11

oemí heard a heart beating, as loud as a drum, calling for her. It woke her up.

Carefully she ventured outside her room to find the place where it was hiding. She felt it beneath her palm, when she pressed her hand against the walls; felt the wallpaper grow slippery, like a strained muscle, and the floor beneath her was wet and soft. It was a sore. A great sore she walked upon, and the walls were sores too. The wallpaper was peeling, revealing underneath sickly organs instead of brick or wooden boards. Veins and arteries clogged with secret excesses.

She followed the beating of the heart and a thread of red on the carpet. Like a gash. A line of crimson. A line of blood. Until she stopped in the middle of the hallway and saw the woman staring back at her.

Ruth, the girl from the photograph. Ruth, in a white dressing gown, her hair like a golden halo, her face bloodless. A slim, alabaster pillar in the darkness of the house. Ruth held a rifle between her hands and she stared at Noemí.

They began walking together, side by side. Their movements

were perfectly synchronized; even their breathing was identical. Ruth brushed a lock of hair away from her face and Noemí brushed her hair too.

The walls around them were glowing, a dim phosphorescence that nevertheless guided their steps, and the carpet underneath their feet was squishy. She noticed, too, markings on the walls—walls that were made of flesh. Traceries of fuzzy mold, as if the house were an overripe fruit.

The heart kept beating faster.

The heart pumped blood and groaned and shivered, and it beat so loudly Noemí thought she'd go deaf.

Ruth opened a door. Noemí grit her teeth because this was the source of the noise, the beating heart lay inside.

The door swung open, and Noemí saw a man on a bed. Only it wasn't truly a man. It was a bloated vision of a man, as if he'd drowned and floated to the surface, his pale body lined with blue veins, tumors flowering on his legs, his hands, his belly. A pustule, not a man, a living, breathing, pustule. His chest rising and falling.

The man could not possibly be alive but he was, and when Ruth opened the door he sat up in bed and extended his arms toward her, as if demanding an embrace. Noemí remained by the doorway, but Ruth approached the bed.

The man extended his hands, his greedy fingers quivering, while the girl stood at the foot of the bed and stared at him.

Ruth raised her rifle, and Noemí turned her head away. She did not want to see. But even as she turned she heard the horrid noise of the rifle, the muffled scream of the man followed by a throaty moan.

*He must be dead*, she thought. *He has to be.*

She looked at Ruth, who had walked past Noemí and was now standing in the hallway, and the young woman looked back at Noemí.

"I'm not sorry," Ruth said, and she pressed the rifle against her chin and pulled the trigger.

There was blood, the dark splatter marking the wall. Noemí

watched Ruth fall, her body bending like the stem of a flower. The suicide, however, did not unnerve Noemí. She felt that this was the way things should be; she felt soothed, she even thought to smile.

But the smile froze on Noemí's face when she saw the figure standing at the end of the hallway, watching her. It was a golden blur, it was the woman with the blur of a face, her whole body rippling, liquid, rushing toward Noemí with a huge open mouth— although she had no mouth—ready to unleash a terrible scream. Ready to eat her alive.

And now Noemí was afraid, now she knew terror, and she raised her palms to desperately ward off—

A firm hand on her arm made Noemí jump back.

"Noemí," Virgil said. She looked quickly behind her, then back at him, trying to make sense of what had happened.

She was standing in the middle of a hallway, and he stood in front of her, holding an oil lamp in his right hand. It was long and ornate, and its glass was milky green.

Noemí stared at him, speechless. The golden creature had been there a second before, but now it was gone! Gone, and in its stead it was him, wearing a plush velvet robe with a pattern of golden vines running up the fabric.

She was in her nightgown. It was supposed to be part of a gown-peignoir set, but she was not wearing the cover-up. Her arms were bare. She felt exposed and she was cold. She rubbed her arms.

"What's happening?" she asked.

"Noemí," he repeated, her name so smooth on his lips, like a piece of silk. "You were sleepwalking. One is not supposed to wake a sleepwalker. They say it can cause the sleeping person a great shock. But I was worried you'd hurt yourself. Did I frighten you?"

She did not understand his question. It took her a minute to comprehend what he was saying.

She shook her head. "No. That's quite impossible. I haven't done that in years. Not since I was a child."

"Maybe you hadn't noticed."

"I would've noticed."

"I've been following you for a few minutes now, trying to decide whether to shake you awake or not."

"I wasn't sleepwalking."

"Then I must have been mistaken, and you were simply walking around in the dark," he said coolly.

God, she felt stupid, standing there in her nightgown, gawping at him. She did not want to argue with him; there was no point in it. He was right, and besides, she dearly wished to get back to her room. It was too cold and dark in this hallway; she could hardly see anything. They could be sitting in the belly of a beast for all she knew.

In the nightmare, they had been in a belly, had they not? No. A cage made of organs. Walls of flesh. That's what she had seen, and who knew. If she tried to touch the wall right now it might ripple beneath her palm. She ran a hand through her hair.

"Fine. Maybe I was sleepwalking. But—"

She heard it then, a throaty moan like in her dream, low but undeniable. It made her jump again, jump back. She almost collided with him.

"What was that?" she asked and looked down the hallway, then turned to stare at him anxiously.

"My father is ill. It's an old wound which never quite healed and pains him. He's been having a rough night," he said, looking very composed, adjusting the flame of the oil lamp, making it bloom a little brighter. She could now see the wallpaper, its drawing of flowers, faint traces of mold marring its surface.

No veins pumping through the walls.

Damn it, and yes, Francis had told her something similar earlier that day, about Howard being ill. But was she in that area of the house, close to the old man's bed? So far from her room? She thought she might have taken a few paces outside her door, not wandered from one side of the house to the other.

"You should call for a doctor."

"Like I explained, sometimes it pains him. We are used to it.

When Dr. Cummins stops by for his weekly visit he can examine him, but my father is simply an old man. I'm sorry if he startled you."

Old, yes; 1885 was when they arrived in Mexico. Even if Howard Doyle had been a young man back then, almost seventy years had passed. And how old was he, exactly? Ninety? Closer to a hundred? He must have been an old man already when he had Virgil. She rubbed her arms again.

"Here, you must be cold," he said, setting the oil lamp down on the floor and untying his robe.

"I'm fine."

"Put this on."

He took off the robe, placing it around her shoulders. It was too large. He was tall and she was not. It never bothered her much, tall men. She simply looked them up and down. But she did not feel very confident right this second, still unnerved by that ridiculous dream. Noemí crossed her arms and looked down at the carpet.

He picked up the oil lamp. "I'll walk you back to your room."

"You don't have to."

"I do. Otherwise you'll be liable to hurt your shins in the dark. And it's quite dark."

He was, once again, correct. The few wall sconces with working bulbs gave off a dim light, but there were large pools of blackness in between them. The glow of Virgil's lamp was an eerie green, but on the other hand she felt grateful for its more potent illumination. This house, she was sure, was haunted. She wasn't one for believing in things that go bump in the night either, but right that second she firmly felt every spook and demon and evil thing might be crawling about the Earth, like in Catalina's stories.

He was quiet as they walked, and even if the silence of the house was unpleasant, and the creaking of each board made her wince, it was better than having to talk to him. She simply could not converse at a time like this.

*I'm a baby*, she thought. Boy, would her brother laugh at her if he saw her. She could picture him, telling everyone Noemí now practically believed in el coco. The memory of her brother, her family, Mexico City, it was good. It warmed her better than the robe.

When they got to her room, she finally felt at ease. She was back. All was well. She opened the door.

"If you want, you can keep this," he said, pointing to the lamp.

"No. Then you'd be the one hitting your shins in the dark. Give me a minute," she said, reaching for the top of the dresser, by the door, where she'd left the gaudy silver candelabra with the cherub. She grabbed the box of matches and lit the candle.

"Let there be light. See? It's fine."

She began to take the robe off. Virgil stilled her, setting a hand on her shoulder and then carefully running his fingers down the edge of the wide lapel. "You look very fine in my clothes," he said with that voice that was made of silk.

The comment was mildly inappropriate. In the daylight, with other people, it might have been a joke. At night, and the way he said it, it didn't seem at all decent. And yet, though subtly wrong, she found herself unable to reply. *Don't be silly*, she thought to say. Or even, *I don't want your clothes.* But she didn't say a thing, because it wasn't really that bad of a comment, a few words, and she didn't wish to start a fight in the middle of a dark hallway over what amounted to almost, but not quite, nothing.

"Well, good night, then," he said, unhurriedly releasing the lapel and taking a step back.

He held the oil lamp at eye level and smiled at her. Virgil was an attractive man and the smile was a pleasant smile—almost teasing, in a good-humored way—but there was an edge to his expression that the smile could not mask. She did not like it. She was suddenly reminded of her dream, and she thought of the man in the bed holding his arms outstretched, and she thought there was a golden cast to his eyes, a glimmer of gold among the blue. She turned her head abruptly, blinking and staring at the floor.

"You won't bid me good night?" he asked, sounding amused. "Nor grant me a thank-you? It would be rude not to."

She turned toward him, looking at him in the eye. "Thanks," she said.

"Better lock your door so you don't end up wandering around the house again, Noemí."

He adjusted the level of the oil lamp once more. His eyes were blue without a hint of gold when he gave her a final glance and stepped away, marching back down the hallway. Noemí watched the green glow float away with him, the sudden flash of color disappearing and plunging the house into darkness.

# 12

I t's funny how daylight could change her mind so utterly. At night, after her sleepwalking episode, Noemí had been scared, pulling the covers up to her chin. Contemplating the sky through her window, scratching her left wrist, she found the whole episode embarrassing and prosaic.

Her room, when viewed with the curtains wide open and the sun streaming in, was worn and sad, but couldn't conceal ghosts or monsters. Hauntings and curses, bah! She dressed in a long-sleeved button-down blouse in pale cream and a navy skirt with a kickpleat, put on a pair of flats, and headed downstairs long before the predetermined hour. Bored, she once again walked around the library, pausing before a bookcase filled with botanical tomes. She imagined Francis must have obtained his knowledge of mushrooms this way, scavenging for wisdom among moth-eaten papers. She brushed a hand along the silver frames of the pictures in the hallways, feeling the whorls and swirls beneath her fingertips. Eventually, Francis came downstairs.

He wasn't very talkative that morning, so she limited herself to a couple of comments and fiddled with her cigarette, not quite willing to light it yet. She didn't like smoking on an empty stomach.

He dropped her off by the church, which, she gathered, was where they'd dropped off Catalina each week when she went into town.

"I'll pick you up at noon," he said. "Will that be sufficient time?"

"Yes, thank you," she told him. He nodded at her and drove away.

She made her way to the healer's house. The woman who had been doing the washing the other day wasn't out; her clothesline lay empty. The town remained quiet, still half asleep. Marta Duval, however, was awake, setting out tortillas to dry in the sun next to her doorway, no doubt to be used for preparing chilaquiles.

"Good morning," Noemí said.

"Hello," the old woman replied with a smile. "You've come back at exactly the right time."

"You have the remedy?"

"I have it. Come inside."

Noemí followed her into the kitchen and sat at the table. The parrot was not there that day. It was only the two of them. The woman wiped her hands against her apron and opened a drawer, then placed a small bottle in front of Noemí.

"One tablespoon before bedtime should be enough for her. I made it stronger this time, but there's no harm in two tablespoons, either."

Noemí held the bottle up, staring at its content. "And it'll help her sleep?"

"Help, yes. It won't solve all her problems."

"Because the house is cursed."

"The family, the house." Marta Duval shrugged. "Makes no difference, does it? Cursed is cursed."

Noemí set the bottle down and ran a nail across the side of it. "Do you know why Ruth Doyle killed her family? Did you ever hear any rumors about that?"

"You hear all kinds of things. Yes, I heard. Do you have any more cigarettes?"

"I'll run out of them if I don't ration them."

"I bet you were going to buy more."

"I don't think you can buy these here," Noemí said. "Your saint has expensive tastes. Where's the parrot, by the way?"

Noemí took out her pack of Gauloises and handed one to Marta, who placed it next to the statuette of the saint. "Still in his cage under his blanket. I'll tell you about Benito. Do you want coffee? It's no good telling tales without a drink."

"Sure," Noemí said. She still wasn't hungry, but she supposed coffee might restore her appetite. It was funny. Her brother said she always breakfasted as if food was going to go out of fashion, and yet for the past two days she'd hardly touched a morsel in the mornings. Not that she'd had much in the evenings, either. She felt slightly ill. Or rather, it was the preface of an illness, like when she could predict she was about to get a cold. She hoped that was not the case.

Marta Duval set a kettle to boil and rummaged among her drawers until she produced a small tin can. When the water boiled, she poured it into two pewter mugs, added the proper amount of coffee, and placed both cups on the table. Marta's house smelled strongly of rosemary, and the scent mixed with the scent of the coffee.

"I take mine black, but do you want sugar in yours?"

"I'm fine," Noemí said.

The woman sat down and settled her hands around her mug.

"Do you want the short version or the long one? Because the long means going back quite a bit. If you want to know about Benito, then you need to know about Aurelio. That is, if you want to tell the tale properly."

"Well, I am running out of cigarettes but not out of time."

The woman smiled and sipped her coffee. Noemí did the same.

"When the mine reopened, it was big news. Mr. Doyle had his workers from England, but those weren't enough to run a mine. They could oversee the work and others could work in the house

he was building, but you can't open a mine and build a house like
· High Place with sixty Englishmen."

"Who used to run the mine before him?"

"Spaniards. But that had been ages ago. People were happy
when the mine reopened. It meant work for the locals, and folks
came from other parts of Hidalgo for the chance at a job too. You
know how it is. Where there's a mine, there's money, the town
grows. But right away folks complained. The work was tough,
but Mr. Doyle was tougher."

"He treated the workers poorly?"

"Like animals, they said. He was better with the ones building
the house. At least they were not in a hole beneath the earth. The
Mexican mining crews, he had no mercy on those. Him, Mr.
Doyle, and his brother, both of them bellowing at the workers."

Francis had pointed Leland, Howard's brother, out in the photos, but she could not recall what he looked like, and anyway, all
the people in the family seemed to have that similar physiognomy,
which she was dubbing in her head "the Doyle look." Like the
Habsburg jaw of Charles II, only not quite as concerning. Now
that had been a case of severe mandibular prognathism.

"He wanted the house built quickly and he wanted a great
garden, in the English style, with rose beds. He even brought
boxes filled with earth from Europe to make sure the flowers
would take. So there they were, working on the house and trying
to mine the silver, when there came a sickness. It hit the workers
at the house first and then the miners, but soon enough they were
all heaving and feverish. Doyle had a doctor, who he'd brought
along, just like his soil, but his precious doctor didn't help much.
They died. Lots of the miners. Some of the people working at the
house, and even Howard Doyle's wife, but mostly a great deal of
miners dropped dead."

"That's when they built the English cemetery," Noemí said.

"Yes. That's right." Marta nodded. "Well, the sickness passed.
New folks were hired. People from Hidalgo, yes, but having heard
there was an Englishman with a mine here, there also came more
Englishmen who were working around other mines, or were sim-

ply trying to make their fortune, lured by silver and a good profit. They say Zacatecas is for silver? Well, Hidalgo does well enough too.

"They came and again there were full crews and by now the house was finished, which meant it had a large staff for a proper large house. Things went along well enough—Doyle was still hard, but he paid on time and the miners also got their little quota of silver, which is the way it's always been done around here—miners expected the partido. But it was around the time Mr. Doyle married again that things started to turn sour."

She recalled the wedding portrait of Doyle's second wife: 1895. Alice, who looked like Agnes. Alice, the little sister. Now that she considered it, it was odd that Agnes had been immortalized with a stone statue, while Alice received no such treatment. Yet Howard Doyle had said he hardly knew her. It was his second wife who had lived with him for many years, who birthed him children. Did Howard Doyle like her even less than his first wife? Or was the statue insignificant, a memorial created on a whim? She tried to remember if there had been a plaque near the statue discussing Agnes. She didn't think so, but there could be. She hadn't looked closely.

"There was another wave of sickness. Lord, it hit them worse than before. They were dropping like flies. Fevers and chills and quickly to their deathbeds they went."

"Is that when they buried them in mass graves?" Noemí asked, remembering what Dr. Camarillo had told her.

The old woman frowned. "Mass graves? No. The locals, their families took them to the cemetery in town. But there were many people without kin working the mines. When someone didn't have family in town, they buried them in the English cemetery. The Mexicans didn't get a headstone, though, not even a cross, which I guess is why people talked about mass graves. A hole in the ground with no wreath nor proper service might as well be a mass grave."

Now that was a depressing thought. All those nameless workers, buried in haste, and no one to ever know where and how their lives had ended. Noemí set her pewter cup down and scratched her wrist.

"Anyway, that was not the only problem at the mine. Doyle had decided to end the custom of letting the workers have a bit of silver along with their wages. There was a man and his name was Aurelio. Aurelio was one of the miners who didn't like the change none, but unlike others who would grumble to themselves, Aurelio grumbled to the others."

"What did he say?"

"Told them what was obvious. That the camp where they worked was shit. That the doctor the Englishman brought with him had never cured anyone and they needed a good doctor. That they were leaving behind widows and orphans and hardly any money for them, and on top of that Doyle wanted to fatten up his pockets more so he'd taken away their partido and was hoarding all the silver. Then he asked the miners to go on strike."

"Did they?"

"Yes, they did. Of course, Doyle thought he could bully them back to work real easy. Doyle's brother and Doyle's trusted men, they went over to the mining camp with rifles and threats, but Aurelio and the others fought back. They threw stones at them. Doyle's brother got away by the skin of his teeth. Soon after that, Aurelio was found dead. They said it was a natural death, but no one really believed that. The strike leader dies one morning? It didn't sound right."

"There was an epidemic, though," Noemí pointed out.

"Sure. But people who saw the body said his face looked awful. You've heard about people dying of fright? Well, they said he died of fright. That his eyes were bulging and his mouth was open and he looked like a man who's seen the devil. It scared everyone good, and it also ended the strike."

Francis had mentioned strikes and the closure of the mine, but Noemí had not thought to ask him more about them. Perhaps she should remedy that, but for now she focused her attention on Marta.

"You said that Aurelio was connected to Benito, though. Who was that?"

"Patience, girl, you'll make me lose my train of thought. At my age, it's no easy thing to try and remember what was when and how it happened." Marta took several long sips of her coffee before speaking. "Where was I? Oh, yes. The mine went on. Doyle had remarried and eventually his new wife gave birth to a girl, Miss Ruth, and many years later a baby boy. Doyle's brother, Mr. Leland, he also had children. A boy and a girl. The boy was engaged to Miss Ruth."

"Kissing cousins, again," Noemí said, disturbed by this notion. The Habsburg jaw was a more apt comparison than she'd thought, and things had not ended well for the Habsburgs.

"Not much kissing, I think. That was the problem. That is where Benito comes in. He was a nephew of Aurelio and went to work in the house. This was years after the strike, so I suppose it's not like Doyle cared that he was related to Aurelio. Or a dead miner didn't matter to him none, or else he didn't know. In any case, he worked in the house, tending to the plants. By that time instead of a garden the Doyles had settled on a greenhouse.

"Benito had a lot in common with his dead uncle. He was smart, he was funny, and he didn't know how to keep out of trouble. His uncle had organized a strike, and he did an even more horrifying thing: he fell in love with Miss Ruth and she fell in love with him."

"I can't imagine her father was pleased," Noemí said.

He'd probably given his daughter the eugenics talk. Superior and inferior specimens. She pictured him by the fireplace in his room admonishing the girl, and she with her eyes fixed on the floor. Poor Benito had not stood a chance. It was funny, though, that if Doyle was truly that interested in eugenics he'd insist on all these marriages to close relations. Maybe he was imitating Darwin, who'd also married within his family.

"They say when he found out he almost killed her," Marta muttered.

Now she pictured Howard Doyle wrapping his fingers around the girl's slim neck. Strong fingers, digging deep, pressing hard, and the girl incapable of even uttering a protest because she couldn't breathe. *Papa, don't.* It was such a vivid image that Noemí had to close her eyes for a moment, gripping the table with one hand.

"Are you all right?" Marta asked.

"Yes," Noemí said, opening her eyes and nodding at the woman. "I'm fine. A little tired."

She raised the cup of coffee to her lips and drank. The warm liquid was pleasant in its bitterness. Noemí set the cup down. "Please, go on," she said.

"There's not much more to say. Ruth was punished, Benito vanished."

"He was killed?"

The old woman leaned forward, her cloudy eyes fixed on Noemí. "Even worse: disappeared, from one day to the next. Folks said he'd run off because he was afraid of what Doyle would do to him, but others said Doyle had done the disappearing.

"Ruth was supposed to get married that summer to Michael, that cousin of hers, and Benito's disappearance didn't change that one bit. Nothing would have changed that. It was the middle of the Revolution, and the upheaval meant the mine was operating with a small crew, but it was still operating. Someone had to keep the machinery going, pumping the water out, or it would flood. It rains so much here.

"And up at the house, someone had to keep changing the linens and dusting the furniture, so in many ways I guess things hadn't changed over a war, so why would they change over a missing man? Howard Doyle ordered trinkets for the wedding, acting as though nothing was amiss. As though Benito's disappearance didn't matter. Well, it must have mattered to Ruth.

"None can be sure what happened, but they said she put a sleeping draught in their food. I don't know where she got it from. She was clever, she knew many things about plants and medicine, so it could be she mixed the draught herself. Or perhaps her lover had procured it for her. Maybe in the beginning she had thought to put them to sleep and run away, but afterward she changed her mind. Once Benito disappeared. She shot her father while he slept, because of what he'd done to her lover."

"But not just her father," Noemí said. "She shot her mother and the others. If she was avenging her dead lover, wouldn't she have only shot her father? What did the others have to do with that?"

"Maybe she thought they were also guilty. Maybe she'd gone mad. We can't know. They're cursed, I tell you, and that house is haunted. You're very silly or very brave living in a haunted house."

*I'm not sorry*, that's what the Ruth in her dream had said. Had Ruth been remorseless as she wandered through the house and delivered a bullet to her kinfolk? Just because Noemí had dreamed it, it didn't mean it had happened that way. After all, in her nightmare the house had been distorted and mutated in impossible ways.

Noemí frowned, looking at her cup of coffee. She'd taken few sips. Her stomach was definitely not cooperating that morning.

"Trouble is there's not much you can do about ghosts nor hauntings. You might burn a candle at night for them and maybe they'd like that. You know about the mal de aire? Your mama ever tell you about that in the city?"

"I've heard one thing or another," she said. "It's supposed to make you sick."

"There're heavy places. Places where the air itself is heavy because an evil weighs it down. Sometimes it's a death, could be it's something else, but the bad air, it'll get into your body and it'll nestle there and weigh you down. That's what's wrong with the Doyles of High Place," the woman said, concluding her tale.

*Like feeding an animal madder plants: it dyes the bones red, it stains everything inside crimson,* she thought.

Marta Duval rose and began opening kitchen drawers. She grabbed a beaded bracelet and brought it back to the table, handing it to Noemí. It had tiny blue and white glass beads, and a larger blue bead with a black center.

"It's against the evil eye."

"Yes, I know," Noemí said, because she had seen such trinkets before.

"You wear it, yes? It might help you, can't hurt. I'll be sure to ask my saints to watch over you too."

Noemí opened her purse and placed the bottle inside. Then, because she didn't want to hurt the old woman's feelings, she tied the bracelet around her wrist as she'd suggested. "Thank you."

Walking back toward the town center, Noemí considered all the things she now knew about the Doyles and how none of it would assist Catalina. Ultimately even a haunting, if you accepted it as real and not the result of a feverish imagination, didn't mean anything. The fear of the previous night had cooled away, and now all there was left was the taste of dissatisfaction.

Noemí pulled her cardigan's sleeve up, scratching her wrist again. It itched something awful. She realized there was a thin, raw, red band of skin around her wrist. As though she'd burned herself. She frowned.

Dr. Camarillo's clinic was nearby, so she decided to stop by and hope he didn't have a patient. She was in luck. The doctor was eating a torta in the reception area. He didn't have his white coat on; instead he wore a simple, single-breasted tweed jacket. When she stopped in front of him, Julio Camarillo quickly set the torta on a table next to him and wiped his mouth and hands on his handkerchief.

"Out for a walk?" he asked.

"Of a sort," she said. "Am I interrupting your breakfast?"

"It's not much of an interruption, seeing as it's not very tasty. I made it myself and did a bad job. How's your cousin? Are they finding a specialist for her?"

"I'm afraid her husband doesn't think she needs any other doctor. Arthur Cummins is enough for them."

"Do you think it might help if I talked to him?"

She shook her head. "It might make it worse, to be honest."

"That's a pity. And how are you?"

"I'm not sure. I have this rash," Noemí said, holding up her wrist for him to see.

Dr. Camarillo inspected her wrist carefully. "Odd," he said. "It almost looks like you came in contact with mala mujer, but that doesn't grow here. It's a sure recipe for dermatitis if you touch the leaves. Do you have allergies?"

"No. My mother says it's almost indecent how healthy I am. She told me when she was a young girl everyone thought it was very fashionable to suffer a bout of appendicitis and girls went on a tapeworm diet."

"She must have been joking about the tapeworm," Dr. Camarillo said. "That's a made-up story."

"It always did sound quite horrifying. Then I'm allergic to something? A plant or shrub?"

"It could be a number of things. We'll wash the hand and put on a soothing ointment. Come in," he said, directing her into his office.

She washed her hands in the little sink in the corner, and Julio applied a zinc paste, bandaged her wrist, and told her she should not scratch the affected area because it would make it worse. He advised her to change the bandage the next day and apply more zinc paste.

"It'll take a few days for the inflammation to go away," he said, walking her back toward the entrance, "but you should be fine after a week. Come see me if it doesn't improve."

"Thanks," she said and placed the tiny jar of zinc paste he'd gifted her inside her purse. "I have another question. Do you know what could cause a person to begin sleepwalking again?"

"Again?"

"I sleepwalked when I was very young, but I haven't done it in ages. But I sleepwalked last night."

"Yes, it's more common for children to sleepwalk. Have you been taking any new medication?"

"No. I told you. I'm scandalously healthy."

"Could be anxiety," the doctor said, and then he smiled a little.

"I had the oddest dream when I was sleepwalking," she said. "It didn't feel like when I was a kid."

It had also been an extremely morbid dream and then, afterward, the chat with Virgil had not helped soothe her. Noemí frowned.

"I see I've failed to be helpful once again."

"Don't say that," she replied quickly.

"Tell you what, if it happens again you come and see me. And you watch that wrist."

"Sure."

Noemí stopped at one of the tiny little stores set around the town square. She bought herself a pack of cigarettes. There were no Lotería cards to be had, but she did find a pack of cheap naipes. Cups, clubs, coins, and swords, to lighten the day. Someone had told her it was possible to read the cards, to tell fortunes, but what Noemí liked to do was play for money with her friends.

The store owner counted her change slowly. He was very old, and his glasses had a crack running down the middle. At the store's entrance sat a yellow dog drinking from a dirty bowl. Noemí scratched its ears on the way out.

The post office was also in the town square, and she sent a short letter to her father informing him of the current situation at High Place: she'd obtained a second opinion from a doctor who said Catalina needed psychiatric care. She did not write that Virgil was extremely reluctant to let anyone see Catalina, because she did not want to worry her father. She also did not mention anything about her nightmares, nor the sleepwalking episode. Those, along with the rash blooming on her wrist, were unpleasant markers of her journey, but they were superfluous details.

Once these tasks were done, she stood in the middle of the town square glancing at the few businesses there. There was no ice cream shop, no souvenir store selling knickknacks, no bandstand for musicians to play their tunes. A couple of storefronts were boarded up, with *For Sale* painted on the outside. The church was still impressive, but the rest was really quite sad. A withered world. Had it looked this way in Ruth's day? Had she

even been allowed to visit the town? Or was she kept locked inside High Place?

Noemí headed back to the exact spot where Francis had
dropped her off. He arrived a couple of minutes later, while she
sat on a wrought-iron bench and was about to light a cigarette.

"You're quick to fetch me," she said.

"My mother doesn't believe in tardiness," he said as he stood
in front of her and took off the felt hat with the navy band he'd
put on that morning.

"Did you tell her where we went?"

"I didn't go back to the house. If I had, my mother or Virgil
might have started asking why I'd left you alone."

"Were you driving around?"

"A bit. I parked under a tree over there and took a nap too.
Did anything happen to you?" he asked, pointing at her bandaged wrist.

"A rash," Noemí said.

She extended her hand so that he might help her up, and he
did. Without her monumental high heels, Noemí's head barely
reached his shoulder. When such a height difference presented
itself, Noemí might stand on her tiptoes. Her cousins teased her
about it, calling her "the ballerina." Not Catalina, because she
was too sweet to tease anyone, but cousin Marilulu did it all the
time. Now, reflexively, she did that, and that little meaningless
motion must have startled him, because he let go with the hand
that had been holding his hat, and a gust of wind blew it away.

"Oh, no," Noemí said.

They chased after the hat, running for a good two blocks before she managed to get hold of it. In her tight skirt and stockings
this was no small feat. The yellow dog she'd seen at the store,
amused by the spectacle, barked at Noemí and circled her. She
pressed the hat against her chest.

"Well, I suppose now I've done my daily calisthenics," she
said, chuckling.

Francis seemed amused too and watched her with an unusual
levity. There was a sad and resigned quality to him that struck

her as odd for someone his age, but the midday sun had washed his melancholy away and gave color to his cheeks. Virgil was good looking, Francis was not. He had an almost nonexistent upper lip, eyebrows that arched a little too much, heavy-lidded eyes. She liked him nevertheless.

He was odd and it was endearing.

She offered him the hat, and Francis turned it in his hands carefully. "What?" he asked, sounding bashful, because she was looking at him.

"Won't you thank me for rescuing your hat, dear sir?"

"Thank you."

"Silly boy," she said, planting a kiss on his cheek.

She was afraid he'd drop the hat and they'd have to chase it again, but he managed to hold on to it and smiled as they walked back to the car.

"You finished the errands you needed to run in town?" he asked.

"Yes. Post office, doctor. I was also talking to someone about High Place, about what happened there. You know, with Ruth," she told him. Her mind kept going back to Ruth. It really should be no concern of hers, this decades-old murder, but there it was, the nagging thought, and she wanted to talk about it. Who better than him?

Francis tapped the hat twice against his leg as they walked. "What about her?"

"She wanted to run away with her lover. Instead, she ended up shooting her whole family. I don't understand why she'd do what she did. Why didn't she run away from High Place? Surely she could have simply left."

"You can't leave High Place."

"But you can. She was an adult woman."

"You're a woman. Can you do anything you want? Even if it upsets your family?"

"Technically I can, even if I wouldn't every single time," Noemí said, though she immediately remembered her father's issues with scandals and the fear of the society pages. Would she ever risk an outright rebellion against her family?

"My mother left High Place, she married. But she came back. There's no escaping it. Ruth knew as much. That's why she did what she did."

"You sound almost proud," she exclaimed.

Francis placed the hat on his head and looked at her gravely. "No. But truth be told Ruth ought to have burnt High Place to the ground."

It was such a shocking pronouncement that she thought she must have heard him wrong, and she would have been able to convince herself this was the case if they had not driven back to the house in a bubble of silence. That piercing silence more than anything affirmed his words. It underlined them and made her turn her face toward the window. In her hand she held her unlit cigarette, watching the trees, light streaming through the branches.

# 13

oemí decided they'd have themselves a mini casino night. She'd always loved casino night. They'd sit in the dining room, and everyone dressed the part, using old clothes picked from their grandparents' trunks, pretending they were high rollers in Monte Carlo or Havana. All the children played, and even when they were way too old for games of pretend, the Taboada cousins would gather around the table and put the record player to good use, tapping their feet to a snappy tune and carefully laying down their cards. It couldn't be quite like that at High Place since they had no records to play, but Noemí decided the spirit of their casino nights could be captured if they tried.

She slipped the deck into one large sweater pocket and the little bottle into the other, and then she peeked her head inside Catalina's room. Her cousin was alone and she was awake. Perfect.

"I have a treat for you," Noemí said.

Catalina was sitting by the window. She turned and looked at Noemí. "Do you, now?"

"You must choose, the left or right pocket, and then you'll have a reward," Noemí said, approaching her.

"What if I choose the wrong one?"

Catalina's hair fell loose past her shoulders. She had never taken to short hairstyles. Noemí was glad. Catalina's hair was sleek and lovely, and she had fond memories of brushing it and braiding it when she was a little girl. Catalina had been so patient with her, allowing Noemí to treat her like a living doll.

"Then you'll never know what was in the other pocket."

"You silly girl," Catalina replied, smiling. "I'll play your game. Right."

"Ta-da."

Noemí placed the pack of cards on Catalina's lap. Her cousin opened the pack and smiled, taking out a card and holding it up.

"We can play a few hands," Noemí said. "I'll even let you win the first one."

"As if! I never met a more competitive child. And it's not like Florence would let us play late into the night."

"We might still play at least a little."

"I have no money to bet, and you don't play if there's no money on the table."

"You're looking for excuses. Are you afraid of that dreadful, nagging Florence?"

Catalina stood up quickly and went to stand by her vanity, tilting its mirror and setting the pack of cards next to a hairbrush while she looked at her reflection. "No. Not at all," she said, grabbing the brush and running it through her hair a couple of times.

"Good. Because I have a second present for you, and I wouldn't give it to a scaredy-cat."

Noemí held the green bottle up. Catalina turned around, wonder in her eyes, and carefully grabbed the bottle. "You did it."

"I told you I would."

"Dearest, thank you, thank you," Catalina said, pulling her into an embrace. "I should know you would never abandon me. We thought monsters and ghosts were found in books, but they're real, you know?"

Her cousin released Noemí and opened a drawer. She took out a couple of handkerchiefs, a pair of white gloves, before finding her prize: a small silver spoon. Then she proceeded to pour herself a teaspoon, her fingers trembling a little, then another and a third. Noemí stopped her at the fourth, taking the bottle from her hands and setting it on the dresser, along with the spoon.

"Jeez, don't have so much. Marta said you might have one tablespoon and that would be enough," Noemí chided her. "I don't want you snoring for ten hours straight before we even get a chance to play a single hand."

"Yes. Yes, of course," Catalina said, smiling weakly.

"Now, shall I shuffle or will you do the honors?"

"Let me see."

Catalina slid a hand across the deck. Then she stopped; she lifted her hand and her fingers remained hovering above the pack of cards, as if she'd been frozen in place. Her hazel eyes were open wide and her mouth was closed tight. She looked so strange. Like a woman who has gone into a trance. Noemí frowned.

"Catalina? Are you unwell? Do you want to sit down?" she asked.

Catalina did not reply. Noemí gently grabbed her by the arm and attempted to maneuver her toward the bed. Catalina wouldn't move. Her fingers curled into a fist, and she continued to stare forward, those large eyes of hers looking wild. Noemí might as well have attempted to shove an elephant. It was impossible to get her to budge a single inch.

"Catalina," Noemí said. "Why don't—"

There was a loud crack—dear God, Noemí thought it might be a joint cracking—and Catalina began to shiver. She shivered from the top of her head to the soles of her feet, one sweeping, rippling motion. Then the shiver became more frenzied, and she was convulsing, she was pressing her hands against her stomach and shaking her head, and the most vicious scream escaped her lungs.

Noemí attempted to hold her, to drag her toward the bed, but Catalina was strong. It was amazing how strong she was considering how frail she looked, yet she managed to resist Noemí, and they both ended up on the floor, Catalina's mouth opening and closing spasmodically, her arms rising and falling, the legs shaking wildly. A trail of saliva slid down the corner of her mouth.

"Help!" Noemí yelled. "Help!"

Noemí had gone to school with a girl who had epilepsy and although the girl never had a fit on school grounds, she remembered how she once told her she carried a little stick in her purse so that she might place it in her mouth if she had a seizure.

With Catalina's attack growing in intensity—which seemed impossible yet was undeniably happening—she snatched the silver spoon from the dresser and placed it in Catalina's mouth to keep her from biting her own tongue. She knocked down the card deck, which had also been resting on the dresser. The cards spilled and fanned out on the floor. The knave of coins stared at Noemí accusingly.

Noemí ran to the hallway and began yelling, "Help me!"

Had no one heard the commotion? She rushed forward, banging on doors, and yelling as loud as she could. Suddenly Francis appeared and behind him came Florence.

"Catalina is having a seizure," she told them.

They all ran back to the room. Catalina was still on the floor; the tremors had not stopped. Francis sprang forward and sat her up, placing his arms around her, attempting to subdue her. Noemí was going to help him, but Florence stood in her way.

"Get out," she ordered.

"I can help."

"Out, out now," she ordered, shoving Noemí back and slamming the door in her face.

Noemí knocked furiously but no one opened. She could hear murmurs and once in a while a loud word or two. She began pacing the hallway.

When Francis came out he quickly closed the door behind him. Noemí hurried to his side.

"What's happening? How is she?"

"She's in bed. I'm going to fetch Dr. Cummins," Francis said.

They walked briskly toward the stairs, his long stride meaning she had to take two to keep up with him.

"I'll go with you."

"No," Francis said.

"I want to do something."

He stopped and shook his head before clutching her hands together. He spoke softly. "You come with me, it'll be worse. Go to the sitting room, and when I return, I'll fetch you. I won't be long."

"Promise?"

"Yes."

He dashed down the stairs. She rushed down the staircase too and pressed her hands against her face when she reached the bottom, tears prickling her eyes. By the time she walked into the sitting room, the tears were falling hard, and she sat on the carpet, clutching her hands together. The minutes ticked by. She wiped her nose with her sweater's sleeve, wiped her tears with the palms of her hand. She stood up and waited.

He lied. It was a long time. What was worse, when Francis returned it was in the company of Dr. Cummins and Florence. At least there had been enough time for Noemí to compose herself.

"How is she?" Noemí asked, swiftly walking up to the doctor.

"She's asleep now. The crisis has passed."

"Thank God," Noemí said, and she sank onto one of the settees. "I don't understand what happened."

"What happened was *this*," Florence said sharply, holding up the bottle Noemí had fetched from Marta Duval. "Where did you get it?"

"It's a sleeping tonic," Noemí said.

"Your sleeping tonic made her sick."

"No." Noemí shook her head. "No, she said she needed it."

"Are you a medical professional?" Dr. Cummins asked her. He was distinctly displeased. Noemí felt her mouth go dry.

"No, but—"

"So you have no idea what was inside this bottle?"

"I told you, Catalina said she needed medicine to help her

sleep. She asked me for it. She's taken it before, it couldn't have made her ill."

"It did," the doctor told her.

"An opium tincture. That's what you shoved down your cousin's throat," Florence added, pointing an accusing finger at Noemí.

"I did no such thing!"

"It was very ill-advised, very ill-advised, indeed," Dr. Cummins muttered. "Why I couldn't begin to understand what you were thinking, procuring a filthy potion like that. And then, attempting to put a spoon in your cousin's mouth. I suppose you heard that silly tale of people swallowing their tongues? Nonsense. All nonsense."

"I—"

"Where did you get the tincture?" Florence asked.

*Tell no one*, Catalina had said, and so Noemí did not reply even if the mention of Marta Duval might have shifted the burden of her guilt. She gripped the back of the settee with one hand, digging her nails into the fabric.

"You could have killed her," the woman said.

"I wouldn't!"

Noemí felt like crying again but could not allow herself this release, not in their presence. Francis had moved to stand behind the settee, and she felt his fingers upon her hand, almost ghostly. It was a comforting gesture, and it gave her the courage to clamp her mouth shut.

"Who did you procure the potion from?" the doctor asked.

Noemí stared at them and kept on gripping the settee.

"I should slap you," Florence said. "I should slap that disrespectful look off your face."

Florence stepped forward. Noemí felt that perhaps she really did mean to slap her. She pushed Francis's hand aside, ready to stand up.

"If you could please go check on my father I would be very grateful, Dr. Cummins. All the noise tonight has him a little anxious," Virgil said.

He had strolled rather casually into the room, and his voice was cool as he ventured toward the sideboard and inspected a decanter, as if he were alone and pouring himself a drink like any other evening.

"Yes. Why yes, of course," the doctor said.

"It's best if you two go with him. I wish to speak to Noemí alone."

"I am not—" Florence began.

"I wish to be alone with her," Virgil replied acridly. The smooth silk of his voice was now sandpaper.

They left, the doctor mumbling a "yes, at once," Florence walking in a somber silence. Francis was the last to step out, slowly closing the doors of the sitting room before throwing her one nervous glance.

Virgil filled his glass, swirling the liquid in it, staring at its contents, before approaching her and taking a place on the same settee she occupied. His leg brushed against hers when he sat down.

"Catalina once told me you were a very strong-willed creature, but I didn't quite understand how strong-willed until now," he said, setting the drink down on an oblong side table. "Your cousin is a bit of a weakling, isn't she? But you have a certain mettle in your bones."

He spoke so blithely it made her gasp. He talked as if this were a game. As if she were not sick with worry. "Have a little respect," she said.

"I think it's another person who should be showing respect. This is my home."

"I'm sorry."

"You're not sorry at all."

She could not read the expression in his eyes. Perhaps it was contempt. "I *am* sorry! But I was trying to help Catalina."

"You have a funny way of showing it. How dare you constantly upset my wife?"

"What do you mean I constantly upset her? She is glad to have me around, she told me so."

"You bring strangers to look at her and then you bring her poison."

"For God's sake," she said and stood up.

He immediately grabbed her by the wrist and yanked her down. It was her bandaged wrist, and it hurt when he touched her; the skin burned for a second and she winced. He tugged at her sleeve, revealing the bandage, and smirked.

"Let go."

"Dr. Camarillo's work, perhaps? Just like the tincture? Was it him?"

"Don't touch me," she ordered.

But he did not release her; instead he leaned forward. He clasped her arm tight. She thought Howard looked like an insect and Florence was an insectivorous plant. But Virgil Doyle, he was a carnivore, high up the food chain.

"Florence is right. You deserve to be slapped and taught a few lessons," he muttered.

"If anyone is slapped in this room, I assure you, it won't be me."

He threw his head back and laughed a loud, savage laugh, and he reached blindly for his drink. A few dark drops of liquor spilled on the side table as he lifted the glass. The sound of his voice practically made her jump. At least he had released her.

"You're mad," she said, rubbing her wrist.

"Mad with worry, yes," he replied, downing the wine. Rather than placing the glass on the table again, he carelessly tossed it on the floor. It did not shatter, but rolled across the carpet. But what if it had shattered? It was his glass. His to break if he wanted. Like everything else in this house.

"Do you think you are the only person who cares what happens to Catalina?" he asked, his eyes fixed on the glass. "I imagine you do. When Catalina wrote to your family, did you think, 'ah, at last we can pry her away from that troublesome man'? And right now you must think 'I knew he was bad.' Your father certainly didn't like me for a groom.

"When the mine was open, he would have been glad to see

Catalina married to me. Back then I would have been worthy. He wouldn't have thought me inconsequential. It must still irk him, and you, to know Catalina picked me. Well, I'm no two-bit fortune hunter, I'm a Doyle. It would be good of you to remember that."

"I don't know why you bring all this up."

"Because you believe I am so inadequate that you had to go and medicate Catalina. You thought the care I give her is so atrocious that you must sneak behind my back and pour garbage into her mouth. Did you think we wouldn't notice? We know everything that goes on in this house."

"She asked for this medicine. I told your aunt and the doctor already, I didn't realize this would happen."

"No, you don't know very much, and yet you act as if you know everything, don't you? You're a spoiled brat and you've hurt my wife," he said with a brutal finality.

He stood up and picked up the glass, setting it upon the fireplace mantel. She felt twin flames inside her heart, anger and shame. She hated the way he was talking to her, hated this entire conversation. And yet had she not done a foolish thing? Hadn't she earned a reprimand? She did not know how to reply and felt tears pooling in her eyes again as she recalled poor Catalina's face.

He must have noticed her turmoil or else he was simply done berating her, because his voice wavered a little. "You almost made me a widower tonight, Noemí. You will forgive me if I don't feel very gracious at this time. I should head to bed. It's been a long day."

He did look tired, frankly exhausted. His blue eyes were very bright, with the brightness of a sudden fever. It made her feel even worse about the whole mess.

"I must ask you to leave Catalina's medical care to Dr. Cummins and never bring any other tonics or remedies into this house. Are you listening to me?"

"I am," she replied.

"Will you follow this simple directive?"

She clenched her hands. "I will," she said, and she felt very much like a child.

He took a step closer to her, carefully looking at her, as though trying to discern a lie, but there was none. She spoke in earnest, and yet he brushed close to her, like a scientist who must analyze and jot down every detail of an organism, taking in her face, her pursed lips.

"Thank you. There are many things you cannot understand, Noemí. But let me make it clear that Catalina's well-being is of the utmost importance to us. You've harmed her and in harming her you've harmed me."

Noemí turned her head away. She thought he'd leave. Instead, he lingered at her side. Then, a small eternity later, he stepped away from her and out of the room.

# 14

*n a sense all dreams foretell events, but some more clearly than others.*

Noemí circled the word *dreams* with her pencil. She enjoyed writing in the margins of her books; she loved reading these anthropological texts, sinking into the lush paragraphs and the forest of footnotes. But not now. Now she couldn't concentrate. She rested her chin on the back of her hand and placed the pencil in her mouth.

She had spent hours in waiting, trying to find things to do, books to read, perfecting tricks to distract herself. She checked her watch and sighed. It was close to five o'clock.

She had attempted to speak to Catalina early in the morning, but Florence had told Noemí that her cousin was resting. Around noon Noemí had tried again. She had been dismissed a second time, and Florence had made it clear there would be no visits with the patient until nighttime.

Noemí must not push and pry and attempt to wedge her way into that room, as much as she wanted to. She simply couldn't.

They'd toss her out if she did, and besides, Virgil was correct. She'd done wrong and felt ashamed.

How she wished there were a radio around the house. She needed music, conversation. She thought of the parties she attended with her friends, leaning against a piano with a cocktail in her hand. Also her classes at the university and the lively discussions at the cafés downtown. What she now had was a silent house and a heart riddled with anxiety.

*. . . and dreams about ghosts, not recorded in this book, inform people about happenings among the dead.*

She took the pencil out of her mouth and put the book aside. Reading about the Azande did her no good. It offered no distraction. She kept remembering her cousin's face, her contorted limbs, the hideous episode of the previous day.

Noemí grabbed a sweater—the one Francis had given her—and stepped outside. She thought to smoke a cigarette, but once she stood in the shadow of the house she decided she needed a bit more distance from it. It lingered too close; it was hostile and cold and she did not wish to parade before its windows, which felt, to her, like lidless, eager eyes. She followed the path that snaked behind the house and led up to the cemetery.

Two, three, four steps, it seemed it didn't take her long until she stood before the iron gates and walked inside. She'd been utterly lost in the mist before, but she did not bother to consider what she'd do if she should lose her way again.

In fact, a part of her very dearly wished to be lost.

Catalina. She'd hurt Catalina, and even now she did not know how her cousin was faring. Florence was tight-lipped; she'd seen nothing of Virgil. Not that she wished to see him very much.

He'd been beastly.

*You almost made me a widower tonight, Noemí.*

She hadn't meant it. But, intent or not, what did it matter? What mattered were the facts. That's what her father would tell her, and now Noemí felt doubly ashamed. She'd been sent to fix a problem, not to make an even bigger mess. Was Catalina angry with her? What might Noemí say when they finally saw each other? Sorry, dear cousin, I almost poisoned you, but you're looking better.

Noemí walked among tombstones and moss and wildflowers, her chin lowered, tucked close against the folds of the sweater. She saw the mausoleum and in front of it the stone statue of Agnes. Noemí peered up at the statue's face and her hands, which were weathered with speckles of black fungus.

She had wondered if there was a plaque or marker with the name of the deceased on it, and she saw that there was. Noemí had overlooked it during her previous visit, although she could hardly be blamed for missing it. The plaque was hidden by an overgrown clump of weeds. She plucked the weeds away and brushed the dirt off the bronze plaque.

*Agnes Doyle. Mother. 1885.* That was all Howard Doyle had chosen to leave behind to commemorate the passing of his first wife. He had said he had not known Agnes well, that she'd died within a year of their marriage, yet it seemed odd to have a statue carved of her and then not even compose a proper line or two about her passing.

It was the nature of the one word etched beneath the woman's name that bothered her too. Mother. But as far as Noemí knew, Howard Doyle's children were born of his second marriage. Why choose "mother" as the epithet, then? Perhaps she was making too much of this. Inside the mausoleum, where the woman's body rested, there might be a proper plaque and a proper message about the deceased. Yet it was unsettling in a way she could not define, like noticing a crooked seam or a tiny stain on a pristine tablecloth.

She sat there, at the statue's feet, and tugged at a blade of grass wondering if someone ever bothered setting flowers inside the mausoleum or at any of the graves. Could the families of everyone buried in the cemetery be gone from the area? But then, most of the English folk must have come alone, and therefore there had been no kin to bother with such things. There were also unmarked graves for the local workers and with no gravestone to their name, there could be no crowns of flowers for them.

*If Catalina dies*, she thought, *she'll be buried here, and her tomb will be bare.*

What a horrid thought. But she was horrid, wasn't she? Simply horrid. Noemí dropped the blade of grass and took a deep breath. The silence in the cemetery was absolute. No birds sang in the trees, no insects flapped their wings. Everything was muffled. It was like sitting at the bottom of a deep well, shielded by the earth and stone, from the world.

The merciless silence was broken by the sound of boots upon grass and the crunching of a twig. She turned her head and there was Francis, hands deep in his thick corduroy jacket's pockets. He looked, as he often did, quite fragile, the faint sketch of a man. Only in a place such as this, in a cemetery with drooping willows and mist licking at the stones, could he acquire any substance. In the city, she thought, he'd be shattered by the banging of the Klaxon and the rumbling of motors. Fine china, tossed against a wall. But she liked the look of him in that old jacket, frail or not, his shoulders hunched a little.

"I thought you'd be here."

"Hunting for mushrooms again?" Noemí asked, setting her hands on her lap and steadying her voice so that it was not strained. She'd nearly wept in front of them last night. She did not wish to do it now.

"I saw you leaving the house," he confessed.

"Did you need anything?"

"My old sweater; you are wearing it," he said.

It wasn't quite the answer she was expecting. She frowned. "You want it back?"

"Not at all."

She hiked up the too-long sleeves and shrugged. Any other day she would have taken this as a cue to engage in charming banter. She would have teased him and enjoyed watching him grow flustered. Now she picked at blades of grass.

He sat down next to her. "It really isn't your fault."

"You'd be the only person who thinks that. Your mother won't even tell me if Catalina is awake, and Virgil wants to throttle me. I wouldn't be surprised if your uncle Howard wished to do the same."

"Catalina woke up for a bit, but then went back to sleep. She had a little broth. She'll be fine."

"Yes, I'm sure," Noemí muttered.

"When I say it's not your fault I truly mean it," he assured her, his hand falling upon her shoulder. "Please, look at me. It isn't. It's not the first time. This happened before."

"What do you mean?"

They stared at each other. It was his turn to pick a blade of grass and spin it between his fingers.

"Well, come on. What do you mean?" she repeated, snatching the piece of grass away.

"She'd taken that tincture . . . she'd had a reaction to it before."

"Are you telling me she's made herself ill, the same way? Or else that she's tried to kill herself? We are Catholic. It's a sin. She wouldn't, never ever."

"I don't think she wants to die. I mention it because you seem to think you did this to her, and you didn't. It's not your presence that has made her ill; it's not you at all. She's miserable here. You should take her away immediately."

"Virgil wouldn't let me do that before and he certainly won't let me do it now," Noemí said. "She's under lock and key, at any rate, isn't she? As if I could even see her for a minute right now. Your mother is furious at me—"

"Then you should leave," he said brusquely.

"I can't leave!"

First she considered the immense disappointment she'd cause her father. He'd sent her as an ambassador, to squelch scandal and provide answers, and she would return home empty-handed. Their deal would be void—no master's degree for her, ever—and worse than that, she hated the taste of failure.

Besides, she didn't dare to go anywhere with Catalina in this state. What if she should need her? How could she hurt Catalina and then run off? How could she leave her all alone, racked in pain?

"She's my family," Noemí said. "You must stand by your family."

"Even if you can't possibly help her?"

"You don't know that."

"This is no place for you," he assured her.

"Have they asked you to chase me away?" she asked, standing up quickly, irritated by his sudden vehemence. "Are you trying to get rid of me? Do you dislike me so much?"

"I like you very much and you know it," he said, his hands sliding into his jacket's pockets again as he looked down.

"Then you'll help me and take me into town now, won't you?"

"Why do you need to go into town?"

"I want to find out what was in the tincture Catalina drank."

"It won't do you any good."

"Even if it doesn't, I want to go. Will you take me?"

"Not today."

"Tomorrow, then."

"The day after tomorrow, perhaps. Perhaps not."

"Why not make it in a month," she replied angrily. "I can walk into town without you if you have no desire to help me."

She meant to stomp away and succeeded only in stumbling. Francis offered her his arm to steady herself, and he let out a sigh when her fingers caught his sleeve.

"I have every desire to help you. I'm tired. We all are. Uncle Howard has been keeping us awake at nights," he said, shaking his head.

His cheeks seemed more hollowed out and the dark circles under his eyes were almost purplish. Again she felt selfish and awful. She thought of no one but herself and did not pause to imagine that other people at High Place had problems of their own. For example, who knew if at nights Francis was called to tend upon his sickly uncle. She could picture Florence, directing her son to hold up an oil lamp as she pressed cold compresses

---

against the old man's face. Or perhaps other tasks were handed to the young men. Virgil and Francis, undressing the frail, bleached body of Howard Doyle, applying ointments and medications in a closed room reeking of impending death.

Noemí flexed her fingers, raising them to her mouth, and recalling, vaguely, that horrid nightmare in which the pale man had extended his arms toward her.

"Virgil said he has an old wound. But what is the injury?"

"Ulcers that won't heal. But it won't be the end of him. It'll never be the end of him." Francis let out a low, sad chuckle, his eyes on the stone statue of Agnes. "I'll take you to town early tomorrow, before the others wake up. Before breakfast, like the last time. And if you should want to take your suitcase—"

"You'll have to think of a more creative way to get me to leave," she replied.

They began to drift, quietly, back toward the iron gates of the cemetery. She brushed the cool tops of the headstones as they walked. At one point they passed a dead gray oak tree that lay upon the ground, clumps of honey-colored mushrooms growing upon the rotten bark. Francis bent down, running a finger across the smooth caps, just as she'd touched the headstones.

"What has made Catalina so miserable?" she asked. "She was happy when she married. Stupidly happy, my father would have said. Is Virgil cruel to her? Last night, when I spoke to him, he was hard, he had no pity."

"It's the house," Francis murmured. By now the black gates with their snakes were in sight. The ouroboros, casting shadows upon the ground. "It wasn't made for love, the house."

"Any place is made for love," she protested.

"Not this place and not us. You look back two, three generations, as far as you can. You won't find love. We are incapable of such a thing."

His fingers curled around the intricate iron bars, and he stood there, for a second, looking at the ground, before he opened the gate for her.

That night she had another curious dream. She could not even classify it as a nightmare because she felt calm. Numb, even.

The house had metamorphosed in the dream, but it was not a thing of meat and sinew on this occasion. She walked upon a carpet of moss, the flowers and vines crept up the walls, and long, thin stacks of mushrooms glowed a pale yellow, lightening up the ceiling and the floor. It was as if the forest had tiptoed into the house in the middle of the night and left a part of itself inside. As Noemí descended the staircase, her hands brushed upon a banister covered in flowers.

She walked down a hallway that was thick with clumps of mushrooms as high as her thighs and peered at paintings that were hidden under layers of leaves.

In the dream she knew where she ought to go. There were no iron gates to greet her at the cemetery, but why would there be any? This was the time before the cemetery, when they were building a rose garden upon the mountain slope.

A garden, though no flowers grew here yet. No flowers had taken. It was peaceful here, at the edge of the pine forest, with the mist shrouding rocks and shrubs.

Noemí heard voices, very loud, and then a piercing scream, but everything was so still, so calm, that it calmed her too. Even when the screams changed in pitch and seemed to grow in intensity she did not fear.

She reached a clearing and beheld a woman who lay on the ground. Her belly was huge and distended, and she appeared to be in the midst of her labor, which would explain the screams. Attending her were several women who were holding her hand, brushing the limp hair from her face, muttering to her. Men held candles in their hands, others carried lanterns.

Noemí noticed a little girl sitting on a chair, her blond hair tied in a pigtail. She carried a white cloth in her arms, meant to swaddle an infant. A man sat behind the child, with his ringed hand on her shoulder. A ring of amber.

The scene was a little ridiculous. A woman, panting and giving birth in the dirt while the man and the child sat in velvet-upholstered chairs, as if they were observing a theater performance.

The man tapped his finger on the child's shoulder. One, two, three times.

How long had they sat there, in the dark? How long since the labor had begun? But it wouldn't be long now. The time had come.

The pregnant woman clutched someone's hand and let out a long, low moan, and there was a wet sound, the slap of flesh against the damp earth.

The man stood up and approached the woman, and when he moved, the people surrounding her stepped aside, as if a sea were parting.

Slowly he bent down and carefully held the child the woman had birthed.

"Death, overcome," the man said.

But when he raised his arms, Noemí saw he held no child. The woman had given birth to a gray lump of flesh, almost egg-shaped, covered in a thick membrane and slick with blood.

It was a tumor. It did not live. Yet it pulsated gently. The lump quivered, and as it did the membrane ruptured and slid aside. It burst, sending a golden cloud of dust into the air, and the man breathed in the dust. The woman's attendants, the people with their candles and lanterns, and all the onlookers moved closer, holding their hands up, as if to touch the golden dust, which slowly, ever so slowly, fell upon the ground.

Everyone had forgotten the woman, focused now, singularly, on the lump that the man was hoisting above his head.

Only the little girl paid the shivering, exhausted figure on the ground any attention. The child approached her, pressed the cloth she had been holding against the woman's face, as if veiling a bride, and held it tight. The woman convulsed, unable to breathe; she tried to scratch the child, but the woman was exhausted and the child, her cheeks red, held on tight. As the woman quivered and suffocated, the man repeated the same words.

"Death, overcome," he said, and he raised his eyes, staring at Noemí.

It was then, when he looked at her, that she remembered to be afraid, that she remembered revulsion and horror, and turned her face away. Her mouth had the coppery taste of blood, and in her ears there was a faint buzzing sound.

When Noemí woke up she was standing at the foot of the stairs, moonlight streaming through the colored glass windows, tinting her pale nightgown yellow and red. A clock struck the hour and floorboards creaked, and she rested a hand on the banister, listening intently.

# 15

oemí knocked and waited, and waited some more, but no one came to the door. She stood outside Marta's house, nervously pulling at her purse's strap before finally conceding defeat and walking back toward Francis, who was looking at her curiously. They'd parked the car near the town square and walked over together, even though she'd told him he could wait for her just like last time. But he said he could use the walk. She wondered if he was trying to keep an eye on her.

"No one seems to be home," Noemí said.

"Do you want to wait?"

"No. I need to stop by the health clinic."

He nodded, and they slowly headed back toward what constituted the downtown section of El Triunfo, where there was a real road instead of muddy paths. Noemí was afraid the doctor wouldn't be in yet either, but as they reached the door of the clinic, Julio Camarillo rounded the corner.

"Dr. Camarillo," she said.

"Good morning," he replied. He was carrying a paper bag

under one arm and his medical bag in the other. "You're up early. Will you hold this for a moment?"

Francis stretched out his hands and grabbed the medical bag. Dr. Camarillo took out a set of keys and unlocked the door, holding it open for them. Then he walked toward the counter, placed the paper bag behind it, and smiled at them.

"I don't think I've met you officially," Julio said, "but I've seen you at the post office before, with Dr. Cummins. You're Francis, aren't you?"

The blond man nodded. "I'm Francis," he said simply.

"Yes, when I took over Dr. Corona's practice in the winter he actually mentioned you and your father. I think they might have played cards together. A good chap, Dr. Corona. But, anyway, is that hand bothering you, Noemí? Is that why you're here?"

"Could we talk? Do you have time?"

"Sure. Come in," the doctor said.

Noemí followed him into his office. She turned her head to see if Francis planned to accompany her, but he was sitting on one of the chairs in the lobby, his hands in his pockets, his gaze on the floor. If he wanted to keep an eye on her, he wasn't doing that good a job; he could easily have eavesdropped on her entire conversation. She was relieved to think he wasn't interested in that. Noemí closed the door and sat across from Dr. Camarillo, who settled behind his desk.

"Now, what is the matter?"

"Catalina had a seizure," Noemí said.

"A seizure? Is she epileptic?"

"No. I purchased a tonic, a medicine from that woman, Marta Duval. Catalina asked me for it, she said it would help her sleep. But when she drank it she had a seizure. I went to see Marta this morning, but she wasn't there. I wanted to ask if you've heard of something like that happening around town before, if her medications have made anyone ill like that."

"Marta goes to Pachuca to see her daughter, or she goes on herb collection trips, which is probably why you didn't find her. But as to this happening before, I haven't heard of such a thing.

Dr. Corona would have mentioned it, I'm sure. Did Arthur Cummins examine your cousin?"

"He said an opium tincture caused the seizure."

Dr. Camarillo grabbed a pen and twirled it between his fingers. "You know, opium was used to *treat* epilepsy not so long ago. There's always the possibility of allergic reactions with any medicine, but Marta is very careful with this sort of stuff."

"Dr. Cummins called her a quack."

He shook his head and set the pen back on the desk. "She's no quack. Many people go to Marta for remedies, and she helps them well enough. If I thought she was endangering the health of the townsfolk I wouldn't allow it."

"But what if Catalina took too much of the tincture?"

"An overdose? Yes, of course an overdose would be quite awful. She might lose consciousness, she might vomit, but the thing is, Marta wouldn't be able to procure an opium tincture."

"What do you mean?"

Dr. Camarillo laced his hands together, his elbows resting on the desk. "It's not the kind of medical care she provides. An opium tincture is a remedy you could find at a drugstore. Marta makes remedies using local herbs and plants. There are no poppies here with which to make a tincture."

"Then you're saying it must have been something else that caused her to be sick?"

"I can't say with certainty."

She frowned, unable to make heads or tails of this information. She'd gone looking for an easy answer, but there was none. Nothing seemed to be easy here.

"I'm sorry I can't be of more help. Maybe I can look at your rash before you leave? Have you changed the bandage?" Dr. Camarillo asked.

"I haven't. It has completely slipped my mind."

She hadn't even opened the little jar with the zinc paste. Julio took off the bandage, and Noemí expected to see the same raw, red skin. Perhaps it would look even worse than the last time.

Instead, her wrist was completely healed. There was not a single bump blemishing her skin. It seemed to startle the doctor.

"Well, this is quite the surprise. Why, it's vanished," Dr. Camarillo said. "I don't think I've seen such a thing before. Usually it takes seven or ten days, sometimes weeks, for the skin to clear. It's barely been two days."

"I must be lucky," she ventured.

"Extremely," he said. "What a thing. Do you need anything else? If not, I can tell Marta you were looking for her."

She thought about her odd dream and the second sleepwalking episode. Yet she didn't feel the doctor would be able to assist her with that either. It was as he'd said: he wasn't very useful at all. She was beginning to think Virgil had been right when he told her Camarillo was too young and inexperienced. Or maybe she was being grumpy. She was most definitely tired. The anxiety of the previous day hit her suddenly.

"That would be an utter kindness," she said.

Noemí had expected to return to her room without anyone noticing, but of course that was too much to ask. Not even an hour after Francis and Noemí had parked the car, Florence came looking for her. She had Noemí's lunch tray with her, which she deposited on the table. She didn't say anything unpleasant, but her face was fiercely sour. It was the face of a warden ready to squelch a riot.

"Virgil would like to speak with you," she said. "I assume you can eat and be presentable in an hour?"

"Of course," Noemí replied.

"Good. I'll come to fetch you."

She did indeed return in exactly one hour and proceeded to guide Noemí to Virgil's room. When they stopped in front of his door, Florence knocked once, her knuckles so soft upon the wooden surface that Noemí thought he'd never hear them, but he spoke, loud and clear.

"Enter."

Florence turned the doorknob and held the door open for Noemí. Once the young woman stepped inside, Florence carefully closed the door again.

The first thing she noticed upon walking into Virgil's room was an imposing painting of Howard Doyle, hands clasped together, an amber ring on his finger, staring down at her across the room. Virgil's bed was half hidden behind a three-fold painted screen depicting branches of lilacs and roses. The divider created a sitting area, with a faded rug and a pair of shabby leather chairs.

"You've gone to town again this morning," Virgil said. His voice came from behind the divider. "Florence dislikes it when you do that. Just off, without a word."

She approached the painted screen. She noticed that among the flowers and the ferns there lay a snake. It was cleverly hidden, the eye peeking from behind a clump of roses. It lay in wait, like the snake in the garden of Eden.

"I thought driving alone into town was the issue," Noemí replied.

"The roads are bad, and the rains will grow stronger any day now. Torrential rains. The soil turns into a sea of mud. The rain flooded the mines the year I was born. We lost everything."

"It does rain, I've noticed. And the road is not good. But the roads are not impassable."

"They will be. There's been a lull in the rain, but it will fall ferociously very soon. Fetch me the robe on the chair, please."

She grabbed the heavy crimson robe that had been left on one of the chairs and walked back toward the wooden screen. She was startled to see Virgil hadn't bothered putting on a shirt and stood there half naked and nonchalant. This was much too casual; it was frankly immodest, and she blushed in shame.

"How, then, will Dr. Cummins make his way here? He's supposed to visit every week," she said, averting her gaze quickly as she held out the robe. She tried to maintain a cool tone of voice despite the warmth on her cheeks. If he wanted to mortify her, he must try harder.

"He has a truck. Do you honestly think the cars we have are fit for driving constantly up and down the mountain?"

"I assumed Francis would let me know if he felt it was hazardous."

"Francis," Virgil said. She glanced at him when he said the name. He tied the robe's belt. "It seems you spend most of your time with him rather than with Catalina."

Was he reproaching her? No, she thought it was slightly different. He was assessing her, the same way a jeweler might gaze at a diamond, trying to measure its clarity or an entomologist would look at a butterfly's wings under the microscope.

"I have spent a reasonable amount of time with him."

Virgil smiled without any pleasure. "You are so careful with your words. So poised in front of me. I picture you, in your city of cocktail parties and careful words. Do you ever lower your mask there?"

He gestured for her to sit down in one of the leather chairs. She pointedly ignored the gesture. "It's funny, here I thought you could teach me a thing or two about masquerades," she replied.

"What do you mean?"

"It's not the first time Catalina was ill like this. She drank the same tincture and had the same bad reaction."

She had thought to say nothing of the matter, but she wanted to gauge his reaction. He'd assessed her. Now it was her turn.

"You have indeed been spending time with Francis," Virgil said, distaste clear on his face. "Yes, I forgot to mention that previous episode."

"How convenient."

"What? The doctor explained to you that she has depressive tendencies, and you thought it was all lies. If I'd told you she was suicidal—"

"She's not suicidal," Noemí protested.

"Well, of course, since you seem to know everything," Virgil muttered. He looked a little bored and waved a hand, as if shooing an invisible insect. Shooing her. The gesture made her furious.

"You took Catalina from the city and brought her here, and if she *is* suicidal then it's *your* fault," she replied.

She wished to be cruel. She wanted to repay him with the same coin he'd used with her before, but once she had spit her venom she regretted the words, because for once he seemed upset. He looked as if she'd physically stricken him, a pure moment of pain or perhaps shame.

"Virgil," she began, but he shook his head, silencing her.

"No, you're correct. It's my fault. Catalina fell in love with me for the wrong reasons." Virgil sat very straight in his seat, his eyes fixed on her, his hands resting on the arms of the chair. "Sit, please."

She was not ready to concede. She did not sit. Instead she stood behind her chair, leaning forward on its back. She had a vague thought that it would also be easier to run out of the room if she was standing. She wasn't sure why she thought this. It was a disquieting thought, that she must be ready to spring up like a gazelle and escape. It was, she concluded, that she did not like to be speaking to him alone in his room.

His terrain. His burrow.

She suspected Catalina had never set foot in this room. Or if she had, it had been a brief invitation. No trace of her remained. The furniture, the great large painting bequeathed by his father, the wooden screen, the ancient wallpaper streaked with faint traces of mold, these all belonged to Virgil Doyle. His taste, his things. Even his features seemed to complement the room. The blond hair was striking against the dark leather, his face seemed made of alabaster when framed with folds of red velvet.

"Your cousin has a wild imagination," Virgil said. "I think she saw in me a tragic, romantic figure. A boy who lost his mother at a young age in a senseless tragedy, whose family's fortune evaporated in the years of the Revolution, who grew up with a sick father in a crumbling mansion in the mountains."

Yes. It must have pleased her. At first. He had a vehemence that Catalina would have found appealing and, in his home, with the mist outside and the glint of silver candelabra inside, he would have shined very brightly. How long, Noemí wondered, until the novelty wore off?

He, perhaps sensing her question, smirked. "No doubt she pictured the house as a delightful, rustic refuge which, with a little effort, could be made cheerier. Of course, it is not as if my father would allow even a single curtain to be changed. We exist at his pleasure."

He turned his head to gaze at the painting bearing Howard Doyle's likeness, a finger tapping gently against the chair's armrest.

"And would you want to change a single curtain?"

"I'd change a number of things. My father hasn't left this house in decades. To him this is the ideal vision of the world and nothing more. I've seen the future and understand our limitations."

"If that is the case, if change is possible—"

"Change of a certain type," Virgil agreed. "But not a change so grand that I'd become something I am not. You can't change the essence of a thing. That is the problem. The point, I suppose, is that Catalina wanted someone else. She didn't want me, flesh and blood and flawed. She was immediately unhappy, and yes, it *is* my fault. I could not live up to her expectations. What she saw in me, it was never there."

*Immediately.* Why, then, had Catalina not returned home? But even as she asked herself the question she knew the answer. The family. Everyone would have been appalled, and the society pages would have been filled with the most poisonous ink. Exactly as her father now feared.

"What did you see in her?"

Noemí's father had been sure it was money. She didn't think Virgil would admit it, but she felt confident that she might be able to discern the truth, to read between the lines. To approach the answer, even if it remained veiled.

"My father is ill. He is, in fact, dying. Before passing away, he wanted to see me married. He wanted to know I would have a wife and children; that the family line would not die out. It was not the first time he asked this of me, and it was not the first time I complied. I was married once before."

"I did not know that," Noemí said. It quite surprised her. "What happened?"

"She was everything my father thought an ideal wife should be, except that he forgot to consult me on the matter," Virgil said with a chuckle. "She was, in fact, Arthur's daughter. My father had gotten it in his head since we were children that we would marry. 'One day, when you're married,' they'd tell us. Such repetition didn't help. It had the opposite effect. When I turned twenty-three we were wed. She disliked me. I found her dull.

"Nevertheless, I suppose we might have managed to build something of value between us if it hadn't been for the miscarriages. She had four of them, and they wore her down. She abandoned me."

"She divorced you?"

He nodded. "Yes, and eventually, implicitly, I realized my father wanted me to remarry. I took a few trips to Guadalajara and then to Mexico City. I met women who were interesting and pretty, who would have no doubt pleased my father. But Catalina was the one who really caught my attention. She was sweet. It's not a quality that is in great abundance at High Place. I liked that. I liked her softness, her romantic notions. She wanted a fairy tale, and I wanted to give her that.

"Then, of course, it all went wrong. Not merely her illness, but her loneliness, her bouts of sadness. I thought she understood what it would mean to live with me and I understood what it would be like living with her. I was wrong. And here we are."

A fairy tale, yes. Snow White with the magical kiss and the beauty who transforms the beast. Catalina had read all those stories for the younger girls, and she had intoned each line with great dramatic conviction. It had been a performance. Here was the result of Catalina's daydreams. Here was her fairy tale. It amounted to a stilted marriage that, coupled with her sickness and her mental tribulations, must place an exhausting burden on her shoulders.

"If it's the house she dislikes, you could take her somewhere else."

"My father wants us at High Place."

"You must make your own life one day, no?"

He smiled. "My own life. I don't know if you've noticed, but none of us can have our own lives. My father needs me here, and now my wife is sick, and it is the same story. We have to stay. You do realize the difficulty of the situation?"

Noemí rubbed her hands together. Yes, she did. She didn't like it, but she did. She was tired. She felt like they kept going in circles. Perhaps Francis was correct, and it was best to pack her bags. But, no, no, she refused.

He turned his gaze on her. Blue and intense, the blue of lapis lazuli, carefully ground. "Well, we seem to have drifted from the topic I had in mind when I called you here. I wanted to apologize to you for my words the last time we met. I was not in a good frame of mind. I still am not. Anyway, if I've upset you then I am very sorry," Virgil said, quite surprising her.

"Thank you," she replied.

"I hope we can be friendly. There is no need to act as though we are enemies."

"I know we aren't."

"We've gotten off on the wrong foot, I'm afraid. Perhaps we might try again. I promise I'll ask Dr. Cummins to begin asking about psychiatrists in Pachuca, as an option down the line. You can help me pick one; we might even write to him together."

"I'd like that."

"A truce, then?"

"We're not at war, remember?"

"Ah, yes. Nevertheless," he said, extending his hand. Noemí hesitated, then stepped from behind the chair and shook it. His grip was firm, the hand large, covering her own tiny one.

She excused herself and left. When she was walking back to her room she saw Francis standing in front of a door, opening it. Her footsteps made him halt, and he looked at her. He inclined his head, in a mute greeting, but said nothing.

She wondered if Florence had chided him for doing Noemí's bidding. Maybe he would be summoned to stand before Virgil, and he'd tell Francis the same thing he'd said to Noemí: It seems you spend most of your time with her. She pictured a quarrel. Muted. Howard didn't like loud noises, and confrontations must take place in whispers.

*He won't help me again*, she thought as she gazed at his hesitant face. *I've exhausted his goodwill.*

"Francis," she said.

He pretended not to hear her. Gently the young man closed the door behind him and disappeared from sight. He was swallowed by one of the many chambers of the house, into one of the bellies of this beast.

She pressed a palm against the door, thought better of it, and kept on walking, keenly aware that she had already caused too much trouble. She wanted to make it better. She decided to seek out Florence and found her talking with Lizzie in the kitchen, their voices a whisper.

"Florence, do you have a minute?" she asked.

"Your cousin is napping. If you want—"

"It's not about Catalina."

Florence gestured toward the maid, then turned to Noemí and motioned for her to follow her. They went into a room she had not visited before. It had a large, solid table with an old-fashioned sewing machine set atop it. Open shelves held sewing baskets and yellowed fashion magazines. On a wall you could see old nails, signaling the spot where there had once been paintings and now there were smudges, faint traces of frames. But the room was very tidy, very clean.

"What do you need?" Florence asked.

"I asked Francis to take me to town this morning. I know you don't like it when we leave without speaking to you. I wanted you to know it was my fault. You shouldn't be angry at him."

Florence sat down on a large chair that was set next to the table, her fingers laced together, and stared at Noemí. "You think me harsh, don't you? No, don't deny it."

"Strict would be the most appropriate word," Noemí said politely.

"It is important to maintain a sense of order in one's house, in one's life. It helps you determine your place in the world, where you belong. Taxonomical classifications help place each creature atop its right branch. It's no good to forget yourself, nor your obligations. Francis has duties, he has chores. You pull him away from those chores. You make him forget his obligations."

"But surely he doesn't have chores all day long."

"Doesn't he? How would you know? Even if his days are made of leisure, why should he spend them with you?"

"I don't mean to take up all his time, but I don't see—"

"He's silly when he is with you. He completely forgets who he's supposed to be. And do you think Howard would let *him* have *you*?" Florence shook her head. "The poor boy," she muttered. "What do you want, hmm? What do you want from us? There's nothing left to give."

"I wanted to apologize," Noemí said.

Florence pressed a hand against her right temple and closed her eyes. "You have. Go, go."

And like the wretched creature that Florence had mentioned, that does not know its place nor how to find it, Noemí sat on the stairs for a while, staring at the nymph on the newel post and contemplating the motes of dust dancing in a ray of light.

# 16

Florence would not let Noemí sit alone with Catalina. One of the maids, Mary, had been ordered to stand guard in a corner. Noemí was not to be trusted ever again. Nobody said that was the case, but while she approached her cousin's bed the maid moved slowly around, arranging the clothes in the armoire, folding a blanket. Needless tasks.

"Could you do that later, please?" she asked Mary.

"No time for it in the morning," the maid replied, her voice even.

"Mary, please."

"Don't worry about her," Catalina said. "Sit."

"Oh, I . . . Yes, it doesn't matter," Noemí said, trying not to be upset about this. She wanted to maintain a positive façade for Catalina. Besides, Florence had said she could have a half hour with Catalina, nothing more, and she wanted to make the best of it. "You look much better."

"Liar," Catalina said, but she smiled.

"Should I fluff your pillows? Hand you your slippers so tonight you can dance like one of the Twelve Dancing Princesses?"

"You liked the illustrations in that book," Catalina said softly. "I did. I admit I'd read it right now if I could."

The maid began fussing with the curtains, turning her back to them, and Catalina gave Noemí an eager look. "Maybe you'd read me poetry? There's my old book of poems there. You know how I like Sor Juana."

She did remember the book, which rested on the night table. Like the tome packed with fairy tales, this was a familiar treasure. "Which one should I read?" Noemí asked.

" 'Foolish Men.' "

Noemí turned the pages. There it was, the well-worn pages as she remembered. And there too was an unusual element. A yellow, folded piece of paper tucked against the pages. Noemí glanced at her cousin. Catalina said nothing, her lips were pressed tight, but in her eyes Noemí read a naked fear. She glanced in Mary's direction. The woman was still busy with the curtains. Noemí pocketed the piece of paper and began reading. She went through several poems, keeping her voice steady. Eventually Florence arrived at the doorway carrying a silver tray with a matching teapot and a cup and a handful of cookies on a porcelain plate.

"It's time to let Catalina rest," Florence said.

"Of course."

Noemí clapped the book shut and docilely bid her cousin goodbye. When Noemí reached her room, she noticed that Florence had been in there. There was a tray with a cup of tea and the handful of cookies, like Catalina's.

Noemí ignored the tea and closed the door. She didn't have an appetite and had forgotten to smoke a cigarette in ages. This whole situation was souring her to everything.

Noemí unfolded the piece of paper. She recognized Catalina's handwriting on a corner. "This is proof," she said. Noemí frowned and unfolded the letter a second time, wondering what Catalina had written. Would it be a repeat of that strange missive she had sent to Noemí's father? The letter that had started it all.

The letter, however, was not her cousin's as she'd thought. It was older, the paper brittle, and it seemed to have been torn from a journal. It was not dated, although it seemed to be the page of a diary entry.

*I put these thoughts down on paper because it is the only way to remain firm in my resolve. Tomorrow I may lose courage but these words should anchor me to the here and now. To the present moment. I hear their voices constantly, whispering. They glow at night. Perhaps that might be endurable, this place would be endurable, if not for him. Our lord and master. Our God. An egg, split asunder, and a mighty serpent rising from it, expanding wide its jaws. Our great legacy, spun in cartilage and blood and roots so very deep. Gods cannot die. That is what we have been told, what Mother believes. But Mother cannot protect me, cannot save any of us. It is up to me. Whether this is sacrilege or simple murder, or both. He beat me when he found out about Benito but I swore there and then that I would never bear a child nor do his will. I believe firmly this death will be no sin. It is a release and my salvation. R.*

R, a single letter as a signature. Ruth. Could this truly be a page from Ruth's journal? She didn't think Catalina would have faked such a thing, even if it bore an uncanny resemblance to the rambling letter her cousin had penned. But where would Catalina have found it? The house was large and old. She could picture Catalina walking the darkened hallways. A loose floorboard lifted, the elusive diary fragment hidden beneath the wooden plank.

Head bent over the letter, she bit her lips. Reading this scrap of paper with those eerie sentences could make anyone start believing in ghosts or curses or both. Of course, she'd never given credence to the idea of things that go bump in the night. Fantasies and fancies, that's what she told herself. She'd read *The Golden Bough*, nodding at its chapter on the expulsion of evils, she'd curiously leafed through a journal detailing the connection between ghosts and sickness in Tonga, and been amused by a letter to the editor of *Folklore* detailing an encounter with a headless spirit. She was not in the habit of believing in the supernatural.

*This is proof*, Catalina had said. But proof of what? She laid the letter on the table and smoothed it out. She read it again.

*Put the facts together, you fool*, she told herself, chewing on a nail. And what were the facts? That her cousin spoke about a presence in this house, including voices. Ruth also described voices. Noemí had heard no voices, but she'd had bad dreams and sleepwalked, which she hadn't done in years.

One could conclude this was a case of three silly, nervous women. Physicians of old would have diagnosed it as hysterics. But one thing Noemí was not was hysterical.

If the three of them were not hysterical, then the three of them had truly come in contact with *something* inside this house. But must it be supernatural? Must it be a curse? A ghost? Could there be a more rational answer? Was she seeing a pattern where there wasn't any? After all, that's what humans did: look for patterns. She could be weaving three disparate stories into a narrative.

She wanted to talk to someone else about this because otherwise she was going to wear the soles of her shoes off walking back and forth in her room. Noemí slid the paper into her sweater's pocket, grabbed her oil lamp, and went to find Francis. He had been avoiding her for the past couple of days—she assumed Florence had also given him the speech about chores and duties—but she didn't think he'd slam the door in her face if she went to him, and, anyway, it wasn't as if she was going to ask him for a favor this time. She simply wished to chat. Emboldened, she sought him out.

He opened his door, and before he could properly greet her she spoke. "May I come in? I need to talk to you."

"Now?"

"Five minutes. Please?"

He blinked, unsure; cleared his throat for good measure. "Yes. Yes, of course."

The walls in his room were covered with colorful drawings

and prints of botanical specimens. She counted a dozen butter-flies carefully pinned under glass and five lovingly painted water-colors of mushrooms, their names in tiny print beneath them. There were two bookcases laden with leather-bound volumes and books stacked on the floor in tidy piles. The smell of weathered pages and ink permeated the room, like the perfume from an exotic bouquet.

Virgil's room had a sitting area, but Francis's did not. She could see the narrow bed with a dark green coverlet and a richly carved headboard festooned with leaves, the pervasive motif of the snake eating its tail at the center. There was a matching desk, covered with more books. On a corner of the desk, an empty cup and a plate. That is where he must have his meals. He didn't uti-lize the table in the middle of the room.

As she walked next to it, she realized why: the table was cov-ered with papers and drawing instruments. She looked at the sharpened pencils, the bottles of india ink, and the nibs of pens. A box with watercolors, the brushes sitting inside a cup. There were many charcoal drawings, but others were inked. Botanical sketches, the lot of them.

"You're an artist," she said, touching the edge of a drawing showing a dandelion while she held the oil lamp with her other hand.

"I draw," he said, sounding abashed. "I'm afraid I have noth-ing to offer you. I've finished my tea."

"I despise the tea they brew here. It's terrible," she said, look-ing at another drawing, this one of a dahlia. "I tried my hand at painting once. I thought it made sense, you know? My father being in the dye and paint business, after all. But I was no good. Plus, I like photos better. They capture the thing in the moment."

"But painting is the repeated exposure to a thing. It captures the essence of the object."

"You're poetic too."

He looked embarrassed. "Let's sit," he said, taking the lantern from her hand and setting it down on the desk where he had al-ready placed a few candles. Another oil lamp, very much like her own, larger, rested on his night table. The glass on it was tinted yellow, and it varnished the room in warm amber tones.

He pointed her to a large chair covered with an antimacassar showcasing a pattern of rose garlands and quickly shoved off a couple of books that he'd left there. He grabbed his desk chair, sitting before her and lacing his hands together, leaning forward a little.

"Do you get to see much of your family's business?" he asked.

"When I was a kid I'd go to my father's office and pretend to type reports and write memos. But I'm not so interested in that anymore."

"You don't want to be involved with it?"

"My brother loves it. But I don't see why if my family has a paint company I should be in paint. Or worse: marry the heir of another paint company so we can have a larger company. Maybe I want to do something else. Maybe I have an amazing secret talent which must be exploited. You could be talking to a top-notch anthropologist here, you know."

"Not a concert pianist, then."

"Why not both?" she asked with a shrug.

"Of course."

The chair was comfortable, and she liked his room. Noemí turned her head, looking at the watercolors of the mushrooms. "Are those yours too?"

"Yes. I did them a few years ago. They're not very good."

"They're beautiful."

"If you say so," he replied, sounding dignified and smiling.

He had a plain face, mismatched even. She had liked Hugo Duarte because he was a pretty boy, and she appreciated a fellow with a certain slickness, who could dress well and play the game of charm. But she liked this man's quirks and imperfections, the lack of playboy smarts coupled with a quiet intelligence.

Francis was wearing his corduroy jacket again, but in the privacy of his room he walked around barefoot and had donned a rumpled old shirt. There was something lovely and intimate when he looked like this.

Noemí was struck with the desire to lean forward and kiss him, a feeling like wishing to light a match, a burning, bright, and eager feeling. Yet she hesitated. It was easy to kiss someone when it didn't matter; it was more difficult when it might be meaningful.

She didn't want to make a further mess of things. She didn't want to play with him.

"You haven't come to compliment my drawings," he said, as if he could sense her hesitation.

She hadn't. Not at all. Noemí cleared her throat and shook her head. "Have you ever thought your home might be haunted?"

Francis gave her a weak smile. "That's an odd thing to say."

"I'm sure it is. But I have a good reason for asking. So, have you?"

There was silence. He slowly slid his hands into his pockets and looked down at the rug under their feet. He frowned.

"I won't laugh at you if you tell me you've observed ghosts," Noemí added.

"There're no such thing as ghosts."

"But what if there were? Have you ever wondered about that? I don't mean ghosts under bedsheets, dragging chains behind them. I read a book about Tibet once. It was written by this woman called Alexandra David-Neel, who said people there were able to create ghosts. They willed them into existence. What did she call them? Tulpa."

"That sounds like a tall tale."

"Of course. But there is this professor at Duke University, J. B. Rhine, who is studying parapsychology. Things like telepathy as a kind of extrasensory perception."

"What are you saying, exactly?" he asked, a terrible caution lacing his words.

"I'm saying maybe my cousin is perfectly sane. Maybe there is a haunting in this house, but it can be explained logically. I don't know quite how yet, maybe it's got nothing to do with parapsychology, but take that old saying: mad as a hatter."

"I don't understand."

"People said hatters were prone to going crazy, but it was the materials they worked with. They inhaled mercury vapors when they made felt hats. You still have to be careful with that stuff nowadays. You can mix mercury into paints to control mildew, but under the right conditions the compounds give off sufficient mercury vapor to make people sick. You could have everyone in a room going mad and it's the paint job."

Francis stood up suddenly and gripped her hands. "Don't speak another word," Francis told her, his voice low. He spoke in Spanish. They'd stuck to English since she'd arrived at the house; she didn't recall him using one word of Spanish at High Place. She couldn't remember him touching her either. If he had, it hadn't been deliberate. But his hands were steady on her wrists now.

"Do you think I'm mad like those hatters?" she asked, also in Spanish.

"Dear God, no. I think you're sane and clever. Much too clever, perhaps. Why won't you listen to me? Really listen. Leave today. Leave right this instant. This is no place for you."

"What do you know that you aren't telling me?"

He stared at her, his hands still gripping her own. "Noemí, just because there are no ghosts it doesn't mean you can't be haunted. Nor that you shouldn't fear the haunting. You are too fearless. My father was the same way, and he paid dearly for it."

"He fell down a ravine," she said. "Or was there more to it?"

"Who told you?"

"I asked a question first."

A cold pinprick of dread touched her heart. He shifted away from her, uneasily, and it was her turn to grip his hands. To hold him in place.

"Will you speak to me?" she insisted. "Was there more to it?"

"He was a drunk and he broke his neck, and he did fall down a ravine. Must we discuss this now?"

"Yes. Because it seems you'll discuss nothing with me at any time."

"That is not true. I've told you plenty. If you'd really listen," he said, his hands extricating themselves from hers and resting on her shoulders in a solemn motion.

"I'm listening."

He made a sound of protest, it was half a sigh, and she thought he might begin to talk to her, but then a loud moan echoed down the hall, and then another. Francis stepped away from her.

The acoustics in this place, they were odd. It made her wonder why sound traveled so well.

"It's Uncle Howard. He's in pain again," Francis said, grimacing, so that it almost looked like he was the one in agony. "He can't hold on much longer."

"I'm sorry. It must be difficult for you."

"You have no idea. If only he'd die."

It was a terrible thing to say, and yet she imagined it must not be easy to live day after day in that creaky, musty house, walking on tiptoes so as to not upset the old man. What resentments could sprout in a young heart when all affection and love had been denied? Because she could not imagine anyone ever loving Francis. Not his uncle, nor his mother. Had Virgil and Francis been friends? Did they ever look at each other, wearily, and confess their dissatisfactions? But Virgil, though perhaps also nursing his own grievances, had gone out into the world. Francis, he was tied to this house.

"Hey," she said, extending a hand to touch his arm.

"I remember, when I was small, how he'd beat me with that cane of his," Francis mused, his voice a hoarse whisper. " 'Teaching me strength,' that's how we put it. And I thought, dear Lord, Ruth was right. She was right. Only she couldn't finish him off. And there's no point in trying, but she was right."

He looked so absolutely wretched, and although what he'd said had been terrible, she felt more pity than horror, and she didn't flinch, her hand steady against his arm. It was Francis who turned his head away, who shirked her.

"Uncle Howard is a monster," Francis told her. "Don't trust Howard, don't trust Florence, and don't trust Virgil. Now you should go. I wish I didn't have to send you off so quickly, but I should."

They were both quiet. He had his head down, his eyes lowered.

"I can stay for a bit, if you want me to," she offered.

He looked at her and smiled faintly. "My mother will have a fit if she finds you here, and she will be here any minute. When Howard is like this she needs us nearby. Go to sleep, Noemí."

"As if I could sleep," she said with a sigh. "Although I could count sheep. Do you think that might help?"

She ran a finger across the cover of a book that lay at the top of a pile, by the chair she had been occupying. She had nothing more to say and was simply delaying her departure, hoping he might speak to her more, despite his reservations; that he'd get to the matter of ghosts and a haunting that she wished to explore, but it was no use.

He caught her hand, lifting it from the book, and looked down at her.

"Noemí, please," he whispered. "I didn't lie when I said they will come and fetch me."

He gave her back the oil lamp and held the door open for her. Noemí stepped out.

She looked over her shoulder before turning a corner. He seemed a bit ghostly, still standing by the doorway, with the glow of the lanterns and candles in his room lighting his blond hair like an unearthly flame. They said, in dusty little towns around the country, that witches could turn into balls of fire and fly through the air. That's how they explained will-o'-the-wisps. And she thought of that, and of the dream she'd had about a golden woman.

# 17

Noemí hadn't been lying about counting sheep. She was too energized by all the thoughts of hauntings, of answers to puzzles, to be lulled into an easy slumber. And that moment when she'd thought to lean forward and plant a kiss on Francis's lips was still bright in her mind, electric.

Noemí decided that the best thing she could do was take a bath.

The bathroom was old, several of the tiles were cracked, but under the light of the oil lamp the tub appeared intact and decidedly clean, even if the ceiling was defaced by unsightly traces of mold.

Noemí set the oil lamp on a chair and her bathrobe on the back of it, and opened the faucet. Florence had told her mild baths were what everyone ought to take, but Noemí didn't intend to soak in a cold pool of water, and whatever issues the boiler might have, she was able to draw a hot bath for herself, the steam quickly filling the room.

Back home she would have sprinkled sweet-smelling oils or

bath salts into the water, but there were none to be had. Noemí
slipped into the bathtub anyway and rested her head back.

High Place wasn't exactly a dump, but there were so many
small things wrong with it. Neglect. Yes, that was the right word.
There was a great amount of neglect. Noemí wondered if Catalina might have turned things around, had the circumstances
been slightly different. She doubted it. Rot had set in in this place.

The thought was unpleasant. She closed her eyes.

The faucet dripped a little. She sank deeper under the water
until her head was completely underwater and she held her breath.
When was the last time she'd gone swimming? She'd have to make
a point to visit Veracruz soon. Better yet, Acapulco. She couldn't
think of a place that would be more different than High Place.
Sun, beaches, cocktails. She could telephone Hugo Duarte and
see if he was available.

When she emerged, Noemí brushed the hair away from her
eyes almost angrily. Hugo Duarte. Who was she kidding? She
wasn't thinking about him these days. That arrow of yearning
that had struck her in Francis's room was worrisome. It felt different from her other excursions into desire. Though a young
woman of her social standing was not supposed to know anything about desire, Noemí had had the chance to experience
kisses, embraces, and certain caresses. That she did not sleep
with any of the men she dated had less to do with a fear of sin
than with the concern that they'd tattle about it to their friends,
or worse, entrap her. There was always this smidgen of fear in her
heart, fear of so many things, but with Francis she forgot to fear.

*You're turning mawkish*, she told herself. *He's not even handsome.*

She slid a hand up and down her breastbone and contemplated
the mold on the ceiling before sighing and turning her head away.

That's when she saw it. The figure by the doorway. Noemí
blinked, thinking for a moment it was an optical illusion. She'd
brought the oil lamp into the bathroom and it provided enough
light, but it wasn't the stark illumination of a light bulb.

The figure stepped forward, and she realized that it was Virgil, in a navy pinstripe suit and a tie, looking nonchalant, as if he'd walked into his bathroom instead of her own.

"There you are, you pretty little thing," he said. "No need to speak, no need to move."

Shame and surprise and anger shot through her body. What the hell did he think he was doing? She was going to yell at him. She was going to yell at him and cover herself, and not only yell. She'd slap him. She'd slap him once she was in her bathrobe.

But she didn't move at all. No sound escaped Noemí's lips.

Virgil stepped forward, a thin smile on his face.

*They can make you think things*, a voice whispered. She'd heard that voice before, somewhere in this house. *They make you do things.*

Her left hand was resting on the edge of the tub, and she managed, with considerable effort, to curl it tighter. She was able to open her mouth a little, but not to speak. She wanted to tell him to get out and couldn't, and it made her tremble with fright.

"You'll be a good girl, won't you?" Virgil said.

He had reached the bathtub and knelt down to look at her, smiling. It was a cunning, crooked smile set in a perfectly sculpted face, and he was so close to her that she could see there were flecks of gold in his eyes.

He tugged at the tie around his neck and took it off, then he unbuttoned his shirt.

She was petrified, like the unwary character in an old myth. She was the victim of the gorgon.

"Such a good girl, I know it. Be good to me."

*Open your eyes*, the voice said.

But her eyes were wide open, and he had woven his fingers into her hair, making her lift her head up. A rough gesture, devoid of any of the kindness he was asking of her. She wanted to shove him away, but she still couldn't move, and his hand clenched in her hair and he was leaning down to kiss her.

Noemí tasted sweetness on his lips. The trace of wine, perhaps. It was pleasant and it made her relax her tense body. She let go of the edge of the bathtub, and the voice that had been whispering to her was gone now. There was the steam from the bath and the man's mouth atop her own, the hands snaking around her body. He kissed down her long neck, pausing to bite at the top of her breast, which drew a gasp from her. His stubble was rough against her skin.

Her neck arched backward. It seemed she could, in fact, move.

She raised her hands to touch his face, to draw him toward her. He wasn't an intruder. He wasn't an enemy. There was no reason to yell or to slap him, while there was every reason to keep touching him.

His hand ran down her stomach and disappeared beneath the water, caressing her thighs. She was not trembling with fright anymore. It was desire making her shiver, delicious and thick, spreading across her limbs, his touch heavy, his fingers toying with her as her breathing hitched. His body was hot against her skin. Another flick of his fingers, a deep exhalation, but then—

*Open your eyes*, hissed the voice, yanking her hard, and she turned her face away from him, staring up again at the ceiling. The ceiling had melted away.

She saw an egg, and from it rose a thin white stalk. A snake. But no, no, she'd seen such an image before. In Francis's room a couple of hours ago. On the walls. The watercolors of mushrooms with their neat labels beneath, and one of them had said "universal veil." Yes. That's what it was. The egg, pierced, the membrane removed, the snake that was the mushroom rising through the ground. Alabaster snake, sliding and knotting itself, devouring its tail.

Then there was darkness. The light from the oil lamp had gone off. She wasn't in the tub anymore. She had been wrapped in a thick cloth that impeded her movement, but she managed to pull it apart, to slide it away, and it slipped from her shoulders as neatly as the membrane she'd observed.

Wood. She could smell damp earth and wood, and when she raised a hand her knuckles hit a hard surface and a splinter cut her skin.

Coffin. It was a coffin. The cloth was a shroud.

But she wasn't dead. She wasn't. And she opened her mouth to yell, to tell them that she wasn't dead even when she knew she'd never die.

A buzzing, like a million bees had suddenly been unleashed, and Noemí pressed her hands against her ears. A blinding golden light shivered; it touched her, moving from the tip of her toes up to her chest until it reached her face, smothering her.

*Open your eyes*, Ruth said. Ruth with blood in her hands and blood on her face and her nails caked with blood, and the bees were inside her head, tunneling through Noemí's ears.

Noemí snapped her eyes open. Water was dripping down her back and her fingertips, and the bathrobe she was wearing was not cinched; it lay loose and open showing her nakedness. She was barefoot.

The room she stood in lay in shadows, but even in the dark the configuration indicated it was obviously not her own room. A dim lamp rose, like a firefly, grew brighter as nimble fingers adjusted it. Virgil Doyle, sitting in his bed, raised the lamp that had been resting at his bedside and regarded her.

"What's this?" she asked, pressing a hand against her throat.

She could speak. Dear God, she could speak, even if her voice was hoarse and she was trembling.

"I believe you managed to sleepwalk into my room."

She was breathing much too quickly. She felt as though she had been running and God knew if she had. Anything was possible. She managed to close her robe with a clumsy motion of her hands.

Virgil pushed the covers away. He put on his velvet robe and approached her. "You're all wet," he said.

"I was taking a bath," Noemí muttered. "What were you doing?"

"I was sleeping," he said, reaching her side.

She thought he meant to touch her and took a step back, almost toppling the painted screen next to her. He steadied it with one hand.

"I'll fetch you a towel. You must be cold."

"Not that cold."

"You're a little liar," he said simply and went rummaging in an armoire.

She was not going to wait for him to find the towel. She meant to walk immediately back to her room, in absolute darkness if necessary. But the night had stunned her, it had reduced Noemí to a state of anxiousness that did not allow her to leave. As in the dream, she was petrified.

"Here," he said, and she clutched the towel for a minute, before finally drying her face and then slowly blotting her hair with it. She wondered how long she had been in the tub, and then how long she'd wandered down the hallways.

Virgil slipped into the shadows, and she heard the clinking of glass. He returned with two glasses in his hand.

"Sit and have a sip of wine," he said. "It'll warm you up."

"Let me borrow your lamp and I'll be out of here."

"Have the wine, Noemí."

He sat in the same chair he'd used the last time, setting the oil lamp on a table, along with her drink, while he nursed his own glass. Noemí twisted the towel between her hands and sat down. She let the towel drop to the floor and picked up the glass, taking a sip—only one, as he'd suggested—very quickly, before setting the glass down again.

She felt as though she were still floating in the dream even though she had woken up. A haze lingered in her mind, and the only clear thing in the room was Virgil, his hair a little wild, his handsome face peering at her intently. He expected her to speak, that much was obvious, and she sought proper words.

"You were in my dream," she said. More for her sake than for his. She wanted to understand what she'd seen, what had happened.

"I hope it wasn't a bad dream," he replied. He smiled. The smile was sly. It was the same smile she'd dreamed. Slightly malicious.

The ardor that she'd felt so vividly and pleasantly was now turning into a sour feeling in the pit of her stomach, but the smile was like a stray spark, reminding Noemí of her eagerness, of his touch.

"Were you in my room?"

"I thought I was in your dream."

"It did not feel like a dream."

"What did it feel like?"

"Like an intrusion," she said.

"I was sleeping. You woke me up. You are the intruder tonight."

She'd seen him rise from his bed and grab his velvet robe and yet she didn't think him innocent. But he couldn't have swept into the bathroom, like a medieval incubus, sitting on her chest as if they were posing for one of Fuseli's paintings. Sneaking into her chamber to ravish her.

She touched her wrist, wanting to feel the blue-and-white beads. She'd taken off the bracelet against the evil eye. Her wrist was bare. So was she, for that matter, wrapped in the white bathrobe, with water droplets still clinging to her body.

She stood up.

"I'll be heading back now," she declared.

"You know, when you wake after sleepwalking you are not supposed to go back to bed right at once," he said. "I really think you could use a little more wine."

"No. I've had a terrible night and don't wish to prolong it."

"Mmm. And yet if I didn't agree to let you take my lamp you'd be forced to remain here for a few more minutes, wouldn't you? Unless you plan to find your way back by touching the walls. This house is very dark."

"Yes. I do plan to do that if you won't be polite and assist me."

"I thought I was assisting you. I've offered you a towel to dry your hair, a chair to sit down, and a drink to calm your nerves."

"My nerves are fine."

He rose with the glass in one hand, eyeing her with a dry amusement. "What did you dream tonight?"

She did not wish to blush in front of him. To turn crimson like an idiot in front of a man who wielded such meticulous hostility toward her. But she thought of his mouth on hers and his hands on her thighs, like it had been in the dream, and an electric thrill ran down her spine. That night, that dream, it had felt like desire, danger, and scandals, and all the secrets her body and her eager mind quietly coveted. The thrill of shamelessness and of him.

She blushed after all.

Virgil smiled. And even though it was impossible, she was sure that he knew exactly what she had dreamed, and that he was waiting for her to give him the smallest hint of an invitation. The fog in her brain was clearing, though, and she remembered the words in her ear. That single phrase. *Open your eyes.*

Noemí curled a hand into a fist, her nails digging into her palm. She shook her head. "Something terrible," she said.

Virgil seemed confused, then disappointed. His face turned ugly as he grimaced. "Perhaps you were hoping to sleepwalk into Francis's room, hmm?" he asked.

The words shocked her, but they also gave her the confidence to stare back at him. How dare he. And after he had said they could be friends. But she understood now. This man was an absolute liar, toying with her, attempting to confuse and distract her. He turned kind for a second when it suited him, granted her an inch of cordiality, then took it away.

"Go to sleep," she said, but in her mind she thought *fuck you,* and her tone plainly indicated that. She snatched the lamp and left him in the shadows.

When she reached her room she realized it had started to rain. The sort of rain that does not ease, a constant patter against the window. She ventured into the bathroom and looked at the bathtub. The water was cold, and the steam had dissipated. She yanked up the plug.

# 18

Noemí slept fitfully, afraid she'd launch into another somnambulistic escapade. Eventually, she dozed off.

There was a rustle of cloth in her room, the creak of a board, and she turned her head in fright toward the door, her hands clutching her bedsheets.

It was Florence in another of her prim dark dresses and her pearls. She had let herself into her room and carried a silver tray in her hands.

"What are you doing?" Noemí asked, sitting up. Her mouth felt dry.

"It's lunchtime," Florence said.

"What?"

It couldn't be that late, could it? Noemí got up and pulled the curtains aside. Light streamed in. It rained still. The morning hours had burned away without her noticing, exhaustion bleeding her dry.

Florence set the lunch tray down. She poured a cup of tea for Noemí.

"Oh, no, thanks," Noemí said, shaking her head. "I wanted to see Catalina before eating."

"She's woken up already and has gone back to bed," Florence replied, setting the teapot down. "Her medication is making her very sleepy."

"In that case, will you tell me when the doctor arrives, then? He is supposed to come today, isn't he?"

"He won't be here today."

"I thought he visited every week."

"It's still raining," Florence said, indifferent. "He won't come up with this rain."

"It might rain tomorrow too. After all, it's the rainy season, isn't it? What'll happen then?"

"We'll get by on our own, we always have."

What neat, crisp answers to everything! Why, it almost felt like Florence had written and memorized all the right things to say.

"Please tell me when my cousin wakes up," Noemí insisted.

"I'm not your servant, Miss Taboada," Florence replied. Her voice lacked animosity, though. It was merely a fact.

"I am well aware of that, but you demand that I not visit Catalina without warning and then you set up an impossible schedule for me. What is your problem?" she asked. She realized she was being incredibly rude, but she wished to draw a crack through Florence's calm façade.

"If you have an issue with that, you'd best bring it up with Virgil."

Virgil. The last thing she wished to do was bring anything up with Virgil. Noemí crossed her arms and stared at the woman. Florence stared back at her, her eyes very cold and her mouth curved a little, the slightest hint of derision.

"Enjoy your lunch," Florence concluded, and there was superiority in her smile, as if she thought she'd won a battle.

Noemí stirred the soup with her spoon and sipped the tea. She quickly gave up on both of them. She felt the beginning of a headache. She ought to eat but stubbornly decided to look around the house.

Noemí grabbed her sweater and walked downstairs. Did she hope to find anything? Ghosts, peeking from behind doors? If there were any, they evaded her.

The rooms with sheets on top of the furniture were dire, and so was the greenhouse with its wilted plants. Aside from evoking a mild sense of depression, they revealed nothing. She ended up seeking refuge in the library. The curtains were drawn, and she pulled them open.

She looked down at the circular rug with the snake she had noticed during her first visit and slowly walked around it. There had been a snake in her dream. It burst from an egg. No, from a fruiting body. If dreams had meaning, what did this one tell her?

Well, she was damn sure one needn't phone a psychoanalyst to determine it had a sexual component to it. Trains going through tunnels make for neat metaphors, thanks, Mr. Freud, and apparently phallic mushrooms straining through the soil served the same purpose.

Virgil Doyle straining against *her*.

That was no metaphor; it was crystal clear.

The memory of him, with his hands in her hair, his lips against her own, made her shiver. But there wasn't anything pleasant in the memory. It was cold and disturbing, and she turned her eyes toward the bookshelves, furiously looking among the tomes for a book to read.

Noemí grabbed a couple of books at random and went back to her room. She stood by the window, looking outside, nibbling on a nail before she decided she was too nervous and needed a smoke. She found the cigarettes, the lighter, and the cup decorated with half-naked cupids that she utilized as an ashtray. After taking a drag, she settled on the bed.

She hadn't even bothered to read the titles of the books she'd picked. *Hereditary Descent: Its Laws and Facts Applied to Human Improvement*, it said. The other book was more interesting, dwelling on Greek and Roman mythology.

She opened it and saw the faint, dark marks of mold upon the first page. She turned the pages carefully. The interior pages were mostly intact, a few tiny spots on a corner or two. They made her think of snatches of Morse code. Nature writing upon paper and leather.

Noemí held the cigarette in her left hand and let the ash drop into the cup, which she'd placed on the side table. Golden-haired Persephone, the book informed her, had been dragged down into the Underworld by Hades. There she ate a few seeds of pomegranate, which chained her to his shadow world.

The book contained an engraving showing the exact moment when Persephone was snatched away by the god. Persephone's hair was strewn with flowers and a few flowers had fallen to the ground; her breasts were bare. Hades, reaching from behind, had picked her up, clutching her in his arms. Persephone had one hand in the air and swooned, a scream on her lips. Her expression was one of horror. The god stared forward.

Noemí clapped the book shut and looked away, her eyes landing on the corner in her room where the rose-colored wallpaper was stained black by mold. And as she looked at it, the mold *moved*.

Christ, what kind of optical illusion was that?!

She sat in the bed and gripped the covers with one hand while with the other she held her cigarette. Slowly she stood and approached the wall, unblinking. The shifting mold was mesmerizing. It rearranged itself into wildly eclectic patterns that reminded her of a kaleidoscope, shifting, changing. Instead of bits of glass reflected by mirrors it was an organic madness that propelled the mold into its dizzy twists and turns, creating swirls and garlands, dissolving, then remerging.

There was color to it too. At first glance it appeared black and gray, yet the longer Noemí looked at the mold, the more it became obvious there was a golden sheen to certain sections of it. Gold and yellow and amber, dulling or intensifying as the patterns remade themselves into a new combination of staggering, symmetrical beauty.

She reached a hand up, as if to touch that section of the wall that was dirtied by the mold. The mold moved again, away from her hand, skittish. Then it seemed to change its mind. It pulsated, as if it was bubbling up, like tar, and it crooked a long, thin finger, beckoning her.

There were a thousand bees hiding in the walls, and she heard them buzzing as she pressed forward drowsily, intending to slide her lips against the mold. She'd run her hands across the shimmering gold patterns, and they would smell of earth and green, of rain, and then they would speak a thousand secrets.

The mold beat to the rhythm of her heart; they beat as one, and her lips parted.

The forgotten cigarette, still in her possession, burned Noemí's skin, and she let go of it with a yelp. She quickly bent down and picked up the cigarette, tossing it into her makeshift ashtray.

She turned around to look at the mold. It was absolutely still. The wall looked like old, dirty wallpaper and had not changed even a little bit.

Noemí rushed into the bathroom and shut the door. She gripped the edge of the sink to keep herself steady. Her legs were about to fail her, and she thought, panicked, that she would faint.

She opened the faucet, splashing cold water against her face, unwilling to collapse even if it took all her damn might. Breathe and breathe again, that's what she did.

"God damn it," Noemí whispered, bracing herself with both hands against the sink. The dizzy spell was passing. But she wasn't going out there. Not for a while, at least. Until she made sure . . . made sure of what? That she'd stopped hallucinating? That she wasn't going mad?

Noemí slid one hand against her neck while she examined the other. She had a great, nasty burn between her index and middle fingers, where the cigarette had burned down to a stub. She'd have to obtain an ointment for that.

Noemí splashed more water against her face and stared into the mirror, her fingertips on her lips.

A loud knock made her jump back.

"Are you in there?" Florence asked. Before Noemí had time to reply, the woman opened the door.

"Give me a minute," Noemí muttered.

"Why are you smoking when it's forbidden?"

Noemí whipped her head up and scoffed at the inane question. "Yeah? I think the more important question is what the fuck is going on in this house?" Noemí said. She wasn't quite yelling, but she was awfully close.

"What language! Watch how you talk to me, young girl."

Noemí shook her head and closed the faucet. "I want to see Catalina, right away."

"Don't you dare order me around. Virgil will be here any minute and you'll see—"

She clutched Florence's arm. "Listen—"

"Take your hands off me!"

Noemí squeezed her fingers harder while Florence tried to push her away.

"What's this?" Virgil asked.

He stood at the doorway, looking at them curiously. He had on the same pinstriped jacket that he'd worn in her dream. It gave her a jolt. She'd likely seen it on him before, which is why she'd pictured him wearing it in the first place, but she didn't like this detail. It blended reality and fantasy together. It unnerved her enough to release Florence.

"She's been breaking the rules, as usual," Florence said, carefully smoothing back her hair even though it did not need to be smoothed. As if their brief confrontation could have upset her well-coiffed head. "She's a nuisance."

"What are you doing here?" Noemí asked, crossing her arms.

"You yelled, and I came to see if anything was amiss," Virgil told her. "I imagine that's the same reason why Florence is here."

"Indeed," Florence replied.

"I didn't yell for anyone."

"We both heard you," Florence insisted.

Noemí had definitely not yelled. There had been noise, but that was the noise from the bees. Of course there were no bees, but that didn't mean she had yelled. She would damn well remember if she yelled. The cigarette had burned her hands, but she hadn't made that much noise and—

They both looked at her. "I want to see my cousin. Now. I swear to God, you let me see her or I'll knock her door down," she demanded.

Virgil shrugged. "There is no need for that. Come."

She followed them. At one point Virgil looked at her over his shoulder and smiled. Noemí rubbed her wrist and looked away. When they walked into Catalina's room she was surprised to see her cousin awake. Mary was also there. It seemed this would be a group reunion.

"Noemí, what is it?" Catalina asked, a book in her hands.

"I wanted to see how you were doing."

"Same as yesterday. Resting, mostly. It seems I'm the Sleeping Beauty."

Sleeping Beauty, Snow White. Noemí couldn't care less about that right now. But Catalina was smiling kindly, like she always used to smile. "You look tired. Anything wrong?"

Noemí hesitated and shook her head. "It's nothing. Do you want me to read to you?" she asked.

"I was going to have a cup of tea. Do you want to join me?"

"No."

Noemí wasn't sure what she had expected to find, but it wasn't Catalina in high spirits, the maid quietly arranging flowers in a vase, the meager blooms from the greenhouse. The scene struck her as artificial and yet there was nothing wrong. She stared at her cousin, trying to find the faintest trace of discomfort in her face.

"Really, Noemí. You seem a little odd. You aren't getting a cold, are you?" Catalina asked.

"I'm fine. I'll let you have your tea," Noemí said, unwilling to reveal more in the presence of the others. Not that they seemed terribly interested in this conversation.

She stepped outside. Virgil exited the room too and closed the door. They looked at each other.

"Are you satisfied?" he asked.

"I'm appeased. For now," she replied tersely, intending to walk back to her room alone, but he was going in the same direction, obviously wishing to continue their conversation and not minding her curtness.

"And I thought there was no appeasing you."

"What's that supposed to mean?" she asked.

"You're on a quest to find faults around you."

"Faults? No. Answers. And let me tell you, they're pretty big ones."

"Are they?"

"I saw this awful thing, moving—"

"Last night or now?"

"Now. And last night too," she muttered, pressing her hand against her forehead.

She realized then that if she headed back to her room she'd have to look at the ugly wallpaper with the hideous black stain on it. She wasn't ready to face it. Noemí changed course, quickly veering toward the stairs. She could always hide in the drawing room. It was the most comfortable room in the house.

"If you're having bad dreams I can ask the doctor for a remedy to help you sleep the next time he visits us," Virgil said.

She walked faster, intent on putting distance between him and her. "That won't do any good since I wasn't dreaming."

"You weren't dreaming last night? But you walked in your sleep."

She turned around. They were standing on the stairs, and he was three steps above her.

"That was different. Today I was awake. Today—"

"It all sounds very confusing," he interjected.

"That's because you're not giving me a chance to speak."

"You're very tired," he said dismissively as he began to descend those steps.

Noemí went down three more steps, attempting to maintain

the same gap between them. "Is that what you told her? You're very tired? Did she believe you?"

A moment later he had reached Noemí and bypassed her, descending the final steps to the ground floor. He turned to look at her.

"I think it's better if we leave it at this for now. You're agitated."

"I don't want to leave it at this," she said.

"Oh?"

Vigil slid a hand over the shoulder of the carved nymph that grasped the newel post at the bottom of the staircase. A sordid spark danced in his eyes. Or was she imagining that too? Was there something else to that casual "oh," to that smile spreading across his face?

She descended the steps, giving him a challenging look. But then her courage evaporated when he leaned forward and she thought he was about to transfer his hand to *her* shoulder.

In the dream there had been a strange taste in his mouth, like ripe fruit, and he, with the pinstriped jacket, hovering above her, taking off his clothes, slipping into the tub and touching her, while Noemí wrapped her arms around him. The memory was tinged with arousal, but also with a terrible humiliation.

*You'll be a good girl, won't you?* He'd told her that. And here they were now, wide awake, and she realized that he was capable of saying exactly that to her in real life. That he'd have no trouble snidely delivering such a line, that his strong hands could find her in the daylight or the dark.

She was afraid he'd touch her and of how she'd react. "I wish to leave High Place. Can you tell someone to drive me back to town?" she asked quickly.

"You're full of impulsiveness today, Noemí," he said. "Why would you be leaving us?"

"I don't need a reason."

She'd come back. Yes, that was right. Or even if she didn't leave, if she could get as far as the train station and write to her father, it would all be better. The world seemed to be collapsing around her, becoming a confused mess, dreams bleeding into her waking hours. If she was able to step out, to discuss the strange experiences she was having at High Place with Dr. Camarillo, then maybe she'd feel like herself again. Camarillo might even be able to help her figure out what was going on, or what she should do. Air. She needed fresh air.

"Of course not. But we can't drive you back with all this rain. I told you, the roads are treacherous."

She could see the raindrops splattered against the colored glass window on the second landing. "Then I'll walk back."

"You'll drag your suitcase in the mud? Perhaps you intend to use it as a boat and paddle away on it? Don't be silly," he said. "The rain must cease today, and we can attempt the drive tomorrow morning. Will that suffice?"

Now that he'd agreed to take her to town she was able to breath and unclench her tense hands. Noemí nodded.

"If you really are leaving us tomorrow, then you should have dinner with us one final time," Virgil said, sliding his hand off the nymph and glancing down the hallway, in the direction of the dining room.

"Very well. And I'll want to talk to Catalina too."

"Of course. Is there anything else?" he asked.

"No," she said. "There's nothing."

It wasn't a lie, but she still avoided his gaze, and for a moment she remained unmoving, not knowing whether he might continue following her as she went toward the sitting room. But remaining wouldn't do her any good either.

She began walking.

"Noemí?" he said.

She paused to look back at him.

"Please don't smoke again. It disturbs us," he said.

"Don't worry," she replied and, remembering the cigarette burn on her hand, she looked at her fingers. But the red, raw mark was gone. There was no sign of it at all.

Noemí held up her other hand, thinking that perhaps she'd mistaken which hand she'd injured. Nothing there either. She flexed her fingers and hurried to the sitting room, her steps loud as she walked. She thought she heard Virgil chuckle, but she wasn't sure. She wasn't sure of anything at all.

# 19

Noemí packed her suitcases slowly, feeling traitorous and second-guessing herself. Yes. No. Perhaps it would be best to remain. She truly did not wish to leave Catalina alone. But she'd said she was going to town, and it was vital that she clear her head. She decided she wouldn't quite return to Mexico City. Instead she would journey to Pachuca, where she'd write to her father and find a good doctor willing to accompany her back to High Place. The Doyles would be reluctant to allow this, but it was better than nothing.

Emboldened, with a plan of attack, she finished her packing and headed to dinner. Because it was her last night at High Place and because she didn't wish to seem haggard or defeated, she decided to wear a party dress. It was a buff-colored embroidered tulle dress with metallic gold accents, a yellow acetate bow at the waist, and a perfectly boned bodice. Not as full a skirt as she normally liked to wear, but very flattering and perfectly adequate for a dinner.

Obviously the Doyles had the same thought, treating this as an important, almost celebratory moment. The tablecloth of white damask was laid out, as were the silver candelabra, and a multitude of candles had been lit. In preparation for Noemí's departure they had lifted the ban on conversation, though this evening she might have enjoyed the silence. Her nerves were still much too raw from the strange hallucination she'd experienced. Even now Noemí wondered what had caused the bizarre episode.

She was getting a headache. Noemí blamed the wine. It was strong and yet very sweet; it lingered on the palate.

The poor company did not make matters any better. She must pretend cordiality for a little bit more, but her patience had been stretched to its limits. Virgil Doyle was a bully and Florence wasn't any better.

She glanced in Francis's direction. By her side sat the member of the Doyle family she appreciated. Poor Francis. He looked rather miserable that evening. She wondered if he'd drive her to town the next morning. She hoped so. It might give them time to speak in private. Could she trust him to take care of Catalina for her? She must ask for his help.

Francis eyed her back, a fleeting look. His lips parted to whisper a word before Virgil's loud voice hushed him. "We'll venture upstairs after supper, of course."

Noemí raised her head. She looked at Virgil. "I'm sorry?"

"I said my father expects us to all pay him a visit after supper. To say his goodbyes to you. You won't mind a short trip to his room, will you?"

"I wouldn't dream of leaving without saying goodbye," she replied.

"And yet you most eloquently wished to walk your way to town a few hours ago," Virgil said. The words had a mordant little twist.

If she liked Francis, then she had decided she could not stomach Virgil. He was hard and unpleasant, and beneath that veneer of wretched civility she knew he could be beastly. Most of all she loathed the way he was looking at her now, which he'd done before, a chilling little smirk on his lips and his eyes fixed on her with a rawness that made her want to cover her face.

In the dream, in the bathtub, she'd felt much the same. Yet there had also been another feeling running all through her. It was pleasurable, but in a terrible way, like when she'd had a cavity and kept pressing her tongue against it.

A panting, ferocious, and sickly lust.

It was a wicked thought to have at the dinner table, with him sitting across from her, and she looked down at her plate. This was a man who could know secrets, who could divine unarticulated desires. She must not look at him.

A long silence stretched between them as the maid walked in and began taking away the dishes.

"You might have trouble getting into town come morning," Florence said once more wine had been poured and dessert was set before them. "The roads will be terrible."

"Yes, all these floods." Noemí nodded. "That is how you lost the mine?"

"Ages ago," Florence replied, waving a hand in the air. "Virgil was a baby."

Virgil nodded. "It was waterlogged. Anyway, it's not like it was being worked on. With the Revolution going on, you couldn't get nearly enough workers here. They'd all be fighting for one side or the other. You need a constant influx of workers at a mine like this."

"I suppose it was impossible to get people back after the Revolution ended? Had they all gone away?" Noemí asked.

"Yes, and besides, we had no way to hire new crews, and my father was ill for a long time, so he couldn't oversee the work. Of course, that'll change soon."

"How so?"

"Catalina hasn't mentioned it? It is our intention to open up the mine again."

"But it's been closed for a very long time. I thought your finances were strained," Noemí protested.

"Catalina has decided to invest in it."

"You didn't mention that before."

"It slipped my mind."

He spoke so casually that one might be tempted to actually believe him. But Noemí was betting he had kept his lips tightly shut knowing the conclusion she would draw based on that: that Catalina was going to serve as a docile piggy bank.

If he was speaking now, it was because he meant to rile her up a little, to throw in her direction that sharp smile he had deftly shown her on more than one occasion. He wished to gloat. Because she was going away, after all, so a little gloating couldn't hurt now.

"Is it very wise to do such a thing?" she asked. "With your wife in her condition?"

"It is not as if it'll make her worse, don't you think?"

"I think it's callous."

"We've long been simply existing at High Place, Noemí. Too long. It is now time to grow again. The plant must find the light, and we must find our way in this world. You may consider that callous. I find it natural. And, in the end, it was you who was speaking of change to me the other day."

How lovely that he should pin this project on her. Noemí pushed her chair back. "Maybe I should say good night to your father now. I'm tired."

Virgil held the stem of his glass and raised an eyebrow at her. "I suppose we could skip dessert."

"Virgil, it's much too early," Francis protested.

He had spoken only those words that evening, but both Virgil and Florence turned their heads in his direction brusquely, as if he'd been saying offensive things all night long. Noemí guessed that he was not supposed to offer any sort of opinions. It did not surprise her.

"I'd say it's about the right time," Virgil replied.

They stood up. Florence led the way, taking an oil lamp that rested on a sideboard. The house was very chilly that evening, and Noemí crossed her arms against her chest, wondering if Howard would want to talk for long. Dear Lord, she hoped not. She wished to sneak under the covers and go to sleep as quickly as possible so that she might wake up early and jump into the blasted car.

Florence opened the door to Howard's room, and Noemí followed her in. A fire was burning, and the curtains around the large bed were closed tight. There was an ugly smell in the air. Too pungent. Like a ripe fruit. Noemí frowned.

"We are here," Florence said, setting her oil lamp down on the mantelpiece above the fireplace. "We have your visitor."

Florence then went by the bed and began peeling the curtains away. Noemí schooled her features into a polite smile, ready for the sight of Howard Doyle tucked neatly under the covers or perhaps lounging against the pillows in his green robe.

She did not expect him to be lying there, over the blankets, naked. His skin was terribly pale and his veins contrasted grotesquely against his whiteness, indigo lines running up and down his body. Yet that was not the worst of it. One of his legs was hideously bloated, crusted over with dozens of large, dark boils.

She had no idea what they were. Not tumors, no, for they pulsed quickly, and their fullness contrasted with his emaciated body, the skin grown taut against the bones except upon that leg where the boils grew, as thick as barnacles upon a ship's hull.

It was horrid, horrid, and she thought he was a corpse, afflicted by the ravages of putrefaction, but he *lived*. His chest rose and dipped, and he breathed.

"You must get closer," Virgil whispered into her ear and clasped her tight by the arm.

The shock had prevented Noemí from moving, but now that she felt his hand closing around her, she attempted to shove Virgil away and rush to the door. He yanked her back, though, with a vicious strength that threatened to snap her bones, and she gasped in pain, but still she fought him.

"Come on, help me here," Virgil said, looking at Francis.

"Let go of me!" she screamed.

Francis did not approach them, but Florence grabbed Noemí's free arm, and together Virgil and the woman dragged Noemí toward the head of the bed. She twisted her body and managed to kick the night table, sending a porcelain chamber pot crashing onto the floor.

"Kneel down," Virgil ordered her.

"No," Noemí said.

They shoved her down, Virgil's fingers digging into her flesh, and he placed a hand behind her neck.

Howard Doyle turned his head upon the pillow and looked at her. His lips were as bloated as his leg, crusted with black growths, and a trail of dark fluid dripped down his chin, staining his bedclothes. This was the source of the bad smell in the room, and up close the stench was so awful she thought she would retch.

"My God," she said and tried to get up, to scuttle away, but Virgil's hand was a band of iron around her neck, and he was pushing her even closer to the old man.

And the man was rising in his bed, turning and stretching out a thin hand, his fingers digging into Noemí's hair and pulling their faces closer.

She was able, at this disgustingly intimate distance, to clearly see the color of his eyes. They were not blue. The color was diluted by a bright, golden sheen, like flecks of molten gold.

Howard Doyle smiled at her, showing off his stained teeth—stained with black—and then he pressed his lips against hers. Noemí felt his tongue in her mouth and then saliva burning down her throat as he pressed himself against her and Virgil propped her in place.

He let go of her after long, agonizing minutes, and Noemí was able to gasp and turn her head.

She closed her eyes.

She felt very light; her thoughts were scattered. Drowsy. *My God*, she told herself, *my God, stand up, run.* Over and over again.

When she looked around, she tried to focus her eyes and saw that she was in a cave. There were people there. A man had been handed a cup, and he was drinking from it. The hideous liquid burned his mouth, and he almost passed out, but the others laughed and they clasped his shoulder in a friendly manner. *They hadn't been so friendly when he'd first arrived, a stranger in these parts. They were skittish, and for good reason.*

The man was fair-haired, and his eyes were blue. He shared a resemblance with Howard, with Virgil. The shape of the jaw, the nose. But his clothes and his shoes and everything about him and the men in the cave pointed to a previous time.

*When is this?* Noemí thought. But she felt dizzy, and the sound of the sea distracted her. This cave, was the ocean nearby? The cave was dark; one of the men held a lantern, but it did not provide much illumination. The others continued with their jokes, and two of them helped the blond man up. He stumbled.

The man wasn't doing very well, but that wasn't their fault. He'd long been ill. His physician said there was no cure. There was no hope, but Doyle had hoped.

*Doyle.* That was him, yes. She was with Doyle.

*Doyle was dying and in his desperation he'd found his way here, seeking a remedy for those who were beyond remedies. Instead of a peregrination to a holy site, he'd come to this wretched cave.*

*They hadn't liked him, no, but these folk were poor, and he had a fat purse of silver. Of course, he'd feared they'd cut his throat and take the silver, but what else was there to be done? All he could manage was to promise them there'd be more where that came from if they kept their end of the bargain.*

*Money wasn't everything, of course. He knew as much. They recognized him as their natural superior. Force of habit, he imagined. My lord spilled from their lips, even though these were scavengers.*

In the corner of the cave Noemí saw a woman. Her hair was stringy, her face plain and pasty. She held a shawl around her shoulders with a bony hand and looked at Doyle with interest. There was a priest too, an old man who tended to the altar of their god. For in the end this *was* indeed a holy site of a strange sort. Instead of candles, the fungus hanging from the cave walls, luminescent, lit a crude altar. Upon it there were a bowl and a cup and a pile of old bones.

*If he died, Doyle thought, his bones would be added to that pile. But he was not afraid. He was half dead already.*

Noemí rubbed a hand against her temples. A terrible headache was building inside her skull. She squinted, and the room wavered, like a flame. She tried to focus on something and fixed her eyes on Doyle.

Doyle. She'd seen him stumbling around, his face worn down by disease, but now he looked so hearty she almost confused him with another man. His vitality restored, one would have expected him to return home at once. But here he was lingering, running a hand down the woman's naked back. They'd married, following the custom of her people. Noemí felt his disgust as he touched the woman, but he kept a smile on his face. He must dissimulate.

*He needed them. Needed to be accepted, needed to be one with these rough folk. For only then could he know all their secrets. Eternal life! It was there for the taking. The fools didn't understand it. They used the fungus to heal their wounds and preserve their health, but it could be so much more. He'd seen it, the evidence was in the priest they blindly obeyed, and what he hadn't witnessed he'd imagined. There were such possibilities!*

*The woman, she wouldn't do. He'd known that from the start. But Doyle had two sisters, back in his great home awaiting his return, and that was the trick. It was in the blood, in his blood, the priest had said so already. And if it could be in his blood it could be in their blood.*

Noemí pressed her fingertips against her forehead. The headache was growing stronger, and her vision blurred.

*Doyle. Sharp, he was. Always had been, and even when his body had failed him, his mind was a blade. Now the body was alive, vital, and he thrummed with eagerness.*

*The priest recognized his strength, whispered that he might be the future of their congregation, that a man like him was necessary. The holy man was old and he feared for the future, for his little flock in the cave, for these timid folk. Picking through wreckage, scrambling in the dirt, that was their life. They'd fled here seeking safety and they'd survived till now, but the world was changing.*

*The holy man was right. Too right, perhaps. For Doyle indeed envisioned a deep change.*

*Lungs filled with water, the priest weighed down. What a simple death!*

*And then it was chaos and violence and smoke. Fire, fire, burning. The cave was deemed almost a fortress by its inhabitants. When the tide came in, it was cut off from land and only approachable by boat, rendering it a cozy, safe hideout. They hadn't much, but they had this.*

*He was a single man and there were three dozen of them, but he'd killed the priest and now he held sway over them. He was holy. They were forced to remain on their knees as he set their bundles of cloth, their possessions, on fire. The cave filled with smoke.*

*There was a boat. He pulled the woman into the boat. She obeyed, numb and afraid. As he rowed off, she stared at him, and he glanced away.*

*He'd thought her unattractive. She was now frightfully ugly, with her belly grown and her eyes dull. But she was necessary. She would serve a purpose.*

And then Noemí wasn't with *him* as she'd been all this time, as close as his shadow. She was with someone else, a woman, with her fair hair falling loose around her shoulders as she spoke to another girl.

"He has changed," the young woman whispered. "Don't you see it? His eyes are not the same."

The other girl, her hair plaited, shook her head.

Noemí shook her head too. Their brother, gone on a long voyage and now returned and there were so many questions to ask, but he wouldn't let them speak. And the first woman, she thought a horror had befallen him, that an evil possessed him, but the other one, she knew this had always been him, under the skin.

*I feared evil long ago. I feared him.*

Under the skin, and Noemí looked down at her hands, at her wrist, which itched terribly. Before she could scratch herself pustules erupted and there rose tendrils, like hairs, upon her skin. Her velvety body fruited. Fleshy, white, fan-shaped caps sliced through her marrow and her muscle, and when she opened her mouth liquid poured up, gold and black, like a river that stained the floor.

A hand on her shoulder and a whisper in her ear.

"Open your eyes," said Noemí reflexively. Her mouth was full of blood and she spat out her own teeth.

# 20

reathe. Just breathe," he told her.

He was a voice. She couldn't see him well, because the pain blurred her eyes and the tears didn't help in that regard. He held her hair back as she vomited and helped her stand up. Black and gold specks danced under her eyelids when she closed them. She'd never felt this sick in her life.

"I'll die," she croaked.

"You won't," he assured her.

Hadn't she died? She thought she had. There had been blood and bile in her mouth.

She stared at the man. She thought she knew him, but his name escaped her. She was having trouble thinking, remembering, separating her thoughts from other thoughts. Other memories. Who was she?

*Doyle*, she'd been Doyle, and Doyle had killed all those people, burned them all.

The snake, it bites its tail.

The young, skinny man walked her out of the bathroom and pressed a glass of water against her lips.

She lay on the bed and turned her head. Francis sat on a chair, close to her, dabbing the sweat that beaded her forehead. Francis, yes. And she was Noemí Taboada, and this was High Place. It came back to her, the horror she'd been subjected to, the bloated body of Howard Doyle and his spit in her mouth.

She recoiled. Francis froze, then slowly handed her the hand-kerchief he'd been holding. She clutched it in one hand.

"What did you do to me?" she asked. It hurt to speak. Her throat felt scratchy. She recalled the filth that had poured into her mouth, and she suddenly wished to run into the bathroom again, to vomit her guts out.

"Do you need to get up?" he asked, readying a hand to help her.

"No," she said, knowing she couldn't reach the bathroom on her own, but also not wanting him to touch her.

He slid his hands into his jacket's pockets. The corduroy jacket she'd thought looked good on him. The bastard. She regretted every nice thing she'd ever thought of him.

"I'm supposed to explain," he said, his voice quiet.

"How the hell are you explaining that?! Howard . . . he . . . you . . . *how?*"

Christ. She couldn't even put it into words. The damn horror of it. Of the black bile in her mouth and then the vision she'd had.

"I'll tell you the story and then you can ask me questions. I think that would be the easiest thing," he said.

Noemí didn't want to do any talking. She didn't think she could talk much, even if she tried. Better to let him speak, even if she felt like punching him. She was so tired, so sick.

"I suppose now you realize we are not like other people and this house is not like other houses. A long time ago, Howard, he found a fungus which is able to extend human life quite a bit. It can cure diseases; it keeps you healthy."

"I saw that. I saw him," she muttered.

"You did?" Francis replied. "I suppose you entered the gloom. How deep have you gone into it?"

She stared at him. He was confusing her more. He shook his head.

"The fungus, it runs under the house, all the way to the cemetery and back. It's in the walls. Like a giant spider's web. In that web we can preserve memories, thoughts, caught like the flies that wander into a real web. We call that repository of our thoughts, of our memories, *the gloom*."

"How is that possible?"

"Fungi can enter into symbiotic relationships with host plants. Mycorrhiza. Well, it turns out that it can also have a symbiotic relationship with humans. The mycorrhiza in this house creates the gloom."

"You have access to ancestral memories because of a fungus."

"Yes. Only some of them are not full memories; you get faint echoes and they're jumbled."

*Like not being able to tune to a radio station,* she thought. Noemí looked at the corner on the wall that was defaced by the black mold. "I've seen and dreamt very strange things. Are you telling me the house has done that? Because there's a fungus running inside of it?"

"Yes."

"Why would it do that to me?"

"It wouldn't be intentional. I guess it's in its nature."

Every damn vision she had experienced had been terrifying. Whatever this *thing's* nature was, she couldn't begin to understand it. A nightmare. That's what it was. A living nightmare, sins and malevolent secrets fastened together.

"Then I was right about your house being haunted. And my cousin is not insane, she's simply seen this gloom."

Francis nodded, and Noemí chuckled. No wonder Francis had been so agitated when she had suggested there was a rational explanation to Catalina's strange behavior and her talk of ghosts. Not that she would have guessed it was all connected to mushrooms.

She glanced at the oil lamp burning by her bedside and realized she had no idea how much time had passed. How long she'd been in the gloom. It could have been hours, it could have been days. She couldn't hear the patter of the rain anymore.

"What did Howard Doyle do to me?" she asked.

"The fungus is in the walls of the house and it's in the air. You don't realize it, but you're breathing it in. Slowly, it has an effect on you. But if you come in contact with it in other ways, the effect can accelerate."

"What did he *do* to me?" she repeated.

"Most people who come in contact with this fungus die. That's what happened to the workers in the mine. It killed them, some faster than others. But obviously not everyone perishes. Some people are more resistant to it. If they don't die, though, it can still affect their mind."

"Like Catalina?"

"Sometimes a little and sometimes worse than Catalina. It can burn out your own self. Our servants, you might have noticed they don't talk much. There's very little of them left. It's almost like their mind has been carved out."

"That's not possible."

Francis shook his head. "Have you ever known an alcoholic? It affects their brain, and so does this."

"Are you telling me that's what's going to happen to Catalina? To me?"

"No!" Francis said quickly. "No, no. They're a special case, Great Uncle Howard calls them his bondservants, and the miners, they were mulch. But you can have a symbiotic relationship with the fungus. None of that will happen to you."

"What *will* happen to me?"

Francis's hands were still firmly in his pockets, but he was fidgeting. She could tell, the fingers clenching and unclenching. He was looking down at the cover on her bed.

"I've told you about the gloom. I haven't told you about the bloodline. We're special. The fungus bonds with us, it's not noxious. It can even make us immortal. Howard has lived many lives, in many different bodies. He transfers his consciousness to the gloom and then from the gloom he can live again, in the body of one of his children."

"He possesses his children?" Noemí said.

"No . . . he becomes . . . they become him . . . they become someone new. Only the children, it goes down the bloodline. And for generations the bloodline has been kept isolated, to ensure we were all able to interact with the fungus, that we would keep this symbiotic relationship. No outsiders."

"Incest. He married two women who were sisters, and he was going to marry Ruth to her cousin, and before that he must have . . . his sisters," Noemí said, suddenly remembering the vision she'd had. The two young women. "He had two sisters. God, he had children with them."

"Yes."

The Doyle look. All the people in those portraits. "How far back?" Noemí asked. "How old is he? How many generations?"

"I don't know. Three hundred years, maybe more."

"Three hundred years. Marrying his own kin, having children with them, then transferring his mind into one of their bodies. Over and over again. And all of you? You allow this?"

"We have no choice. He's a god."

"You have a damn choice! And that sick fuck is not a god!"

Francis stared at her. He had taken his hands out of his pockets and was now clutching them together. He looked tired. Slowly he slid a hand up and touched his forehead; he shook his head.

"He is to us," he said. "And he wants you to be part of our family."

"Then that's why he poured that black sludge down my throat."

"They were afraid you were going to leave. They couldn't let you do that. Now you won't be able to go anywhere."

"I don't want to be part of your god damn family, Francis," she said. "And believe me, I'm going to go back home and I'm going to—"

"It won't let you go. My father, I don't think I told you about him, did I?"

She had been looking at the black marks on the wall, the mold in the corner of her room, but she slowly turned her head to look at him. He had taken out a little portrait from his pocket. This is what he clutched in his hand, she thought. The little picture nestling in his jacket's pocket.

"Richard," Francis whispered, allowing her to look at the black-and-white photograph of a man. "His name was Richard."

The sharpness of Francis's sallow face vaguely reminded her of Virgil Doyle, but now she could see the traces of his father: the pointed chin, the broad forehead.

"Ruth caused a lot of damage. It wasn't just the people she killed; she hurt Howard very badly. No *normal* man would have survived after she shot him, not the way she did it. He survived. But his grip, his power, decreased. That's why we lost all our workers."

"They were all hypnotized? Like your three servants?"

"No. Not quite. He couldn't possibly manipulate that many people at once. It was a more subtle push and pull. It affected them, though. The house, the fungus, it affected the miners. It was a fog that could dull your senses when he needed it."

"What about your father?" she asked, handing him back the portrait, which he tucked in his pocket.

"After Howard was shot, he slowly began to heal himself. It has been hard, in recent generations, for the family to have children. When my mother came of age, Howard tried to . . . but he was too old, too damaged, to give her a child. And there were other troubles too."

*His niece. He tried to have a child with his niece*, Noemí thought, and the fleeting idea of that hideous thing she'd seen naked laboring over a woman, pressing its emaciated body against Florence, made her want to hurl again. She pressed the handkerchief to her mouth.

"Noemí?" Francis asked.

"What troubles?" she replied, urging him on.

"Money. The remaining workers all left when Howard's control over them snapped, and there was no one to watch the mine, so it flooded. There was no money coming in, and the Revolution had already ruined much of our finances. They needed money and they needed children. Otherwise, what would happen to the bloodline? My mother found my father, and she thought he'd do. He had a little money. Not a huge fortune, but enough to tide us over, and most important she thought he could get her with child. He came to live here, to High Place. They had me. I was a boy, but the idea was that he might give her more children, that he might give her girls.

"The gloom, it affected him. He felt himself going mad. He wanted to leave, but he couldn't. He never could get far. He threw himself down a ravine in the end. If you fight it, then it will hurt. It will be bad," Francis warned her. "But if you obey, if you bond with it, if you agree to be part of the family, then it will be fine."

"Catalina fights it, doesn't she?"

"Yes," Francis admitted. "But it's also that she is not . . . she's not quite as compatible—"

Noemí shook her head. "What makes you think I'll comply any more than she has?"

"You're compatible. Virgil, he picked Catalina because he knew she'd be compatible, but when you came here, it became obvious you're even more suitable than her. I guess they hope you'll be more understanding."

"That I'll be happy to join your family. That I'll be happy to what? Give you my money? Maybe give you children?"

"Yes. Yes, to both."

"You're a pack of monsters. And you! I trusted you."

He stared at her intently, his mouth quivering. She thought he might cry. It made her furious. That he should be the one breaking down and weeping. *Don't you dare*, she thought.

"I'm so sorry."

"Sorry! You god damn bastard!" she yelled, and despite the fact that her body still throbbed with a horrible, dull pain she stood up.

"I am sorry. I didn't want this," he said, pushing his chair back, getting up too.

"Then help me! Get me out of here!"

"I can't."

She hit him. It wasn't a good punch, and as soon as she threw it she thought she was going to collapse on the floor. It robbed her of all strength, and she felt suddenly boneless. If he hadn't caught her, surely she'd have cracked her head open. Yet she scrambled against him, trying to shove him off.

"Let go," she demanded, but her voice was muffled against the folds of his jacket. She couldn't pull her head up.

"You need to rest. I'll think of a solution, but you need to rest," he whispered.

"Go to hell!"

He deposited her carefully on the bed again, pulling the covers up, and she wanted to tell him to go to hell one last time, but her eyes were closing, and in the corner of the room the mold was beating like a heart, stretching out, making the wallpaper ripple. The floorboards also swayed, trembling like the skin of a living thing.

A great snake rose from under the floorboards, slick and black, and slid over the covers. Noemí stared at it as it touched her legs, its skin cool against her feverish flesh, and she didn't move, fearing it would rear its head back and bite her. And upon the snake's skin there were a thousand tiny little growths, tiny pulsating points, which quivered and unleashed spores.

*It's another dream*, she thought. *It's the gloom, and the gloom isn't real.*

But she didn't want to see this, she didn't want to, and she moved her legs at last, trying to kick the thing away. When she touched the snake its skin split open, and it was white and dead, the carcass of a snake ravaged by decay. Life teemed upon this white corpse, mold blooming all over it.

*Et Verbum caro factum est,* said the snake.

She was on her knees now. The chamber was cold and made of stone. It was dark; there were no windows. They'd set candles upon an altar, but it was still much too dark. The altar was more elaborate than the one she'd spied in the caves. The table was covered with a red velvet cloth and silver candelabra. But it was still dark and humid and cold.

Howard Doyle had added tapestries too. Red and black, the ouroboros displayed on them. Pageantry, Doyle understood pageantry was an important part of this game. There he was, Doyle, clad in crimson. Next to him stood the woman from the caves, heavily pregnant, and looking ill.

*Et Verbum caro factum est,* the snake told her, whispering secrets in her ear. The snake was gone, but she could still hear it. It had a peculiar, hoarse voice, and Noemí had no idea what it was telling her.

Two women were helping her down a dais, to lie down at the foot of the altar. Two blond women. She'd seen them too, before. The sisters. And she'd seen this ritual before. In the cemetery. The woman giving birth in the cemetery.

Birth. The child cried out, and Doyle held the child. And then she knew.

*Et Verbum caro factum est.*

She knew what she had not properly seen in her previous dreams, and she did not wish to see now, but there it was. The knife and the child. Noemí closed her eyes, but even behind her eyelids she saw it all, crimson and black and the child torn apart and they were *eating* him.

Flesh of the gods.

They held their hands up, and Doyle deposited bits of flesh, bits of bone, into their hands and they chewed this pale meat.

They'd done this before, in the caves. But it had been the priests, when they died, who offered their flesh. Doyle had perfected the ritual. Clever Doyle, who was well learned, and had read plenty of books on theology, biology, medicine, looking for answers, and now he'd found them.

Noemí's eyes were still closed, and the woman's eyes were closed too. They pressed a cloth against her face, and Noemí thought they would kill the woman now, they would also cut up her body and ingest it. But she was wrong on this point. They swaddled the body. Swaddled it tight, and there was a pit by the altar, and they were throwing her into it but she was *alive*.

*She's not dead*, Noemí told them. But it didn't matter. It was a memory.

*It was necessary, always is. The fungus would erupt up, from her body, up through the soil, weaving itself into the walls, extending itself into the foundations of the building. And the gloom needed a mind. It needed her. The gloom was alive. It was alive in more than one way; at its rotten core there was the corpse of a woman, her limbs twisted, her hair brittle against the skull. And the corpse stretched its jaws open, screaming inside the earth, and from her dried lips emerged the pale mushroom.*

*The priest would have sacrificed himself: part of the body devoured, the rest buried. Life erupting from those remains, and the congregation tied to him. Tied ultimately to their god. But Doyle was no fool who would offer himself in sacrifice.*

*Doyle could be a god without having to obey their arcane, foolish rules.*

*Doyle was a god.*

*Doyle existed, persisted.*

*Doyle always is.*

*Monsters. Monstrum, ah, is that what you think of me, Noemí?*

"Have you seen enough, curious girl?" Doyle asked.

He was playing cards in a corner of her room. She watched his wrinkled hands, the amber ring upon his index finger flashing bright under the light of the candles as he shuffled the cards. He raised his head to look at her. She stared at him. It was the Doyle of now. Howard Doyle, his spine bent, his breath labored. He placed three cards down, carefully turning each one. A knight with a sword and a page holding a coin. She could see, through the thin shirt he wore, the black boils dotting his back.

"Why do you show me this?" she asked.

"The house shows you. The house loves you. Are you enjoying our hospitality? Would you like to play with me?" he asked.

"No."

"A pity," he said, revealing the third card: a single, empty cup. "You'll still renounce yourself in the end. You're already like us, you're family. You don't know it."

"You don't scare me, you piece of shit monster, with your dreams and your tricks. This isn't real, and you'll never keep me here."

"You really think that?" he asked, and the boils rippled down his back. A trickle of black liquid, as black as ink, dripped onto the floor beneath him. "I can make you do anything I want."

He sliced one of the pustules in his hands with a long nail, pressing it against a silver cup—it looked like the goblet in the card he'd been holding—and it broke, filling the cup with a foul liquid. "Have a drink," he said, and for a second she felt compelled to step forward and take a sip, before revulsion and alarm froze her limbs.

He smiled. He was trying to show her his power; even in dreams he was the master.

"I'll kill you when I wake up. Give me a chance, I'll kill you," she swore.

She threw herself at him, sinking her fingers into his flesh, wringing the thin neck. It was like parchment, it tore beneath her hands, muscle and blood vessels showing. He grinned at her, with Virgil's brutish smile. He was Virgil. She squeezed harder, and then he was pushing her back, his thumb pressing against her lips, against her teeth.

Francis looked at her, his eyes wide with pain, his hand sliding down. She let go of him and stepped back. Francis opened his mouth, to plead with her, and a hundred maggots crawled out of his maw.

Worms, stems, the snake in the grass rose and wrapped itself around Noemí's neck.

*You're ours, like it or not. You're ours and you're us.*

She tried to peel the snake off her, but it knotted itself tight, digging into her flesh, and it opened its jaws, ready to devour her whole. Noemí dug her nails into the snake, and it whispered "*Et Verbum caro factum est.*"

But a woman's voice also spoke, and she said, "Open your eyes."

*I must remember that,* she thought. *I must remember to open my eyes.*

aylight. She'd never been more thankful for such an ordinary sight, the beams of light filtering under the curtains making her heart soar. Noemí flung the curtain aside and pressed her palms against the window. She tried the door. It was, predictably, locked.

They had left a tray with food for her. The tea had gone cold, and she didn't dare drink it, wondering what might be in it. Even the toast gave her pause. She ended up nibbling at the edges of the slice of bread and drinking water from the bathroom's faucet.

If the fungus was in the air, though, did it matter? She was inhaling it anyway. The closet door was open, and she could see they'd emptied her suitcase and returned all her dresses to their hangers.

It was cold, so she put on her long-sleeved plaid dress with the Peter Pan collar and the matching white cuffs. It was warm enough, even if she had never quite favored plaid. She couldn't even remember why she'd packed it, but she was glad she had.

Once she'd combed her hair and put on her shoes, Noemí tried to open the window again, but it didn't budge. Neither did the door. The cutlery they'd left included a spoon, which would be of no help to her. Just as she was wondering if the spoon could be used to pry the door open, the key turned in the lock, and Florence stood at the doorway. As usual, she seemed extremely peeved to see Noemí. The feeling, that day, was entirely mutual.

"Do you intend to starve yourself?" Florence asked, eyeing the tray by the door, which Noemí had barely touched.

"Can't say I have much of an appetite after what happened," Noemí replied flatly.

"You'll have to eat. In any case, Virgil wants to see you. He's waiting in the library. Come along."

Noemí followed the woman down the hallways and down the stairs. Florence did not speak to her, and Noemí moved two steps behind her at all times, until they reached the ground floor and Noemí dashed toward the front door. She feared they might have locked it, but the door handle turned, and she burst out into the misty morning. It was quite thick, this mist, but it didn't matter. She dashed blindly into it.

Tall grasses brushed her body, and her dress caught on something. She heard it ripping, but she tugged at the skirt and kept going. It was raining, the slightest drizzle dampening her hair. And even if there had been thunder and lightning and hail she wouldn't have stopped.

But Noemí did in fact stop. She was suddenly out of breath, and even when she stood still, tried to calm herself and breathe in, she could hardly accomplish it. She felt as though a hand were squeezing her throat and she gasped, stumbling against a tree, its low branches scratching her temple, and let out a sharp hiss, touching her head, feeling blood under her fingertips.

She needed to walk more slowly, needed to see where she was going, but the mist was thick, and the breathlessness did not subside. She slipped, tumbling to the ground, and lost a shoe. It was there and suddenly gone.

Noemí attempted to push herself up to her feet again, but the relentless pressure against her throat made it difficult to summon the necessary strength. She managed to get on her knees. Blindly she tried to reach for the missing shoe and gave up on it. It didn't matter where it was. She tugged the other shoe off.

Barefoot, she'd continue on barefoot. She clutched her remaining shoe in one hand, trying to think. The mist shrouded everything. The trees and the shrubs and the house. She had no idea in which direction she should go, but she could hear the grasses rustling, and she was certain someone was coming for her.

She still couldn't breathe, her throat was on fire. She gasped, trying to force air into her lungs. Noemí dug her fingers into the wet earth and stood up, dragging herself forward. Four, five, six steps before she stumbled again and was back on her knees.

It was too late by then. Through the mist came a tall, dark figure, which bent down next to her. She raised her hands, to ward it off, to no avail. He bent down, the man, he picked her up as easily as one lifted a rag doll, and she shook her head.

She struck, blindly, the shoe hitting his face, and he let out an angry grunt. He released her, dropping her in the mud. Noemí shifted forward, ready to crawl away if it came to it, but she hadn't really hurt him, and he clutched her, pulled her into his arms.

He was taking her back to the house, and she couldn't even protest; it was as if in the struggle her throat had been sealed almost completely shut and now she could barely draw in any air. To make it even worse, she realized how close the house really was, how she'd scarcely walked more than a few meters before collapsing on the ground.

She saw the porch, the front entrance, and turned her head to look up at the man.

Virgil. He'd opened the door and now they were going up the stairs. The round, colored glass window at the top of the staircase had a thin snake etched in red around the rim. She hadn't noticed it before, but now the image was clear: the snake was biting its tail.

They headed to her room and into the bathroom. He gingerly placed her in the bathtub, and she gasped as he opened the tap and water began to flow into the tub.

"Get out of those clothes and clean yourself," he said.

The shortness of breath was gone. Like flipping a switch. But her heart was still racing, and she stared at him, her mouth slightly open, her hands holding on to the sides of the bathtub.

"You'll catch a cold," he said simply, and he stretched out a hand, as if to undo the top button of her dress.

Noemí slapped his hand away and clutched the collar of her dress. "Don't!" she yelled, and it hurt to speak, that one word slicing her tongue.

He chuckled, amused. "This is your fault, Noemí. You decided to take a tumble in the mud, in the rain, and now you must wash yourself. So, get out of those clothes before I make you," he said. There was no threat in his voice; he sounded very measured, but his face was infused with a simmering animosity.

She undid the buttons with shaky hands and took the dress off, crumpling it into a ball and tossing it on the floor. She was left in her underthings. She thought that humiliation would be enough for him, but he leaned against the wall and cocked his head, looking at her.

"Well?" he said. "You're filthy. Take off everything and wash yourself. Your hair is a mess."

"As soon as you step out of the bathroom."

He grabbed the three-legged stool and sat down, looking unperturbed. "I'm not going anywhere."

"I'm not getting naked in front of you."

He leaned forward, as if to share a secret with her. "I can *make you* get out of those clothes. It won't take me a minute, and I will hurt you. Or you can take them off yourself, like a good girl."

He meant it. She still felt light-headed, and the water was too hot, but she peeled off her undergarments and tossed them away, to rest in a corner of the bathroom. She grabbed the bar of soap sitting on a porcelain dish and scrubbed her head, soaped her arms and her hands. She worked quickly, rinsing the soap out.

Virgil had closed the tap, his left elbow resting on the edge of the tub. At least he was looking at the floor rather than at her, apparently content to admire the tiles. He rubbed his mouth with his fingers.

"You cut my lip with your shoe," he said.

There was a trail of blood on his lips, and Noemí was glad that at least she'd managed that. "Is that why you're torturing me?"

"Torture? I wanted to make sure you didn't faint in the bath. It would be a pity if you drowned while in the tub."

"You could have stood guard outside the door, you pig," she told him, brushing a wet strand of her hair away from her face.

"Yes. But that wouldn't be half as much fun," he replied. His grin would have been charming if she'd met him at a party, if she didn't know him. He had fooled Catalina with that smile, but it was a predator's grin. It made her want to hit him again, to beat him in the name of her cousin.

The faucet was dripping. *Plop, plop, plop.* It was the only noise in the bathroom. She raised a hand, pointed behind him.

"You can pass me the robe now."

He didn't reply.

"I said, you can—"

His hand dipped into the water, settling on her leg, and Noemí pushed herself back, slamming against the tub, making water splash onto the floor. Her instinct was to stand up, jump out of the tub, and run out of the room. But the position he occupied meant her path would be blocked if she did. He knew it too. The tub, the water, seemed to the young woman her shield, and she drew her knees against her chest.

"Get out," she said, trying to sound firm rather than afraid.

"What? Are you suddenly bashful?" he asked. "Last time we were here it wasn't the case."

"That was a dream," she stammered.

"It doesn't mean it wasn't real."

She blinked incredulously at him, and she opened her mouth to protest. Virgil leaned forward, his hand settling on the back of her neck, and she shrieked, pushing him away, but he'd gotten hold of her hair and was tipping her head back, pulling it hard.

He'd done that in the dream, or a similar motion. Pulled her head up and kissed her, and afterward she'd wanted him.

She tried to turn her head away.

"Virgil," Francis said loudly. He was standing by the doorway, his hands curled into tight fists at his side.

Virgil turned his head toward his cousin. "Yes?" he said, his voice hard.

"Dr. Cummins is here. He's ready to see her."

Virgil let out a sigh and gave Noemí a shrug, releasing her. "Well, it seems we'll continue our chat some other time," he declared and walked out of the bathroom.

She had not expected him to release her, and her relief was so profound she pressed both hands against her mouth and bent forward, gasping.

"Dr. Cummins wants to check up on you. Do you need help getting out of the tub?" Francis asked. He spoke softly.

She shook her head. Her face was burning, flushed with mortification.

Francis had grabbed a folded towel from a pile upon a shelf, and he wordlessly handed it to her. She looked up at him and clutched the towel.

"I'll be in the room," Francis said.

He walked out of the bathroom and closed the door behind him. Noemí dried herself and put on her robe.

When she stepped out of the bathroom Dr. Cummins was standing by the bed and gestured for her to sit down on it. He took Noemí's pulse, checked her heartbeat, then opened a bottle with rubbing alcohol and dampened a ball of cotton with it. He pressed the piece of cotton against her temple. Noemí had forgotten about the scratch she'd incurred, and she winced.

"How is she?" Francis asked. He was standing behind the doctor, looking anxious.

"She'll be fine. There's nothing but a couple of scrapes. It won't even necessitate a bandage. But it shouldn't have happened. I thought you had explained to her the situation already," the doctor said. "If she'd damaged her face Howard would have been very sore about it."

"You shouldn't be mad at him. Francis did explain that I'm in a house full of incestuous monsters and their toadies," Noemí replied.

Dr. Cummins stilled his fingers and frowned. "Well. You haven't lost that charming way of addressing your elders. Fill a glass with water, Francis," the doctor said as he continued dabbing at her hairline. "The girl is dehydrated."

"I can manage," she replied, snatching away the piece of cotton and pressing it against her head.

The doctor shrugged and tossed his stethoscope in his black bag. "Francis was supposed to talk to you, but he must not have made himself clear last night. You can't leave this house, Miss Taboada. No one can. It won't let you. If you try to run off, you'll suffer another attack like the one you had."

"How can a house do that?"

"It can. That is all that matters."

Francis approached the bed with the glass of water and handed it to her. Noemí took a couple of sips, carefully eyeing both men. Cummins's face caught her eye; there was a detail she had not noticed before and which now seemed obvious.

"You're related to them, aren't you? You're another Doyle."

"Distantly, which is why I live in the village, managing the family's affairs," the doctor replied.

Distantly. That sounded like a joke. She didn't think there was any distance in the Doyle family tree. It didn't branch at all. Virgil had said he'd married Dr. Cummins's daughter, which meant that, to boot, they'd attempted to pull that "distant" relation back into their bosom.

*He wants you to be part of our family*, Francis had said. Noemí clutched the glass with both hands.

"You must have your breakfast. Francis, bring the tray here," the doctor commanded.

"I've lost my appetite."

"Don't be silly. Francis, the tray."

"Is the tea warm? I'll very much enjoy tossing a scalding cup in the good doctor's face," she said lightly.

The doctor took off his glasses and began cleaning them with a handkerchief, his brow furrowed. "It seems you are determined to be difficult today. I shouldn't be surprised. Women can be terribly mercurial."

"Was your *daughter* difficult?" Noemí asked. The doctor raised his head sharply and stared at her, and she knew she'd struck a nerve. "You gave them your own *daughter.*"

"I have no idea what you are talking about," he muttered.

"Virgil said she ran away, but it's not true. No one leaves this place, you said so. It would never have let her go. She's dead, isn't she? Did he kill her?"

Noemí and the doctor stared at each other. The doctor stood up stiffly, snatching the glass from her hands and setting it on the night table.

"Perhaps if you'd let us speak, the two of us alone," Francis told the older man.

Dr. Cummins clasped Francis by the arm and gave Noemí a narrow look. "Yes. You must talk sense into her. He won't tolerate this behavior, you know it."

Before exiting the room, the doctor paused at the foot of the bed, his medical bag held tight in one hand, and addressed Noemí. "My daughter died in childbirth, if you must know. She couldn't give the family the child they needed. Howard thinks you and Catalina will be hardier. Different blood. We'll see."

He closed the door behind him.

Francis grabbed the silver tray and brought it to the bed. Noemí clutched the covers. "You really must eat," he told her.

"Isn't it poisoned?" she asked.

He leaned down, set the tray upon her lap, whispering in Spanish to her ear. "The food you've had, the tea, they've been laced with something, yes. But the egg is fine, start eating. I'll tell you."

"What—"

"In Spanish," he said. "He can hear, through the walls, through the house, but he doesn't speak Spanish. He won't understand. Keep your voice low and eat, I'm serious. You *are* dehydrated and you vomited so much last night."

Noemí stared at him. Slowly she grabbed a spoon and tapped the hard-boiled egg's shell without taking her eyes off him.

"I want to help you," he said, "but it's difficult. You've seen what the house can do."

"Keep you inside, apparently. Is it true I can't leave?"

"It can induce you to do certain things and stop you from doing others."

"Control your mind."

"In a way. It's more rudimentary than that. There's certain instincts it triggers."

"I couldn't breathe."

"I know."

Slowly Noemí nibbled at a bit of egg. When she was done he pointed at the toast, nodding, but shook his head at the jam.

"There must be a way to get out of here."

"There might be." He took out a little flask from his pocket and showed it to her. "Recognize this?"

"It's the medicine I gave my cousin. What are you doing with it?"

"Dr. Cummins told me to get rid of it after that episode, but I didn't. The fungus, it's in the air, and my mother makes sure it's in your food. That's how, slowly, it gets a hold of you. But it's very sensitive to certain triggers. It doesn't really like light much, nor certain scents."

"My cigarettes," she said, snapping her fingers. "It irritates the house. And this tincture, it must irritate it too."

Did the healer in town know this? Or had it been a happy accident? Catalina had figured out the tincture had an effect on the house, that was certain. Accidental or intentional, her cousin had discovered the key even if she had been prevented from turning it.

"It does more than that," Francis said. "It interferes with it. You take this tincture, the house, the fungus, will loosen its hold on you."

"How can you be sure about that?"

"Catalina. She tried to run away, but Virgil and Arthur caught her and brought her back. They found the draught she'd been taking and determined it was affecting the house's control on her, so they took it away. But they didn't realize this had been going on for a little while, and she must have asked someone in town to post a letter for her."

Catalina, clever girl. She'd devised a fail-safe mechanism and had summoned help. Unfortunately, now Noemí, the would-be rescuer, was also trapped.

She reached for the flask, but he caught her hand and shook his head. "Remember what happened to your cousin? Take too much at once and you'll have a seizure."

"Then it's useless."

"Far from it. You'll have to drink a little bit each time. Look, Dr. Cummins is here for a reason. Great Uncle Howard is going to die. There's no stopping it. The fungus extends your life, but it can't keep you going forever. His body will give way soon, and afterward he'll begin the transmigration. He will take possession of Virgil's body. When that happens, when he dies, everyone will be distracted. They'll be busy clustering around both of them. And the house will be weakened."

"When will this happen?"

"It can't be too long," Francis said. "You've seen Howard."

Noemí didn't really want to remember what she'd seen. She put down the bit of egg she had been nibbling and frowned.

"He wants you to be part of the family. Go along with it, be patient, and I'll get you out of here. There are tunnels, they lead to the cemetery, and I think I can hide supplies in them."

"What does 'go along with it' mean exactly?" Noemí asked, because Francis was evading her eyes.

She caught his chin with one hand, made him look at her. He stood perfectly still, holding his breath.

"He'd like you to marry me. He'd like you to have children with me. He wants you to be one of us," Francis said at last.

"And if I say no? What then?"

"He'll have his way."

"He'll carve my mind out, like the servants? Or simply rape me?" she asked.

"It won't come to that," Francis muttered.

"Why?"

"Because he enjoys controlling people in other ways. It would be too coarse. He let my father go to town for years, he let Catalina go to church. He even let Virgil and my mother get far away from town and find spouses. He knows he needs people to obey his will and do his bidding, and they must welcome it, otherwise it's too exhausting."

"And he can't control them all the time," Noemí ventured. "Ruth was able to grab a rifle, after all, and Catalina tried to tell me the truth."

"That's right. And Catalina wouldn't reveal who'd given her the tonic, no matter how much Howard tried to wrestle that information from her."

Plus the miners had organized a strike. As much as Howard Doyle would like to believe himself a god, he couldn't push and force everyone to submit to him every hour of the day. And yet, in decades past, he must have been able to subtly manipulate a great number of people, and when that wasn't enough he could kill them or make them disappear, like with Benito.

"Outright confrontation won't work," Francis said.

Noemí examined the butter knife and knew he was right. What could she do? Kick and punch and she'd end up right where she was, perhaps even worse off. "If I agree to go along with this charade, then you must get Catalina out too."

Francis did not reply, but she could guess that he wasn't enjoying the idea of springing two people out by the way he frowned.

"I can't leave her behind," she said, clutching the hand in which he still held the bottle. "You must also give her the tincture, you must also break her free."

"Yes, fine. Keep your voice down."

She let go of his hand and lowered her voice. "You must promise, on your life."

"I'm promising. Now, shall we give it a try?" he asked, taking out the bottle's glass stopper. "It'll make you a little sleepy, but you probably need the rest."

"Virgil can see my dreams," she muttered, pressing her knuckles against her mouth for a moment. "Won't he know, if he can see my dreams? Won't he know what I'm thinking?"

"They're not really dreams. It's the gloom. But be careful when you're there."

"I don't know if I can trust you," she said. "Why would you help me?"

He was unlike his cousin in a thousand tiny ways, with his slim hands and his weak mouth, spindly where Virgil was solid forcefulness. He was young and wan, and infected with kindness. But who could say if it was all for show, if he couldn't sink into ruthless indifference. After all, nothing in this place was what it seemed. There were secrets upon secrets.

She touched the back of her neck, the place where Virgil's fingers had dug into her hair.

Francis twirled the glass stopper in one hand. It caught a stray ray of light, filtering through the curtains; a tiny prism, painting a rainbow on the edge of her bed.

"There's a cicada fungus. *Massospora cicadina*. I remember reading a journal article which discussed its appearance: the fungus sprouts along the abdomen of the cicada. It turns it into a mass of yellow powder. The journal said the cicadas, which had been so grossly infected, were still 'singing,' as their body was consumed from within. Singing, calling for a mate, half dead. Can you imagine?" Francis said. "You're right, I do have a choice. I'm not going to end my life singing a tune, pretending everything is fine."

He ceased toying with the glass stopper and glanced at her.

"You managed to pretend so far."

She stared at him, and he stared back at her gravely. "Yes," he said. "And now you're here and I can't anymore."

She watched him, silent, as he poured out a minute amount of liquid onto a spoon. Noemí swallowed the tincture. It was bitter. He offered her the napkin that had been set by her plate, and Noemí wiped her mouth clean.

"Let me take this away," Francis said, placing the bottle back in his pocket and picking up her tray. She touched his arm, and he stopped.

"Thanks."

"Don't thank me," he replied. "I should have spoken sooner, but I'm a coward."

She pressed her head back against the pillows after that and let the drowsiness take over. Later—she wasn't sure how much later—she heard a rustling of cloth and sat up. Ruth Doyle was perched at the foot of her bed, looking down at the floor.

Not Ruth. A memory? A ghost? Not quite a ghost. She realized that what she had been seeing, the voice whispering to her, urging her to open her eyes, was the mind of Ruth, which still nestled in the gloom, in the crevices and mold-covered walls. There must be other minds, bits of persons, hidden underneath the wallpaper, but none as solid, as tangible as Ruth. Except, perhaps, for that golden presence that she still could not identify and that she could not even declare a *person*. It didn't feel like a person. Not like Ruth.

"Can you hear me?" she asked. "Or are you like the grooves in a vinyl record?"

She wasn't afraid of the girl. She was a young woman, abused and abandoned. Her presence wasn't malicious, merely anxious.

"I'm not sorry," Ruth said.

"My name is Noemí. I've seen you before, but I'm not sure you understand me."

"Not sorry."

Noemí didn't think the girl was going to offer her more than those scant words, but suddenly Ruth lifted her head and stared at her.

"Mother cannot, will not protect you. No one will protect you."

*Mother is dead*, Noemí thought. *You killed her.* But she doubted there was any point in reminding someone who was a corpse, long buried, about such things. Noemí stretched out a hand, touching the girl's shoulder. She felt real under her fingers.

"You have to kill him. Father will never let you go. That was my mistake. I didn't do it right." The girl shook her head.

"How should you have done it?" Noemí asked.

"I didn't do it right. He is a god! He is a god!"

The girl began sobbing and clasped both hands against her mouth, rocking back and forth. Noemí tried to embrace her, but Ruth flung herself against the floor and curled up there, her hands still covering her mouth. Noemí knelt down next to her.

"Ruth, don't cry," she said, and as she spoke Ruth's body turned gray, white speckles of mold spreading across her face and hands, and the girl wept, black tears sliding down her cheeks, bile trickling out of her mouth and nose.

Ruth began to tear at herself with her nails, letting out a hoarse scream. Noemí pushed herself backward, bumping against the bed. The girl was writhing; now she scratched at the floor, her nails tearing at the wood, driving splinters into her palms.

Noemí clacked her teeth together in fear and thought to cry too, but then she recalled the words, the mantra.

"Open your eyes," Noemí said.

And Noemí did. She opened her eyes, and the room was dark. She was alone. It rained again. She stood up and slid the curtain away. The distant sound of thunder was unsettling. Where was her bracelet? The bracelet against the evil eye. But that would do no good now. Inside the night table's drawer she found her pack of cigarettes and her lighter; those were still there.

Noemí flicked the lighter on, watching the flame bloom, and then closed it, returning it to the drawer.

# 22

rancis came back to see her the next morning, giving her another small amount of the tincture and pointing out the items that were safe to eat. When night fell, he reappeared with a tray of food and told her that after she finished her dinner they were supposed to speak with Virgil, who awaited them in the office.

It was too dark, even with the oil lamp in Francis's hands, to look at the portraits running along the wall that led toward the library, but she wished she could have stopped and gazed at Ruth's picture. It was an impulse born of curiosity and sympathy. She had been a prisoner, like her.

Noemí was struck by the unpleasant scent of moldy books as soon as Francis opened the door to the office. Funny how she'd gotten used to it and barely noticed it in days past. She wondered if that meant the tincture was doing its job.

Virgil sat behind the desk. The subdued lighting in the paneled room gave him the appearance of a Caravaggio painting and rendered his face almost bloodless. There was a stillness to his body, like that of a wild animal camouflaging itself. His fingers were laced together, and when he saw them he leaned forward in greeting, smiling.

"You seem to be doing better," Virgil said. Noemí sat before him, Francis at her side, her mute stare the one answer to his question. "I've asked you here because we need to clarify a few points. Francis says you understand the situation and you're willing to cooperate with us," Virgil continued.

"If you mean I realize I can't leave this horrid house, yes, that has become unfortunately clear."

"Don't be sore about it, Noemí—it's quite a lovely house once it gets to know you. Now, I guess the question is whether you are determined to be a nuisance or whether you'll willingly join the family?"

On the walls the three deer heads cast long shadows. "You have a very interesting notion of 'willingly,'" Noemí said. "Are you offering any other option to me? I don't think so. I've decided to stay alive, if that is what you'd like to know. I wouldn't want to end up in a pit, like those poor miners."

"We didn't dump them in a pit. They're all buried in the cemetery. And they needed to die. You must make the soil fertile."

"With human bodies. *Mulch*, isn't that right?"

"They would have died anyway. It was an assortment of underfed peasants, riddled with lice."

"Was your first wife also a peasant, riddled with lice? Did you also use her to make the soil more fertile?" Noemí asked. She wondered if her portrait was hanging outside, with the pictures of all the other Doyles. A wretched young woman with her chin up, trying to maintain her smile for the camera.

Virgil shrugged. "No. But she was inadequate all the same, and I can't say that I miss her."

"How charming."

"You won't make me feel bad about that, Noemí. The strong survive, the weak are left behind. I think you're quite strong," he said. "And what a pretty face you have. Dark skin, dark eyes. Such a novelty."

*Dark meat*, she thought. Nothing but meat, she was the equivalent of a cut of beef inspected by the butcher and wrapped up in waxed paper. An exotic little something to stir the loins and make the mouth water.

Virgil stood up, rounding the desk and standing behind them, a firm hand resting on the back of each of their chairs. "My family, as you might know, has strived to keep the bloodline clean. Our selective breeding has allowed us to transmit the most desirable traits. Our compatibility with the fungi in this house is the result of that. There's one tiny problem."

Virgil began walking around, circling them, looking down at the desk and toying with a pencil. "Do you know that chestnut trees that stand alone are sterile? They require cross-pollination from another tree. This seems to have become the case with us too. My mother gave my father two living children, yes, but she had many stillbirths. It's the same story when you look back in time. Stillbirths, crib deaths. Before Agnes, my father had two other wives, neither of which was any good.

"On occasion you need to inject new blood into the mix, so to speak. Of course my father has always been very stubborn about these things, insisting that we must not mingle with the rabble."

"Superior and inferior traits, after all," Noemí said dryly.

Virgil smiled. "Exactly. The old man even brought earth from England to ensure the conditions here would be like the ones in our motherland; he wasn't about to entertain the locals. But the way things have gone, it has become a necessity. A question of survival."

"Hence Richard," Noemí said. "And hence Catalina."

"Yes. Although if I'd seen you before, I might have picked you rather than her. You're healthy, young, and the gloom rather likes you."

"I suppose my money doesn't hurt."

"Well, that's obviously a prerequisite. Your stupid Revolution robbed us of our fortune. We must get it back. Survival, as I said."

"Murder, I think that's the word. You murdered all those miners. You made them sick, you didn't tell them what was wrong with them, and your doctor, he let them die. And you must have killed Ruth's lover too. Although she paid you back for that."

"You're not being very nice, Noemí," he said, his eyes fixed on hers. He sounded peeved and turned to Francis. "I thought you had smoothed things out with her."

"Noemí won't try running again," Francis said, sliding his hand upon her own.

"That's a good first step. The second step is that you are going to write a letter to your father, explaining that you will remain here until Christmas, to keep Catalina company. Come Christmas, you'll inform him that you've been married and intend to live with us."

"My father will be upset."

"Then you'll have to write a few more letters, to assuage his concerns," Virgil said smoothly. "Now, why don't you start writing that first letter."

"Now?"

"Yes. Come here," Virgil said, patting the chair he had been occupying behind the desk.

Noemí hesitated but stood up and took the seat he was offering. There was a sheet of paper ready and a pen. Noemí stared at the writing instruments but did not pick them up.

"Go on," Virgil said.

"I don't know what to say."

"Write a convincing message. Because we wouldn't want your father visiting us and maybe falling ill with an odd disease, would we?"

"You wouldn't," she whispered.

Virgil leaned down, gripping her shoulder tight. "There's plenty of space in the mausoleum, and as you pointed out, our physician is not very good at treating illnesses."

Noemí shoved his hand aside and began writing. Virgil turned away.

She kept scribbling, finally signing the letter. When she was done Virgil came back to her side and read the letter, nodding.

"Are you happy?" Francis asked. "She's done her bit."

"She's far from done her bit," Virgil muttered. "Florence is rummaging around the house, trying to find Ruth's old wedding dress. We're to have ourselves a wedding ceremony."

"Why?" Noemí asked. Her mouth felt dry.

"Howard is a stickler for those kind of details. Ceremonies. He does love them."

"Where will you find a priest?"

"My father can officiate; he's done so before."

"So I'll be wed in the Church of the Holy Incestuous Mushroom?" she intoned. "I doubt that's valid."

"Don't worry, we will of course drag you to the magistrate at one point."

"*Drag* is the right word."

Virgil slammed the letter down on the desk, startling Noemí. She winced. She recalled his strength. He'd carried her into the house as if she were as light as a feather. His hand, resting against the desk, was large, capable of inflicting tremendous damage.

"You should consider yourself lucky. I did tell my father Francis might as well tie you to the bed and fuck you tonight, without any preamble, but he doesn't think that would be right. You're a lady, after all. I disagree. Ladies are not wanton, and as we both know, you aren't exactly a little innocent lamb."

"I have no idea—"

"Oh, you definitely have *a few* ideas."

Virgil's fingers grazed her hair. The slightest touch, which sent a shiver down her body, a dark and delicious feeling coursing down her veins, like imbibing champagne much too quickly. Like in her dreams. She thought of sinking her teeth into his shoulder and biting down, hard. A ferocious pang of desire and hatred.

Noemí jumped up, pushing the chair between herself and Virgil. "Don't!"

"Don't what?"

"Stop this," Francis said, hurrying to her side. He clutched her hand, assuaging her, quickly reminding her with one look that they had, after all, a plan, and then, turning to Virgil, he spoke firmly. "She's my bride. You need to show her respect."

Virgil seemed unamused by his cousin's words, that thin, tart smile of his widening, ready to turn into a snarl. She was certain he would push back, but he surprised her by raising his hands in the air in sudden, theatrical surrender.

"Well, I guess for once in your life you've actually grown a pair of balls. Fine," Virgil said. "I'll be polite. But she needs to mind her words and learn her place."

"She will. Come," Francis said, quickly guiding her out of the office, oil lamp in hand, shadows wavering and shifting due to the sudden movement of the light source.

Once outside, he turned to her. "Are you all right?" he asked in a whisper, switching to Spanish.

She did not reply. Noemí pulled him down the hallway, into one of the unused, dusty rooms with chairs and settees covered by white sheets. A huge floor-to-ceiling mirror reflected them, its top embellished with elaborate carvings of fruits and flowers and the ever-present snake that lurked around every corner in this house. Noemí stopped in her tracks as she stared at the snake, and Francis almost bumped into her, whispering an apology.

"You said you'd get supplies for us," she told him, her eyes on the decoration surrounding the mirror, the fearful snake. "But what about weapons?"

"Weapons?"

"Yes. Rifles and guns?"

"There are no rifles, not after what happened with Ruth. My uncle Howard keeps a gun in his room, but I wouldn't be able to have access to it."

"There must be something!"

She was startled by her own vehemence. In the mirror, Noemí saw her face reflected, anxious, and turned away, disgusted by the sight of it. Her hands were trembling, and she had to hold on to the back of a chair to steady herself.

"Noemí? What is it?"

"I don't feel safe."

"I reali—"

"It's a trick. I don't understand your mind games, but I know

I'm not entirely *me* when Virgil is around," she said, her hands fluttering up as she brushed the hair away from her face nervously. "Not lately. Magnetic. That's how Catalina described him. Well, no wonder. But it's not charm alone, is it? You said the house can induce you to do certain things . . ."

She trailed off. Virgil brought out the worst in Noemí, she disliked him immensely, and yet as of late he also awoke a depraved thrill in her. Freud talked of death drives: that impulse that makes someone, standing at the edge of a cliff, suddenly want to jump off it. It was surely this ancient principle at work, Virgil tugging at a subconscious string she'd been ignorant of. Playing with her.

She wondered if it was like this for the cicadas Francis had mentioned. Singing their mating songs even as they were consumed alive from within, their organs turning to powder while they rocked against each other. Perhaps chirping even more loudly, the shadow of death creating a frenzy of need inside their small bodies, urging them on toward their own destruction.

What Virgil inspired was violence and carnality, but also a heady delight. The joy of cruelty and a velvet black decadence she had tasted only slightly before. This was her greedy, most impulsive self.

"Nothing will happen to you," Francis assured her, setting down his oil lamp on a table shrouded in white.

"You don't know that."

"Not when I'm around."

"You can't be around all the time. You weren't there when he grabbed me in the bathroom," she said.

Francis clenched his jaw, almost imperceptibly, shame and anger washing over his features, his face flushing richly. His gallantry was misplaced. He wanted to be her knight and could not. Noemí crossed her arms, tucking her chin down.

"There must be a weapon, please, Francis," she insisted.

"My straight razor, perhaps. I could give you that. If it would make you feel safer."

"It would."

"Then you can have it," he said; he sounded genuine.

She realized this was but a small gesture, which did not solve her problems. Ruth had carried a rifle, and that did not save her. If this was truly a death drive, a defect of her psyche now amplified or twisted by the house, then no ordinary weapon could protect her. Yet she appreciated his willingness to help her.

"Thank you."

"It's nothing. I hope you don't mind bearded men, since I won't be able to shave if you've got my razor," he said, trying to make a quip, trying to lighten the mood.

"A bit of stubble now and then never hurt anyone," she replied, matching his tone.

He smiled, and the smile, like his voice, was genuine. Everything in High Place was gnarled and begrimed, but he'd been able to grow bright and mindful, like an odd plant that is carried onto the wrong flower bed.

"You truly are my friend, aren't you?" she said. She hadn't quite believed it, half expecting a ruse, but she didn't think there was one.

"You should know the answer by now," he replied, but not unkindly.

"It's very difficult, in this place, to discern what's real from what's false."

"I know."

They looked at each other, quiet. Noemí began walking around the room, running her hand atop the shrouded furniture, feeling the decorations carved into the wood beneath, upsetting the dust that had collected upon the drop-sheets. She raised her head and saw him staring at her, his hands in his pockets. Noemí tugged at one of the white sheets, revealing a sofa upholstered in blue, and sat on it, her feet tucked up under her.

He sat next to her. The mirror that dominated the room was now right in front of them, but it was cloudy with age and distorted their reflections, turning them into phantoms.

"Who taught you Spanish?" she asked.

"My father. He liked learning new things, learning languages. He used to tutor me; he even tried tutoring Virgil a little, but he had no interest in such lessons. After he died, I'd help Arthur with documents or errands. Since he also speaks Spanish, I was able to practice with him. I always assumed I'd take Arthur's place."

"Serving in town as your family's middleman."

"It's what I was given to expect."

"You've had no other desire but that? To serve your family?"

"When I was younger I dreamed I'd go away. But it was the sort of dream only a small child can have, like thinking one day you might join the circus. I didn't pay it any heed, lately. It was pointless. After what became of my father, I figured, well, he had a stronger personality than I have, he was more audacious, and even he could do nothing but obey the will of High Place."

As he spoke, Francis reached into his jacket's pocket and took out the little portrait she'd seen before. She leaned down, looking at it with more care than the first time. It was part of an enamel locket, one side painted blue, decorated with golden lilies of the valley. She traced a flower with a nail.

"Did your father know about the gloom?"

"Before coming to High Place, you mean? No. He married my mother, and she brought him here, but she obviously didn't mention it. He didn't know for a while. By the time he learned the whole truth it was too late, and he eventually agreed to stay."

"The same setup that they are offering me, I suppose," Noemí said. "A chance to be a part of the family. Not that he had much of a choice."

"He loved her, I guess. He loved me. I don't know."

Noemí handed him back the locket, and he tucked it into his pocket. "Will there truly be a wedding ceremony? A bridal dress?" she asked.

She recalled the rows of pictures in the hallways, fixing each generation in time. And the bridal portraits in Howard's room. If they could, they would have painted Catalina's portrait in the same style. They would have painted Noemí's portrait too. Both paintings would have hung side by side atop a mantelpiece. There would also have been a photo of the newlyweds, decked in their fine silks and velvet.

The mirror offered her a vague impression of what such a wedding picture might have looked like, for it captured both Noemí and Francis, their faces solemn.

"It's tradition. In the old days there would have been a great feast, and every person attending would have given you a gift of silver. Mining has always been our trade, and it all began with silver."

"In England?"

"Yes."

"And you came chasing more silver here."

"It had run out, over there. Silver, tin, and our luck. And the people back in England, they suspected us of odd doings. Howard thought they'd ask fewer questions here, that he'd be able to do as he wished. He wasn't wrong."

"How many workers died?"

"It's impossible to know."

"Have you wondered about it?"

"Yes," he whispered, his voice thick with shame.

This house had been built atop bones. And no one had noticed such an atrocity, rows and rows of people streaming into the house, into the mine, and never leaving. Never to be mourned, never to be found. The serpent does not devour its tail, it devours everything around it, voracious, its appetite never quenched.

She gazed at the wide-open fangs of the snake surrounding the mirror, and she turned her face and rested her chin on his shoulder. And like that they sat for a long time, she dark and he pale, making an odd contrast amidst all the snowy-white sheets, and around them, like a vignette, the darkness of the house blurring the borders.

# 23

ow that there was no need for pretense, they let her talk to Catalina without the watchful maid to spy on them. Francis was her companion instead. She supposed they saw them as a unit. Two symbiotic organisms, tethered together. Or else, jailer and prisoner. Whatever their reasoning, she appreciated the chance to speak to her cousin and pulled her chair closer to the bed where Catalina was resting. Francis stood on the other side of the room, glancing out the window and tacitly offering them privacy as they spoke in whispers.

"I'm sorry I didn't believe you when I read the letter," Noemí said. "I should have known."

"You couldn't know," Catalina said.

"Still, if I'd simply fetched you, despite their protestations, we wouldn't be here."

"They wouldn't have let you. Noemí, it's enough that you came. Your presence makes me better. It's like in those stories I used to read: it's as if you've broken a spell."

More likely it was the tincture Francis was administering, but

Noemí nodded and grasped her cousin's hands. How she wished that it were true, though! The fairy tales Catalina had shared with her always had good endings. The wicked were punished, order was restored. A prince climbed a tower and fetched down the princess. Even the dark details, such as the cutting of the wicked stepsisters' heels, faded into oblivion once Catalina declared that everyone lived happily ever after.

Catalina could not recite those magical words—happily ever after—and Noemí had to hope the escape they had formulated was not a tall tale. Hope was all they had.

"He knows something is wrong," Catalina said suddenly, blinking slowly.

The words unsettled Noemí. "Who?"

Catalina pressed her lips shut. This had happened before too, that she suddenly, dramatically grew quiet or seemed to lose her train of thought. As much as Catalina might want to say that she was getting better, she was not herself yet. Noemí brushed a strand of hair behind Catalina's ear.

"Catalina? What's wrong?"

Catalina shook her head and then lay back on the bed, turning her back toward Noemí. Noemí touched her cousin's shoulder, but Catalina shoved her hand away. Francis walked over toward the bed.

"I think she's tired," he said. "We should walk back to your room. My mother said she wanted you to try that dress on."

She had not really pictured the dress. It had been the furthest thing from her mind. Having no preconceptions, anything should have sufficed. Yet she was still surprised when she saw it laid out on her bed, and she regarded it with worry. She did not wish to touch it.

The dress was silky chiffon and satin, the high neck adorned with a collar of Guipure lace, and a long line of tiny mother-of-pearl buttons running down the back. It had rested in a large, dusty box for years and years, and one might have expected moths to have feasted on this creation, but although the fabric had yellowed a little, it was intact.

It wasn't ugly. That wasn't what repulsed her. But it seemed to her it represented the youthful fancies of another girl, of a dead girl. Perhaps two girls. Had Virgil's first wife worn this too?

It reminded her of an abandoned snake's skin. Howard would slough off his own skin, would sink into a new body, like a blade entering warm flesh. Ouroboros.

"You must try it on so the alterations can be made," Florence said.

"I have nice dresses. My purple taffeta—"

Florence stood very straight, her chin slightly raised, her hands clasped beneath her bosom. "The lace at the collar, you see it? That was taken from an older dress, incorporated in the final design. And the buttons, they came from another dress too. Your children will reuse this dress. It is the way things are done."

Leaning down carefully, Noemí noticed there was a tear on the waist and a couple of small holes on the bodice. The dress's perfection was deceiving.

She grabbed the dress and ventured into the bathroom, changing there, and when she emerged Florence regarded her with a critical eye. Measurements were taken, alterations indicated with the required pins; tuck this, tuck that. Florence muttered a few words to Mary, and the maid opened another dusty box, producing a pair of shoes and a veil. The veil was in a much sorrier state than the dress. It had aged to a creamy ivory color, and the lovely flower-and-scroll design running near the edges had been marred by ugly mildew stains. The shoes were also hopeless, and besides, they were a size too big.

"It will do," Florence said. "As shall you," she added derisively.

"If you find me displeasing, maybe you could kindly ask your uncle to stop this wedding."

"You silly creature. You think he'd desist? His appetite has been whetted," she said, touching a lock of Noemí's hair.

Virgil had touched her hair too, but the gesture had had a different meaning. Florence was inspecting her. "Fitness, he says. Germ plasm and the quality of the bloodstream." She let go of

Noemí's hair and gave her a hard look. "It's the common lust of all men. He simply wants to have you, like a little butterfly in his collection. One more pretty girl."

Mary was quietly putting aside the veil, folding it as though it were a precious treasure and not a stained, wrecked bit of clothing.

"God knows what degenerative strain runs through your body. An outsider, a member of a disharmonic race," Florence said, flinging the soiled shoes on the bed. "But we must accept it. He has spoken."

"*Et Verbum caro factum est*," Noemí said automatically, remembering the phrase. He was lord and priest and father, and they were all his children and acolytes, blindly obeying him.

"Well. At least you're learning," Florence replied, a slight smile on her face.

Noemí did not reply, instead locking herself in the bathroom again and peeling off the dress. She changed back into her clothes and was glad when the women laid the dress back in its box and silently departed.

She put on the heavy sweater Francis had gifted her and reached into a pocket, clutching the lighter and the crumpled pack of cigarettes she'd taken to hiding there. Touching these objects made her feel more secure; they reminded her of home. With the mist outside obscuring the view, trapped between the walls of High Place, it seemed very easy to forget that she'd come from a different city and that she would ever see it again.

Francis came by a little while later. He brought with him a tray with her dinner and his razor wrapped in a handkerchief. Noemí joked that it was a terrible wedding present, and he chuckled. They sat side by side on the floor as she ate, the tray on her lap, and he managed a few more quips, and she smiled.

A distant, unpleasant groan dried up their mirth. The noise seemed to send a shiver down the house. It was followed by more groans, then silence. Noemí had heard such moaning before, but it seemed especially acute tonight.

"The transmigration must take place soon," Francis said, as if reading the question in her eyes. "His body is falling apart. It never healed right since that day when Ruth shot him; the damage was too awful."

"Why did he never transmigrate before? When he was shot, then?" she asked.

"He couldn't. There was no new body he could inhabit. He needs an adult body. The brain must grow up to a certain point. Twenty-four, twenty-five, that's the point at which the transmigration may take place. Virgil was a baby. Florence was still a girl, and even if she'd been older, he would never transmigrate into a woman's body. So he held on, and his body stitched itself back together into a semblance of health."

"But he could have transmigrated as soon as Virgil turned twenty-four or twenty-five instead of staying an old man."

"It's all connected. The house, the fungus running through it, the people. You hurt the family, you hurt the fungus. Ruth damaged the whole fabric of our existence. Howard wasn't healing alone, everything was healing. But now he's strong enough and he will die, his body will fruit, and he'll begin a new cycle."

She thought of the house growing scar tissue, breathing slowly, blood flowing between the floorboards. It reminded her of one of her dreams, in which the walls palpitated.

"And that's why I won't go with you," Francis continued, fiddling with the cutlery, spinning a fork between his fingers and setting it down, ready to grab the tray and depart. "We're all interconnected, and if I fled, they'd know, maybe even follow us and find us with ease."

"But you can't stay here. What will they do to you?"

"Probably nothing. If they do, it won't be your problem anymore." He clutched the tray. "Let me take that and I'll—"

"You can't be serious," she said, snatching the tray away and laying it on the floor, shoving it aside.

He shrugged. "I've been gathering supplies for you. Catalina tried to run away, but she was ill prepared. Two oil lamps, a compass, a map, perhaps a pair of warm coats so that you can walk to town without freezing. You have to think about yourself and your cousin. Not about me. I don't really count. The fact of the matter is this is all the world I've ever known."

"Wood and glass and a roof do not constitute a world," she countered. "You're not an orchid growing in a hothouse. I'm not letting you stay. Pack your prints or your favorite book or whatever you wish, you are coming with us."

"You don't belong here, Noemí. But I do. What would I do outside?" he asked.

"Anything you want."

"But that is a deceiving idea. You are right to think that I was grown like an orchid. Carefully manufactured, carefully reared. I am, yes, like an orchid. Accustomed to a certain climate, a certain amount of light and heat. I've been fashioned for a single end. A fish can't breathe out of water. I belong with the family."

"You're not an orchid or a fish."

"My father tried to escape, and you see how he fared," he countered. "My mother and Virgil, they came back."

He laughed without joy, and she could very well believe he would stay behind, a cephalophore martyr of cold marble who'd let the dust accumulate on his shoulders, who'd allow the house to gently, slowly devour him.

"You'll come with me."

"But—"

"But nothing! Don't you want to leave this place?" she insisted.

His shoulders were hunched, and he looked as if he would bolt out the door any second, but then he took a shaky breath.

"For God's sake, you can't be that blind?" he replied, his voice low and harrowed. "I want to follow you, wherever you may go. To the damn Antarctic, even if I'd freeze my toes off, who cares? But the tincture can sever *your* link between you and the house, not mine. I've lived too long with it. Ruth tried to find a way around it, tried to kill Howard to escape. That didn't

work. And my father's gambit didn't work either. There's no solution."

What he said made a terrible amount of sense. Yet she stubbornly refused to concede. Was everyone in this house a moth
caught in a killing jar and then pinned against a board?

"Listen," she said. "Follow me. I'll be your pied piper."

"Those who follow the pied piper don't meet a good end."

"I forget which fairy tale it is," Noemí said angrily. "But follow me all the same."

"Noemí—"

She raised a hand and touched his face, her fingers gliding
along his jaw.

He looked at her, mutely, his lips moving though he uttered
no words, gathering his courage. He reached out for her, pulling
her closer to him in a gentle motion. His hand trailed down her
back, palm pressed flat, and she rested her cheek against his
chest.

The house was quiet, a quiet that she disliked, for it seemed to
her all the boards that normally creaked and groaned had stopped
creaking, the clocks on the walls did not tick, and even the rain
against the window panes was shushed. It was as if an animal
waited to pounce on them.

"They're listening, aren't they?" she whispered. They couldn't
understand them since they were speaking in Spanish. Yet it still
disturbed her.

"Yes," he said.

He was scared too, she could tell. In the silence his heart beat
loud against her ear. At length she lifted her head and looked at
him, and he pressed his index finger to his lips, rising and stepping back from her. And she wondered if in addition to being able
to listen, the house might not have eyes too.

The gloom, shivering and waiting, like a spider's web, and
them sitting on a silvery bit of silk. The lightest movement would
reveal their presence and the spider would pounce on them. Such
a dreadful thought, and yet she considered the possibility of en-

tering that cold, foreign space willingly, which she'd never done before.

It terrified her.

But Ruth existed in the gloom, after all, and she wanted to speak to her again. She wasn't sure how to accomplish that. After Francis left, Noemí lay in bed with her hands at her side, listening to her own breathing, and tried to visualize the young woman's face as it looked in her portrait.

Eventually she dreamed. They were in the cemetery, she and Ruth, walking among the tombstones. The mist was thick around them, and Ruth carried a lantern, which glowed a sickly yellow. They paused before the entrance to the mausoleum, and Ruth raised the lantern, and they both raised their heads to look at the statue of Agnes. The lantern could not provide sufficient illumination, and the statue remained half in shadow.

"This is our mother," Ruth said. "She sleeps."

*Not your mother*, Noemí thought, for Agnes had died young, as had her child.

"Our father is a monster who comes at night, creeping around this house. You can hear his footsteps outside the door," Ruth said, and she raised the lantern higher, the light shifting the pattern of lights and shadow, obscuring the statue's hands, her body, but revealing the face. Unseeing eyes and the lips pressed tightly together.

"Your father can't hurt you anymore," Noemí said. Because at least there was that mercy, she supposed. Ghosts cannot be tortured.

But the girl grimaced. "He can always hurt us. He never stops hurting us. He will never stop."

Ruth turned her lantern toward Noemí, making her squint and hold a hand up to shield her eyes. "Never, ever, never. I've seen you. I think I know you."

The conversation was fragmented, yet it remained more coherent than any other exchange Noemí had conducted with the girl before. In fact, it was the first time she had the impression

she was speaking to an actual person rather than the faint carbon copy of one. But that's what she was, wasn't she? A faded
carbon copy, the original manuscript long destroyed. One could
not blame Ruth if she didn't make much sense, if she muttered
and lowered the lantern and raised it again repeatedly like a
wind-up doll.

"Yes, you've seen me around the house," Noemí said, stilling
Ruth with a gentle touch on the arm. "I need to ask you a question, and I hope you'll have an answer. How strong is the bond
between the house and your family? Could a Doyle leave and
never come back?" she asked, because she kept thinking about
what Francis had told her.

Ruth tilted her head and looked at Noemí. "Father is power-
ful. He knew something was wrong, sent Mother to stop me . . .
and the others, the others too. I tried to keep my mind clear. I
wrote my plan down, concentrated on my words."

The diary page. Like a mnemonic device? Was that the key to
the gloom? Tricking it in such a way? Focus on commands and
instructions and let them lead your steps?

"Ruth, could a Doyle ever leave this house?"

Ruth had stopped listening to her; her eyes were glassy. Noemí
stood directly in front of her.

"You thought about running away, no? With Benito?"

And the young woman blinked and nodded. "Yes, I did," she
whispered. "Perhaps you could. I thought I could. But it's a compulsion. It's in the blood."

Like the cicadas Francis talked about. *I'll carry him out if I
need to*, she thought and her resolve grew firmer even if Ruth's
words had hardly been the solid reassurance she'd sought. There
was at least a possibility he could be pulled from the grip of Howard Doyle and his noxious house.

"It's dark here, isn't it?" Ruth said, looking up at the sky.
There were no stars, no moon. Only mist and night. "Take this,"
Ruth said and handed Noemí the lantern.

Noemí grabbed it, her fingers curling around the metal handle. Ruth sat down at the foot of the statue, touching its feet and contemplating it. She lay next to the base of the statue, as if she were about to take a nap on a bed made of mist and grass.

"Remember to open your eyes," Ruth told her.

"Open your eyes," Noemí whispered.

When she did, turning her head toward the window, she saw that the sun was out. She was to be married that evening.

# 24

t occurred in reverse, the farce of a marriage. First the banquet, then the ceremony.

They gathered in the dining room, Francis and Noemí sitting side by side, Florence and Catalina across from the groom and bride, and Virgil at the head of the table. Neither Howard nor Dr. Cummins was present.

The servants had lit many candles, and dishes were piled upon the white damask tablecloth. Wildflowers were crammed into high turquoise glass vases. The plates and the cups that evening were silver, and though carefully polished, they looked very old, older than the silver Noemí had cleaned. They must have used these to feast some four hundred years ago. Perhaps even more. Treasure troves from their vault, carefully placed in crates, just like the dark earth Howard had packed, so that they might reassemble the world where they'd reigned as masters.

At Noemí's right Francis sat dressed in his double-breasted gray frock coat suit, white waistcoat and dark gray necktie. She wondered if this outfit had belonged to Ruth's groom, or whether it was a relic of another relative. In Noemí's case, they had found a proper veil for her somewhere in a chest. It was a white tulle bandeau that covered her forehead, head combs and pins holding it in place.

Noemí did not eat, and she drank only water; she did not speak, and neither did the others. The magic rule of silence had been reinstated, the susurrus of hands upon a napkin the only interruption. Noemí glanced in Catalina's direction, and her cousin looked back at her.

The scene reminded her of a picture in one of her childhood fairy tale books, when the wedding banquet is in place and an evil fairy walks into the room. She recalled the table laden with meats and pies, the women wearing high headdresses, and the men in box coats with huge sleeves. She touched her silver cup and once again wondered at the age of it and whether Howard had been born three hundred, four hundred, five hundred years in the past and might have walked around in a jerkin and hose. She'd seen him in a dream, but the dream had been vague, or it had grown vaguer in the days since. How many times had he died, acquired a new body? She looked at Virgil, and he returned the look, raising his cup, which prompted Noemí to stare at her plate.

The clock marked the hour, and that was their cue. They rose. Francis took her hand and they walked together, up the stairs, a tiny wedding procession winding its way to Howard's room. She'd known instinctively that this must be their destination, yet she still recoiled at the entrance and clutched Francis's hand so hard she must have hurt him. He whispered in her ear.

"We're together," he said.

They walked in. The air was foul with the stench of food gone sour, and Howard still lay on the bed, his lips black and covered with pustules, but this time he was under the covers and Dr. Cummins stood at his side. In a church there would have been the smell of incense. Here was the perfume of putrefaction.

When Howard caught sight of Noemí, the old man grinned.

"You look beautiful, my dear," he said. "One of the prettiest brides I've had the chance to gaze upon."

She considered exactly how many that might be. Another pretty girl for his collection, Florence had said.

"Loyalty to the family is rewarded, and impertinence is punished. Remember that and you shall be very happy," the old man continued. "And now, here, the two of you must be wed. Come."

Cummins stepped aside, and they took his place by the bed. Howard proceeded to speak in Latin. Noemí had no idea what he said, but at one point Francis knelt, and she knelt with him. This choreographed obeisance to the father had meaning. *Repetition*, Noemí thought. *Tracing the same path over and over again. Circles.*

Howard offered Francis a lacquered box, and the young man opened it. On plush velvet rested two tiny, dried pieces of yellow mushrooms.

"You must eat," Howard said.

Noemí held a tiny mushroom piece in her hand and Francis did the same. She was reluctant to place it in her mouth, lest it inhibit or reduce the progress of the tincture she'd been secretly imbibing, but more than that its provenance disturbed her. Had it been collected from the grounds near the house, or had it come from the cemetery, riddled with corpses? Or else had it grown upon Howard's flesh and been plucked with nimble fingers, blood flowing when the stem was severed?

Francis touched her wrist, motioning for her to feed him the mushroom, and then it was her turn, he placing the mushroom in her mouth. It seemed to her this was a strange parody of the communion wafer, and the thought of it almost made her giggle. She was so nervous.

She swallowed quickly. The mushroom had no taste, but the cup of wine that Francis pressed against her lips was sickly sweet, though she hardly had a sip. It was more the scent of it that assailed her nostrils, mixing with that other scent pervading the room, the miasma of sickness and decay.

"May I kiss you?" Francis asked, and she nodded.

Francis leaned forward, and it was a delicate touch, barely there, like gossamer, before he stood up and gave her his hand so that she might rise with ease.

"Let us instruct the young couple," Howard said, "that they may be bountiful."

They had exchanged only a handful of words through the wedding ceremony, and it was apparently all over. Virgil now motioned for Francis to follow him, while Florence took hold of Noemí and led her out of the room and into her own chamber. In Noemí's absence one of the servants had decorated it. They'd placed flowers in more of those tall vases, left a bouquet tied with an old ribbon on the bed, and lit many long candles. It was a parody of romanticism. The scent here was of misplaced spring, of flowers and wax.

"What instruction did he mean?" Noemí asked.

"The Doyle brides are proper girls, chaste and modest. What happens between a man and a woman is a great mystery to them."

Noemí doubted that was the case. Howard had been a lecher, Virgil the same. Maybe they saved certain bits for last, but they did not deny themselves entirely.

"I can name all body parts," Noemí replied.

"Then you'll do fine." Florence raised her hands to help Noemí take off her veil, but she brushed the woman's hand away even though she suddenly felt a bit unsteady, and the assistance might have proven useful.

"I can manage alone. You can go."

Florence, hands clasped under her breast, stared at Noemí and walked out.

*Thank God*, Noemí thought.

Noemí ventured into the bathroom and looked in the mirror, removing pins and head combs and tossing the piece of tulle to the ground. The temperature had dropped. She walked back into the bedroom and put on the sweater she liked to wear. Her lighter was hard and cold against her fingers as she shoved her hands into her pockets.

She felt a little light-headed. Nothing unpleasant, nothing like what had happened the last time she'd been in Howard's room. This was the buzz of alcohol, although she'd not had any wine, except for that one sip during the ceremony.

In the corner of the room she noticed that same stain on the wallpaper that had scared her. It wasn't moving now, but there were tiny golden points dancing at the edge of it. When she closed her eyes, however, it became obvious that the golden points were in her eyes, as if she'd stared at a light bulb.

She sat down on the bed, eyes still closed, and wondered where Francis was right now and what they were saying to him, and whether he also felt pinpricks running down his spine.

She had a vague impression of a different wedding, a different bride with a garland of pearls. *On the morning of her wedding she'd received a silver wedding casket and inside there had been colored ribbons and jewels and a coral necklace. Howard's hand on her own, the amber ring, and she did not wish for this but she must* . . . Was this . . . was she Agnes or Alice? Noemí was unsure. Alice, probably, because the girl thought of her sister.

*Sister.*

This made Noemí remember Catalina, and she opened her eyes, staring up at the ceiling. She wished they might have had a word. A single word, to soothe both of their nerves.

Noemí rubbed a hand against her mouth. It was considerably warmer in the room, where before it had felt like morning frost. She turned her head and saw Virgil standing next to the bed.

For a second she thought she was mistaken, that it was Francis and she was seeing wrong or else it was the gloom, confusing her once more. After all, why would Virgil be in her room? But then Virgil grinned, and Francis would never smile at her like that. He was leering at her.

She jumped to her feet, intending to flee, but she stumbled, and he caught her in two quick movements, grabbing hold of her arm.

"Noemí, here we are again," he said.

His grip was firm, and she knew she couldn't fight him using physical force alone. She took a breath. "Where's Francis?"

"Busy being reprimanded. Did you think we wouldn't find out?" Virgil asked, reaching into his pocket and showing her the glass vial with the tincture. "It wouldn't have worked, anyway. How do you feel?"

"Drunk. Did you poison us?"

He tucked the vial back in his pocket. "No. It was a little wedding gift, a little aphrodisiac. It's a pity Francis won't be able to enjoy it."

She had a razor, she recalled. Hidden under the mattress. It would count for something. If she could get to it. But his hand was still on her arm with an iron grip, and when she tried to brush it away he wouldn't allow it.

"I'm married to Francis."

"He's not here."

"But your father—"

"He's not here either. How funny, they're all busy right now." He tilted his head. "Francis is a little green boy of no experience, but I know what I'm doing. I know what you want."

"You don't know anything," she whispered.

"You dream of me, you come looking for me as you dream," he said. "Life bores you, Noemí. You like a hint of danger, but back home they wrap you in gauze, to keep you from breaking. But you'd like to break, wouldn't you? You play with people and you wish someone would have the guts to play with you."

It was not a real question, he awaited no answer, and his mouth covered hers. She bit him, but it was not in an attempt to deter his actions, and he knew it. He was right that she liked to play, that she enjoyed flirting and teasing and dancing, that they were so careful around her because she was a Taboada, and once in a while a coil of darkness wrapped itself around her heart and she wished to strike, like a cat.

But even as she was admitting this, even as Noemí knew this was a part of her, she also knew it was not *her*.

She must have said that out loud without realizing, because he chuckled.

"Of course it's you. I can nudge you, but it's you."

"No."

"It's me you want, me you fantasize about. We have an understanding, don't we? We know each other, really know each other. Underneath the layers of decorum all you do is *want*."

She slapped him. It accomplished nothing. There was the briefest pause, and he caught her face between his hands and turned her head, running his thumb along her neck. Lust, thick and heady, made her gasp in ruinous delight.

The mold in the corner of the room was shifting and blurring, and his fingers were clenching hard into her flesh, pulling her tighter against him. The mold was streaked with veins of gold, and he was trying to gather up her skirts, shoving her against the bed, touching her between her thighs. The motion made her panic.

"Wait!" she said, as he pressed down on her, undaunted, impatient.

"No waiting, you tease."

"The dress!" He frowned, annoyed, but Noemí spoke again, hoping to buy time. "You'd better help me take off the dress."

This seemed to improve his mood, and he gave her a radiant smile. She managed to stand up, and he peeled off her sweater, tossing it on the bed, and pushed her hair away from her nape as she furiously tried to think of a way out of—

In the corner of her eye the mold, with its streaks of gold, had spread across the wall and was dripping onto the floor. It refracted and changed, a pattern of triangles turning to diamonds and then whorls. She nodded, feeling as if a great hand were pressed against her face, quietly smothering her.

She was never getting out of this house. To have considered it had been a folly. To have wanted to leave had been a mistake. And she wished to be a part of this, wanted to be one with the strange machinery and the veins and the muscles and the marrow of High Place. She wanted to be one with Virgil.

*Want.*

He had undone the top buttons on the back of the dress. She could have left long ago. Should have left in the beginning, when the first tingle of disquiet assailed her, but there had been a thrill to it, hadn't there? A curse, maybe a haunting. She had even been excited to tell Francis about it. A haunting, a mystery to solve.

All along, the sickly pull of this. And why not? Why not.

*Why not. Want.*

Her body, which had been cold, now felt too hot, and the mold dripped down, forming a black puddle in the corner. It reminded her of the black bile that Howard had spit down her throat, and that memory awoke a wave of disgust, her mouth tasting sour, and she thought of Catalina and Ruth and Agnes and the terrible things they'd done to them, which they'd now do to her.

She turned around, away from the shimmering, changing mold, and shoved Virgil away with all her might. Virgil stumbled against the chest at the foot of her bed and fell down. She immediately knelt by the bed and stretched an arm under the mattress, clumsy fingers grabbing the razor she'd hidden there.

Noemí clutched the razor and looked at Virgil, who was sprawled on the floor. He'd hit his head, and his eyes were closed. Here was luck at last. Noemí breathed in slowly and leaned down next to his body, reaching into his pocket for the tincture. She found it, uncapped it, and drank a little from it, wiping her mouth with the back of her hand.

The effect was immediate and noticeable. She felt a wave of nausea, her hands trembled, and the flask slipped from her fingers and shattered on the floor. She held on to one of the bedposts and breathed quickly. *My God.* She thought she'd faint. She bit her hand hard to jolt herself into wakefulness. It worked.

The black puddles of mold that had accumulated on the floor were receding, and the fog in her mind was evaporating. Noemí put on her sweater, tucked the razor in one pocket and the lighter in another.

She looked at Virgil still sprawled on the floor and considered sticking the knife into his skull, but her hands were trembling again, and she needed to get out of there and away from him. She must fetch Catalina. There was no time to waste.

# 25

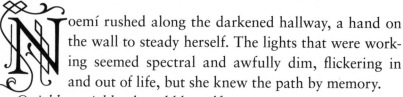oemí rushed along the darkened hallway, a hand on the wall to steady herself. The lights that were working seemed spectral and awfully dim, flickering in and out of life, but she knew the path by memory.

*Quickly, quickly,* she told herself.

Noemí feared her cousin's room would be locked, but she turned the doorknob and yanked the door open.

Catalina sat on the bed in a white nightgown. She was not alone. Mary kept her company, her eyes fixed on the floor.

"Catalina, we're leaving," Noemí said, extending a hand in her cousin's direction while she held the razor in the other.

Catalina did not move; she did not even acknowledge Noemí, her gaze lost.

"Catalina," she repeated. The young woman didn't budge.

Noemí bit her lip and walked in, her eyes fixed on the maid sitting in the corner, her hand trembling as she gripped the razor. "For God's sake, Catalina, snap out of it," she said.

But it was the maid who raised her head, golden eyes zeroing in on Noemí, and rushed toward her, shoving her against the vanity. Her hands wrapped around Noemí's throat. It was such a startling attack, the strength of the woman unthinkable for someone her age, that Noemí dropped the blade. Several items on the vanity also clattered and fell: perfume bottles and a hair comb and a picture of Catalina in a silver frame.

The maid pushed harder, forcing Noemí to step back, the hands at her throat squeezing tight and wood digging against her back. She tried to grasp something, anything as a weapon, but her fingers found nothing suitable, tugging at a doily, overturning a porcelain pitcher that rolled upon the ground and cracked.

"Ours," the maid said. It didn't sound like the woman's voice. It was an odd, raspy sound. It was the voice of the house, the voice of someone or something else, reproduced and approximated by these vocal cords.

Noemí attempted to pry the fingers off her neck, but those hands were more like claws, and all Noemí managed was to gasp and tug at the woman's hair, which accomplished nothing.

"Ours," Mary repeated, then clenched her teeth like a wild animal, and Noemí could hardly see, so bad was the pain. Her eyes watered, her throat was on fire.

Suddenly the woman was yanked away and Noemí was able to breathe, taking in air in huge, desperate gulps as she gripped the dresser with one hand.

Francis had walked in, and he had pulled the maid off Noemí, but now the woman was clawing at him, her mouth opening wide to unleash a hideous screech. She shoved him down, onto the floor, her hands around his neck, bent over him like a bird of prey ready to devour a piece of carrion.

Noemí picked up the straight razor and approached them. "Stop!" she cried out, and the woman turned around, screeching at Noemí, ready to sink those hands into her neck again and crush her windpipe.

She knew then a dizzy sort of terror, pure and overwhelming, and she slashed at the woman's throat. Once, twice, three times, blade meeting flesh, and the woman did not cry out. She fell to the ground in silence, face-first.

Blood dripped down Noemí's fingers, and Francis raised his head and looked up at her, dazed. He stood up and stepped toward her. "Are you hurt?"

She rubbed her neck with her free hand and stared at the dead woman on the floor. She must be dead. Noemí dare not turn the body over to look at her face, but there was a pool of blood growing underneath her.

Her heart beat with a terrible, thundering force, and the blood dripped down, dirtying the pretty antique dress, dirtying her fingers. She slid the blade into her pocket, rubbed the tears from her eyes.

"Noemí?"

He was now in front of her, blocking her view, and she snapped her eyes up to stare into his wan face. "Where were you?" she asked, fingers furiously clutching the lapels of his frock coat, and she wanted to beat him for not being with her, for leaving her alone.

"Locked in my room," he said. "I had to break out. I had to find you."

"You aren't lying? You didn't abandon me?"

"No! Please, are you hurt?"

She chuckled. A ghastly chuckle, since she had fended off a rapist and escaped being choked to death.

"Noemí," he said.

He sounded worried. He should be. They should all be terribly worried. She let go of him. "We have to get out of here."

She turned to Catalina. Her cousin was still sitting on the bed. She had not moved, except to press a hand against her open mouth. Her eyes were fixed on the lifeless body of the maid. Noemí pulled the covers away and grabbed her cousin's hand.

"Come on," she said, and when Catalina wouldn't move, she turned to Francis, whose suit was now smeared with her bloody fingerprints. "What's wrong with her?"

"They must have drugged her again. Without the tincture—"

Noemí took her cousin's face between her hands and spoke firmly. "We're leaving."

Catalina did not react. She wasn't looking at Noemí. Her eyes were glassy. Noemí saw a pair of slippers by the bed and grabbed them, fitting them on Catalina's feet. Then Noemí yanked Catalina by the arm, pulling her out of the bed. Catalina followed her, docile.

They hurried down the hallway. In her white nightgown Catalina looked like a second bride. *Two ghost brides*, Noemí thought.

Ahead of them a shadow emerged from within a pool of darkness, darting onto their path and startling Noemí.

"Stop," Florence said. Her face was very composed. Her voice did not sound anxious. She carried a gun in her hand rather casually, as if this were a regular occurrence.

They stood still. Noemí had the razor, but even as she tightened her grip around its wood handle she knew she didn't stand much of a chance, and Florence was aiming squarely at her.

"Drop that," Florence said.

Noemí's hand trembled, and the blood made the handle slick, difficult to hold, but she held it up. At her side, Catalina was trembling too.

"You can't make me."

"Drop it, I said," Florence repeated.

Her preternaturally calm voice had not wavered, but in her cold eyes Noemí could read savage murder, yet Noemí did not let go of the weapon until the woman shifted her aim, pointing at Catalina. The threat was clear, there was no need to speak it.

Noemí swallowed and dropped the weapon.

"Turn around and start walking," Florence commanded.

They did. Back the way they'd come, until they reached Howard's room with the fireplace and the twin paintings of his wives. The old man lay in the ornate bed, as before, and Dr. Cummins sat at his side. The doctor's bag was open, resting upon a side table, and now he took out a scalpel from it and pricked a couple of boils on Howard's lips and cut through a thin film that seemed to cover his mouth.

This must have eased the man's pain, for Howard sighed. Dr. Cummins placed the scalpel next to the bag and wiped his forehead with the back of his hand and let out a grunt.

"There you are," he said, rounding the bed. "It has accelerated. He can't breathe properly. We need to begin."

"It's her," Florence said, "and the trouble she has caused. Mary is dead."

Howard lay propped against a considerable number of pillows. His mouth was open, and he was making a wheezing sound as he clutched at the covers with his gnarled hands. His skin seemed the color of wax, the veins very dark, standing out against such paleness, a trickle of black bile falling down his chin.

Dr. Cummins raised a hand, pointing a finger at Francis. "You get over here," he told the young man. "Where's Virgil?"

"Hurt. I felt his pain earlier," Florence said.

"There's no time to fetch him. The transmigration must take place now," the doctor muttered, sinking his hands into a small basin with water and washing them clean. "Francis is here, and that's what matters."

"You can't mean him," Noemí said, shaking her head. "It's not supposed to be him."

"Of course it's him," Florence said. Her countenance was cool and collected.

Suddenly Noemí understood. Why would Howard have forfeited his son, his favorite? It made sense that he would pick the boy he cared little about, whose mind he might obliterate without remorse. Had this, then, been their game all along? To slide Howard into Francis's skin in the middle of the night and then for him to slide into Noemí's bed? An impostor. But she wouldn't have known at once, and maybe they figured afterward it wouldn't matter. That she would be content, having taken a liking to Francis's shell.

"But you can't," Noemí mumbled.

Francis was walking meekly toward the doctor. Noemí tried to grab his arm, but Florence intercepted her and pulled her toward a black velvet chair, forcing her to sit down. Catalina trailed around the room looking lost, standing at the foot of the bed, before walking a bit more and settling at the head of it.

"It could have all been easy and quiet," Florence said, staring at Noemí. "You could be sitting calmly in your room, but you had to cause a ruckus."

"Virgil tried to rape me," Noemí said. "He tried to rape me, and I should have killed him back there."

"Shush," Florence replied, looking disgusted. Things were never spoken at High Place, not even now.

Noemí made a motion as if to rise, but Florence pointed the gun at her. She sat back again, gripping the chair's arms. Francis had now reached Howard's bedside and was speaking to the doctor, their voices low.

"He's your son," Noemí whispered.

"It's a body," Florence replied, her face stiff.

A body. That's what they all were to them. The bodies of miners in the cemetery, the bodies of women who gave birth to their children, and the bodies of those children who were simply the fresh skin of the snake. And there on the bed lay the body that mattered. The father.

Dr. Cummins placed a hand on Francis's shoulder, pushing him down. Francis fell to his knees and clutched his hands together, penitent.

"Bow your head, we will pray," Florence ordered.

Noemí did not obey at once, but then Florence smacked her head, hard. The woman's hand felt well practiced. The sting of the blow made black dots dance before Noemí's eyes. She wondered if they had also delivered such blows upon Ruth, teaching her obedience.

Noemí clutched her hands together.

On the other side of the bed, Catalina, mute still, imitated them, also clasping her hands. Her cousin did not look distressed. Her face was immutable.

"*Et Verbum caro factum est*," Howard said, his voice thick and low, his amber ring flashing as he raised a hand in the air.

Howard recited a series of words that Noemí could not understand, yet she realized that understanding was not necessary. Obedience, acceptance, that was what he required. For the old man, there was pleasure in witnessing this submission.

*Renounce yourself,* that's what he had demanded in the dream. That's what mattered now. There was a physical component to this process, but there was also a mental one. A surrender that must be granted. Perhaps there was even pleasure in such submission.

*Renounce yourself.*

Noemí looked up. Francis was whispering, his lips moving softly. Dr. Cummins and Florence and Howard were also whispering, all of them speaking in unison. This low whisper sounded, oddly, like a single voice. As if all their voices had coalesced into one mouth and it was that mouth that spoke, growing louder, rising like the tide.

The buzzing that Noemí had heard before began now, also growing louder. It sounded like hundreds of bees were hiding beneath the floorboards and the walls.

Howard had raised his hands, as if to cup the young man's head between them. Noemí recalled the kiss the old man had given her. But this would be worse. Howard's body was covered with boils and he smelled of rot, and he would fruit and he would die. He would die, he would slide into a new body, and Francis would cease to exist. A demented cycle. Children devoured as babes, children devoured as adults. Children are but food. Food for a cruel god.

Catalina, softly, quietly, had edged closer to the bed. Her movements had gone unnoticed. All heads were down, after all, all except for Noemí's.

Then she saw it. Catalina had seized the doctor's scalpel and was looking at it, very much like a dreamer, very much like someone who does not recognize the object in her hands, still caught in a vague, soporific state.

Then her expression changed. A startled flash of recognition came over her and then a spark of rage. Noemí wasn't aware that Catalina could be capable of such rage. It was naked hatred, it made Noemí gasp, and at last Howard seemed to notice something amiss and turned his head, only to feel the scalpel descend into his face.

The blow was fierce, going straight into an eye.

Catalina became a maenad, her frenzied stabbing—the scalpel bit the neck, the ear, the shoulder—brought forth a river of black pus and dark blood, splattering the covers. Howard yelled and shook as if an electric current ran through his body, and the others in the room echoed him, their bodies convulsing. The doctor, Florence, Francis, they fell upon the floor, seized by a terrible paroxysm.

Catalina stepped back, dropping the scalpel and slowly moving toward the doorway, where she remained, staring at the room.

Noemí jumped to her feet and rushed to Francis's side. She could see nothing but the white in his eyes, and she grasped his shoulders and tried to pull him up into a sitting position.

"Let's go!" she said, giving him a hard slap. "Come on, let's go!"

Though dazed, he stood up and clutched her hand, trying to make his way across the room with her. But then Florence's hand clawed at Noemí's leg, and she stumbled and lost her footing. Francis tumbled down with her.

Noemí attempted to stand again, but there was Florence holding her ankle tight. Noemí saw the gun on the floor and tried to reach for it. Florence, noticing this, leaped upon her like a wild animal, and as Noemí's fingers closed upon the weapon, Florence's hand closed around Noemí's hand, clutching it with a grip so strong Noemí yelped as she heard the cruel, hard cracking of bones.

The pain was atrocious, and her eyes watered as Florence pulled the gun out of her useless hand.

"There's no way you can leave us," Florence said. "Ever."

Florence pointed the gun at her, and Noemí knew this bullet would kill, not wound, for the woman's face was eager, the mouth a vicious snarl.

They'd cleanse the house afterward, she thought. A mad

thought, but it was there, that they'd wash the floors and the linens and scrape off the blood, and toss her into a pit in the cemetery without a cross, like they had so many others.

Noemí raised her injured hand, as if to shield herself, which could do no good. There was no way to dodge a bullet at this range.

"No!" Francis yelled.

Francis lunged toward his mother, and they both crashed against the black velvet chair where Noemí had been sitting, toppling it. There was the noise of the gun going off. It was loud. She pressed her hands against her ears and winced.

She held her breath. Francis lay under the weight of his mother. From the angle where she was sitting Noemí couldn't see who had been shot, but then Francis rolled Florence away, stood up, and he had the gun in his hands. His eyes were bright with tears and he was shivering, but it wasn't like the previous monstrous shivers that had wracked his body.

On the floor, Florence's body lay still.

He stumbled in Noemí's direction and shook his head helplessly. Perhaps he meant to speak, to give himself into the fullness of grief. But a groan made them both turn their heads toward the bed as Howard extended his hands in their direction. He'd lost an eye, and the cuts from the scalpel marred his face. But the other eye remained open and monstrous and golden, staring at them. He spat out blood, spat out black mucus.

"You're mine. Your body is mine," he said.

He held out his hands, like claws, commanding Francis to approach the bed, and Francis took a step, and Noemí knew in that moment that this compulsion could not abate, that Francis was primed to obey. There was a pull there that could not be ignored. She had assumed, until now, that Ruth had committed suicide, that, horrified by her actions, she'd shot herself.

*I'm not sorry*, she'd said, after all. But now Noemí realized it had probably been Howard who had pushed her to do this. He had incited Ruth to turn the rifle onto herself in a last, desperate attempt to survive. The Doyles could do such things.

They could push you in the desired direction, like Virgil had pushed Noemí.

Ruth, she thought, had been murdered.

Now Francis shuffled forward, and Howard grinned. "Come here," he said.

*It's the right time*, Noemí thought. *A tree ripens and one must pluck the fruit.*

It was like that, and now Howard was sliding his amber ring off his finger, now he was holding it up for Francis, so that Francis might slide it onto his own hand. A symbol. Of respect, of transference, of acquiescence.

"Francis!" she yelled, but he didn't look at her.

Dr. Cummins was moaning. He'd be on his feet any second, and Howard, he was staring at them with that single golden eye, and she needed Francis to turn around and leave. She needed him to step out of there now, because the walls were beginning to palpitate softly all around them, alive, rising and falling, like a great, heaving beast, and the bees had returned.

The maddening movement of a thousand tiny wings.

Noemí leaped forward and dug her nails into Francis's shoulder.

He turned, he turned and looked at her, and his eyes were fluttering, beginning to roll up.

"Francis!"

"Boy!" Howard yelled. His voice shouldn't have sounded so loud. It bounced all around them, off the walls, the wood groaning and repeating it while the bees buzzed, their wings flapping in the dark.

*Boy boy boy.*

*It's in the blood*, Ruth had said—but you can cut out a tumor.

Francis's fingers were slack around the gun, and Noemí pulled it out of his hand easily. She had shot once in her life before. It had been that trip to El Desierto de los Leones, and her brother had set little target pieces up and their friends had applauded her accurate aim, and then they'd all laughed and gone horseback riding. She remembered the instructions well enough.

Noemí raised the gun and shot Howard twice. Something snapped in Francis. He blinked and stared at Noemí, his mouth open. Then she pulled the trigger again, but she'd run out of bullets.

Howard began to convulse and shriek. Once, when Noemí's family had gone to the coast on vacation, they'd eaten stew, and she recalled her grandmother slicing the head off a large fish for their dinner with one steady swoop of the knife. The fish had been slippery and fierce, and even after its head had been chopped off it wriggled and attempted to escape. Howard reminded her of the fish, his body rippling violently, wracked with such violence even the bed shook.

Noemí dropped the gun, grabbed Francis by the hand and pulled him out of the room. Catalina was standing in the hallway, both hands clasped against her mouth, staring at them, staring over Noemí's shoulder at what lay on the bed, kicking and screaming and dying. Noemí didn't dare to look back at it.

# 26

They stopped running when they reached the top of the staircase. Lizzie and Charles, the other two servants at High Place, were standing a few steps below, looking up at them. They shivered, their heads lolling to the side, their hands opening and closing spasmodically, their mouths frozen in a stark grin. It was like observing a couple of wind-up toys that had fallen apart. Noemí guessed that the events that had transpired had affected every family member. It had not, however, destroyed them, for these two were there, staring at them.

"What's wrong with them?" Noemí whispered.

"Howard lost control of them. They're stuck. For now. We could attempt to walk past them. But the front entrance might be locked. My mother would have the keys."

"We are not headed back for the keys," Noemí said. She was also unwilling to walk past those two, and she was not heading into Howard's room again to rifle through a corpse's pockets.

Catalina moved to stand next to Noemí, staring back at both of the servants, and shook her head. It didn't look like her cousin was eager to go down the main staircase either.

"There's another way," Francis said. "We can take the back stairs."

He rushed down a hallway, and the women followed him. "Here," he said, opening a door.

The back stairs were narrow and the illumination was poor, only a couple of sconces with light bulbs to guide them all the way down. Noemí reached into her pocket and lifted her lighter while holding onto the bannister with her other hand.

As they were winding their way down, the bannister seemed to grow slippery under her fingers, like the body of a slick eel. It was alive, it breathed, and rose, and Noemí lowered the lighter and stared at the bannister. Her injured hand was throbbing in unison with the house.

"It's not real," Francis said.

"But can you see it?" Noemí asked.

"It's the gloom. It wants to make us believe things. Go, go quickly."

She walked faster and reached the bottom of the stairs. Catalina came walking right behind her and then Francis, who sounded out of breath.

"Are you all right?" Noemí asked him.

"I'm not feeling great," he said. "We need to keep moving. Ahead it seems to be a dead end; there's a walk-in pantry and inside it there's a cupboard. It's painted yellow. It can be moved aside."

She found a door and inside it the walk-in pantry he had mentioned. The floor was made of stone, and there were hooks to hang meat. A naked light bulb with a long chain dangled from the ceiling. She pulled the chain, illuminating the small space. All the shelves were empty. If this place had stored food, it had been a long time ago, for there was dark mold running up and down the walls, which would have rendered it completely unsuitable for such use.

She saw the yellow cupboard. Its top was arched, and it had two glazed doors and two large drawers at the bottom, marks and scuffs marring its surface. It had been lined in yellow fabric, to better match its outside.

"We should be able to push it to the left," Francis said. "And there, in the bottom of the cupboard, there's a bag." He still sounded like he was trying to catch his breath.

Noemí bent down and pulled open the cupboard's bottom drawer. She found a brown canvas bag. Catalina unzipped it for her. Inside of this bag there was an oil lamp, a compass, two sweaters. It was Francis's unfinished escape kit. It would have to do.

"We push it left?" she asked, stuffing the compass in her pocket.

Francis nodded. "But first, we should block the entrance here," he said, pointing at the door where they'd come in.

"There's that bookcase there we can use," she replied.

Catalina and Francis proceeded to drag a rickety wooden bookcase against the door. It was not a perfect barricade, but it did the job well enough.

Safely hidden in the small room, Noemí handed one sweater to Catalina and the other to Francis, for it would no doubt be chilly outside. Then it was time to tackle the cupboard. It looked heavy, but surprisingly they were able to slide it to the side with less effort than the bookcase. A dark, weathered door was revealed.

"It leads to the family crypt," Francis said. "Then it's a question of walking down the mountain to the town."

"I don't want to go there," Catalina whispered. She had not spoken until now, and the sound startled Noemí. Catalina pointed at the door. "The dead sleep there. I don't want to go. Listen."

Noemí heard it then, a deep, deep groan. It seemed to make the ceiling above them shiver, and the light bulb flickered, the cord moving a little. A chill went down Noemí's spine.

"What's that?" she asked.

Francis looked up and inhaled. "Howard, he's alive."

"We shot him," Noemí said. "He's dead—"

"No." Francis shook his head. "He's weakened and in pain and he's angry. He's not dead. The whole house is in pain."

"I'm scared," Catalina said, her voice small.

Noemí turned to her cousin and hugged her tight. "We'll soon be out of here, you hear me?"

"I guess so," Catalina muttered.

Noemí bent down to pick up the oil lamp. Lighting it proved a problem with her injured hand, but she offered Francis her lighter and he helped her.

He carefully put the glass chimney back on the oil lamp, glancing at her hand, which she had pressed against her chest. "Want me to hold it?" he asked.

"I can do it," she told him, because she'd broken two fingers on her left hand, not both her arms, and also because it made her feel safer to carry the lamp.

With the lamp lit, she turned toward her cousin. Catalina nodded and Noemí smiled. Francis turned the doorknob. A long tunnel stretched out ahead of them. She had expected it to be very rudimentary, the sort of thing the miners might have roughly carved.

It was not the case.

The walls had been decorated with yellow tiles, and upon those tiles were painted flower patterns and green, curling vines. On the walls there were graceful silver sconces shaped like snakes. Their open jaws would have held wax candles if they had not been tarnished and covered with dust.

On the ground and on the walls she noticed a few tiny yellow-ish mushrooms popping up between stone cracks. It was cold and damp, and no doubt the mushrooms found the conditions underground deeply inviting, for as they advanced they seemed to multiply, clustering together in small clumps.

Noemí began to notice something else as their numbers grew: they seemed to have a glow to them, a vague luminescence.

"I'm not imagining it, am I?" she asked Francis. "They light up."

"Yes. They do."

"It's so odd."

"It's not that unusual. Honey mushrooms and bitter oyster mushrooms both glow. People call it foxfire. But that glow is green."

"These are the mushrooms he found in the cave," Noemí said, looking up at the ceiling. It was like looking at dozens of tiny stars. "Immortality. In this."

Francis raised a hand, grasping one of the silver sconces as if to support himself, and looked down at the ground. He ran trembling fingers through his hair and let out a low sigh.

"What's wrong?" she asked.

"It's the house. It's upset and aching. It affects me too."

"Can you go on?"

"I think so," he said. "I'm not sure. If I faint—"

"We can stop for a minute," she offered.

"No, it's fine," he said.

"Lean on me. Come on."

"You're hurt."

"So are you."

He hesitated, but did rest a hand on her shoulder, and they walked together, with Catalina ahead of them. The mushrooms continued to multiply and grow in size, the soft glow now coming from the ceiling and the walls.

Catalina stopped abruptly. Noemí almost bumped into her and clutched the lamp harder.

"What is it?"

Catalina raised a hand, pointing ahead. She could see now why her cousin had halted in her steps. The passageway widened and gave way to two massive double doors of a very dark, very thick wood. Upon the doors was an inlaid silver snake, biting its tail in a perfect circle, and two large door-knockers, twin circles of silver hanging from the jaws of amber-eyed matching snake heads.

"It leads to a chamber beneath the crypt," Francis said. "We must go in there and up."

Francis pulled one of the door-knockers. The door was heavy, but it yielded after he gave it a harsh tug, and Noemí walked in, her lamp held high. She walked in four paces and lowered the lamp. There was no need for it, no need to light the way.

The chamber was festooned with mushrooms of varying sizes, a living, organic tapestry gracing the walls. They ran up and down the high walls, like barnacles on the hull of an ancient ship run aground, and they glowed, furnishing the large room with an unwavering source of light, stronger than candles or torches. It was the light of a moribund sun.

A metal gate to the right of the chamber had been spared the mushroom growth, and the chandelier above their heads, with its coiling metal snakes and candles reduced to stubs, evidenced no mushrooms either. The stone floor was almost bare of the luxurious mushroom growth, a scant few popping up here and there among loose tiles, and it was easy to see the gigantic mosaic that served as a decoration. It was a black snake, viciously biting its tail, its eyes aglow, and around the reptile there was a curling pattern of vines and flowers. It resembled the ouroboros she'd seen in the greenhouse. This one was larger, more magnificent, and the glow of the mushrooms gave it an ominous appearance.

The chamber was bare, except for a table set upon a stone dais. The table was covered with a yellow cloth, and upon it there sat a silver cup and a silver box. Behind the table a long, flowing drape, also of yellow silk, served as a backdrop. It might be a portiere that would hide a doorway.

"The gate, it leads up to the mausoleum," Francis said. "We should take it."

She could indeed see stone steps behind the metal gate, but rather than attempting to open it Noemí walked up to the stone dais, frowning. She set her lamp down on the floor and ran a hand over the table, lifting the lid of the box. Inside she found a knife with a jeweled handle and held it up.

"I've seen this," she said, "in my dreams."

Francis and Catalina had slowly walked into the chamber and were both looking at her. "He killed children with this," she continued.

"He did many things," Francis replied.

"Casual cannibalism."

"A communion. Our children are born infected with the fungus, and ingesting their flesh means ingesting the fungus; ingesting the fungus makes us stronger and in turn it binds us more closely to the gloom. Binds us to Howard."

Francis winced suddenly and bent down. Noemí thought he was about to retch, but he stood like that, with his arms wrapped around his belly. Noemí dropped the knife on the table and walked down the dais, back to his side.

"What is it?" she asked.

"It's painful," he said. "She's in pain."

"Who?"

"She's speaking."

Noemí became aware of a sound. It had been there all along, but she had not paid attention to it. It was very low, almost inaudible, and it would have been easy to think she was imagining it. It was a hum and also very much unlike a hum. The buzzing noise she'd heard on other occasions, only the pitch this time seemed higher.

*Don't look.*

Noemí turned around. The hum seemed to be coming from the dais, and she walked up to it. As she moved closer, the hum grew stronger.

It was behind the yellow drape. Noemí raised a hand.

"Don't," Catalina said. "You don't want to see."

Her fingers touched the drape, and the buzzing became the beating of a thousand frenetic insects against glass, the sound of a swarm caught inside her head, so strong she could almost feel it like a vibration cutting through the air, and she lifted her head.

*Don't look.*

Bees seemed to flutter against her fingertips, the air alive with unseen wings, and her instinct was to step back, to turn away and shield her eyes, but she clutched the fabric and yanked it aside with such force she almost ripped it to the ground.

Noemí stared straight into the face of death.

It was the open, screaming maw of a woman, frozen in time. A mummy, a few teeth dangling from her mouth, her skin yellow. The clothing in which she had been buried had long dissolved into dust, and instead she was clothed in a different finery: mushrooms hid her nakedness. They grew from her torso and her belly, they grew down her arms and her legs, they clustered around her head creating a crown, a halo, of glowing gold. The mushrooms held her upright, anchored her to the wall, like a monstrous Virgin in a cathedral of mycelium.

And it was this thing, dead and buried for years and years, that made that buzzing noise. It made that terrible sound. This was the golden blur she'd seen in her dreams, the terrifying creature that lived in the walls of the house. It held out an outstretched hand, and upon that hand it wore an amber ring. She recognized it.

"Agnes," Noemí said.

And the buzzing, it was terrible and sharp and it pulled her down and it made her see and it made her *know*.

*Look.*

The pressure of the cloth against her face, suffocating her, until she lost consciousness, only to wake up in a coffin. Her startled gasps, because despite being prepared for this, despite knowing what must happen, she was scared. Her palms pressing against the lid of the coffin, again and again, splinters digging into her skin, and she screamed, tried to push her way out, but the coffin did not yield. She screamed and screamed but nobody came. Nobody was supposed to come. This was the way it was meant to be.

*Look.*

He needed her. Needed her mind. The fungus by itself, it had no mind. It held no real thoughts, no real consciousness. Faint traces, like the faded scent of roses. Even the cannibalization of the priests' remains could not bring true immortality; it augmented the potency of the mushrooms, it created a soft link between all the people present. It united but it could not preserve for all eternity, and the mushrooms themselves could heal, they could extend life, but they could not offer immortality.

Doyle, however, clever, clever Doyle, with his knowledge of scientific and alchemical matters, with his fascination with biological processes, Doyle had understood all the possibilities nobody else had grasped.

A mind.

The fungus needed a human mind that could serve as a vessel for memories, that could offer control. The fungus and the proper human mind, fused together, were like wax, and Howard was like a seal, and he imprinted himself upon new bodies like a seal on paper.

*Look.*

The priests had managed to transmit a few stray memories from one to the other through the mushrooms, through the lineage of their people, but they were crude and random occurrences. Doyle systematized. And all he had needed were people like Agnes.

His wife. His kin.

But now there was no Agnes. Agnes was the gloom and the gloom was Agnes, and Howard Doyle, if he perished this instant, would still exist in the gloom, for he had created wax and a seal and paper.

And it hurt. It was in pain. The gloom. Agnes. The mushrooms. The house, heavy with rot, with hidden tendrils extending beneath and up its walls feeding on all manner of dead matter.

*He is hurt. We are hurt. Look, look, look. Look!*

The buzzing had acquired a fever pitch; it was so loud Noemí covered her ears and screamed, and inside her head a voice bellowed.

Francis grabbed her by the shoulders and turned her around.

"Don't look at her," he said. "We are never supposed to look at her."

The buzzing had ceased all of a sudden, and she raised her

head and looked at Catalina, who was staring at the floor, and she looked back at Francis in horror.

A sob stuck in her throat. "They buried her alive," Noemí said. "They buried her alive and she died, and the fungus sprouted from her body and . . . dear God . . . it's not a human mind anymore . . . he remade her. He remade her."

She was breathing very fast. Too fast, and the buzzing had ceased, but the woman was still there. Noemí turned her head, tempted to stare again at that hideous skull, but he caught her chin in his hand. "No, no, look at me. Stay here with me."

She took a deep breath, feeling like a diver who was surfacing again. Noemí stared into Francis's eyes. "She's the gloom. Did you know?"

"Only Howard and Virgil come here," Francis said. He was shivering.

"But you knew!"

All the ghosts were Agnes. Or rather, all the ghosts lived inside Agnes. No, that wasn't right either. What had once been Agnes had become the gloom, and inside the gloom there lived ghosts. It was maddening. It was not a haunting. It was possession and not even that, but something she couldn't even begin to describe. The creation of an afterlife, furnished with the marrow and the bones and the neurons of a woman, made of stems and spores.

"Ruth knew too, and we couldn't do anything. She keeps us here, she's how Howard controls everything. We can't leave. They don't let us, ever."

He was sweating and then he was sliding down onto his knees, grasping Noemí's arms. "What is it? You must get up," she said, also sliding to her knees, touching his face.

"He's right, he can't leave. Neither can you, for that matter."

It was Virgil who had spoken. He was swinging the metal gate open and walking in. Strolling in. Very casually. Perhaps he was a hallucination. Perhaps he wasn't even there. Noemí stared at him. *It can't be,* she thought.

"What?" he said with a shrug, letting the gate close behind

him with a loud clang. He was there. It was no hallucination. Rather than following them down the tunnel he had simply gone aboveground, through the cemetery, and descended the steps from the crypt.

"Poor girl. You actually look shocked. You didn't *really* think you had killed me. You also didn't think I accidentally happened to carry that tincture in my pocket, did you? I let you have it, I let you snap out of our hold for a few moments. I let you cause this mayhem."

She swallowed. Next to her Francis was shivering. "Why?"

"Isn't it obvious? So you could hurt my father. I couldn't. Francis couldn't. The old man ensured none of us could raise a hand against him. You saw how he forced Ruth to kill herself. When I learned what Francis was up to I thought: here's my chance. Let the girl escape her bonds, let's see what she can do, this outsider who isn't subject to our rules quite yet, who can still fight back. And now he's dying. Feel it? Hmm? His body is falling apart."

"That can't be good for you," Noemí said. "If you hurt him, you hurt the gloom, and besides, even if his body dies, he'll still exist in the gloom. His mind—"

"He's weakened. I control the gloom now," Virgil said angrily. "When he dies, he'll die forever. I won't let him have a new body. Change. That's what you wanted, no? Turns out we want the same."

Virgil had reached Catalina's side and was glancing at her with a smirk. "There you are, dear wife. Thank you for your contribution to the evening's entertainment," he said, squeezing her arm in a gesture of mock affection. Catalina winced, but did not move.

"Don't touch her," Noemí said, standing up and reaching for the knife in the silver box.

"Don't be meddlesome. She's my wife."

Noemí closed her fingers around the knife. "You better not—"

"You better drop that knife," Virgil replied.

*Never*, she thought, yet her hand was shaking and there was this terrible impulse rushing through her body, pushing her to obey.

"I drank the tincture. You can't control me."

"Funny, that," Virgil said, letting go of Catalina and looking at Noemí. "You did snap out of our control back there. But the tincture doesn't seem to last that long, and walking all around the house, down into this chamber, you've been exposed to the gloom's influence again. You're breathing it in, all these tiny, invisible spores. You're in the heart of the house. All three of you."

"The gloom is hurt. You can't—"

"We've all taken a beating today," Virgil said, and she could now see there were beads of sweat dotting his forehead and his blue eyes had a feverish sheen to them. "But I'm in control now, and you're going to do as I say."

Her fingers ached, and suddenly it felt like she was holding a hot coal in her hand. Noemí let the knife fall to the floor with a loud clang and a yelp.

"Told you," Virgil said mockingly.

She looked down at the knife, which lay by her foot. It was so close, yet she could not pick it up. She felt pins and needles running down her arms, making her fingers twitch. Her hand hurt, the broken bones ached with a terrible, burning pain.

"Look at this place," Virgil said, glancing at the chandelier above their heads with distaste. "Howard was caught in the past, but I look forward to the future. We'll have to reopen the mine, see about getting new furniture in here, real electric power. We'll need servants, of course, new automobiles, and children. I expect you'll have no problem giving me many children."

"No," she said, but it was a whisper, and she could sense his grip on her, like an invisible hand settling on her shoulder.

"Come here," Virgil ordered. "You've been mine since the beginning."

The mushrooms on the walls swayed, as if they were alive, like anemones rippling under water. They released clouds of golden dust and they sighed. Or it was she who sighed, for there was that sweet, dark feeling she had felt before enveloping her once again, and she was suddenly light-headed. The troublesome pain of her left hand lifted and vanished.

Virgil was holding his arms out to her, and Noemí thought of those arms twined around her and how good it would be to surrender to his will. Deep down she wished to be torn apart, to scream in shame; his palm muffling that scream against her mouth.

The mushrooms glowed brighter, and she thought perhaps later she might touch them, running her hands against the wall and settling her face against the softness of their flesh. It would be good to rest there, skin pressed tight against their slick bodies, and maybe they'd cover her, the lovely fungi, and cram into her mouth, into her nostrils and eye sockets until she could not breathe and they nestled in her belly and bloomed along her thighs. And Virgil, too, driving deep within her, and the world would be a blur of gold.

"Don't," Francis said.

She had taken one step down the dais, but Francis had reached out a hand and clasped her injured fingers, the pain of his touch making her wince. She looked down at him, blinking, and froze.

"Don't," he whispered, and she could tell he was afraid. Nevertheless, he descended the steps ahead of her, as if he might shield her. His voice sounded frail and strained, ready to splinter. "Let them go."

"Why would I ever do that?" Virgil asked innocently.

"It's wrong. Everything we do is wrong."

Virgil pointed over his shoulder, toward the tunnel they had followed. "Hear that? That's my father dying, and when his body finally collapses I will have absolute power over the gloom. I'll need an ally. We are kin, after all."

Noemí thought that she could indeed hear something, that in the distance Howard Doyle groaned and spat blood, and black fluid leaked from his body as he strained to keep breathing.

"Look, Francis, I'm not a selfish man. We can share," Virgil said expansively. "You want the girl, I want the girl. It's no reason to fight, huh? And Catalina is a sweet thing too. Come, come, don't be dull."

Francis had picked up the knife she had dropped, and now he held it up. "You won't hurt them."

"Are you going to try and stab me? I should warn you I'm a little harder to kill than a woman. Yes, Francis, you managed to kill your mother. Over what? A girl? And now? It's my turn?"

"Go to hell!"

Francis rushed toward Virgil, but he suddenly halted, his hand frozen in midair, the knife tight in his grip. Noemí couldn't see his face but she could imagine it. It must mirror her expression, for she too had become a statue, and Catalina stood in absolute stillness.

The bees stirred, the buzzing began. *Look.*

"Don't make me kill you," Virgil warned him, and his hand fell upon Francis's trembling hand. "Yield."

Francis shoved Virgil away, sending Virgil crashing against the wall with a strength that seemed impossible.

For one split second she felt Virgil's pain, the tug of adrenaline rushing through her veins, his fury mingled with her own. *Francis, you little shit.* It was the gloom, connecting them for a brief instant, and she yelped, almost biting her tongue. She stepped back, her feet slowly obeying her. One, two steps.

Virgil frowned. His eyes seemed to glow gold as he stepped forward and brushed off tiny bits of mushrooms and dust that had adhered to his jacket.

The buzzing bubbled up, first low, then rumbling into life, and she winced.

"Yield."

Francis groaned his answer and flung himself against Virgil once more. His cousin stopped him with ease. He was much stronger, and this time he was prepared for an attack. He caught Francis's desperate punch, returning it with vicious abandon, hitting Francis in the head. Francis stumbled yet managed to regain his balance and struck back. His fist connected with Virgil's mouth, and Virgil let out an angry, startled gasp.

Virgil's eyes narrowed as he wiped his mouth clean.

"I'll make you bite off your own tongue," Virgil said simply.

The men had changed positions, and now Noemí could see Francis's face, the blood welling down his temple as he heaved and shook his head, and Noemí saw the way his eyes were open wide and the way his hands were shaking and how his mouth was opening and closing, like a fish gasping for air.

Dear God, Virgil was going to make him do it. He would make him eat his own tongue.

Noemí heard the growing buzzing of bees behind her.

*Look.*

She turned around, and her eyes fell on the face of Agnes, her lipless mouth set in an eternal circle of pain, and she pressed her hands against her ears, furiously wondering why it wouldn't stop. Why that noise wouldn't cease, returning over and over again.

And it struck her all of a sudden this fact that she had missed, which should have been obvious from the very beginning: that the frightening and twisted gloom that surrounded them was the manifestation of all the suffering that had been inflicted on this woman. Agnes. Driven to madness, driven to anger, driven to despair, and even now a sliver of that woman remained, and that sliver was still screaming in agony.

She was the snake biting its tail.

She was a dreamer, eternally bound to a nightmare, eyes closed even when her eyes had turned to dust.

The buzzing was her voice. She could not communicate properly any longer but could still scream of unspeakable horrors inflicted on her, of ruin and pain. Even when coherent memory and thought had been scraped away, this searing rage remained, burning the minds of any who wandered near it. What did she wish?

Simply to be released from this torment.

Simply to wake up. But she couldn't. She couldn't ever wake.

The buzzing was growing, threatening to hurt Noemí again and overwhelm her mind, but she reached down and grabbed the oil lamp with quick, rough fingers and rather than thinking about what she was about to do, she thought of that single phrase that Ruth had spoken. *Open your eyes, open your eyes,* and her steps were quick and determined, and for each step she whispered *open your eyes.*

Until she was staring at Agnes again.

"Sleepwalker," she whispered. "Time to open your eyes."

She tossed the lamp against the corpse's face. It instantly ignited the mushrooms around Agnes's head, creating a halo of fire, and then tongues of fire began to spread quickly down the wall, the organic matter apparently as good as kindling, making the mushrooms blacken and pop.

Virgil screamed. It was a hoarse, terrible scream, and he collapsed upon the floor and scratched at the tiles, attempting to stand up. Francis also collapsed. Agnes was the gloom and the gloom was part of them, and this sudden damage to Agnes, to the web of mushrooms, must be like neurons igniting. Noemí for her part felt jolted into complete awareness, the gloom shoving her away.

She rushed down the dais and immediately went to her cousin, pressing her hand against Catalina's face.

"Are you all right?" she asked.

"Yes," Catalina said, nodding vigorously. "Yes."

On the floor, both Virgil and Francis were moaning. Virgil tried to reach for her, tried to lift himself up, and Noemí kicked him in the face, but he clawed at her, scrabbled to grab hold of her leg. Noemí stepped back, and he was extending a hand, still grasping and pulling himself forward even though he couldn't walk. He crawled toward her, gritting his teeth.

Noemí took another step back, fearing he'd pounce upon her.

Catalina picked up the knife Francis had dropped, and now she stood over her husband and brought the knife down into his face when he turned to look at her, piercing an eye, in imitation of what she'd done to Howard Doyle.

Virgil fell down with a muffled groan, and Catalina pressed the knife in deeper, her lips closed together, not a single word or sob escaping them. Virgil twitched and his mouth fell open, spitting and gasping. Then he lay still.

The women held hands and looked down at Virgil. His blood was smearing the black head of the snake, painting it red, and Noemí wished they'd had a great big knife, for she would have cut off his head if she could, like her grandmother had cut off the head of the fish.

She knew, by the way Catalina clutched her hand, that she wished for the same.

Then Francis muttered a word, and Noemí knelt next to him and tried to get him to stand up. "Come on," she told him, "we need to run."

"It's dying, we are dying," Francis said.

"Yes, we are going to die if we don't get out quickly," Noemí agreed. The whole room was quickly catching on fire, patches and patches of mushrooms bursting into flames, and the yellow curtains she had pulled aside were also burning.

"I can't leave."

"Yes, you can," Noemí said, gritting her teeth and coaxing him to his feet. She couldn't make him walk, though.

"Catalina, help us!" she yelled.

They each took one of Francis's arms and placed it over their shoulders, half lifting, half dragging him toward the metal gate. It was easy to swing it open, but then Noemí eyed the steps leading up and wondered how they were going to manage that climb. But there was no other way. When she looked back, she saw Virgil on the ground, stray sparks falling upon him, and the chamber burning bright. There were also mushrooms growing on the walls of the staircase, and these too seemed to be catching fire. They had to hurry.

Up they went, as fast as they could, and Noemí pinched Francis to get him to open his eyes and assist them. He managed to climb several steps with their aid before Noemí was forced to literally drag him up the last couple of steps, stumbling into a dusty chamber with crypts running from one side to the other. Noemí glimpsed silver plaques, rotting coffins, empty vases that might once have contained flowers, a few of the little glowing mushrooms upon the ground, providing the faintest illumination.

The door leading to the mausoleum was mercifully open, courtesy of Virgil. When they stepped out, the mist and the night were waiting to embrace them.

"The gate," she told Catalina, "do you know the way to the gate?"

"It's too dark, the mist," her cousin said.

Yes, the mist that had frightened Noemí with its mysterious golden blur, that buzzing that had been Agnes. But Agnes was a pillar of fire beneath their feet now, and they must find their way out of this place.

"Francis, you need to guide us to the gate," Noemí said. The young man turned his head and looked at Noemí with half-lidded eyes and managed to nod and point to the left. They went in that direction, him leaning on Noemí and Catalina, stumbling often. The gravestones rose like broken teeth from the earth, and he grunted, pointed another way. Noemí had no idea where they were headed. It could be they were walking in circles. And wouldn't that be ironic? Circles.

The mist gave them no quarter until, at last, she saw the iron gates of the cemetery rising in front of them, the serpent eating its tail greeting the trio. Catalina pushed the door open and they were on the path that led back to the house.

"The house is burning," Francis said as they stood by the gates, catching their breath.

Noemí realized this was the case. There was a distant glow, visible even through the mist. She couldn't see High Place, but she could picture it. The ancient books in the library quickly catching fire, paper and leather burning fast, mahogany furniture and heavy curtains with tassels smoldering, glass cases filled with precious silver objects crackling, the nymph and her newel post shrouded in flames as bits of the ceiling fell at her feet. The fire, flowing up the staircase like a relentless river, making floorboards snap while the Doyles' servants still stood on the steps, frozen.

Old paintings bubbling, faded photographs curling into nothingness, doorways arched with fire. Howard Doyle's portraits of his wives were consumed by flames and his bed now a bed of fire, and his decayed and heaving body choked by smoke, while on the floor his physician lay immobile and the fire began to lick at the bedcovers, began to eat Howard Doyle inch by inch, and the old man screamed, but there was no one who would assist him.

Invisible, beneath the paintings and the linens and plates and glass, she imagined masses of fine threads, delicate mycelium, also burning and snapping, fueling the conflagration.

The house blazed in the distance. Let it burn until it was all reduced to ashes.

"Let's go," Noemí muttered.

# 27

He was asleep, the covers pulled up to his chin. It was a small room with scarcely space for a chair and a dresser, and she occupied that chair, right by the bed. Atop the dresser sat a little figurine of San Judas Tadeo, and Noemí had found herself praying to it more than once, placing a cigarette before its feet as an offering. She was staring at the figurine, her lips moving slowly, when the door opened and Catalina walked in. She wore a cotton nightgown that belonged to one of Dr. Camarillo's friends and a thick brown shawl.

"I came to see if you needed anything before I go to bed."

"I'm fine."

"You should go to bed too," her cousin said, setting a hand on her shoulder. "You've hardly had any rest."

Noemí patted her hand. "I don't want him to wake up alone."

"It's been two days."

"I know," Noemí said. "I wish it were like in the fairy tales you read to us. It was very easy in them: all you had to do was kiss the princess."

They both looked at Francis, his face as pale as the pillowcase on which his head rested. Dr. Camarillo had tended to all of them. He'd seen to their wounds, given them a chance to clean themselves and change their clothes, prepared rooms for them to stay, called for Marta to bring her tincture when Noemí quietly explained they needed it. After imbibing it, they had all experienced headaches and nausea, which quickly eased. Except for Francis. Francis had drifted into a deep slumber from which he couldn't be roused.

"Tiring yourself won't help him," Catalina said.

Noemí crossed her arms. "I know, I know."

"Do you want me to keep you company?"

"I'm fine. I swear, I'll go to bed soon. I also don't really want to. I'm not tired."

Catalina nodded. They were both quiet. Francis's chest rose and fell steadily. If he was dreaming, the dreams were not unpleasant. She almost felt sorry for wishing him awake.

The truth was she was afraid of going to bed, of what nightmares might uncoil in the dark. What did people do after witnessing the horrors they had seen? Was it possible to slip back into normality, to play pretend and go on? She wanted to think this was exactly the case, but she was afraid sleep would prove her wrong.

"The doctor says two police officers and a magistrate are arriving tomorrow from Pachuca and your father will be here too." Catalina adjusted her shawl. "What will we say to them? I don't think they'll believe us."

Upon stumbling onto a pair of farmers with their donkeys behind them, the bloodied, bruised, and tired trio had not really agreed what tale they would tell, and the farmers were too shocked by the sight of them to ask much. Instead they quietly guided them to El Triunfo. Later, as they were ushered into Dr. Camarillo's house, it had been necessary to fabricate a story, and Noemí had simplified their tale, saying that Virgil had gone mad and attempted to repeat his sister's murderous actions, killing all the inhabitants of High Place, this time by setting the house on fire.

This, however, did not explain why Noemí had been wearing an old wedding dress and Francis was in a matching wedding suit, nor why both women's clothes were stained with so much blood.

Noemí was pretty sure Camarillo didn't believe their version of events, but he pretended to. In his weary eyes Noemí had read a tacit understanding.

"My father will help smooth things out."

"I hope so," Catalina said. "What if they should charge us? You know."

Noemí doubted anyone could hold them in place; there wasn't even a jail in El Triunfo. If anything, they'd be sent to Pachuca, but she didn't think they'd do such a thing. Statements would be taken, a cursory report would be typed up, but they couldn't really prove much.

"Tomorrow we'll go home," Noemí said firmly.

Catalina smiled, and Noemí, though tired, was glad to see that smile. It was the smile of the sweet young woman she'd grown up with. It was her Catalina.

"Well, then, get some sleep," Catalina said, leaning down to kiss her cheek. "They'll be here early in the morning."

The women hugged, one long, tight embrace, Noemí unwilling to cry. Not now. Then Catalina gently brushed the hair from her face and smiled again.

"I'm down the hall if you need me," she said.

Catalina took one last look at the young man and closed the door behind her.

Noemí placed her hand in the pocket of her sweater and felt the lighter there. Her lucky talisman. Finally she took out a crumpled pack of cigarettes that Camarillo had given her the previous day.

She lit the cigarette, tapped her foot, and let the ashes fall into an empty bowl. Her back ached. She had been sitting in that uncomfortable chair for a long time but refused to go away even though first Camarillo and then Catalina had come to poke at her. When she had taken but a few puffs of the cigarette Francis stirred, and she dropped the cigarette onto the bowl and placed the bowl on the dresser, waiting.

He had moved like this before, a faint tilting of the head, but this time she thought it was different. She touched his hand.

"Open your eyes," she whispered. Ruth had said the same words to her many times, in fear and terror, but Noemí's voice was warm.

She was rewarded by his eyes fluttering a little, then more, until they focused on her.

"Hello there," she said.

"Hi."

"Let me get you some water."

There was a carafe on the dresser. She filled a glass and helped him drink.

"You hungry?" she asked.

"God, no. Maybe later. I feel terrible."

"You look terrible," she replied.

His lips formed a fragile smile, and he let out a chuckle. "Yes, I suppose so."

"You slept two whole days. I thought I'd have to dislodge an apple from your throat, like a poor imitation of Sleeping Beauty."

"Snow White."

"Well. You look pale enough."

He smiled anew and attempted to position himself better against the headboard, his smile waning. "Is it all gone?" he asked, his voice a worried, anxious whisper.

"A couple of townspeople went up the mountain to see what was left of the house. They told us it was a bunch of smoldering ruins. High Place is gone, and the fungus must be gone with it."

"Yes, I think it is. Although . . . mycelia can be pretty resistant to fire. And I've heard that certain mushrooms . . . like . . . like morels, they'll sprout more easily after a forest fire."

"It wasn't a morel and it wasn't a forest fire," she said. "If there's anything left we could find it and burn it."

"I suppose we could."

The thought seemed to relax him; he had been clutching the

covers quite fiercely and now he released them and sighed, his eyes settling on her.

"What happens tomorrow, then, when your father arrives?" he asked.

"You sneaky man. Were you listening to us the whole time?"

He seemed abashed and shook his head. "No. I suppose you woke me up or I was half awake already. Anyway, I heard your cousin say your father is arriving in the morning."

"That's right. He'll be here soon. I think you'll like him. And you're going to love Mexico City."

"I'm going with you?"

"We can't leave you here. Besides, I dragged you down a mountain. I think in cases such as this I'm supposed to guard you. There must be a law about that," she said with that genial tone of hers. It had been a while since she had employed it. It felt stale and difficult to sound so carefree, it almost hurt her tongue, but she managed a smile, and he looked pleased.

She must practice, she thought. It was all practice. She'd learn to live without worry, without fears, without any darkness chasing after her.

"Mexico City, then," he said. "It's very large."

"You'll get the hang of it," she replied, stifling a yawn with her injured hand.

His eyes fixed on Noemí's splinted fingers. "Does it hurt very badly?" he asked quietly.

"It hurts a little. No sonatas for me for a while. Maybe we can play a duet and you help me with the left hand."

"Seriously, Noemí."

"Seriously? Everything hurts. It'll mend."

Maybe it wouldn't, and maybe she'd never be able to coax notes out of a piano the same way she used to, maybe she would never be able to vanquish this experience, but she didn't want to say that. There was no point in saying that.

"I did hear your cousin telling you to sleep. It sounded like a good idea."

"Bah. Sleep is boring," she proclaimed and fidgeted with her pack of cigarettes.

"Do you have nightmares?"

She shrugged and did not reply, tapping her index finger against the box.

"I didn't have nightmares about my mother. Maybe I will dream of her later," Francis said. "But I did dream the house had stitched itself together and I was inside of it, and this time there was no way out. I was alone in the house, and all the doors were sealed."

She crushed the box. "It's all gone. I told you, it's all gone."

"It was grander than before. It was the house before it had fallen into disrepair; the colors were vivid and there were flowers growing in the greenhouse, but flowers also grew inside, and there were forests of mushrooms up the staircase and in the rooms," he said, his voice infinitely calm. "And when I walked, mushrooms sprouted from my footsteps."

"Please, be quiet," she said, and she wished he had dreamed of murder, of blood and viscera. This dream was much more disquieting.

She dropped her box of cigarettes. They both looked down at the ground, where it had landed between her chair and his bed.

"What if it's never gone? What if it's in me?" he asked, and there was a hitch in his voice.

"I don't know," she said. They'd done everything they could. Burned all the mushrooms, destroyed the gloom, ingested Marta's tincture. It ought to be gone. Yet, *in the blood*.

He shook his head with a heavy exhalation. "If it's in me, then I should put an end to it, and you shouldn't be so close to me, it's not—"

"It was a dream."

"Noemí—"

"You're not listening."

"No! It was a dream. Dreams can't hurt you."

"Then why won't you go to sleep?"

"I don't want to, and it has nothing to do with this. Nightmares mean nothing."

He intended to protest, she pulled herself closer to him, settled on the bed and finally under the covers, bidding him to hush as she embraced him. She felt his hand ghosting against her hair, heard his heart stuttering and smoothing into a steady beat.

She looked up at him. Francis's eyes were shiny with unshed tears.

"I don't want to be like him," he whispered. "Maybe I'll die soon. Maybe you can cremate me."

"You won't."

"You can't promise that."

"We'll stay together," she said firmly. "We'll stay together and you won't be alone. I can promise you that."

"How can you make such a promise?"

She whispered that the city was wonderful and bright, and there were areas of it where buildings were rising up, fresh and new, places that had been open fields and held no secret histories. There were other cities too, where the sun could scorch out the land and bring color to his cheeks. They could live by the sea, in a building with large windows and no curtains.

"Spinning fairy tales," he murmured, but he embraced her.

Catalina was the one who made stories up. Tales of black mares with jeweled riders, princesses in towers, and Kublai Khan's messengers. But he needed a story and she needed to tell one, so she did until he didn't care whether she was lying or speaking the truth.

He tightened his arms around her and buried his face in the crook of her neck.

Eventually, she slept and did not dream. When she woke up to the half-light of the early morning, Francis turned his wan face toward Noemí and locked his blue eyes on her. She wondered whether one day, if she looked carefully, she might notice a golden sheen to them. Or maybe she'd catch her own reflection staring back at her with eyes of molten gold. The world might indeed be a cursed circle; the snake swallowed its tail and there could be no end, only an eternal ruination and endless devouring.

"I thought I dreamed you," he said, still a little sleepy.

"I'm real," she replied, a murmur.

They were quiet. Slowly she leaned forward, kissing him on the mouth so he'd know she was truly there, and he sighed, intertwining his fingers with hers and closing his eyes.

The future, she thought, could not be predicted, and the shape of things could not be divined. To think otherwise was absurd. But they were young that morning, and they could cling to hope. Hope that the world could be remade, kinder and sweeter. So she kissed him a second time, for luck. When he looked at her again his face was filled with such an extraordinary gladness, and the third time she kissed him it was for love.

# ACKNOWLEDGMENTS

Thanks to my agent, Eddie Schneider; my editor, Tricia Narwani; and the Del Rey team. Thanks also to my mother for letting me watch scary movies and read scary books as a kid. And as always, thanks to my husband, who reads every single word I write.

# ABOUT THE AUTHOR

SILVIA MORENO-GARCIA is the author of the critically acclaimed speculative novels *Gods of Jade and Shadow*, *Signal to Noise*, *Certain Dark Things*, and *The Beautiful Ones*; and the crime novel *Untamed Shore*. She has edited several anthologies, including the World Fantasy Award–winning *She Walks in Shadows* (aka *Cthulhu's Daughters*). She lives in Vancouver, British Columbia.

silviamoreno-garcia.com
Facebook.com/smorenogarcia
Twitter: @silviamg

# ABOUT THE TYPE

This book was set in Sabon, a typeface designed by the well-known German typographer Jan Tschichold (1902–74). Sabon's design is based upon the original letter forms of sixteenth-century French type designer Claude Garamond and was created specifically to be used for three sources: foundry type for hand composition, Linotype, and Monotype. Tschichold named his typeface for the famous Frankfurt typefounder Jacques Sabon (c. 1520–80).